PRAISE FOR "THE DARK BEFORE DAWN" THE DEBUT NOVEL OF THE GABRIEL MCRAY SERIES

"Stevens sets the stage for graphic sensory details and a fast-paced, tantalizing mystery that utilizes her passion and research in forensics and psychology... Memorable characters, macabre scenes, and a dazzling portrayal of reality will leave readers anxious for book two in the Gabriel McRay series."
Kirkus Reviews

"This is a very unique, nuanced thriller with multiple layers of intrigue... had me hooked from the first page."
Writer's Digest

"Laurie Stevens does a masterful job of developing both the characters and the plot... This is definitely not your typical psychological thriller. This is a must read novel."
Sheila Rae Meyers, Shelfari Reviewer

"*The Dark Before Dawn*_is a psychologically accurate and profound thriller and has gripped us like *The Hunger Games*."
Dr. Christina L. Cassel, Psy.D., Mft

"Twists and turns abound in this book... it was a nail-biting race to the finish. I couldn't put this book down because I simply had to know what would happen next. This was an excellent mystery thriller and I thoroughly enjoyed it."
My Fiction Nook

"This blood-curdling thriller kept me up at night"
Suspense Magazine

"Frighteningly great Indie title... Be sure to leave a light on!"
The Huffington Post

Named to Kirkus Reviews Best of 2011/Indie
Recipient of the Kirkus Star of Merit
2012 Hollywood Book Festival Honoree

Deep into

Dusk

A GABRIEL McRAY NOVEL

....

By Laurie Stevens

To a talented author—
Bev!
love
Laurie Stevens

Published by Follow Your Dreams Publishing
19411 Londelius Street
Northridge, California 91324

ISBN: 0989163407
ISBN 13: 9780989163408
LCCN: 2013938682

Where She Goes
Words and Music by Dave de Castro
Copyright Dave de Castro
Reprinted by permission

ACKNOWLEDGEMENTS

This book was made possible by a wonderful team of people. Thanks to Dr. Stephen Kibrick, Colleen Kelly MFT, Dr. Christine Cassel, and Dr. Bob Weathers for their invaluable insight into the realm of psychology. With regards to forensics, a giant thank you goes to the lovely Sarah Robertson. *Gracias a Vianca Osorio por su ayuda*. Thanks also to Jody Hepps and Sara and Anne at Victory Editing, and a huge hug to David Vieira for generously providing his artistic talents. Thanks always to my friend and mentor Ronald Jacobs, for his patient way of imparting wisdom. Suzanne Kalb and Debbie Birenbaum -- thank you fellow authors and discerning content editors. Mickley Gantman, Scott Templeton, Petra Vieira, Glenn and Laura Goodstein, your support for the arts (mine) is, as it's always been, very much appreciated. Barbara and Bob Price, not only do you cheer on my endeavors, you both are the best family publicists an author could hope for. Joyce and David Birenbaum your love and influence are something I have always cherished. Thanks for being such wonderful parents. And Kathy Magallanes, honestly, what would I do without you? Jonathan and Alanna -- I may be your mom, but you two are your own excellent creations. It's a pleasure to watch you live your own life story. Finally, thank you to Steven, an incredible life partner, (an endeared critic), and my own true love.

For Carole Marsh
Because you always love more

CHAPTER 1

His pretty hands tied a thin nylon rope around her wrists. As her hands came together, he gave an extra pull, knowing it would hurt. Tara Samuels refused to give him the satisfaction of a whimper, but her breath caught in her throat just the same.

Her assailant immediately looked at her face, searching for the fright he heard in her gasp. Amused by her struggle to keep composed, he purposefully pulled and twisted the rope and then shoved her down on the filthy green carpeting that smelled like a nest of insects.

"You're gonna yell for it, you worthless whore. I know you live for this..." He dropped to his knees and leaned over her, his hungry eyes roving over her body. He caught her staring at him. "What are you looking at? You know not to look at me."

Tara watched his hand rise to strike her and she braced for the blow, when an ugly gurgling sound cut through the room. His hand froze in the air, and they both turned toward the sound.

The dead girl's eyes were staring. She was naked and facing them from about three feet away. A drowning, ominous click-click-click issued from her open mouth. The wet rattling of her final exhalation filled the loft and then there was silence.

After the moment of surprise passed, he guffawed at the dead girl. "Nice timing." He shot out a booted foot and kicked at the girl's cooling flesh. "Got anything else to say?"

Tara's eyes slid to the side of the loft. No railing lined the edge. The drop wasn't too far. Tara's hands fervently worked to loosen her bonds as she slowly inched her body across the worn carpeting.

"Even when she's dead," her tormenter stated as he amused himself with the dead girl. "She can't shut up."

Tara felt the rope slide gracefully from her wrists and without a second thought, she launched herself over the edge of the loft.

Somewhere beyond the storm of her own desperation she heard him yell, robbed of his moment. She hit the carpeted floor on her right hip and felt her insides jostle. Ignoring the pain, Tara lurched toward the front door, threw it open, and ran for the tall chaparral outside.

A light rain blurred her eyes, making the green mountains beyond her an impressionistic watercolor. He was right behind her—she could hear him thrashing furiously through the underbrush.

Tara slashed through the sumac and deer weed, using her bare arms as machetes. Pushing blindly ahead, she suddenly smashed face-first into a chain-link fence. Tara's grappling fingers led her along the rusted links to the end post. She swung wildly around it and then tumbled out onto wet asphalt.

A passing motorcyclist saw what appeared to be Botticelli's Venus, blond hair, naked, standing frozen and wild-eyed. The helmeted man instantly swerved on the wet pavement and his bike spun out from under him.

Breathless, Tara sat down in a heap on the asphalt and hugged her knees to her chest. She was naked but she didn't care. Her stomach clenched at the sound of the approaching male footfalls and she closed her eyes. At any moment, she would be hoisted upwards by her hair to face the consequences of what she'd done.

"Lady, are you all right?"

Tara opened her eyes. Standing above her was the motorcyclist, surveying her with wide eyes. The next thing Tara knew, a leather jacket was being draped over her bare shoulders.

The motorcyclist fumbled for his cell phone.

"I'll get help," he assured her, nodding.

Tara's face hurt, and when she touched her lips, she saw blood on her fingertips. She warily looked over her shoulder. Nothing moved in the hills but the falling rain.

❧ ❧ ❧

Detective Gabriel McRay pulled into the driveway of the Peninsula Hotel in Beverly Hills, struggling with his bowtie. Tuxes were never his style; they looked better on playboys. At least his body was fit due to regular gym workouts, but his efforts didn't show under the flabby folds of his cheap rental suit.

He tried reminding himself that all that glittered wasn't gold as he walked through the hotel, passing the bar festooned with celebrities. Gabriel ran his hands self-consciously over the lapel of his tuxedo, breathing in the scent of expensive cologne, freshly polished marble, and the large flower arrangement centered in the lobby. The reservation clerk, looking like a runway model, offered him a disapproving glance. Even the bellboys pursed their lips. Los Angeles could make anybody feel like a nobody.

If he had come to this place to investigate a murder or to interview a witness, Gabriel would have been in his element. Faced with having to impress his girlfriend's fancy colleagues today made him feel as awkward as a teenager, and his rented penguin suit wasn't helping matters.

Gabriel walked toward the ballroom and saw a sign that read: "Southern California Pathology Convention."

From inside the ballroom came murmuring and the genteel chink of cutlery. He entered a large salon and found himself in the middle of a sea of tables. A stage at far right held a few chairs and an empty podium. The speech giving was over.

Gabriel groaned inwardly and his discomfort must have made him look completely out of place for an Armani suit immediately detached itself from the nearest table and strode toward him.

"This is a private function," the man in Armani said. His light brown, blow-dried hair leaned to the right. "You may want to double-check the sign outside for your party."

A flame of fire licked Gabriel's insides: the old rage. *Keep it at bay,* Gabriel warned himself.

"This is my party."

Gabriel purposely brushed the man aside, satisfied to see the Armani stumble backwards. It was his insecurity, of course, that was riling up the anger. Armani quickly sought the aid of a few cohorts and they approached Gabriel, who shook his head and turned, ready for a skirmish.

"That's okay, Jim. He's with me."

Gabriel heard the familiar wind-chime voice and watched the Armani gang raise their eyebrows in surprise. They backed off. Gabriel turned around to see Dr. Ming Li standing behind him. The thick black hair inherited from her Mexican mother was pulled up into a sweeping twist. Her rose sheath dress hugged her slim, curvy figure, giving her a conservative, yet sexy look. But the almond-shaped orbs Ming inherited from her Chinese father were full of cold anger.

"You're late," she stated bluntly.

"There was an accident on the freeway—the rain."

"You should have left enough time!" Ming caught herself, glancing around at the onlookers who were observing their scuffle.

Ming sidled closer to Gabriel and whispered, "This is important to me."

Gabriel tried to keep his voice low. "You think I like sitting on the freeway with my thumb up my ass?"

"I don't know what you like."

Feeling a dozen pairs of eyes on him, Gabriel wanted to end this argument now. "I said I was sorry."

"No, you didn't. Well, at least you're here now." She took a controlled breath and then surveyed Gabriel with a wry smile. "Nice tux."

Grateful to see a glimpse of her humor, he leaned close to Ming. "I'm a lot more attractive out of it."

"Yes, you are."

Gabriel inhaled the spice of her perfume, envisioning the smooth skin hiding under the silk. He slid an arm around her waist and felt her soften under his touch.

"I'm sorry I missed your speech," he said, truly apologetic now. "Tell you what; you finish lunch, I'll book a room."

"I've already taken care of that. Come," Ming said, and took Gabriel's arm to lead him through the round-table obstacle course.

Ming was the chief Los Angeles County medical examiner whose word was solid in court, and Gabriel had always enjoyed working with her. Last summer, when the two of them worked side-by-side on the Malibu Canyon Murder case, their professional relationship had turned personal. Ming's self-assuredness never bothered Gabriel, although most men found it annoying. What did annoy Gabriel was the fact that Ming had already bought and paid for their hotel room. He'd wanted that to be his move.

"Right here," Ming said, halting at a table with a tall centerpiece: a single rare orchid amid a twig concoction that probably cost a fortune and looked like a dry weed. Enough crystal and china lay on the table to blind Gabriel. He went to pull the chair out for Ming, but she was already taking her seat. Standing like a fool, feeling like an idiot, Gabriel sat down.

"Everybody, I'd like to introduce, Detective Sergeant Gabriel McRay."

Gabriel nodded and extended his hand to four other couples seated at the table.

"Ron Wasserstein," a trim gentleman in his late forties told him. "And this is my wife, Claire."

Wasserstein had graying temples and charcoal-colored hair. His gray-and-black pinstriped suit matched him perfectly. His wife might have been beautiful once, but plastic surgery had given her face a perpetually surprised expression.

Another man, identifying himself as Dr. Darren Darnell, was diving into the breadbasket, even as his stomach blocked his access to the table. His wife, whom no one bothered introducing, was downing martinis.

Ming introduced Gabriel to the four other people seated at their table, only he instantly forgot their names. It was okay because three of them never paused in their discourse about the calcification on rotator cuffs. The other doctor, who bore an uncanny resemblance to the Frankenstein monster, nodded ever so slightly at Gabriel and then stared morosely at the silver fork in his hand.

Gabriel whispered to Ming, "Maybe the bolts in his neck need tightening."

She elbowed him. "Mathias is a pioneer on heart transplants."

"I don't doubt he knows all about transplants." Gabriel suppressed a chuckle as he took his seat. "That, and the reanimation of dead tissue."

Ming shushed him.

"So," Ron Wasserstein said, addressing Gabriel. "Detective McRay, huh?"

"That's right."

A waiter placed a green salad in front of Gabriel: two long pieces of lettuce accompanied by grape tomatoes and a goat cheese crostini. Gabriel knew food. Gourmet cooking was his hobby. Still, two measly pieces of lettuce weren't going to suffice for the appetite he'd worked up in traffic. Gabriel reached for the breadbasket and played tug-of-war with the pudgy doctor.

"Any interesting cases?" Wasserstein addressed Gabriel.

Gabriel felt the fingers of discomfort creep over his ill-fitting clothes. Still, he shrugged as if he were important.

"I was the lead investigator on the Malibu Canyon Murder case."

Okay, Gabriel confessed silently, I'm bragging. Sometimes it's hard not to get sucked in, especially when you're wearing a cheap rented tux among a sea of designer threads.

"I think I remember your name," Wasserstein said.

"Maybe," Gabriel murmured in reply, cutting his salad leaf with his knife. "It did make the papers occasionally."

Cut it out. Gabriel stuffed a salad leaf in his mouth to keep from talking. *You sure did make the papers and most of it was nothing to brag about.*

The pudgy doctor, Dr. Darnell, miffed about losing the breadbasket to Gabriel, said evenly, "I heard the killer is going to go free."

Gabriel reached for the pad of butter. "No, he's awaiting trial."

Darnell squinted in memory. "I know who you are. You're that cop who was fired for punching an old lady. They hired you back to work the Malibu Canyon case because you were friends with the killer."

The conversation seemed to die then and all of them turned their attention to Gabriel. Ming's naturally mocha-colored skin went a shade paler.

"What was his name again?" Darnell asked the now silent table. "Hector something?"

"Victor Archwood," Gabriel told Darnell and then glanced at Ming. "He wasn't my friend. He was someone from my past."

Ming took a shaky sip of water and looked as if she might choke. Wasserstein, noticing the change in his normally confident colleague, laughed to break the ice.

"Don't mind Darren," he told Gabriel. "He thinks all cops plant evidence."

Gabriel frowned and concentrated on buttering his bread roll.

Darnell smirked as he chewed his food. "Would it be surprising with the LAPD? Would it now, ha?"

Gabriel put down the bread. "I'm with the Sheriff's Department, not LAPD."

Darnell gave Gabriel a sullen what's-the-difference shrug.

"The Sheriff's Department handles all the contract cities of Los Angeles County," Gabriel explained. "LAPD handles the city of Los Angeles."

Dr. Darnell stared blankly at Gabriel for a moment and then turned to the Frankenstein doctor. "Hey Mathias, did you catch Cameron Diaz in the lobby?"

Gabriel sat back and wondered if his temper would make it through lunch.

☙ ☙ ☙

Jonelle Williams carried a sealed rape kit in one hand and her camera in the other as she walked through the Tarzana Medical Center. Her polyester, navy blue skirt hugged her wide hips tightly and the matching blazer's one fastened button was coming loose with every step. She nodded a greeting to the orderlies she vaguely remembered and kept her maroon lips closed tight. Jonelle Williams was with the Sheriff's Department's Sex Crimes Division and her business here today was nobody else's.

She headed to a private room at the very back of the emergency ward, bypassing a crying child. Hating the antiseptic smell of hospitals, especially on Sundays, Jonelle entered the room and found an Iranian doctor and a nurse conferring quietly in one corner. The doctor nodded to Jonelle.

"Detective Williams?" he asked in a thick Farsi accent.

"Yes," Jonelle said, extending her hand. "Nice to meet you."

The doctor limply shook her hand and dropped it. "Dr. Farad." He seemed to zone in on the gold bicuspid cap Jonelle proudly wore. "The patient, she is in there." He motioned to the closed beige curtain. "She's told us nothing about what happened to her. We can only assume from the fact that she was found without clothes…"

"I understand." Jonelle set her camera down on an orange vinyl chair and then broke the seal on the rape kit. "We'll try to get through this quickly. What's her name?"

"Tara Samuels," the nurse offered. "She did say that."

"Have you called her relatives?"

"Her husband. He is on his way," said Dr. Farad.

The nurse, a gangly woman whose white skin looked pasty under her dyed black hair, said to Jonelle in a low voice, "I don't think you're going to get much from her."

Jonelle eyed the nurse confidently as she opened the curtain. The woman sitting on the bed wore a hospital gown over her wraithlike body. Shagged gold hair fell about her face in perky little wisps.

The blond woman looked up at Jonelle. Her eyes, the color of light sapphires, were vacant.

"Mrs. Samuels? I'm Detective Jonelle Williams with the Los Angeles County Sheriff's Sex Crimes Division. I'm going to ask you some very personal questions and I hope that—"

"He's going to kill me."

Jonelle looked at Tara for a moment and nodded. "The perpetrator? He threatened you after the attack?"

Tara stared at Jonelle and then looked down. "I'm so stupid."

"No, you're not. You're safe is what you are." Jonelle set the rape kit on the bed. "I'm going to take some pictures and collect evidence. Can I ask you, Ms. Samuels, did the perpetrator penetrate you orally?"

Tara Samuels did not reply.

"Was it a vaginal penetration then? Where exactly did he touch you?"

Jonelle received no answer.

"You see, if there was no oral penetration, I don't have to take a sample from your mouth. Ms. Samuels?"

Tara studied the linoleum, seeming to count the pattern repeats.

"Ms. Samuels, do you know who your attacker was? Could you identify him?"

Nothing. Jonelle exhaled loudly and exchanged looks with Dr. Farad, who shrugged.

One day I won't be working these assault cases. Jonelle had a hankering to join the homicide bureau.

The nurse attempted to help Tara out of the hospital gown, but Tara resisted. "I've got to go now."

Jonelle glanced at her watch, a Gucci knockoff. The husband could have been some support. Where was he?

"Please, Ms. Samuels," Jonelle said. "To catch your assailant, we must do this."

Tara's shoulders dropped and she reluctantly let the nurse undress her.

Dr. Farad drew the curtain closed behind him. Jonelle removed the camera from its case. "Ms. Samuels, I'm gonna take some photographs of you. May I begin?"

Tara nodded once and kept her eyes glued on the floor.

"Can you look up at me, please, so we can record any facial discolorations?"

Eyes the color of aquamarine ice met Jonelle's and for a moment, the detective's heart quaked in empathy.

"May I ask how you got that cut on your lip?"

"I ran into a fence."

Jonelle made notes. No other contusions marked Tara's face.

Dr. Farad approached Tara. "Can you uncross your arms please so that I can see your chest area?" Tara uncrossed her arms shyly. Dr. Farad inspected Tara's breasts. Jonelle could not see any particular bruises on the victim's breasts—usually the battleground for sexual assaults.

"Here," Dr. Farad said, gently turning Tara's limp wrist.

As Tara stared into space, Jonelle zoomed in on bracelets of ligature scrapes along both wrists. The shutter snapped in quick succession.

"Here," Dr. Farad said again, turning Tara around and Jonelle swallowed. A large blue-and-yellow bruise was blooming on Tara's right hip. Jonelle quickly shot photos from every angle.

"Can you tell me what caused that bruise?"

The curtain was suddenly torn aside and Jonelle jerked her head toward the intruder. A man, billboard handsome, stood under the blinking fluorescents, holding a bundle of clothes.

"Tara?"

Jonelle surmised from his anxious expression that this must be the husband.

"Mr. Samuels?" Dr. Farad asked.

The man didn't respond, staring only at his wife, and then he appeared to collect himself. Jonelle felt a prickling silence invade the room and glanced at Tara, who simply looked terrified.

"Marc, I'm so sorry!" Tara cried.

Marc shook his head, his features pained. He quickly went to his wife's side and put his arms around her. "Shhh, don't talk, baby. Everything is okay now."

Tall and brown-haired, Marc wore a solid gold Rolex President wristwatch with a diamond bezel that Jonelle just bet was real. The rest of his attire smacked of money and adorned a physique only a private trainer could create. Jonelle cleared her throat. No more waiting. Tara's body was surely breaking down the components found in seminal fluid.

"I know this is very upsetting, Mr. Samuels," Jonelle said in a polite but determined voice. "However, we must continue the examination to help catch your wife's assailant."

Marc Samuels slowly released his wife and stood up, turning his broad shoulders toward Jonelle. "Okay, now what?"

Not used to capturing the attention of male model types, Jonelle eagerly showed off her expertise. She pointed to the rape kit. "Each of these envelopes contains items central to collecting evidence—evidence that will be used for a conviction in court."

Jonelle opened the first envelope, which contained a paper towel and a comb. She glanced at Marc to see if he was watching. He was.

Dr. Farad tucked the paper towel under Tara's derriere and then methodically ran the comb through her pubic hairs. Jonelle watched the couple's eyes lock worriedly.

The towel and combings were returned to the envelope, sealed by Jonelle, initialed, and dated.

Tara Samuels stared into space as Dr. Farad took up another envelope and began scraping material from underneath her fingernails.

Twelve hairs were cut from Tara's head and put into another envelope, which was also sealed, initialed and dated by Jonelle.

"Can you please lie back," Dr. Farad said to Tara. "Yes, please. Lay back. Can you—" He gently pried at Tara's legs, but she crossed them tightly like a little child. Dr. Farad tried to gently coax her but she squirmed away.

"Tara," Marc said, biting his lower lip. "Lean back."

Jonelle threw Marc a sharp glance, but Tara reached out for her husband, who immediately took her hand.

The nurse reached for another envelope, tied a tube around Tara's arm, and began drawing blood. Dr. Farad wiped a vaginal specimen onto a slide and handed it to the nurse, who whisked it out of the room.

"Where's she going with that?" Marc asked.

"To analyze it for mobile sperm," Jonelle answered. "If we find semen, we'll run DNA on it."

Anxiety twisted Marc's beautifully sculpted features and Jonelle was certain the realization had finally hit him: a rapist could have impregnated his pretty wife.

One by one the envelopes were filled with samples. When Tara was finally allowed to shower in peace, Marc Samuels approached Jonelle as she collected the envelopes.

"Will you be able to find her attacker?"

"I'm afraid Mrs. Samuels wasn't able to furnish us with much information. Maybe you can get her to talk to you. Meanwhile, there were no apparent traces of seminal fluid, but we'll run the swab through the lab and see what comes up."

"And if you get his DNA...?"

"If I can get a genetic profile of the assailant, the first thing I'll do is run it through CODIS. That's the Combined DNA Index System, which is a data bank of DNA profiles of sex offenders. It's a start."

Marc Samuels studied Jonelle. "What else did you find?"

"She was bound at the wrists at one point and she has a good-size bruise on her hip. It doesn't appear that Mrs. Samuels was beaten on any other part of her body."

Marc stared at Jonelle, his dimpled chin jutting toward her like a weapon. "But you can't identify him?"

"It simply doesn't happen that fast, sir." Jonelle surveyed Marc Samuels with a mixture of envy and sympathy. Here was a man, Jonelle presumed, who was obviously used to getting his own way, right away.

"Your wife needs you to be strong," Jonelle told him and reached into her purse. "Here is my card. I will be in touch as I'm the detective on this case. You will be contacted by a state social worker, a rape counselor. I highly advise that you meet with her."

Tara Samuels timidly exited the bathroom, dressed in a pink Juicy Couture jogging suit brought by her husband.

"You can go home now, Ms. Samuels." Jonelle snapped shut her evidence collection kit and replaced the camera in its case.

Tara allowed Marc to help her into a jacket and said in a small voice, "She wanted to go home, too."

Heading out the door, Jonelle Williams stopped in her tracks and turned back toward Tara. "She?"

Marc gaped at his wife and then stammered, "One of your friends? Were you with someone?" He glanced, concerned, at Jonelle.

Jonelle slowly approached the couple, aware her loafers were making clicking sounds in the quiet room. "There was another female with you, Ms. Samuels? Where?"

Tara focused on her and Jonelle suddenly felt frightened under the strange blue headlights. "In the house. Only she can't go home because she's not moving."

"Oh, good Lord," Jonelle said. She flipped open her cell phone and dialed the Sheriff's Department operator to dispatch a search and rescue.

CHAPTER

The green helicopter sent by the Aero Bureau of the Sheriff's Department hovered low over the stretching oak trees, kicking up a tornado of sharp brown leaves and new green grass. The rain, having abated somewhat, allowed the officers better visibility to search for suspects, vehicles, tire tracks, and even more importantly, bodies.

The Wagon Wheel Ranch was a sixteen-acre abandoned movie set at the end of a quarter-mile dirt road. From above, the deputies spied a house, corrals, stables, and an empty pool. They touched down in the middle of a large riding ring bordered by broken wood fencing. Deputy Donald Hart radioed their position to the Malibu substation.

Deputy Tony Velasquez killed the engine and exited the helicopter along with Hart. The two men surveyed the lonely mist-laden ranch.

"Where do you want to start?" Hart asked.

A coyote bayed from a surrounding hill. The two men looked toward the sound, seeing nothing but wet chaparral.

"Didn't the victim say where the other girl was?" Hart did not like coyotes.

"They got nothing out of her," Velasquez said, eyeing the howling hill. "Some guy on a motorcycle said she came running out of the drive."

Hart shook his head and lifted his parka hood against the wetness. "Sixteen acres, huh? We might as well start there." He nodded to the barn before them. The dilapidated doors hung open in a forlorn welcome.

The two men entered stables that smelled like mildewed hay and the ghosts of long ago horses. Innumerous holes punctured the walls, piercing their bodies with vapory light as they walked from stall to stall, hands on weapons, alert for any sounds. The coyote issued another passionate wail, and Hart swallowed as his foot kicked a cracked leather bridle.

Finding the barn empty, the two deputies trudged through soft mud toward the ranch house. True to its name, an ancient wagon wheel rested against the home's stone exterior.

Hart pushed open a whitewashed front door, which gave with no hesitation. The inside smelled surprisingly fresh, the reason apparent when the two men looked up and saw a huge hole in the roof through which a light rain sprinkled. An elaborate stone fireplace loomed to the right, its firebox empty save for a rustling wind.

Velasquez peeked into a small kitchen. Pipes jutted from the yellowed walls and the tile floor was brown where appliances once stood.

"Tony."

Hearing his name, Velasquez exited the kitchen and joined Hart who stood in the living room. He followed Hart's gaze. A ladder rose up to a loft. Next to the ladder was a closed, narrow door.

Tony Velasquez nudged his partner and they pulled their guns, approaching the door.

"Anybody in there?" Hart called.

A whispery silence answered him.

Velasquez quietly counted off and Donald Hart took the cover position. Velasquez kicked in the door, which immediately hit the wall with a loud crack.

The two deputies exchanged glances. They stood before a tiny bathroom. The ceramic tub was religiously chipped and brown with age. A spider scuttled from the drain when they inspected it. The sink held nothing but a drain surrounded by a corona of ancient rust. For show, Hart turned the squeaking faucet and a groan was heard in the bowels of the house.

Shrugging, Hart turned to his partner. "Well, looks like we've got sixteen acres to search. Think we need help?"

"I would say so," Velasquez said and then narrowed his eyes as a drop of red magically appeared on Hart's hood. He was about to inquire whether his partner was hurt when another drop suddenly fell with a soft plop. Velasquez jerked his head upwards and saw a bloodstain pooling on the yellowed popcorn ceiling. Hart followed his gaze and was met with another droplet, this one catching the bridge of his nose.

❧ ❧ ❧

Dr. Ming Li stood at the window of her hotel room and watched the mist come in from the ocean and creep over the city. Behind her, Gabriel kissed her neck and gently pulled down the zipper of her dress. He laid her shoulders bare and kissed the soft skin of her back. Ming shivered beneath his lips. The dress fell to her feet, and Gabriel's hands traced the outline of her figure. He pressed himself close to her as his breath deepened and his hands meandered to the front of her body.

"Why were you late?" Ming asked.

Gabriel paused. "You want to start this now?"

"I want to know what you found more important than me. I specifically asked you to support me today and you were late. And I don't buy your traffic excuse. You could have made it from your place to here in no time."

Gabriel sighed into her neck. "I wasn't coming from Santa Monica. I was coming from Dr. B's."

Dr. Raymond Berkowitz had been working with Gabriel since he'd been ordered into therapy for police brutality. Although Gabriel's sessions were no longer mandatory, Gabriel continued to seek therapy to help him deal with the fact he'd been molested as a child. Both Dr. B and the Malibu Canyon Murder case had brought that sad fact to light last summer. For most of his life, Gabriel had blocked out the memory of his rape.

Ming turned to face him. "Why didn't you say so?"

"I wasn't going to announce it, especially with those people listening."

"What do you mean 'those people'?"

Gabriel let his hands drop.

"I'm one of those people," Ming said more emphatically.

Gabriel shook his head, feeling his arousal tight in his pants. He sighed again and sat on the bed, thinking that if only Ming could keep her mouth shut the two of them could be between the sheets right now.

"Are you intimidated by my professional friends, Gabriel?" Standing in her satiny bra and panties, Ming put her hands on her hips and stared him down. "Is that the real reason you were late?"

He gave her an exasperated look as his cell phone began to ring. He reached for it.

"McRay," he answered hollowly.

A voice on the line said, "I need you, Hiker Joe."

Gabriel recognized the Chicano accent of his Team Lieutenant, Miguel Ramirez, and figured that something had happened in the Santa Monica Mountains.

"What's going on?" he asked.

"A dead girl off Topanga Canyon. I know you're not on duty right now, but—"

"No problem," Gabriel said, eager to escape Ming's interrogation. "I'm on my way."

"I'm not interrupting one of your 'sessions,' am I?"

Ramirez always had to stick one in.

"No," Gabriel answered and kept a wary eye on Ming, "but I'll have to call you back."

He ended the call. Once upon a time, Gabriel and Ramirez used to be at each other's throats, but the two had forged a grudging respect for one another. While they still butted heads, they did so with less-than-sharp horns.

"I've got to go," he told Ming as he pulled on his tuxedo jacket. "I've been assigned a new case."

"You're leaving?"

"Sorry."

Ming's high cheekbones burned scarlet, but she said nothing. Gabriel gave her a peck on the cheek, and wondered why all their conversations ended in arguments lately. Feeling powerless to stop the pattern, Gabriel left the hotel room with nothing to look forward to except a murder.

CHAPTER 3

The low clouds spread fingers of white mist between the green, tree-studded hills. Gabriel drove along the bumpy, mud-churned drive of Wagon Wheel Road. He passed a shed that might have once served as a gatehouse and a rusted Volkswagen bug that peeked like an animal through the thistle that had overgrown it. The Celica's tires skidded, and Gabriel commanded himself to slow down.

The road ended in a circular valley surrounded by hills, with stables on one side and a farmhouse on the other. The farmhouse would have been charming were it not hiding the body of a dead person.

Two flashing black and white units were there; the officers just finished taping off the perimeter. A coroner's wagon, fire truck, and an ambulance were parked outside the farmhouse, along with a Mobile Crime Scene Unit van. The bad visibility brought on by the low clouds caused a helicopter to idle uselessly in the dead center of a decrepit riding ring.

As Gabriel removed his evidence case from the Celica's trunk, he saw his partner approaching. Michael Starkweather was nicknamed "Dash" for the bottle of salt-free seasoning he always carried with him. Dash was reed-thin, with bulging brown eyes, peach-colored skin, and a prominent Adam's apple.

"Hey." Dash smiled and the Adam's apple bobbed in amusement. "You didn't have to dress up on my account."

Gabriel looked down at his tuxedo, now getting ruined in the moist air. "You're a real joker. I just came from a luncheon."

"Charity?"

"Yeah, Doctors Plagued with Big Egos." Gabriel looked heavenward, reminded again of the grief he would get later from Ming. Dash didn't press the subject.

"What have we got?" Gabriel asked him.

"A woman was sexually assaulted here. She was seen running from this road out onto Topanga Canyon Boulevard. She mentioned there being another female involved." Dash looked back to the house. "The guys from Aero found a woman's body in an upstairs loft about two hours ago."

"Okay, let's go."

As lead investigator, Gabriel assumed control, ensuring the safety of personnel and security at the scene. Gabriel began his preliminary walk-through. The partners entered the house and heard the murmur of voices coming from an upstairs loft. A ladder was nailed to the wall next to a bathroom door. Hooking his hands on each side of the rails, Gabriel hoisted himself upwards and found himself staring into the blue face of a young woman.

Her eyes, dotted with burst blood vessels, bulged unnaturally from their sockets. Her tongue protruded from her mouth like a purple flag. Gabriel looked up and saw a CSI officer, Jonelle Williams from Sex Crimes, and a coroner standing over the body.

"Hello," Gabriel said to them genially as he carefully climbed over the corpse.

"Greetings," replied the coroner. "Upon preliminary inspection, I'd say strangulation was the cause of death. Garroted. She's been dead about ten hours."

Gabriel snapped on latex gloves, pulled his camera from the evidence case, and looked where the coroner gently lifted the folds of jet-black hair. At first Gabriel could not see the weapon used to choke the woman since her neck was so encrusted with drying blood; then the coroner displayed two ends of a wire protruding from the back of the head. With gloved fingers, Gabriel inspected the wound and his stomach did a somersault.

"She's nearly decapitated."

"The murder weapon appears to be common baling wire," the coroner told him.

Gabriel backed away, swallowing. Most killers this furious would make use of something convenient, and Gabriel thought of the barn outside.

"Dash," he called to his partner below. "Conduct a thorough search of those stables. Collect any remnants of baling wire." Gabriel caught sight of Tony Velasquez loitering near the whistling stone fireplace. "Tell me you didn't touch anything in the stables."

Velasquez held his hands up defensively. "Not me, man. We did a walk-through though."

A rumbling of thunder rolled over them.

"Shit," muttered the CSI officer. "Better get started right away. This whole place could get soaked in a New York minute."

The CSI unit dusted for fingerprints and Gabriel began photographing the victim in situ. She wore white lace panties. The band over the right hip was twisted, as if the panties had been yanked up her body. Ligature marks encircled her wrists, but nothing bound them now. A pair of boots stood neatly on the other side of the loft next to a folded pair of jeans, a black biker's jacket, and a polka-dotted retro shirt. Another pair of jeans, with thong panties still visible inside, and a white ruffled blouse lay crumpled nearby.

After Gabriel photographed their position, he picked up the white ruffled blouse with his gloved hand.

Jonelle Williams, who had been intently watching Gabriel work, finally spoke. "The witness claims to have worn jeans and a white shirt. I'd like them bagged for her."

"Okay," Gabriel nodded. "The other clothes must belong to the dead girl."

He rifled through them, searching for a wallet or ID and found none. The living girl who had pulled on her boots that morning was now unknown, a Jane Doe. Gabriel let his eyes roam the loft.

The loft's green shag carpeting was strewn with empty tin cans, faded fast food wrappers, and broken glass. Garbage left by junkies and vagrants. Gabriel spied a syringe and ordered all garbage collected, including fiber samples from the carpet.

He photographed the crime scene from all angles, including the eye-level encounter he'd first had with the dead girl, and began his written narrative of the crime scene by pulling out a spiral notepad and a pencil.

Gabriel noted the location, date, time, weather, and lighting, while Dash, the more artistic of the two, sketched the basic perimeter, fixing objects in detail, from the boots in the loft to the fireplace down below.

It was dark when Gabriel mapped out a grid for the other officers to use in order to conduct an extensive evidence search of the property.

"I'm gonna need to talk to our witness, Jonelle," he said, noting how the Sex Crimes investigator had stayed around much longer than she needed to.

"You can't do that yet, Gabe. She's a victim herself."

"She's not dead like her friend. What time can you have her in my office tomorrow?"

Jonelle, haughty behind her dark brown eyes, replied, "She's not going to your office. You go to her."

Gabriel eyed Jonelle with some irritation and a little admiration. She was like Ming, a tough cookie.

"Okay," he acquiesced.

Ten hours of rain had washed any tire tracks from the mud and Gabriel was left with countless questions. Did the two victims walk the long road to the house or were they driven? Was the assailant with them or did they encounter him at the ranch? Only the rape victim could provide these answers and Gabriel planned on quizzing her tomorrow.

The following day, Gabriel headed to the guard-gated community of Hidden Springs.

He thought of Ming's invulnerable beauty as he drove along a comfortable road bordered by white corral fencing and pastoral trails. Out his window, Gabriel viewed mansions of varying designs. Ming also had a big house. She had all the trappings of success. She'd been right, of course, when she accused him of being intimidated by her fellow professionals. Sometimes Gabriel wondered if Ming categorized him as an emotionally dented, uncouth cop.

Refusing to delve further into his aching pride, Gabriel concentrated instead on his case. He drove up the Samuels' long driveway that wound around a wide lawn flush with valley oaks. He parked near a koi pond with a waterfall in the center and looked mutely at a sprawling ranch house. Gabriel exited his car, walked up a brick path lined with potted flowers of Evening Primrose, and rang a doorbell that chimed "Silent Night."

The clouds above him were bilious and bright white. Gabriel studied them and could make out the shapes of a caboose, a poodle, and—

His eyebrows furrowed. In the vaporous forms, Gabriel saw the face of Andrew Pierce, a neighbor from his childhood. Andrew Pierce had—

He had raped me.

Gabriel quickly dropped his gaze to the bricks at his feet. The beautiful clouds were deceiving; they warned of approaching storms.

The door swung open to reveal a squat woman with a wide, easy face and short dark hair.

"Mrs. Samuels?" he asked her.

The woman looked suspiciously at him and Gabriel showed her his identification.

"Is Tara Samuels at home? I'm Detective Gabriel McRay, Los Angeles County Sheriff's Department."

"*¿Mande?*"

Jonelle Williams poked her face next to the squat woman. "It's okay, Rosa. Come on in, Gabriel."

A little acid burned in her invitation. Gabriel responded by slipping his card in her jacket pocket as he stepped by her.

"Where's your sword and shield, Jonelle?"

"Watch yourself," Jonelle warned him. Nylons shaded her large calves, and red lipstick shone fresh on her full lips.

Highly polished wood floorboards covered the entry hall and extended out into a large living room. A den and spacious kitchen spanned to the left where Gabriel could make out a portion of a large central island, a Viking range, Sub-Zero refrigerator, and miles of expensive granite countertops. A hallway veering to the right seemed to lead to another country.

A tall, good-looking man with pecan-colored eyes and an unseasonable tan rounded the kitchen entrance and took

Gabriel's hand in his smooth one, shaking it hard. He held a can of Coke Zero in his other hand.

"Detective McRay, right? Marc Samuels, Tara's husband. Listen, you make this quick. My wife is in no condition to entertain visitors."

"I'm not a visitor," Gabriel told him squarely. "And I don't need entertainment. Your wife is a witness to a homicide I'm investigating, and I need to ask her a few questions."

Marc Samuels rubbed his chiseled jaw, sizing up Gabriel, who stoically weathered Marc's gaze. Finally Marc tossed Jonelle a pleading look. She took the bait and ambled forward.

"Mrs. Samuel's condition is very delicate, Gabe. Go easy, huh?"

"Of course," Gabriel told her.

Jonelle looked at him doubtfully and then turned her solid frame to Marc. "Sergeant McRay will keep it brief."

Marc crunched the can in his fist and made a perfect basket into the kitchen sink. His show of confidence reminded Gabriel of Ming.

Marc led Jonelle and Gabriel through a set of gleaming French doors into a vast backyard containing an over-sized pool, complete with a slide, a waterfall, and a view of the mountains beyond. An outdoor kitchen and fireplace stood ready for entertaining al fresco.

The trio continued past a large pool house through whose glass doors Gabriel spied not one, but two pool tables. Marc motioned them down a small hill to the stables.

"Tara!" Marc called loudly, cupping his hands around his mouth.

From over a small rise, backed by blue sky and white clouds, emerged a woman on horseback. Her gold hair was elfish, playing around her face in the crisp winter breeze. She rode slowly toward the group, and Marc moved to help his wife dismount her Palomino.

Tara Samuels appeared to be fragile, but the frailty seemed to come less from her attractive body and more from some inner melancholy.

Understandable for what she's gone through, Gabriel thought.

He could clearly make out, under the cable knit sweater Tara wore, breasts too voluptuous for such a slender reed. She's had augmentation, Gabriel surmised, unable to stop his eyes from surveying her body.

Pulling out his identification, Gabriel fumbled and dropped it. When Marc Samuels retrieved the ID and handed it back, Gabriel read amusement in Samuels's nut-colored eyes. Obviously, Marc Samuels enjoyed seeing other men falter around his gorgeous wife.

"Can I talk to Mrs. Samuels in private, please?"

"I can hear whatever my wife has to say."

"Mrs. Samuels?" Gabriel said, turning to Tara. Maybe she wouldn't want her husband to hear the lurid details of her rape.

"I want Marc to stay." Tara's voice, wan like a child's, seemed tinged with the lull of an anti-depressant.

Marc tossed Gabriel an "I-told-you-so" smirk. Unfazed, Gabriel tucked his badge away and pulled out a pencil and his dog-eared notepad. He felt the anger brewing but he willed it down.

"Mrs. Samuels," Gabriel began. "You told Detective Williams here that you do not know the identity of the woman found."

Tara regarded her short nails.

No polish, also like a young girl, Gabriel thought. He cleared his throat. "You don't know her?"

Tara shook her head and absently petted the horse's light mane. The Palomino was a beautiful animal. Gabriel's eyes left the horse and traveled once again to Tara and how well she wore her jodhpurs.

"Can you tell me what you remember about that day, Mrs. Samuels," Gabriel asked. "You were abducted—where?"

Tara slowly removed the horse's bridle. "I was horseback riding. I have another horse boarded at Blue Sage Stables. Dorrie."

"We have two horses there," Marc added with a sniff of pride. "Both have championship lineages."

Gabriel ignored Marc and said to Tara, "You often ride alone?"

"It's very peaceful there." She walked the horse into the stall. Gabriel followed, catching a scent of lavender coming from underneath her sweater.

"I've never had a problem," Tara said. She peeled a flake of hay from the stack and lovingly fed her horse.

"Let Gilberto do that, honey," Marc said.

Tara didn't seem to hear him. "I was returning from my ride. I wasn't far from the equestrian center when something spooked my horse." Tara licked her lips once and she seemed to wince internally. "A masked man came out of the brush and my horse reared and I fell off."

"You fell off into the brush?"

"What the hell else would she fall into?" Marc cried.

Gabriel took his time regarding Marc Samuels and then made a note to have Tara's pants checked by a forensic botanist.

"Gabriel, we wanted this to be short," Jonelle said.

"A man came out of the brush," Gabriel pressed onward. "You say he was wearing a mask. What kind?"

"A ski mask."

"What color?"

"Navy blue."

That line of questioning went well despite Tara's Zoloft fog. Navy blue ski masks, however, were a dime a dozen. "About how tall was he?"

In a drifting voice, not looking at either man, Tara replied, "Taller than you, more like Marc's height."

Did she have to notice that Gabriel wasn't as tall as her husband? Feeling a little sheepish that he cared at all if Tara Samuels found him attractive, Gabriel asked, "And his hands, did you notice his hands?"

Gabriel was hoping she would have noticed if he were black, white, tattooed…

"He was completely clothed in black, except for that navy mask."

Gabriel saw Tara look at her husband for help, but Marc seemed too concerned to come to her rescue.

"He wore gloves," Tara said. "Black leather gloves and he grabbed me before I could scream. He grabbed me while I was still sitting down from where I fell. He grabbed me and he tied my wrists behind my back. He—" Tara looked up at the burst of clouds in the sky and then slowly put her face into her hands. Marc put an arm around her shoulders.

"What did he tie your hands with?" Gabriel pressed.

Tara shook her head violently.

"What did he say to you?"

"Nothing." Tara's voice was muffled through her hands.

"Okay, Sergeant, time to leave," Marc declared.

Gabriel turned to Marc. "There's a girl with no name down at the county morgue who can't tell anybody anything. Your wife is my only witness."

"My wife is in no shape to continue."

Gabriel turned toward Tara. "Mrs. Samuels, I'm sorry to press you like this, but can you tell me anything more about this person? Did he have an accent?"

"I don't know!" Tara cried. "He tied my hands and stuffed something in my mouth! It was awful! He dragged me to his car."

"Where was his car parked?" Gabriel made a note to hike around Blue Sage Stables and the surrounding area.

"Time to leave, Mr. McRay," Marc said.

Tara fidgeted out from under Marc's arm. "He dragged me through some bushes!"

"Did he drag you back to the equestrian center parking lot?"

"No!"

"Where then?"

"I don't know!"

"Was the other girl in the car?"

"I can't—" Tara looked miserably from the stables to her horse to Marc. "She was already at the house. He parked on the road and we walked up the driveway. She told me she wanted to go home."

Not quite following her train of thought, Gabriel shook his head to clear it. "What happened then?"

"She was tied up."

"No—okay. What happened when you got to the ranch house?"

"Hey!" Marc said. "You're not welcome anymore!"

"Please, Mr. Samuels." Gabriel stepped closer to Tara. "You entered the house and then what happened?"

"He tied my hands."

"In the house? You said he tied your hands on the trail."

"In the car!"

Gabriel paused, looking at her. Don't bother to ask the anti-depressant too many questions, he thought. "Did you see the assailant kill the other woman?"

Tara shook her head and crossed her arms tightly.

"Mrs. Samuels," Gabriel ventured.

"This is torturing my wife!" Marc stepped toward Gabriel. "Hasn't she been through enough?"

The anger hit, a devil on Gabriel's shoulder, on his back, in his head. Gabriel swiveled his body toward the taller man. "Would you please stay out of this?"

Marc Samuels slammed his hands on Gabriel's shoulders. "I'm going to escort you out now, Sergeant Jerko."

"Get your hands off me," Gabriel said through clenched teeth. "Get them off now."

"What kind of cop are you? I'm reporting you, you fucking nutcase!"

"Oh, great, Gabriel!" Jonelle said, coming between them.

"He told me to turn my head away!" Tara screamed suddenly. "I didn't want to look. She made the most hideous sound. I could hear her choking! I knew she was dying!"

Gabriel, who previously felt pressured to slam his fist into Marc's handsome features, went limp. Jonelle and Marc stood by dumbly and looked at Tara, who fell into convulsing sobs and knelt down in the mud. Marc went to his wife and gently picked her up.

"It's okay, baby," Marc reassured her and then glared furiously at Gabriel.

Jonelle walked Gabriel past the swimming pool, through the Native American motif of the living room, and finally halted him at the front door. "Can't you control yourself, Gabe?"

"I'm sorry. Dash is better in sensitive situations."

"I'll try to get something more from her," Jonelle told him. "Assuming the rapist is unknown to her, he's most likely been assaulting other women. I accessed the NCIC, but no similar crimes surfaced."

Gabriel gazed at the flowing waterfall in the koi pond. "A guy with a ski mask and leather gloves forces her into a car after toppling her from her horse. How could he have been following on foot while she was on a horse?"

"Maybe this was an opportunistic sex offender. He sees a woman alone on a horse. Maybe he was hiking."

"Dressed as he was?" Gabriel studied a cloud. "Nah, he was dressed for action. He had a car, a place picked out."

"He still could be opportunistic. He could be a park ranger, a worker at the equestrian center."

Gabriel acquiesced with a nod. "True. Then he drives her to an abandoned house where he—what? Did he assault Mrs. Samuels there or in the car? Did he kill the other woman first and then assault Mrs. Samuels? How did Mrs. Samuels get away? Did he let her go? Her information was sketchy at best."

"What do you expect? The woman's been violated and witnessed a horrible murder. You think people can turn off and on like machines? Don't you have a heart?"

Gabriel swallowed, and said nothing as Jonelle closed the door. He wandered slowly to his car. Dark clouds began blotting out the sapphire sky, and despite all his unanswered questions, Gabriel could only think of Tara's striking blue eyes.

❦ ❦ ❦

Gabriel lived at one of the last rent-controlled apartments in Santa Monica. Although it was old, it was near enough to the beach and that suited Gabriel fine. The temperate weather calmed him and the strong and steady Pacific Ocean was a much-needed constant in his life.

He heard a knock at the door and he opened it to find Ming, holding a bottle of Macallan whiskey.

"I'm sorry I ruined our afternoon delight," she said.

"I was the one who had to leave." Gabriel took the proffered whiskey.

"I made you want to get away from me." Ming sighed as she peeled off her coat and then sat down on the worn couch.

Gabriel checked the bottle's label. "Eighteen years old. You shouldn't have."

"I thought we both could use a drink."

Gabriel reached into his cabinet for two tumblers, which he filled with ice. Ming shivered and crossed her arms. Raindrops glistened on her dark hair.

Ming—a bulwark of professionalism, even as her nipples hardened under her blouse. Try as she might, Gabriel observed, Dr. Li couldn't shirk her own femininity.

He set the glasses down on the coffee table in front of her and she automatically reached for the bottle to pour. Gabriel stopped her hand and picked up the bottle.

"Why don't you let me do it?"

He poured their drinks and gave her a glass. She gazed at him with a strange expression.

"What?" he asked her.

Ming looked like she wanted to say a smart remark; instead, she raised the glass to her lips and took a long drink. Gabriel took a seat next to her and finished off nearly half his glass.

"Can we continue," Ming asked, "from where we left off?"

He opened his arms to her and she moved in, snuggling against him. He held her as she laid her head upon his chest.

"Don't move," she whispered.

He didn't.

A minute or so passed and then she lifted her face up to his and he kissed her. It was a long kiss, filled with the longing to forget past arguments. Soon, Gabriel's hands were running along and under her blouse, becoming more determined. Ming kicked off her shoes and pulled at his shirt, kneading the taut muscles underneath. Gabriel hiked up her skirt and Ming arched her back to give him free reign.

His hand found its way between her legs and Ming's hand covered his, urging him on. Gabriel moved on top of her, his tongue exploring her mouth while his fingers moved rhythmically. He felt the heat running through her body and moving into his—her moans moving down his throat. And then Gabriel realized Ming was struggling away from him, and her moans were not pleasurable, but panicked.

"I can't breathe!" she cried and threw herself to the opposite end of the couch.

Gabriel lay stupefied with his hard-on.

"I can't breathe with you on top of me like that!"

Gabriel stared at her, too astonished to reply. Ming gagged and grabbed her throat.

Her choking gesture suddenly reminded Gabriel of the girl with the baling wire twisted mercilessly around her bloodied neck. Cold water couldn't have been more effective in cooling his heat.

He moved to comfort Ming, but she jerked away and leaped to her feet. Gabriel watched in wonder as she began to frantically dress herself.

"What is it?" he asked.

"Nothing!" Tears began slipping from Ming's eyes. Gabriel rose and went to her.

"This is something. What's wrong?"

Ming ducked away from him, ran to a corner of the room, and then stood there, half-dressed and shaking. "Sometimes I get claustrophobic. I get... I remember that—that fucker Archwood and how I couldn't breathe!"

She put her face into her hands and began to sob.

Gabriel gazed at his girlfriend. He had never seen Ming like this except last summer when—

In a dark cave filling with icy seawater, Gabriel caught sight of a PVC pipe jutting from the sandy floor. The scent of fog was thick in his nostrils and he felt creeping terror at his back. The pipe suddenly moved erratically and he realized in horror that someone was buried there. Digging frenziedly through the muck, he found Ming soaking, buried alive, struggling to breathe through the pipe lodged between her teeth.

"Ming, sit down," Gabriel told her.

"No."

"You want another drink?"

"No."

All along Gabriel had convinced himself that Ming was a medical professional and could better understand the complexities of human catastrophe. She had dealt so well with Gabriel's own problems. Obviously, she was less adept at handling her own issues.

"Why don't you see Dr. B about this?" he suggested gently.

Ming wiped her running nose. "I don't need his help."

"Apparently, you do."

"I'm handling it!"

Gabriel ran a frustrated hand through his hair and felt the whiskey speak through him. "Always have to be perfect, don't you?"

Ming shot him a severe look and swiped up the rest of her clothes.

"How long has this been going on?" Gabriel asked her.

"You're not a therapist, Gabriel. Quit trying to act like one."

Hurt, Gabriel grabbed his pants and yanked them on. "Jesus, you don't talk anymore, you just attack."

"I'm not attacking you!" she yelled. "Not everything is about you!"

Gabriel wanted to yell back, he could feel the anger surging through him, but he controlled himself and took a deep breath.

The hour was late, a young woman had died a violent death, and Gabriel's mind was overtired.

"This isn't working," he announced quietly.

Ming looked at him, wobbling slightly from the liquor and her meltdown.

He slowly met her eyes. "I think we should take some time apart."

She did not reply. Instead, Ming collected her coat and walked out the door.

CHAPTER 4

D r. Raymond Berkowitz began his career as a psychological profiler for the FBI but had eventually tired of probing the minds of the violent. Although Dr. B still profiled big cases, his emphasis now was on helping the good guys—the men in blue—or as he put it: the men with the blues.

He sat in his office at Sheriff's headquarters in Monterey Park, holding the phone to his ear and speaking with his son, Isaac.

"It's not anything important," he told his son. "I just called to say hello."

Dr. B listened as Isaac related the long list of plans he had for that afternoon.

"Well, give my regards to the coffee house crowd," Dr. B finished pensively. "You call me when you get time. Yes, I'll tell Mother hello."

Dr. B hung up the phone and gazed at a photo of his curly-haired boy. Isaac was at Stanford University deep into his graduate studies and Dr. B was left with a yearning he had never thought possible. The empty nest had liberated his wife,

Maureen, who was now rampaging through life, taking art classes, playing mah-jongg, and learning karate.

Dr. B simply felt left out.

A knock on his office door prompted the doctor to look up. He saw Gabriel McRay poke his head inside.

"May I come in?"

"Come in, come in," Dr. B said genially. Gabriel was making great progress in his therapy, much more so than Dr. B had anticipated. Then again, Gabriel was a man who wanted to get better. Attitude was half the cure.

Gabriel entered the office and hung a rain parka on the coat rack. He took his seat in one of two comfortable armchairs in front of Dr. B's desk.

Dr. B was an Adlerian psychologist. Alfred Adler, a peer of Freud, practiced a personable approach with his patients. The armchairs provided an amicable forum where patient and doctor could discourse as pals.

"How's biz?" Dr. B shook Gabriel's hand. "Any headaches lately?"

Headaches, nightmares, even severe loss of memory, were all symptomatic of the post-traumatic stress disorder, which had plagued Gabriel until recently.

"My headaches are only those brought on by simple stress." Gabriel poured himself a cup of water from a pitcher on a side table. He held the pitcher up toward Dr. B.

Dr. B shook his head, declining the water. "Is stress ever simple?"

Gabriel shrugged and sat down with his drink.

His patient wasn't talking, so Dr. B thought he would prompt him a little. "I read in the paper that the D.A. is almost ready to have their case tried against Victor Archwood."

Gabriel nodded, silent, focusing on the revolving second hand of Dr. B's wooden desk clock.

"Any thoughts about that?" Dr. B asked.

Gabriel had thought plenty about the Malibu Canyon Murderer. Ming's reenactment of her trauma last night had been an unhappy reminder.

"I don't want to think about him anymore."

"Fair enough." Dr. B chose a new subject. "Have you opened communication with your parents?"

Gabriel shrugged again, non-committal.

"It's important for you to make that effort, Gabriel. They need to hear what you have to tell them. They need to know about the molestation."

Gabriel remained silent. A minute ticked by.

"How is Ming?" Dr. B asked, switching gears.

"Not too good, I'm afraid."

"Really?"

"She's suffering, Raymond. You should have seen her last night. She's very traumatized."

Dr. B knew why Ming was traumatized. For years, Dr. Ming Li had been an audience member to the human dramas wheeled into her autopsy room. But last summer, when Victor Archwood had kidnapped her, Ming's role went from clinical pathologist to victim.

"What happened to her was my fault," Gabriel told him.

"It wasn't your fault. You rescued her."

"No. Archwood had been after me and used her as bait." Gabriel's eyes locked onto Dr. B's. "Ming thinks she can handle everything herself, but she can't. When I point that out to her, she makes me her verbal punching bag."

"Boyfriends, children, spouses—people who love us are easy targets. Strangers don't care enough about us to put up with our afflictions."

Gabriel smoothed his black curls with his hand. "I want to feel good. I want someone who makes me feel important.

I went for years feeling like a werewolf; like someone the villagers would want to kill."

"A werewolf?" Dr. B had to smile.

Gabriel pointed at his psychiatrist. "And don't hand me that Eleanor Roosevelt crap about the only person who can make you feel inferior is yourself."

Dr. B's smile widened. "I wasn't going to quote Eleanor Roosevelt. And it's 'no one can make you feel inferior without your consent.'

Gabriel did not reply, so Dr. B brought up what he felt was the central issue. "So you would like to be in a relationship with someone who empowers you, correct?"

"It'd be nice," Gabriel answered with a sharp edge to his voice.

Dr. B regarded his patient. "What kind of woman would be your ideal partner?"

"Someone not so self-assured. Someone who gives me a little room to be strong."

"Have you discussed this with Ming?"

"And give her further confirmation that I'm weak? No thanks."

"How do you know she'd consider you weak for opening up to her?"

"I just know, okay?"

"What's the alternative then?" Dr. B asked.

Gabriel shrugged. "Maybe someone else. Someone more like me."

CHAPTER 5

The girl brought in toe-tagged as Jane Doe #874 lay on a steel table in the examination room. At her head was a scale to weigh her internal organs; at her feet was a smaller table, used for dissection. X-rays had already been taken to reveal knives, needles, or any other items that might be embedded in her body. Photos had been snapped of the victim, clothed and then naked.

Ming attached a microphone to her surgical greens to record her observations and then proceeded with the external examination. The girl's clothing had been analyzed at the lab for semen and bloodstains, and Ming had the initial report. Unfortunately, the technicians had found no trace of foreign fluids.

Ming carefully unwound the baling wire that encircled the girl's throat like a feral necklace. She noted the cyanotic cast to the girl's face. Cyanosis was caused by a lack of oxygen in the blood, which gave the victim a bluish appearance. Ming knew that in most manual strangulation cases, assailants used more force than necessary to kill their victims, and this often resulted in deep contusions around the neck. The internal structure would be damaged as well, fracturing the small bone at the base of the tongue, called the hyoid. But as Ming counted the twists in the wire, even she was impressed by the fury of this garroting.

The girl's jet-black hair looked inexpensively dyed. Her chipped nails were painted a metallic green. Ming wondered who she might be and how she ended up in the morgue.

Geoffrey, a deputy coroner with wiry red hair, assisted Ming. He began collecting residue from under the girl's fingernails. Perhaps a few skin cells would ID the girl's assailant. Maybe one tiny thread caught on a hangnail would blow open the case. These possibilities reminded Ming of how much she enjoyed her job.

Sometimes, she needed to be reminded. The prosecutors, the police, the defense lawyers, and even the victim's families had little respect for the dead. Lawyers often pressured Ming to contort the truth to better suit their cases. Oftentimes, the victim's own families pressured her to erase embarrassing causes of death from the record. As chief medical examiner, Ming had successfully juggled the political rigors of her profession, managing to tell the truth and keep her job at the same time. Through all the noise that accompanied a death, Ming never lost sight of one key factor: she alone could make the dead speak.

Ming scanned the woman's torso, looking for signs that would reveal something about the girl. Various fresh bruises marred the young woman's breasts. A small hole poked through the girl's left nipple, which Ming first mistook as a wound inflicted by the attacker. But upon closer inspection, she saw that the hole was open but healed. A piercing, Ming surmised.

Going on instinct, Ming checked the girl's nostrils and belly button and found tiny holes there too. Still scanning the body for skin perforations, Ming's eyes fell on a circlet of holes adorning the dead girl's right thigh. They were large in diameter and seemed to be old scars.

Not dismissing foul play, Ming went to her toolbox and brought out a sampling of nails. She discovered the wound holes matched two-inch double-grip nails with smooth shanks.

Ming stepped back and surveyed Jane Doe, putting her age at about nineteen or twenty. Ming adjusted the microphone on her tape recorder. "On the upper right thigh, there are five healed wounds forming a circle. These might have been formed by nails..." Ming glanced hopefully toward the door.

Normally, investigators attended the autopsies of their case victims. Gabriel, however, hadn't shown up, nor had he called. Ming sighed worriedly into her microphone.

Had he been serious when he said they should take some time apart?

How selfish he was! Didn't she have the right to lose her temper now and then? Gabriel could be a little more understanding.

Still, when her world had crashed down, Gabriel had caught her like a knight in shining armor. Ming smiled sadly behind her mask. Gabriel McRay was more Night with Shiny Gun. He carried darkness on his shoulder, but he always held out for the coming dawn. Gabriel's strange optimism attracted Ming. That, and the way his hands felt on her body.

Was he no longer her boyfriend as of today?

Ming regarded the dead girl and commanded herself to concentrate less on Gabriel and more on her work. She took up a glass slide to collect a specimen swab, when the slide slipped from her grasp and shattered on the floor.

Ming bent down to collect the broken glass and then froze.

She was under black water and sand again, thrashing vainly and fighting for air.

Ming stared at the tiled floor and forced herself to breathe. In the shards of glass, she saw Victor Archwood's face; the stranger who had attacked her so suddenly that her brain hadn't had time to process what was happening to her.

It's processing everything now, Ming thought, and tore off her mask. She spat into her gloved palm; sure she would see the seawater of the San Francisco Bay. Feeling miserable, she trashed the glass shards and snapped on a new glove. She turned back to the young, violated girl lying placidly on the table with her dyed hair, chipped nails, and toe ring that glinted off the steel sink.

Ming could now relate to that stilled heart within the girl's chest, to the bulging eyes whose last vision was her attacker's face.

Victor Archwood had furiously rammed the pipe into her mouth as if she were a piece of meat, cutting her lip, chipping her tooth and then burying her beneath the earth. He had worked fervently, unmindful of her pleading eyes, the screams behind her gag. And then she was alone, underground, and knowing the tide was coming in.

Suddenly overcome, Ming missed Gabriel terribly, the man who wasn't afraid of monsters. She wanted nothing more than to have Gabriel hold her and listen to his soothing voice. A runaway teardrop escaped her eye. Geoffrey looked at her in concern, but he knew better than to get personal with his touchy boss, so he kept his questions to himself.

Ming replaced her mask and mustered her usual emotional distance, telling herself she must identify this girl and give closure to the family. She began combing the pubic hairs for evidence, and hoped to find her usual refuge in her work.

A sudden glimpse of bright gold between the black curls caught Ming's eye. Curious, she pulled the hairs apart and saw more vivid color. Taking up a razor, Ming carefully shaved the groin area.

"Check this out," she said to Geoffrey. "Get a photo of it."

Ming took out a ruler as a scale device and put it against the flesh. Bending over the body with a camera, Geoffrey immortalized a previously hidden tattoo that now stood out in vibrant color: a golden cross with a black snake draped across it.

❦ ❦ ❦

Gabriel headed to the house in Hidden Springs. The weather was dry and the morning sunshine sparkled off every wet surface. Driving over the Sepulveda Pass, Gabriel was treated to a clear view of the sweeping San Fernando Valley, with the snow-tipped San Gabriel Mountains to the east and the Simi Hills to the west, newly minted with fresh green grass and noble oaks. The Spanish settlers who first crossed the pass had seen this vista, minus the endless field of suburban houses and mini-malls, and surely thought they were entering Eden's meadows.

Gabriel parked his ancient Celica under the thick branches of a hanging oak tree and squinted jealously at the mansion sprawling before him.

How could Marc Samuels have been dealt every good card; incredible looks and incredible wealth?

At the front door, Rosa answered his knock. "*¿Sí?*"

"Is Mrs. Samuels here?"

"*Momentito.*"

He stood in the entry facing a large mirror that reflected his cheap shirt and tie; his Dockers that were wrinkled from the car ride. Rosa reappeared at the end of the hall leading to the right wing of the house.

"*Ella dice*—," She caught herself speaking Spanish and reddened under her café-au-lait skin. "The Missus, she say wait. You unnerstand, Mister?"

Gabriel nodded. Rosa retreated down the hallway, and he wandered into the den with its broad armchairs and Navajo rugs, dark wood tables and thick pillar candlesticks. On an intricately carved end table lay a white satin photo album entitled "Our Wedding." Gabriel fidgeted momentarily and then, unable to resist, he opened the album.

One photo showed Tara in a Cinderella wedding dress, beaded bodice, white puffy sleeves, and infinitely long train. Marc Samuels stood beside her, straight out of a magazine ad: custom tuxedo, chiseled jaw, long lashes, white teeth, and thick, curling brown hair. Both wore diamond-encrusted wedding bands. A carriage pulled by white horses brought in the bride. The banquet tables were strewn with crab, shrimp, lobster, and caviar. A stretch Hummer limo carried the bride and groom away...

"Hello, Sergeant McRay."

Gabriel turned to see Tara, wearing lavender cashmere and distressed jeans. Her blond hair played gracefully around her elfin face as she hugged her delicate body. Again her mix of beauty and vulnerability struck Gabriel.

He promptly shut the wedding album. "Thank you for seeing me, Mrs. Samuels."

She shrugged. "Please call me Tara."

Gabriel nodded, embarrassed to be caught thumbing through her photos.

Tara deposited herself into one of the Native American patterned chairs while Gabriel took a seat on a plush, color-coordinated sofa.

"Your house is very beautiful."

"Thank you. I had a designer."

The whisper of a drug haunted her inflection and she stared through Gabriel as if he were a ghost. He fought the urge to wave his palm in front of her face. Instead, he cleared his throat and pulled out his pad and pencil.

"How are you feeling?" he asked, mimicking Dr. B.

"Better, thank you."

"That's good..." Gabriel trailed off, not knowing where to begin. The house was very quiet. "Your husband is at work?"

She nodded and then focused an intense look on Gabriel.

Discomfited, Gabriel studied his notepad. "You often ride horses alone in the mountains?"

"Yes."

"Any stable personnel, male, who might have struck up conversations with you? Acted a bit too interested? Anybody at the equestrian center who is aware you ride alone?" He looked up at Tara and felt a stirring in his groin.

"Jonelle already asked me that. I told her I don't talk to anyone except Lynn Traxler, who owns the place. There are some laborers, but they don't bother me." Tara licked her lips. "There is one guy..."

"His name?"

She shook her head, as if to jar loose the memory. "Rob, Ross, maybe."

Gabriel nodded and wrote in his notebook: *horse center/ laborer—Rob, Ross made conversation*. To Tara he said, "You said that your horse was spooked and that you fell off. Were you grabbed from behind or did he rush at you from one side?"

"I can't remember," Tara said, inhaling deeply. "He was there all of a sudden, wearing a ski mask and pulling my arm, pulling me away from Dorrie."

Gabriel nodded. "So he abducted you, tied your hands, and forced you into a car. What kind of car was it?"

"A white car."

"A van?" Gabriel shrugged, wanting answers. "A convertible?"

"Jonelle already asked me," Tara said, becoming agitated. "It was a sedan."

"Four doors? Two doors?"

"Four—no, I mean two."

Gabriel looked at her, brows furrowed.

Tara suddenly stood up sighing and began pacing. "How am I supposed to remember every detail? I was shocked. One minute I'm on my horse and the next minute… I didn't get any details!" She wrung her hands. "I sat in the front seat where he could keep the gun on me."

"He abducted you at gunpoint?"

"Yes!" Tara nodded her head. "And he drove with one hand on the wheel."

"An automatic transmission then," Gabriel surmised. "I mean, if it were a stick shift he couldn't hold the gun." Gabriel scribbled in his pad and asked, "Can you describe the gun at all? Was it a revolver or…?"

He glanced up at Tara and saw her staring at him in exasperation.

Gabriel liked his job, sometimes too much and often at the expense of another's feelings. Dash was the sensitive one.

"I'm sorry," Gabriel said.

Tara pressed her hands to her forehead, drumming delicate fingers lightly against her flesh. "Can we get out of this house for a while?" She appraised Gabriel with her sky blue eyes. "Can we go somewhere else to talk?"

Gabriel gazed back at her. "Sure."

They went to an outdoor mall in Calabasas where Gabriel treated them both to beverages at a bakery. They took a table outside, hoping to soak in the meager sunshine. A few yards to the right, a manmade waterfall tumbled with recycled water. Tara drank hot chocolate heaped with whipped cream. A little girl's drink, observed Gabriel.

"Don't you think hot chocolate is good on a cold day?" she said with the water rushing loudly behind her.

Gabriel drank from his steaming black coffee. "I don't go much for sweet drinks myself, but I suppose hot chocolate is good on a cold day."

"On the ranch where I grew up, my mother used to make homemade hot chocolate for us kids."

Gabriel wiped a napkin under his nose against the cold. "You grew up on a ranch?"

Tara nodded, smiling around the rim of her cup. "Just outside of Las Vegas. We had a big rambling house. We had dogs and horses and lots of land to explore. We're the Bannings. Perhaps you've heard of my family?"

"I'm afraid I don't move in society circles."

"Of course, we're the Nevada Bannings. Are you a California native?"

Gabriel's head moved forward an inch in surprise. He wasn't used to witnesses interviewing him. "Yes. I lived in San Francisco until my late teens." Thinking of San Francisco made his voice curt. "Our open space was Golden Gate Park. My family home was a two story flat."

Across the street had lived Andrew Pierce in a pastel-colored house that looked no different than thirty others in the neighborhood. But what went on inside that house had been different, very different indeed.

Each day Gabriel remembered more and more wretched details of that house: the tired couch in the den, the rabbit-eared TV, reruns of Gilligan's Island, and Andrew playing the Skipper.

Gabriel shut his eyes tightly for a moment, willing the memory to leave him.

"Where do you live now?" Tara asked.

"In Santa Monica."

He used to live in a house in Culver City, but that now belonged to his ex-wife.

"On Christmas," Tara said dreamily, "Daddy said we could have any tree we wanted, no matter how big or fancy. Money was never an object with our family." Tara studied the waterfall thoughtfully. "But we kids always thought decorating one of the trees on our property and leaving it alive was a better idea."

Gabriel pulled out his notebook. Tara had gone away again and it was time to bring her back.

"Mrs. Samuels,"

"Tara."

"I know this is difficult for you, but please try to help me. When you got into the house, did your assailant direct you into the loft?"

"Yes," she whispered and averted her eyes.

"Did you see the other girl there?"

"Yes."

"Can you describe what you saw?"

"She was tied up, but she wasn't gagged. She had no clothes on. It was cold and the rain was coming in." Tara spoke in a monotone voice and examined her whipped cream.

"Was there any conversation between the young woman and the man who abducted you?"

Tara shook her head.

"Did he call her by a name?"

"No."

"Did she say anything to you?"

"She said she wanted to go home." Tara looked over the whipped cream to Gabriel. Tears welled in her eyes.

Gabriel wondered if he should back off. Too bad Dash hadn't joined them. He was always better in emotional situations.

"He called her a lousy bitch and a bad lay!" Tara yelled suddenly.

A couple walking by glanced at Tara. Gabriel's frown sent them on their way. Tara's shoulders bunched together and the tears spilled down her face.

Keep on track, Gabriel decided. His witness was communicating. "And then what happened?"

"He tied my wrists. He was furious and h-happy all at the same time. He scared me." Her breath came out in ragged shards that cut her words. "But before he tied my wrists he—he pulled off my shirt. I didn't fight him. I was scared. She was bleeding from her neck. He pulled down my pants."

The hot chocolate shook in her hands, sloshing dangerously over the rim. Gabriel watched her shudder and shake.

"He—took—the—gun—" Tara stammered, her face twisting. "He—shoved it in—in and he—said—he said, 'you should see what happens when it cums—'" The hot chocolate exploded in her grip and she yelled in pain as the brown liquid coursed down her hand like the nearby rushing waterfall.

Gabriel jumped out of his seat and came around the table with some napkins.

He wiped the spilled chocolate from the table before it could land on her clothes, and cursed himself for pushing her too far. He grabbed more napkins and caught Tara staring at him. Slowly, she held out her wet hand to him. Gabriel regarded her tear-streaked face, and recalled how difficult it was for him to discuss his own molestation. Gabriel gently took her hand and began dabbing the chocolate away.

※　※　※

Ranger Dan Gordon enjoyed being stationed at Tapia Park off Malibu Canyon Road. Filled with oak trees and wild flowers, Tapia Park was popular with picnickers and day hikers alike.

After chasing off a couple of potheads smoking near the creek, Dan walked along the bank. Malibu Creek, which cut a swath through the park and eventually spilled into the Pacific, was stoked with rainwater. A host of unusual items were surfacing along the sandy banks, old arrowheads, nails from fallen adobe ranchos. No matter how many times Dan patrolled the area, he always discovered something new.

Hugging his bomber jacket close to his body, Dan caught sight of something white embedded in the rocks on the opposite bank. Curious, he carefully crossed the creek to investigate. As he approached, he saw the unmistakable grin of a human skull. No other bones were present other than the skull and the spinal column, caught against the shifting algae.

Dan Gordon knelt down for a closer inspection and then swallowed hard to keep back bile. Rusty wire encircled the neck bones. Two long ends protruded toward the sky like antennae to another world.

CHAPTER 6

"Anything you can tell me that could help identify her?"

"Who?" Ming asked into the phone.

"Who do you think?" Gabriel asked.

"Sorry, I didn't realize we were going to talk shop." Ming held the phone and juggled Jane Doe's open case file at the same time. "She was a Goth girl. You know, dyed black hair, metallic colored fingernails not very well manicured. A silver toe ring. A few piercings."

"Any inscriptions on the ring?"

"No."

Ming was disappointed in Gabriel's distant tone, the fact that his call was strictly business.

"She had no distinguishing marks," Ming continued, "except for a tattoo in her groin area—a gold cross with a snake over the top. Does it mean anything to you?"

"No. Hold on a minute."

Ming waited as Gabriel put her on hold. *When he returns, I'm going to tell him I'll make time for a weekend getaway.*

"Ming," Gabriel said, back on the line. "I have to go. Ramirez just paged me. A ranger found human remains in Tapia Park. The corpse has baling wire tied around the neck."

"Uh, oh." Ming slowly closed the Wagon Wheel Ranch victim's file. "I guess I'll see you in the lab then."

She waited for a response and then realized Gabriel had already hung up.

The moon was high when Gabriel arrived at Tapia Park and he ordered a couple of floodlights to be brought in. He used his own flashlight to search the creek bank. The water gurgled past him and Gabriel stumbled on a wet rock, sending his right loafer into the water.

"Wonderful," he muttered.

As he searched, Dan Gordon, the ranger who had discovered the bones, walked with him.

"The body could have come from anywhere, traveling down the creek, being washed up by the rain," Dan said. "We can inspect some coyote dens in the morning. You know, coyotes and other animals tend to drag stuff off..."

Gabriel nodded, listening to the bubbling creek and searching for anything out of the ordinary.

Unable to find anything further, the men returned to the skull, mandible, and spine, which were now laid out on a folding table under a makeshift tent fitted with lights. A coroner was inspecting the bones, joined by Dash.

"We've got a repeater, don't we?" Dash asked, indicating the twisted wire.

"Looks like it."

Circling the neck bones, the wire seemed the obvious murder weapon. Of course, Ming would make the final judgment call. *Ming...*

I shouldn't have been so brusque with her, Gabriel admonished himself.

In the back of his mind, however, he was still annoyed with Ming, and the therapy session had done nothing to placate him. Intellectually, he knew he should open up and discuss his feelings with her, but Gabriel was tired of looking weak in Ming's eyes.

And then there was that odd moment with Tara. The childlike way she gazed at him when he cleaned her hands, as if Gabriel was some sort of guardian angel.

Dash nudged him and Gabriel, still thinking about Tara, quickly turned his attention back to the corpse.

❦ ❦ ❦

Through the haze of the crack smoke, Paula May leaned back. She had taken Ecstasy earlier and was feeling warm, sexy, and adventurous. The drug moved through her body in a welcomed, slow wave and she took in the present company with half-lidded eyes.

"Want to play?" he asked.

"Sure." Paula felt pretty high. She unsnapped her lacey bra, and her breasts, freed from the constraints of the underwire, bounced in the open air. She looked curiously at the man, but he still wasn't aroused. Paula thought of limp noodles and giggled.

"You are ready to play," the man said, mistaking her laughter for coyness. He turned on the stereo and Kid Cudi's "Alive" thrummed through the room.

"Only if you can get it up," Paula teased and leaned seductively back on the pillows. She nestled against the soft yellow blanket below her.

"Bitch, I can get it up."

Paula giggled again, unable to think of any words. She vaguely wondered if he'd mixed the drug with something else, but she was too high to care—and she was horny.

He got up from where he sat on the bed and hooked a handcuff over her wrist, snapping it shut. Paula could see the cuff was connected to the bed frame. Chains of various lengths dangled from a grid above the bed. Beyond the grid was a ceiling mirror. Looking up through the grid at her naked reflection made Paula dizzy.

Smiling, the man gently cuffed her ankles. Paula glanced at him. How had he gotten to the other end of the bed so fast? She was too stoned. Paula forgave herself though; they'd all been high when they arrived. How was she supposed to notice anything? The cold metal of the cuffs was a delicious sensation. She giggled again with anticipation.

Paula felt her arm swing up as he cuffed her other hand. Her heart picked up a beat. She let her eyes drift around the room and saw the red light blinking on a camcorder that was mounted on a tripod, facing her.

"Is that digital?"

"No," the man said and moved to a counter. "You don't need firewalls with videotape."

Paula guffawed and her eyelids drooped to half-mast. "Who uses video?"

The man did not answer. He had his back to her. Paula heard a hissing noise. Was he taking a piss on the floor?

"What's that sound?" she called out dreamily.

"Acid," he replied, and turned to face her with a prominent erection and a menacing smile. "Now, I'm ready."

The Sheriff's homicide bureau was in an L-shaped room located in an obscure industrial park in Commerce, a city east of downtown Los Angeles. A morning rain fell between the low-lying buildings, tapping on the flat roofs.

A task force had been set up to review the two homicides. Dr. B, on hand as a profiler today, sat next to Gabriel at a long table. Across from Gabriel sat Ming who, in Dr. B's opinion, was in full mental armor, shielding herself with a mass of files and case photos. Gabriel protected himself with his own reports.

Jonelle Williams sat next to Ming, eyeing Gabriel and his case notes with something that, to Dr. B, might have been envy. Next to her was Dash, who appeared to be mulling over which donut to choose from a large pink box.

Dr. B looked toward the head of the table where Lieutenant Ramirez finished an entire jelly donut in two bites and then slurped coffee from a mug that read "I'm The Boss."

"All right, folks," Ramirez began, wiping his mouth with a paper napkin. "I've got two dead bodies, both with wire around their necks. What have you got?"

Dr. B glanced at Gabriel, but his patient's eyes were glued on the Formica tabletop.

Ming spoke first. "I've determined that the Tapia Park remains belong to a Caucasian female. I'd put her age at early to mid-twenties. The water, the elements, the advanced state of decomposition, all make it difficult to decipher an exact manner of death, but that wire around the neck makes a tight enough garrote. I'd say she's been dead at least six months. I found marks on the bone; no surprise given the rocky terrain and the animal activity. The marks do not appear to have been caused by a knife or tool."

Ramirez mused, frowning. "Dead since July, huh? I don't like that. Anybody thinking what I'm thinking?"

Gabriel lifted his eyes to Ming, who looked back at him with a pensive expression.

"We've got a repeater," Dash said, taking Ramirez's cue.

"You're using your brain today, Señor Spiceless." Ramirez walked around to Dash and knocked him gently on his head. "Got to exercise that muscle once in a while, *vato*."

Dash pasted a goofy smile on his face and Dr. B shook his head. Ramirez was in fine form today.

The Chicano strolled over to Ming, who was concentrating on her coffee. "I have a question for you, Dr. Frankenstein, since this recent corpse was so decayed; can you tell us more about the girl at the Wagon Wheel Ranch? Dr. Li? *Hola!*"

Ming jerked her eyes from her coffee cup. "Uh, which girl?"

Ramirez shook his head disdainfully. "The Wagon Wheel Ranch girl."

Ming straightened up. "I have photos of the wounds, the baling wire which nearly severed her head." Ming passed out 8x10 photographs to the present company. "I also have photos of some small punctures, old wounds really, that were on the victim's thigh."

"Old wounds?" Gabriel asked.

Dr. B saw a wave of hurt douse Ming's features as she made eye contact with Gabriel, but then her professionalism took precedent. "Some are only about a week healed. Others are older."

Dash asked for the photo of the puncture marks. "They're all in a round pattern. Does anyone agree this guy might have kept this victim, torturing her before he killed her?"

"It's a strong possibility," Dr. B said, leaning over Dash to gaze at the photo.

Dash passed the photo to Gabriel. "We found no baling wire in the barn at the Wagon Wheel Ranch."

"Which means either the suspect used up what was conveniently there or he took it with him," Ramirez stated and then addressed Ming. "What about the lab tests?"

"There is evidence Jane Doe from the Wagon Wheel house was sodomized shortly before death. I found a couple of yellow fibers in one wound, which are being analyzed. The tests from the lab came up negative regarding any foreign fluids. No semen, no suspect blood, nothing."

Jonelle tapped the gold tooth in her mouth with a thoughtful finger and turned to Dr. B. "If we include Mrs. Samuels, we've got two rapes, no ejaculation. He's careful, isn't he?"

The psychiatrist pushed his ever-slipping wire-rim glasses up the bridge of his nose and said, "There are several sexual predator types. The power-reassurance rapist's fantasy involves consensual relationships with his victims. He's often termed the gentleman rapist. The power-assertive rapist is the individual who believes he's simply entitled to what he wants from women and goes after it. His fantasies are minimal. The anger-retaliatory rapist is a person who assaults because he's motivated by anger and he's getting even with women. But I think the attacker in this case is more dangerous. His type falls under anger-excitation. Simply put, he's a sexual sadist."

Dash reached for a rainbow sprinkled donut. "What about choking them with wire? That's pretty retaliatory in my book. He's an angry som'bitch. Wouldn't that be the anger-retaliatory type?"

Dr. B stood up to take coffee from a machine on a side table. "The fact that the victim, according to Mrs. Samuels, said she wanted to go home indicates to me that perhaps the attacker allowed her to think that going home was an option." After spooning a generous dollop of cream into his coffee, Dr. B went back to his seat. "That sort of behavior is tortuous and cruel. He uses pain, physical or psychological, as a tool to elicit suffering from his victim. And the suffering is what fuels his fantasy."

Dr. B sipped his coffee, burned his mouth, and quickly put a hand on his lips. He turned to Jonelle. "You remarked, Sergeant Williams, how careful the suspect was that no trace of semen was found in two rape cases. Maybe he's careful, maybe not. A sexual sadist does not rape for the sheer joy of sex. He rapes to fulfill fantasies that in turn fuel his psychological need for dominance and control. Maybe physical ejaculation is what he expects, but it's the mental orgasm he achieves during these acts that satisfies him, at least temporarily."

Ramirez reached for another donut. "And we all know what that means."

"Exactly. A sexual sadist rarely strikes once." Dr. B took another, more careful sip of his coffee. "The more fuel for his fantasy he gets, the more he wants, and on a bigger and grander scale every time. We have two, possibly three victims we can now attribute to the same man." He turned to Gabriel. "Were any weapons found at the scene? How about foreign objects used to assault the women?"

Gabriel shook his head, so Dr. B continued. "No weapons were found at the scene because this type of predator is careful. He rehearses every detail and has all the equipment necessary to play out his fantasies. The equipment, of course, goes with him when he's done. There was a trucker who was raping and killing women along the interstate in Texas, he had a rape kit complete with everything he needed to subdue and torture his victims. He even outfitted his truck's cab with shackles."

Ramirez shook his head and gazed pensively at the photos of Wagon Wheel Jane Doe's neck wound. Gabriel had seen his team lieutenant parade indifferently over the many scattered pictures of dead men and women. But something about rape victims, taunted, tortured and then killed, brought out the macho gentleman in him. It was a strange but admirable side Gabriel was not familiar with.

"Let's contact the park rangers and have them step up security," Ramirez told his crew. "I think we'll need to start combing the area for any other bodies. Dash, you contact Missing Persons and check out any other women gone missing from July. And get a 3-D model made from that Tapia Park skull. I want photos of the reconstructed head plus a description of the Wagon Wheel girl sent out to the press." Ramirez swigged more coffee. "Baling wire is his signature. McRay, you check out that equestrian center. Jonelle, please get that Samuels woman to give us something more. She's the only person alive to see this dude in action, and so far she's given us *nada*."

Jonelle shrugged lightly. "With all due respect, Lieutenant, McRay here seems to get more out of the witness than I do."

Ramirez turned to Gabriel and said, "You stick like glue to Tara Samuels until she gives us something we can work with."

Gabriel felt his cheeks go hot. "I'll give it my best."

CHAPTER 7

While Dash took the skull of the Tapia Park corpse to a forensic anthropologist, Gabriel headed west toward the Santa Monica Mountains. The rain had cleared and now the sun was breaking through the clouds, throwing heavenly rays over the Blue Sage Equestrian Center.

Gabriel drove past the sign of a rearing horse and parked. He walked by the stalls, and petted immaculately clean horses that stuck out their heads to greet him. From the tidy appearance of the stalls and the satin coats of the horses, Gabriel surmised boarding at Blue Sage was an expensive endeavor.

As a thoroughbred nibbled at his jacket pocket, Gabriel noticed two double doors of a tack room standing open. He walked over and peered inside.

The various equestrian implements, harnesses, reins, and halters hung neatly on the walls. The calming scent of leather mingled with fresh oats gave the dark room a comforting feel.

A woman, dressed in jodhpurs and English attire, posted by him on a stallion with a braided mane and tail.

"Felipe," the woman said looking just past Gabriel, "Andromeda's hooves need better cleaning. Can you oil the pads as well?"

"Yes, Mrs. Matheson."

Mrs. Matheson posted away, heading toward a large arena where various jumps were positioned.

Gabriel looked behind the tack room and saw Felipe, a mustachioed Guatemalan with friendly eyes.

"Hello, Felipe." Gabriel displayed his badge.

Felipe eyed him quizzically. "Yes?"

"Are you the manager here?"

"No' really. I guess I'm the head of maintenance, though."

"Are the owners here?"

"Mrs. Traxler is in her office, I think."

Gabriel didn't budge. A round bundle of baling wire stared at him like a silver eye from Felipe's feet. "Do you know a Mrs. Samuels?"

"She a blonde? With short hair?" Felipe held his hand to his hair. "Sure I know her. No' well, but the owners prefer to keep it that way. You know, two weeks ago her horse come running back here alone! I had to calm Dorrie down myself. Did Mrs. Samuels have an accident? Nobody tole us nothing."

"Mrs. Samuels is fine. You say the horse returned here by itself?"

"The trainers teach them right away how to come home."

"Mrs. Samuels, she comes here on a regular basis?"

"Every week. Her two horses are champions."

"So I've heard. Have you exchanged a lot of words with her?"

"No' really."

"How about some of the others who work here?"

Felipe's eyes made a quick scan of the immediate area and then he said in a low voice, "The honly one I know that likes to talk more than he should is Ross. He's the boss's nephew and he..." Felipe made a sour face.

Tara had mentioned a Ross. Gabriel wrote in his notepad and then smiled reassuringly. "We can keep it confidential, okay, Felipe?"

The Guatemalan stepped near to Gabriel and whispered, "Between you and me, I would never hire him. He's lazy and he talks too much to the boarders. The Traxlers, who own this place, they tole me to give him a job. But he's lazy." He leaned even closer to Gabriel. "And I think he got other problems, too."

Felipe pointed a finger and poked it at the vein of his other arm. "*Drogas.*"

He gave Gabriel a slow, serious nod and then looked apprehensive. "You no going to tell Mrs. Traxler, are you? I been here for eleven years, but I don't think she like me talking bad about her nephew."

"It's between us. You ever notice Ross talking to Mrs. Samuels."

"He talks to all the pretty girls. He's lazy!"

"Does Ross have access to the tools around here? Does he have a key to this room, for instance?" Gabriel glanced once more at the baling wire.

"I don't know for sure. He'd know where to find a key. He lives here."

"Whereabouts?"

Felipe told Gabriel about a cabin at the far end of the stables.

"Good," Gabriel said and nodded his thanks to Felipe. He then headed toward the Blue Sage office.

The door was open and Gabriel entered a tidy room of rich, dark wood, green leather, and genteel paintings of jumping horses.

He heard water running from behind a closed door that Gabriel assumed led to a bathroom. A moment later the water stopped and the door opened. A smart-looking brunette wearing jodhpurs and dusty riding boots exited the bathroom, wiping her hands on a paper towel. She started in surprise upon seeing Gabriel.

"Oh!"

Gabriel took out his ID. "Sorry to have scared you. I'm Detective McRay. Mrs. Traxler, correct?"

"Yes, I'm Lynn Traxler." Lynn offered her damp hand, which Gabriel shook. Her grip was firm.

"I wanted to talk to you about—"

"—the incident with Mrs. Samuels, yes…" Lynn seemed to wither into her boots.

"Well, it was a little more than an incident."

Lynn sank into one of her leather armchairs. "Please sit."

Gabriel did not sit but leaned against her desk. "How long has Mrs. Samuels been boarding horses here?"

"Oh, God; a year maybe? Not long after she married her husband. Maybe a year and a half. I can check if you really need—"

"That won't be necessary. Did you ever receive complaints from any of the female riders; complaints that someone was hanging out on the trail or around the barn?"

"If you're asking if I anticipated the assault on Mrs. Samuels, the answer is no. This is a Class 1 equestrian center. The assault happened somewhere on Topanga Canyon, not here. I would really like you to keep that clear."

Gabriel nodded, studying Lynn. "May I speak with your nephew? Ross, is it?"

Lynn appeared taken aback. "Why do you need to speak with him?"

"I understand Mrs. Samuels and he have met."

Lynn Traxler stood up. "Look, Sergeant…"

"McRay."

"McRay." Lynn sighed. "Ross is my sister's son. He's had a bit of a problem, so she asked if we could let him stay here. She thought working in the fresh air would benefit him, and it seems to be helping."

"A problem..." Gabriel repeated. "Does he have a habit?"

She shook her head vehemently. "No. He's been clean since he's been here. He may have been smoking pot at one time, but I guarantee you, Sergeant, he is no criminal. He's just a kid that needs to mature."

"His mother sent him to you for smoking pot?"

Lynn's blinking eyes told Gabriel there had been more to it.

"May I talk to him?" Gabriel asked again.

"Be my guest. He may not be home yet; I needed him to run some errands in the city for me."

"I'll check just the same. Thanks for your time." Gabriel placed a business card in her hand.

"My husband, Jim, was a Gulf War vet. He knows how to keep people in line. Don't think Ross had anything to do with the abduction of Mrs. Samuels, Sergeant. Ross is a sweet boy."

Gabriel eyed her passively and then left her standing in her boots.

He wandered past the arena where Mrs. Matheson was doing her jumps. He heard the gentle whinny of a horse and the light patter of a water fountain. He visualized Tara on her mount with the winter sun on her hair.

Gabriel followed a stream to the outskirts of the stables where he found a small cabin nestled in a grove of sycamores. The windows were shuttered and the door was locked. No one answered Gabriel's knock.

Unwilling to give up, he decided to follow the path where Tara was abducted. He trekked up the trail at a steady pace, flicking ticks off his pant legs every so often. The sun ducked down a notch and the marine layer began creeping in, cooling the sweat that dampened his shirt collar. Gabriel kept an eye out for anything that didn't belong—a torn piece of fabric or a cigarette butt.

The trail forked and Gabriel soon realized he'd taken the wrong path because the trail seemed to disappear under his feet. He moved through a vine-like bush made up of pretty fall-colored leaves and found himself in a clearing between a large sumac and a coastal oak.

"Great, Sherlock. Now where are you?" he said aloud.

Isolated in the mountains, Gabriel found it hard to believe that the urban sprawl of Los Angeles lay only a few miles away. Gabriel craned his neck for the trail from which he'd strayed

and he saw Andrew Pierce leaning against the oak.

"Little Buddy."

Gabriel felt the tops of his hands tingle. Pain bloomed behind his eyes and he shivered involuntarily. Andrew was chewing a piece of black licorice. Gabriel swallowed and blinked. Then Andrew was gone.

Gabriel walked over to the oak where he'd seen his mental apparition and laid a shaking hand on the tree bark. He wondered silently if he would ever be a completely sane man. Andrew, of course, was no longer the teenage predator that had just materialized in front of Gabriel. Andrew Pierce could no longer harm anyone because he was dead.

A subtle stirring in the thistle opposite him made Gabriel reach for the Redhawk concealed in his holster. His eyes burned into the thick chaparral. The leaves of the bush parted and a deer emerged.

Proud antlers touched the earth as the stag pulled at the shoots of meadow grass. Gabriel exhaled in relief.

Fascinated by the beautiful animal, Gabriel carefully slid to a seated position. He put his hand on the ground for support and immediately felt a sharp prick. Bringing up his hand, Gabriel stared in horror at a syringe dangling from his palm.

"Shit!" Gabriel rocketed up which sent the stag leaping into the underbrush. He violently shook off the syringe and squeezed the blood from his hand, immediately thinking of deadly communicable diseases. A burned patch in the grass suggested a dropped match.

His evidence kit was inconveniently stored in his car and Gabriel's heart hammered as he pulled a tissue from his pocket. He carefully wrapped the syringe.

Cursing under his breath, Gabriel searched the area for any other useful trash. An empty Mickey's malt liquor can sat a few yards away.

Easy throwing distance from the oak tree, Gabriel reckoned angrily. He snatched up the beer can as well.

A breeze kicked up as Gabriel stomped back to the equestrian center. The sycamore trees surrounding Ross's cabin rustled impatiently. Gabriel slid his card under the locked door of the cabin and then headed to his car.

He would make a point to look into Ross; the lazy nephew of the Traxler's who liked sticking needles into his arm and talking too much to pretty ladies.

⚜ ⚜ ⚜

"Thanks for seeing me on such short notice."

Gabriel watched as Ming pushed the hypodermic needle into his vein. Gabriel had decided to bypass his house and head straight toward L.A. County General to get tested for HIV.

Standing in her surgical scrubs with a bemused look in her eyes, Ming said, "You said it was a matter of life or death."

"I might have overreacted."

"For a homicide detective who's been knifed before," Ming told him, "I'd say you're reaction is bordering on hysteria. At the very least, you sound a lot like Dash."

"Dash would have already died from the stress."

Ming laughed and Gabriel felt comforted. She always had a way of reassuring him. Watching his blood fill the tube reminded Gabriel of the last time Ming had drawn blood from him. During the Malibu Canyon Murder case, Gabriel had been forced to give a DNA sample because he had been considered a suspect. It had been a humiliating experience, but Ming had been there for him. She had never wavered in her friendship and Gabriel felt like a heel for not being more patient with her.

She pulled the needle from his arm.

"Well?" he asked her in concern.

Ming's long hair was pinned up on her head but a few escaped strands pleasantly framed her high cheekbones. "Except for the gangrene, you'll be alright."

"Funny."

She placed a small, round Band-Aid over the puncture and gently closed his arm. Her hands seemed to want to stay on his muscles, but then she pulled away.

"Keep it like that for minute, okay? The syringe doesn't look fresh so I doubt any hepatitis or HIV survived."

"I can't believe I got stuck."

Ming released the tube containing Gabriel's blood from the syringe and marked it with an adhesive label. "We'll know something in a week or so."

"Can't you push it any sooner?"

Ming stripped off her latex gloves and raised her arched eyebrows. "And what's in it for me if I do?"

Gabriel surveyed her with an approving eye. Standing before him, she seemed to be the woman he'd fallen in love with. He took Ming into his arms. Gabriel smoothed her errant strands and studied her intelligent eyes. After a moment, he tilted her chin up and planted a kiss on her lips.

"Uh-uh," Ming said. "That wasn't payment enough."

Pleased to hear it, Gabriel shut the door with his foot.

❧ ❧ ❧

Jean Piper, a Southern flame-haired woman whose ass was the size of Alabama or so her teenage kids told her, had a penchant for both candy and talking too much.

Jean's incessant babbling never bothered anybody because the only people she talked to were dead and usually missing their bodies. As a forensic anthropologist, Jean did a lot of work with human heads.

The candy never bothered anybody either, and Jean always had an open box of Sees chocolates in her lab, or 'artist studio' as she preferred to call it.

When the Tapia Park skull arrived, it was brought in by investigator Michael "Dash" Starkweather, who looked blown inside out from the wind that had kicked up outside.

"It's getting ugly out there," Dash told her, handing Jean a brief report on the victim, the little they knew of her and how she had died.

"Try living near the gulf coast during a hurricane. Would you like a candy, Sergeant?" Jean asked in her sweet southern drawl.

The detective reminded her of that skinny man at the beach who always got sand kicked in his face. The one in that muscle man Charles Atlas ad that graced the backs of the comic books Jean used to read as a kid.

"You're just as skinny as a beanpole, bless your heart. If you don't get some meat on those bones, Sergeant, you might just dry up and blow away."

His masculinity insulted, Dash replied curtly, "I don't eat chocolate! It gives me diarrhea."

Jean gave him a sugary smile as she showed him the door. "Why thank you for sharing that, Sergeant. I'll get back to you on the young lady here just as fast as I can. Now, was that a three-dimensional facial reconstruction or a two-dimensional photographic model?"

"The Lieutenant wants 3-D. The techs and the dentist have already examined the bones and don't need the skull."

"Well, I'm just set, then." Jean pushed Dash into the blowing wind and closed the door. To herself she said, "Diarrhea. Well, didn't that just make my day?"

Jean popped a Scotchmallow into her mouth, and placed the skull on a workable stand where it could easily be tilted and turned in all directions. Jean then reviewed the scant information in the report and decided to go on the assumption that the victim was Caucasian, female, and between the ages of twenty and thirty. This gave her some idea of the proper tissue depth and she began gluing tissue markers directly onto the skull.

She took a break to drink chamomile tea and consume a Rum Nougat, an Almond Royal, and a Toffee-ette while listening to the pleasant patter of the rain outside. On a sugar high, Jean systematically applied clay to the skull, following its contours, minding the tissue markers. While the wind whipped outside, Jean Piper worked as the hours passed. She spoke gently to the face taking form.

"Where are you from, honey?"

Jean had to guess at the details since nobody knew the geographic origins of the young lady or her lifestyle. The teeth had been well taken care of, that was obvious, and Jean placed her bets that the unknown woman wasn't homeless or a drug addict. Perhaps the woman had taken good care of her skin as well as her teeth.

Jean lifted her sizeable derriere from the swivel stool and hit the candy box again, this time selecting a Buttercream and a Divinity Puff.

"Don't you worry now. Pretty soon we'll be able to call your family and you can rest in peace."

The wind sang outside but the unknown girl remained silent. She simply waited for the chubby, cheery anthropologist to give her back her identity.

CHAPTER 8

Gabriel sat at his laptop, accessing the NCIC, the National Crime Information Center, which was a database of felons, stolen vehicles and weapons that fed into every law enforcement agency in the United States. Gabriel had two unidentified female corpses in the morgue and wanted to know if a similar crime had occurred elsewhere.

Scratching an itch on his arm, Gabriel waited out the computer's search. He had typed in all the pertinent information, including the killer's particular brand of weapon: a wire garrote. He sat back and waited. After a minute or so, he pulled out his cell phone. He scrolled through his contacts and stopped at Ming's number. She had invited him to an event tonight, but he had backed out. He knew he owed her an explanation and pressed the call button.

At the same time, Ming Li walked toward the entry hall of her Los Feliz home. The sound of her high heels tapping the dark wood floor echoed through the large house. She was going to another charity dinner tonight and wore a clingy black dress that Gabriel found sexy. Ming paused before an ornate Moroccan mirror that hung near the front door and regarded her reflection.

Looking at herself, Ming imagined Gabriel walking up behind her and wrapping his strong arms around her waist. She could almost smell the cologne he wore and felt an incredible longing for him. She loved the way he would tentatively brush his lips against her ear, her neck, and then softly run his hands over her body.

While Ming thought his manner was sensuous, deep down she knew he had reasons for this careful approach. She guessed it was a leftover inhibition, a symptom that stemmed from the sexual abuse he had endured as a child.

Ming closed her eyes and found her own hand wrinkling her dress luxuriously. Ming selfishly never encouraged Gabriel to come on to her any differently. Only when he drank a glass or two of liquor did he loosen up and forget himself, but those times were rare.

A car's engine gunned outside and Ming looked hopefully at the front door, thinking of Gabriel's chugging Celica. Then the sound passed and Ming's eyes drifted back to her reflection. Gabriel wasn't coming over.

She had invited him to this dinner, of course, but he had declined the invitation. Ming was disappointed and a little angry. She had thought their lovemaking session in the lab had patched things up between them. Apparently, she was wrong.

With a defiant toss of her long dark hair, Ming picked up her car keys. As soon as the door closed behind her, the house phone began to ring.

Gabriel waited through each ring until Ming's voicemail picked up. He had every intention of telling her that she was right, that being around her colleagues made him feel uncomfortable. But when he heard the beep, he ended the call without leaving a message.

Another beep sounded and a dialogue box appeared on his laptop monitor. No matches. No similar crimes.

Rubbing his arm, Gabriel glanced solemnly at the clock. It was time for another "session," as Miguel Ramirez liked to call them.

Gabriel left Commerce; feeling annoyed by a growing itch on his arms and the fact that he wasn't gaining ground on the case. He took Atlantic Boulevard down to Monterey Park for his evening appointment with Dr. B.

His arms itched more tenaciously as he took a seat in his usual chair. Trying not to scratch himself, Gabriel told Dr. B about visualizing Andrew on the trail.

"It's important you address all the aspects of the trauma," Dr. B said. "This is one aspect."

Gabriel fought the urge to rip off his shirt and claw at his flesh. "It's not exactly a clear memory or anything like that. I just keep seeing him."

Gabriel felt a headache stirring. Whenever he thought of Andrew Pierce, his skull protested, as if all those vile memories threatened to contaminate his brain.

It didn't happen to me. It couldn't have happened.

Gabriel studied the carpet, understanding completely why Tara Samuels would refuse to recount her trauma.

"The image is your fear solidified," Dr. B said, eyeing him. "Are you comfortable in that chair?"

"I'm itchy as hell," Gabriel confessed and rubbed his arms. "I guess I hit some poison oak."

"Can I get you something?"

"There's nothing for it, so I'm told. Go on. Talking will get my mind off it."

Dr. B pushed his glasses up the bridge of his nose, still watching Gabriel with concern. "Memories get misty. You've created a character, a monster from your fear that you can look at. But it's important to hook into some solid recollections. Andrew cannot hurt you anymore."

Gabriel looked into Dr. B's brown eyes and suddenly thought of his father.

His dad knocking on the bathroom door, asking what was wrong, as young Gabriel sat on a towel to catch the blood that fell from his body after Andrew had...

"Andrew can't hurt you anymore?" Gabriel mocked and scratched furiously at his arm. "What the fuck do you know about it? How can you possibly identify with any of this?"

Dr. B chewed his lower lip and tapped a pencil against his desk. "I'm merely asking you to look at everything Andrew did to you. We both know you remember."

Gabriel stopped scratching and turned his attention to the fat round face of the wooden desk clock, wishing the hour would pass faster.

"Remember," Dr. B prodded gently.

Gabriel envisioned the locked door in his mind, the one covered in the rust of excuses and the graffiti of his fear. He imagined taking a mental crowbar and slamming the padlock over and over until the door swung wide open on creaking hinges. A wind caught his shoulders, instantly pulling Gabriel into the swirling blackness, where a roaring threatened to bust open his brain like a pumpkin—where all the seeds of his thoughts would scatter on the carpet. *The ugly shag carpeting in Andrew Pierce's house.*

See it from the distance of a football field. Be a spectator, only a spectator watching something far away—far enough away so that it cannot hurt you.

Gilligan's Island played on an old television set and Ginger, wearing her white sequined gown, sang on a stage while Maryann's ponytails bobbed and the Skipper sat next to Gabriel on the worn padded couch.

Just sit right back and you'll hear a tale...

At first the rapes had been quick and violent—at the beginning when the Skipper worried about getting caught. But as the weeks wore on, Andrew became more confident. "Don't worry, Little Buddy, my ma won't be home for another hour."

Andrew would open his fly and touch himself, biding his time. Eventually, he would turn his attention from the TV to the little boy sitting next to him. Knowing what was coming was more torturous for Gabriel than when Andrew had thrown his earlier surprise attacks.

"This is positive, Gabe." Dr. B said earnestly. "Your ability to discuss these details is very positive. Only months ago you had no recollection any of this had transpired. Please feel proud of yourself because you are progressing."

"I'm having headaches again. That's not progress."

"You had the headache when you visualized Andrew Pierce on the trail?"

Gabriel nodded.

Dr. B studied Gabriel for a moment and then penned a note in Gabriel's file: *respite*.

Perhaps Gabriel needed to take a break. They could reframe the trauma at a later date. For now, Gabriel needed space in which to process what he was dealing with. Dr. B switched gears.

"Have you spoken to your family lately?"

Gabriel shook his head, mindlessly scratching his arms again.

"I thought you and your parents were talking now."

Gabriel shrugged. "They call me."

"And?"

Gabriel shrugged again and glanced once more at the desk clock.

"When they call and they want you to call back," Dr. B continued, "what do you feel initially?"

"Like they can wait. I'm working on a multiple murder case right now."

"Gabe…"

"They can wait, okay? I'm glad they're calling but I don't have anything to say."

"But you like when they call. You wouldn't like it if they didn't call you, right?"

"What are you getting at, Raymond?"

Dr. B took a deep breath. Adlerian practitioners were supposed to be lean on advice. "You still harbor underlying hostilities toward your parents for letting you down. You want them to call you, but you won't return the favor. You're testing their love for you."

The detective shook his head, looked at the clock one final time and then promptly stood up.

"Time to go," Gabriel announced. He pulled on his coat and left without another word.

The psychiatrist gazed at the closed door for some time afterward. Something interesting had happened today, something that most analysts were warned against: transference. Gabriel had projected his anger onto Dr. B and saw his psychiatrist as an antagonist who had joined forces with the other antagonists from Gabriel's childhood. Whether Gabriel saw Dr. B as an attacking Andrew Pierce or a negligent parental figure was unknown, but the projected anger had been quite apparent.

Was this part of the natural progression of his therapy or was something else pressuring Gabriel? At any rate, Dr. B mused, it might be interesting to use the transference. Using

Gabriel's own rage as a vehicle was risky business, but Dr. B was willing to take the chance.

❦   ❦   ❦

Gabriel returned home feeling like he needed to punch something. Why did he have to be born? Why couldn't he have an easy life like Marc Samuels? Why did he have to live alone in this old apartment with an old car and old, horrible memories that were popping up like new every day?

He was raped.

The phone rang. Gabriel ignored it. He carefully lifted his sleeve and saw angry red blisters cropping up on his arm. His first instinct was to call Ming, but he fended off that option. Instead, he scanned his medicine cabinet and rubbed Calamine lotion over his arms until his flesh was stained pink. Unable to do anything more, pacing like a caged animal, Gabriel retreated to his kitchen.

Maybe he would put something together for dinner. Maybe that would cage the burgeoning rage and the interminable prickling of his skin. Gabriel moved to his pantry, but the door stuck from layers of old paint. Furiously, Gabriel shook it.

"You can't open? You got a problem opening? Here, I'll help you fucking open!" Gabriel grabbed the door and tore it off its hinges. He stared at the gaping pantry in stormy satisfaction. "Now, you're open."

The phone continued to ring incessantly. Gabriel glared at it and strode over, furiously yanking the receiver to his ear. "Who the hell is this?"

"Excuse *me,* Gabriel," Ming said.

Gabriel, shaking with anger, ran a trembling hand through his hair. "Not a good time, Ming."

"I called to say hello," she said, but ice sharpened her words.

"Okay, hello." Gabriel could hear cutlery clinking and the sound of happy voices. Oh, yeah. The charity dinner. Was she calling to tell him about all the VIPs she was chilling with? He simply didn't need that aggravation.

"So, what's your problem now?" Ming asked tightly.

Gabriel fought for control. "There's too many to list. What do you need?"

"Screw you." Ming hung up.

Gabriel threw the phone to the opposite wall where it crashed; then he sat on the stained linoleum and put his head in his hands. He took several deep inhalations and calmness slowly settled upon him.

He should call Ming back. He shouldn't let his anger get the better of him. He had done so much work to contain it. Gabriel rose and went to his jacket pocket, taking out his notebook.

Call Ming, he wrote. And then:

Call Mom and Dad. Gabriel underlined it for emphasis.

Sometime he was going to have to talk to his parents about what Andrew had done to him. Had they known about his molestation? Andrew had always assured him they did. Gabriel gazed at the words "mom and dad" and then at the phone. He tucked the notepad away. He'd call them—later.

And he was through with therapy.

After all, Internal Affairs was no longer pressuring him. Why should he go?

Gabriel turned on the television and listened to the weather report on the local news. More rain expected. Thunder showers. Someone had drowned in the L.A. River, that cement trough that usually held a junk-fest of broken bottles and the decrepit belongings of the homeless. Gabriel switched the set off. The weather kept fluctuating like some menopausal housewife. Half the officers he knew were sick with colds, and it seemed like the whole world was going to hell.

His pager went off, and rolling his eyes, Gabriel checked it and saw a message from his office. He picked up his stricken telephone and plugged it back into the jack, feeling relieved and a little shameful that it still worked. He called his voicemail, knowing, just knowing, it would be Ramirez wanting to harass him for the sheer pleasure of it.

Gabriel was surprised to hear Tara Samuel's voice.

She said she desperately needed to talk to him and had left her cell phone number.

Popping open a Dos Equis for confidence, Gabriel drank most of it down before he called her.

"Hello?" Her voice sounded thin.

"Hello, Mrs. Samuels. This is Detective McRay. You wanted to talk to me?"

"Yes, I do. Can we meet somewhere?"

Gabriel didn't relish going back to the San Fernando Valley, but before he could speak, Tara informed him that she was in Westwood, not too far from him.

"I really need to talk to you," she pleaded.

"Okay," Gabriel said, finishing off the beer. "Tell me where you are."

CHAPTER

They met at the corner of Gayley and Le Conte, at the foot of UCLA's Fraternity Row. From up the street came the sound of male catcalling and boisterous music, festivities heralding the approach of winter break. Tara was dressed in black pants with a black shirt-coat. The moon was full behind dark, passing clouds, which in turn lit her features and then shaded them.

"I guess I should be heading home," Tara told him, "but there's so much traffic. I thought maybe I could take you to dinner."

"That's very kind of you to offer, but I'm—"

"Won't you please, Detective McRay? Marc is away on business, and I don't want to go home to that empty house. Please keep me company." Tara gestured down the street. "There's a nice restaurant on Westwood Boulevard we can walk to, right over there."

Tempting, Gabriel thought. His witness was willing to talk, but he wasn't dressed appropriately. He wore an old summer jacket over his itching arms that barely kept out the cold. Besides that, he felt beat up from his meeting with Dr. B.

"I can't, Mrs. Samuels. What exactly did you want to talk to me about?"

"Tara. Are you on duty or off duty?"

"I'm not officially on duty. No."

"Then?" Tara took his arm and steered him down the street.

He glanced at her arm entwined in his. Her touch was feathery light and the scent of lavender drifted from under her black coat. Gabriel allowed himself to be led away.

The restaurant served light Asian fare. They ordered a shrimp and candied walnut dish, noodles, and two lychee nut martinis, which Tara had insisted upon. Before their drinks arrived, Tara excused herself to go to the restroom.

Gabriel felt out of place sitting in this modish eatery with its open spaces, lit see-through floors, and patrons cut from celebrity mags. But as Tara approached him, Gabriel saw people stare approvingly at her and then turn to regard him as if to commend him on his choice of women.

"Thanks for keeping me company," Tara said as she took her seat. "I really didn't want to drive during rush hour."

Gabriel agreed with a nod.

"Have you made any progress?"

Feeling it was premature to discuss Ross with Tara, Gabriel answered, "We're still exploring the equestrian center."

"Why? Do you think Ross did it?" Tara asked, surprising him.

"I can't say that with certainty. Can you?"

Tara shook her head.

The waiter set down the drinks and assured them their food would be right out.

"Can you remember anything more, anything at all about the man who attacked you?" Gabriel pushed Tara's martini toward her.

"He wore a ski mask and he told me to keep my head turned. He seemed rather thin to me." She avoided Gabriel's eyes and drank from her martini. Suddenly, she signaled the waiter. "Could you please bring me another one?" She looked back at Gabriel. "Each time I feel ready to talk about this, I can't. I have nightmares where I think I'm paralyzed. I'm afraid if I sleep, I'll die."

Gabriel nodded. Nightmares had afflicted him for years. He took a large gulp of the lychee nut martini and grimaced from the sweet vodka. The waiter brought Tara's second martini, which she grasped eagerly. Sipping from the glass, she asked demurely, "Would you like my lychee nut, Detective?"

"Sure." He didn't like lychee nuts, but Gabriel was relieved to see Tara so alert. He spooned it into his mouth and forced himself to swallow.

"I'm making you uncomfortable, aren't I?" Tara smiled sadly. "I think I make everyone uncomfortable now. I made a big mistake telling anyone about this."

Gabriel rushed a sip of water into his mouth. "No, don't think that. You can't let your assailant walk away."

Tara stared at Gabriel. Netted by her gaze, he could only stare back. Finally, he drained the rest of his martini and ordered a beer from the waiter.

The beer felt good when it arrived, and soon afterwards the food came. The two of them ate in silence. Gabriel could empathize with this witness more than any he had ever dealt with. Tara had gone through the horror of rape. Just like him.

Gabriel felt something on his hand and was startled to see Tara's own tapered fingers resting there.

"You have nice hands, Detective McRay."

Feeling a bit buzzed off the booze, Gabriel allowed her butterfly touch to remain.

"They're strong, but beautifully shaped," Tara ran a finger along his flesh. "Did anyone ever tell you that?"

Gabriel shook his head, inhaling lavender.

Her fingers laced through his. "Strong and nice, the perfect combination. Do you think I'm pretty, Detective McRay?"

"You know you're very attractive, Mrs. Samuels."

"Tara. I'm actually the ugly duckling of my family. My parents look like movie stars."

"Then the apple didn't fall far from the tree." Gabriel watched Tara's lips and felt the warmth of the liquor working through him.

"Will you walk me back to my car?" she asked.

The fraternity party had died and the college town was unusually quiet. Low clouds had settled wetly on the tree branches and the parked cars. Gabriel felt stupidly numb from the martini and beer mixture. Tara was staring fixedly at a point somewhere behind him and Gabriel turned around, curious as to what had captured her attention.

"That's a graveyard back there," she said with a bleak expression.

Gabriel felt a raindrop fall on his head. "The Veteran's Cemetery, yes."

Tara continued looking past him. "I've seen it before. Rows and rows of tombstones. Almost as far as the eye can see." Her eyes shifted to Gabriel. "It's starting to rain."

Gabriel ventured an arm around her. "Here, let me get you inside your car."

"Can you sit with me for a minute?"

He hesitated. "It's getting late and you have a bit of a drive."

Tara clutched at his jacket. "Please?" she begged. "I'm a little tipsy."

Gabriel regarded her grasp on his clothing. The lavender, the alcohol, the secretive silence of a wet sky about to burst played with his judgment. "All right."

Three more raindrops hit his head as Gabriel moved into the passenger seat of the Jaguar. Brand new, Gabriel wagered, from the smell of fresh leather. Again, Gabriel felt envious of Marc Samuels.

"You take your work seriously, don't you?" Tara asked once they'd closed out the damp.

"I do," Gabriel admitted, "I tend to focus hard on the matter at hand."

"Then I'm in good hands." Tara took Gabriel's arms and drew them around her, placing her face very close to his.

Gabriel swallowed, feeling the pressure building in his chest, in his slacks. A flurry of raindrops splashed on the windshield.

"Mrs. Samuels," he said weakly. "I think you better go on home."

"Not yet. Hold me. I'm so frightened. I don't like to be alone."

Gabriel tightened his arms around her and breathed in her lavender scent. She pressed closer. He could feel the outline of her body, her breasts, and the delicate bones of her pelvis. Outside, he heard a rumble of thunder.

"You make me feel safe." Tara placed her lips on his.

Unable to resist, Gabriel kissed her.

Hungry for her, he wove his fingers through her black coat, her silken bra, and caressed her warm breast. She sighed in response and her body melded close to his. She moved her hand to his groin.

"Do you live far from here?" Tara asked breathlessly.

They hit the sheets as the storm broke, pelting the L.A. basin, dumping water in a torrent. Tara and Gabriel fused together, hands and mouths searching like thirsty nomads eager for water to fill empty gourds.

Her body was firm and welcoming. At first, she took his hands and ran them over the contours of her figure as she straddled him naked. And then Tara leaned back submissively, encouraging Gabriel to take full control. The rain beat angrily outside, and the thunder rolled like a cannon. He couldn't grasp enough of her. His tongue explored every physical avenue and his hands followed suit. Finally, when he plunged into her and felt her body melt around him, he knew Tara Samuels was a rare jewel. He watched her, strobe-lit by lightning, as she danced beneath him.

When the sun rose, in the fickle manner of Los Angeles winters, it rose high and strong, causing a ghostly steam to rise from the asphalt outside. The storm had passed.

Tara rose from the bed like an apparition and Gabriel watched her, feeling light and powerful at the same time. She stood naked at the window, opening the pane and letting the cool morning air harden her nipples and ruffle her blond hair.

"Thank goodness the rain is gone," she said in plain voice. "Winter is not my favorite season." She breathed in the salty air of the neighboring Pacific Ocean. "I could live all year long where it's hot. Some place like Mexico, where nobody speaks my language."

Sleepy-eyed, Gabriel gazed at her. When she looked back at him, backlit by the sun and looking like a shimmering angel, he patted the empty side of the bed. She walked slowly toward him, fixing Gabriel with her azure eyes. For a moment, the hairs on the back of his neck stood up, always a red flag for him, but then he drifted into Tara, content to take refuge in the dusk of her body once more.

Jean Piper crunched a piece of peanut brittle between her teeth as she finished applying makeup to the face of the Tapia Park girl.

"There now," Jean said, proud to see the girl's features come alive. "You're quite a pretty thing, aren't you? You should have seen me in my prime. I turned a lot of heads in my day." Jean laughed. "No pun intended."

While Jean talked about her transition from life in the South to life in California, she went through her cache of wigs, searching for a hairpiece that was similar enough in texture and color to what Jean supposed was the girl's true hair color before six months' worth of sun and the elements had bleached it dry.

"Did you wear glasses, sweet pea? How about hats? I wore hats—I was a member of the Red Hat Society. Still am!"

Jean fit a wig onto the reconstructed head and then stepped back to survey her work. She smiled.

"Welcome back to the world, sweet pea."

❧   ❧   ❧

"What are you whistling about?" Dash asked suspiciously.

Gabriel looked up at his partner. Dash was standing at Gabriel's desk in the long L-shaped room that made up homicide bureau. Gabriel blinked. Had he been whistling?

"You haven't bothered me yet today." Gabriel grinned at him. "So, I'm happy."

"We could always go to lunch." Dash set down a large box on the floor next to Gabriel.

"Thanks, but I don't need that torture."

Mealtimes were something of a trial with Dash. So worried was the thin man about the heart problems that ran in his family, he gave the waiters and chefs a run for their money and drove his fellow diners crazy. Of course, Gabriel had gotten used to the finicky habits of his partner and had learned to ignore them. Truth be told, Gabriel was feeling good. He felt as if he had sprung from a coffin where he'd lain decaying for years. Besides, the itching on his arms had stopped.

"Jonelle's been trying to reach you," Dash told him. "She said she interviewed Ross, that stable guy…"

"Stable, he's not," Gabriel piped. "Good for her that she got a hold of him."

"Yeah, well the interview didn't go well for Ross and he's high on her list of probables. Turns out he bothers a lot of the female riders around the place. He got all agitated talking about Tara Samuels."

A nervous flutter ran through Gabriel at the mention of her name. He had slept with a witness – a married rape victim. Why had he done that? Gabriel could blame it on the alcohol, but he knew better. He was drawn to Tara Samuels, and Gabriel could only surmise it was because she seemed so vulnerable—so attacked. He'd once been vulnerable and attacked. Tara felt safe around Gabriel, and that made him feel better… Stronger.

Gabriel checked his schedule and saw he had an appointment that afternoon with Dr. B. He wondered if he should tell Dr. B about his tryst with Tara.

He picked up the phone and dialed the psychiatrist's office.

"Yes, this is Gabriel McRay. I have an appointment with Dr. Berkowitz today, which I'm afraid I have to cancel."

Gabriel replaced the receiver and pensively studied the phone, ignoring Dash who peered at him inquiringly. Gabriel wanted to revel in this newfound feeling of power and didn't need a therapy session to remind him of all his weaknesses.

Nobody had to know. It was a one-time thing, that's all.

The phone buzzed.

"Gabriel McRay," he answered.

"Hi," Tara said.

Holding the phone to his ear, Gabriel glanced at Dash who was typing on his computer keyboard. Gabriel swiveled his body away to face the gray, textured wall of the cubicle.

"Hey."

"Thank you for last night."

"Don't thank me." Gabriel stole another look at Dash—still busy.

"Can we meet tonight?" Tara asked.

"Uhhh..." Gabriel tried to lasso his stampeding thoughts.

"Look, Gabriel, if you're worried about Marc..." She paused and then said rapidly, "Marc's been afraid to touch me. He's making me feel like I'm damaged goods. I need to be around someone who understands what I went through. Can I see you again?"

The memory of her body was still fresh. Gabriel, however, attempted to do the right thing.

"Come to my office," he told her.

"Couldn't we meet somewhere else? Somewhere a little below radar? I need to talk to you in private."

Gabriel caught Dash glance at him, and lowered his voice. "There's a coffee and poetry place I know of in Venice, very bohemian."

"Bohemian is perfect!"

"I'll call your cell with details later." Gabriel hung up. So much for doing the right thing.

"That Ming?" Dash asked him.

Gabriel shrugged, nodding absently. "Yeah. Whatcha got?"

"Two things. First..." Dash lifted the lid on the large box he had placed in front of Gabriel and pulled out the reconstructed head of Tapia Park Jane Doe.

"Pretty, isn't she?"

Gabriel would have to agree. Under the auburn wig was the visage of an attractive Caucasian woman between her mid to late twenties. She fixed Gabriel with a glass-eyed stare. "Who is she?"

"That, my dear Watson," Dash told him, "is something we're going to have to find out. I've already sent a picture of her to Missing Persons."

"Good man."

Dash reached around to his desk and unclasped a manila envelope. "And running the photo of Wagon Wheel Jane Doe in the papers paid off. I received a call from Children of the Night."

"Isn't that a line from Dracula?" Gabriel asked, recalling something about howling wolves.

Dash shook his head. "This group keeps kids off the Hollywood streets. A shelter volunteer saw our girl's photo and called me. She sent me this."

He passed Gabriel a fuzzy Polaroid of a girl leaning against a wall. Gabriel instantly recognized the violated, black-haired young woman found at the Wagon Wheel Ranch house.

"Her name is Regina Jones from Morro Bay," Dash said. "The shelter says she stayed with them for a couple of months. The lady there is willing to be interviewed. I did some checking, and so far there are no Joneses in Morro Bay who own up to knowing a Regina."

Gabriel mused. "If she's a runaway, she would use a fake name."

"Why don't we put a team on researching dental records at Morro Bay. Hopefully we'll get a match with our Regina Jones."

"Well, that's one down," Gabriel said and his cell phone interrupted. He answered it anxiously, thinking it might be Tara again. "McRay."

"Hi, it's Ming."

Gabriel froze and then composed himself. "Hi."

"Are you okay?"

"I'm all right," he answered. "You?"

"I'm well. I just wanted to know what you were doing tonight. I thought we should get together and talk."

"Oh." Gabriel swallowed. "I've got plans."

A minute of silence passed between them and then Ming spoke in her full professional voice.

"Busy boy. Okay, no problem. Hey, I've got the lab results on your AIDS test. No antibodies were found. You're negative. I thought you'd want to know."

Gabriel stiffened. He had forgotten all about the possibility of sexually transmitted diseases. He'd slept with Tara.

"Hello?" Ming asked.

"Thanks so much, Ming. I mean it."

Ming seemed to waver over the phone. "I kind of thought we could celebrate with some safe sex."

Now that sounded like the old Ming. Gabriel forced a chuckle, a hilarity that he didn't feel. "Sounds like a 'safe' plan. But like I said, I'm busy tonight."

Dash crossed his arms, brows furrowed. Gabriel ignored his questioning look.

"I've got some more news," Ming said, cutting him a break, which made Gabriel feel even more like a jerk. "I've got the report on the syringe found at the Wagon Wheel crime scene. The lab found traces of methamphetamine plus a small sampling of blood inside the needle. The blood was AB, which is the same type in that syringe you found in the forest."

Gabriel nodded. "That's great. I'd love to tie the two syringes to Ross."

"Ross?" Ming asked.

"A person of interest."

"I'll need his blood sample or a syringe in his possession. A saliva swab would do for DNA testing."

"I'll work on it. Thanks, Ming. Again, sorry about tonight."

"And if you get me about one hundred milligrams of his hair, cut close to the scalp, I can determine if he was using meth at the time your girl was killed at the Wagon Wheel."

"I'll do my best. Thanks again, and you have a good night, okay?"

"Who are your plans with?"

"Ming, Dash is about to show me something—"

"Are we broken up?"

"Okay, let me call you about this later."

"Asshole." Ming hung up.

Gabriel sighed at the phone in his hand.

"Everything okay?" Dash asked.

Gabriel nodded without looking up. "We've got to get a search warrant for Ross's place. We need to find another syringe to tie directly to him. We'll also need to get a DNA sample."

"I'll let the lieutenant know," Dash told him. "You sure you're all right?"

"Never been better," Gabriel lied.

CHAPTER 10

The Venice boardwalk was quiet and the beach lay dormant beneath a shroud of clouds. Light issued from under the doorway of "Shakespeare's Cup," a hole-in-the-wall café that served organic sandwiches and a variety of coffee beverages. A cluster of souls surrounded the small stage at the back. A bespectacled man with blond hair and a Gibson guitar, sat on a bar stool and strummed pretty chords. He sang an original composition about a woman with a faraway look in her eyes.

"Who knows where she goes when she stares as she's all alone?" he sang softly. "Come back from where you've been. Is it the only place you're really in?"

Gabriel and Tara watched the lone singer as they sat in comfortable chairs and sipped espresso drinks. Gabriel was intent on staying away from booze so he could keep his wits about him.

He studied Tara through the steam rising from her drink. Her porcelain skin, the tight sweater cupping breasts that rode high above her small waist; the body of a woman with the delicate psyche of a little girl. Gabriel found Tara irresistible.

The song ended and Tara grinned, clapping. The performer bowed slightly and then began to play an instrumental.

"That was nice," Tara said, sipping her coffee.

Gabriel gazed at her. "You said you wanted to talk, Tara."

"Did I?" Tara's eyes were on the stage.

"I'm here and it's private," he told her. "Talk to me."

The song ended and Tara clapped euphorically. She didn't seem to hear Gabriel.

"Mrs. Samuels?"

She turned to Gabriel with a perplexed expression. "Aren't we passed that? I told you to call me Tara."

Gabriel sighed. "Look, about what we did the other night... I owe you an apology. I shouldn't have crossed that line."

"What are you sorry for? I crossed a line, too." Tara looked back at the singer, who began a song about voyages to far off places.

"Oh, don't you just love to travel?" she asked Gabriel eagerly. "Marc and I watched this old movie called '10' once and I fell in love with that resort in the movie. It's in Mexico, right on the ocean. Hot sand and blue water. Tropical drinks. It's so sensual. That's just what I consider heaven."

Gabriel watched her, figuring her pole-vaulting between subjects was due to her trauma or the effect of some medication. He motioned the waiter over and asked for the bill. Obviously, Tara had changed her mind about needing to talk.

Tara watched Gabriel pay the tab and her face grew serious. After he'd tucked his wallet into his pocket, she reached over and took his hand. She held it momentarily then placed it between her legs.

"Tara..." Gabriel shook his head.

She moved his hand further up her dress and Gabriel felt heat spread through his body as his fingers touched moist skin. Tara wasn't wearing panties. She lifted his fingers to her mouth and gently sucked on them.

"Would you mind if we left?" she murmured.

Gabriel couldn't answer. He was too busy watching her mouth.

She walked with him to his car and he was mildly surprised to see her crawl into his backseat. She motioned for him to join her. Gabriel shifted uneasily. He didn't want anyone in the backseat of his old car. He couldn't remember the last time he'd had his car washed.

Tara pulled at his arm and he fell inside, forcing a laugh. She didn't seem to mind the gum wrappers, scraps of paper, and empty Styrofoam cups that Gabriel had tossed back there since God-knew-when. She turned her back to him and hoisted up her wool skirt. She planted her palms against the window for support.

Gabriel surveyed her, knowing what she wanted, knowing he wanted it too, and knowing that this was stupid and crazy.

She looked back at him. "What are you waiting for?"

"Are you sure this—" he began tentatively.

"I want you to! Just do it!" She smiled. "And do it like you mean it."

So Gabriel did. He could not see her face. He could only watch her soft blond hair and hear her cries. The woman herself seemed to disappear, so Gabriel experimented, no longer self-conscious. Tara urged him to be more forceful, so he rammed into her body as hard as he could.

Afterwards, when he'd poured himself into her and lay against her with deep breaths, Tara pulled away and gave him a quick peck on the cheek. Gently pushing Gabriel aside, she collected her things and slipped out of his car like a whore. Quickly zipping up his pants, Gabriel exited the car also, if anything just to kiss her goodbye. Before he could reach her, Tara scrambled to the haven of her own car and left him standing awkwardly in the damp parking lot. He watched her drive off.

Bewildered, Gabriel returned to the driver's seat of his Celica with his head feeling stuffed and his body feeling empty. He rolled down the steamed-up window and hoped the night's cold air might give him some clarity. Why was it so easy to fall from grace? Why did he give in again when he knew that this was a dangerous game to play?

For years, sex had been a degrading act; that was the legacy Andrew had left him. Gabriel had never felt in control when it came to sex. With his previous lovers and his ex-wife, he simply went through the motions and felt nothing. He had built a shell around himself. Ming had come around about the same time Gabriel had started therapy. Until lately, they seemed quite good for each other. Now here was Tara, a woman who encouraged Gabriel to dominate, to take control, but it didn't feel right.

He'd fucked her, plain and simple. Apparently, that's how she wanted it. In fact, the more Gabriel could cheapen the experience, the more Tara seemed to get off on it.

Why would she want a man to cheapen her in the backseat of a beat-up car? Was she perhaps subconsciously working out the trauma of her rape? Mulling over these thoughts, Gabriel headed for home and the blissful ignorance of sleep.

ᴥ ᴥ ᴥ

The morning sun sparkled off the white plastered walls of the Hindu Temple, a destination for Hindus and tourists alike. The main Temple boasted a tall white spire intricately adorned with carved gods and goddesses. Lesser buildings housed ornately dressed images of the deities.

Anju Rajamani walked out the main gate with her new husband, Parveen, whom she preferred to call Paul, a decidedly more western name. Still high off her honeymoon, still getting to know her spouse, Anju was jittery. Nerves made her act immature.

Paul played it off by smoking, something Anju couldn't tolerate and was not informed about when they were betrothed.

"Cigarettes cause cancer," she said, watching him light up. They walked toward their parked car.

Paul ignored her, so Anju playfully grabbed the pack from him and sprinted away.

"Anju, that's a brand new pack. Give it to me," he pleaded, following her.

She laughed, shaking her head, running toward the brush lining the paved road.

"Anju!"

He chased her and found her pouting prettily between two monkey bushes. "Okay, hand over the pack."

"My goodness you are addicted. Go get it." She promptly tossed the cigarettes into the farthest bush.

"I can't believe you!" he yelled, glaring at her as he stomped over to the green, thrusting branches.

She laughed, dancing around him, and Parveen wondered if his parents had made a mistake. She was so juvenile. Not like the more sophisticated American women he worked with.

He muttered under his breath, letting her know he was angry. Anju seemed to get the message and knelt at the bush with him. "You want help?"

"Just stay back, okay? You've been enough help." He began combing through the brush.

"Paul, do you think there are snakes this time of year?"

"Now that would be a good one, wouldn't it? A rattler bites me while you laugh like an idiot." Behind his own cigarette smoke, Parveen smelled a rank odor.

He put his hand into the bush and pulled out an empty plastic water bottle. Parveen pushed his torso further into the monkey bush, his arm reaching inside.

"They're only cigarettes!" Anju cried. "Forget it!"

Annoyed with her, Parveen pulled back a thick branch and suddenly, the body of a woman thudded against his chest. He yelped and scrambled backwards as the corpse fell on top of him. Coarse hair touched his face as a slew of ants rained down from under her hairline. One of her eyes was missing, a string of optic nerve hung down her cheek. The other eye was open, red, and staring at him. Parveen gasped; a choker of wire encircled the dead girl's throat.

Somewhere behind him, Parveen heard his new bride screaming. He couldn't move. A fetid odor reeked from the corpse's mouth, which was kissing-close to his. Parveen watched in horror as the corpse's blue lips began to quiver. He felt his bladder release. From out of the dead woman's mouth crawled a shiny black beetle.

✿   ✿   ✿

The crime scene had been taped, but that didn't stop the news helicopters from buzzing overhead. Drivers drawn by the revolving emergency lights slowed down for a better view, halting traffic. Dusk had moved into the mountains, casting the oaks and eucalyptus in a violet hue.

While Dash spoke with the distraught Indian couple that had found the body, Gabriel stood beside the corpse, taking photographs. This girl had been horribly violated. The amount of blood covering her and the expression in her one eye spoke volumes. Tara had been at the mercy of this sadist. No wonder she acted peculiar.

Guilt rolled through Gabriel. He had been rough with Tara the other night in his car. He wasn't an animal, and yet he felt he had acted like one.

Leaves crunched next to Gabriel and a spicy fragrance filled the sour air surrounding the corpse. Ming gave him a brief smile.

"Hi," he said, somewhat surprised and pleased to see her.

"I thought I'd come and see this one myself."

Seeing Ming slide into her usual, capable role once again gave Gabriel comfort. Ming was calm in the midst of tragedy and somehow found humor in a humorless world, so unlike him, definitely unlike Tara. Ming would sooner get impaled on an anthill than encourage a man to demean her.

She knelt to inspect the dead girl and Gabriel crouched down as well, causing their sleeves to brush.

"Note the baling wire," Gabriel said.

"And I see she has ligature marks on both wrists."

Continuing her initial examination under the narrow margin of daylight, Ming pressed her gloved finger against the discolored dark skin of the girl's back. There was no blanching. "There's fixed lividity involving the dorsal aspect. You should make note of that."

Gabriel nodded. From experience, he knew this to mean that the blood had pooled at the victim's back right after death. The witness had claimed the body was draped on the branches, lying on her stomach, which most likely meant the girl had been killed somewhere else and then eventually dumped here.

Like a piece of discarded trash. Like the way I treated Tara.

Gabriel caught Ming studying him.

Ask me, Ming. Be nosy like you used to be. Tell me to tell you what's on my mind.

Ming rose and peeled off her latex gloves. "I'd say she's been dead at least sixteen hours, probably longer." She scanned the dripping chaparral. "I'll know more when we get her downtown. It's the same killer, isn't it?"

Gabriel nodded and stood up as well.

"Did you get me a syringe from your person of interest?" Ming asked.

"We'll be going through his place tomorrow, as soon as the warrant comes through." He regarded her gently. "How're you doing, Ming?"

"We're broken up. You don't have to care." She turned and headed toward the coroner's van.

CHAPTER

11

Two days later, Gabriel called Tara on his cell phone as he drove to the Malibu substation where Ross was being detained. He hadn't spoken to her since their rendezvous on Venice Beach. He had wanted to avoid the temptation of being near her. The case, however, needed her witness account and Gabriel could not afford to hide any longer. Tara answered on the second ring.

"Your attacker has struck again," he stated.

Tara was silent.

"I'm on my way to interview Ross."

"Really?"

"Do you have any more comments about Ross?"

He could hear her fidgeting over the phone. "I can't be sure. I mean, Marc says I have to be sure."

Gabriel was irked. Tara had so much respect for Marc, yet she was real quick to sleep with Gabriel.

"I'm not interested in what Marc has to say."

A nervous laugh escaped her. "Where are you?"

"Not too far."

He didn't know why he told her that. He shouldn't have.

"Come over," she begged. "And I'll tell you my comments about Ross."

Gabriel glanced at his watch. "I don't have a lot of time, Tara."

But the line was already dead.

Gabriel rang the bell and stood waiting until he noticed that the front door was ajar. He pushed it open and entered the foyer.

"Hello?"

He was met with silence. Rosa did not appear to be around.

"Mrs. Samuels?" he called out.

From the far reaches of the house, he heard, "In here!"

Gabriel walked down a long hallway, turned a corner, and opened a double door. Tara was lying on her big bed wearing only lace panties. She smiled and patted the mattress, a clear invitation for Gabriel to join her.

Gabriel's eyes scanned her body. "Tara, what are you doing?"

She gave him a girlish giggle, turned over onto her back, and stretched out luxuriously. "Come over and find out."

He stayed right where he was.

"Please come here." Tara pouted and held out her arms to him like a child. "You know how to make me feel normal."

"Where is your husband? Where's your housekeeper?"

"Away. Please, Gabriel. I know you're going to talk to Ross today and..." She paused and lines of worry marked her pretty face. "Anything that has to do with that day makes me feel like screaming."

He walked over and stood at the edge of the bed. He knew he should run for the nearest exit, but he didn't. He couldn't.

Tara grasped Gabriel's tie and pulled him down on the bed. "Why are you acting so distant?" She wrapped her legs around his body and kissed him. "Can't you act like you like me just a little?"

She began undoing his shirt buttons and Gabriel's resolve faded. In no time, his clothes lay wrinkling on the floor. No comments were made about Ross. Determined to show her he was a generous lover, Gabriel moved down Tara's body and spread her thighs apart. He knelt between her legs, but Tara pushed him away.

"Don't. Marc would be mad."

Gabriel gaped at her, astonished. Suddenly, he felt like an interloper, lying naked on the bed Tara shared with her husband. He immediately made a move to get up, but Tara laughed and pulled him back down. She positioned herself over him and took him into her mouth. Gabriel sat back, feeling the heat. Her ministrations brought him to the brink of orgasm and when he was about to explode, she stopped. He looked at Tara and she grinned. A dreamy haze traveled over her eyes.

Gabriel was puzzled. Tara reached for his hand and locked his fingers onto her hair.

"Make me," she stated simply. She forced his fingers into a clenched fist, which drew her hair up at painful angles.

Gabriel eyed the veins in his fist. "Stop it."

She lowered her head in answer, and soon Gabriel could think of nothing, he just held tight to her hair. Burning like a furnace, eyes closed in ecstasy, Gabriel felt Tara creep up his naked torso until she was a breath from his face.

"What do you want me to do?" she asked.

Gabriel whispered, "Anything you like."

She dug her nails in his shoulder and his eyes flew open in pain.

"Christ!" Gabriel hunched forward as Tara dragged her nails down his bicep, drawing blood.

Before he could protest Tara was astride him, mounting and riding, and Gabriel, caught in the pain of his shoulder and fervor of her sex, did nothing but push into her.

"That's it," she said huskily. "Make me. Hit me."

Moving below her, Gabriel jerked his eyes to her face, wondering if he'd heard her correctly. She brought her head down, blond shag swaying, until her lips tickled his earlobe.

"Do it," she whispered and then sunk her teeth into his flesh like a panther.

Gabriel howled, launching himself upwards.

"Fucking hit me!" she yelled.

Gabriel smacked Tara across the face. Immediately, he recoiled from her, ashamed, and watched her walk her fingers along a rash-red cheek.

"Tara..." Gabriel touched his ear and saw blood on his hand.

Catching him with her pinwheel eyes, Tara reached over and gently kissed his other hand. "I'm sorry. I'm so sorry."

Her light kisses traveled the length of his arm across his chest where she dipped her finger into his blood and drew a heart around his nipple. Giggling, she pulled Gabriel on top of her.

"What the hell are you doing?" Gabriel said crossly as he felt himself guided back inside her.

"Shhh," Tara told him.

He was about to protest, but she moved against him so well and felt so good, that he breathed in her lavender scent and hid in her body once more.

Later, Gabriel climbed out of her bed and dragged himself to the bathroom to wash up. In the mirror, he saw remnants of a flaking brown heart around his nipple. His bicep was carved with deep scratches. A line of dried blood ran from his ear to his collarbone. Gabriel put a hand to his earlobe and winced as he stared at his reflection.

Looking at himself, Gabriel felt his previous feeling of strength evaporate and a sense of dread took its place. She's seriously traumatized, he silently told his reflection. That's what it is. She needs help.

His reflection asked, "Are you sure that's what it is?"

Unsettled, Gabriel turned away from the mirror and got dressed.

✿ ✿ ✿

One hour later, Gabriel stood with Dash and Ross in an interrogation room at the Malibu substation.

"How long have you been a tweaker, Ross?" Gabriel asked.

"I don't do drugs."

Ross, wearing dirty jeans and a white long-sleeved T-shirt with a Quiksilver logo, was sweating profusely and fidgeting around the small room like a trapped terrier. Eager to be on equal footing with their prey, Gabriel and Dash stood on either side of the small conference table, their bodies framed by the mirrored glass of an observation window behind them.

"Would you roll up your sleeve for me?" Gabriel asked, indicating Ross's skinny arm.

The young, dark-haired man nervously licked his lips and rolled his eyes. He pushed up his sleeve for a millisecond and then pulled it down, pacing the room again.

"What's that stuff on your arm?" Gabriel asked calmly. "Acne?"

"Look, why are you hassling me?" Ross turned around and faced the detectives.

"What else are you into, Ross?" Gabriel rested his hands on the table and hoped the scratches on his own arm wouldn't bleed through his shirt.

Ross seemed to be the embodiment of Gabriel's own craving for Tara—an addict never satisfied. Gabriel was ashamed that he hit her. He was confused at his own behavior. And the ugly thought of Ross holding a gun to Tara's head and raping her caused cold fury to swell in Gabriel's unrequited breast.

Ross's nails dragged along the erupted flesh of his forearm again. Sweat made tracks down the degenerated pretty-boy looks of his face. "I don't have to answer any questions."

"You like sticking needles into your arms?" Gabriel taunted. "How about sticking nails into a girl's thigh?"

Dash frowned at him; a clear signal to Gabriel that his partner felt the acid was coming on too strong too soon.

The young oily man sneered at him. "Fuck you."'

Gabriel shoved Ross across the room. Dash shot Gabriel a more emphatic warning look and quickly caught Ross by the collar, easing him into a chair. Gabriel backed off and let Dash talk softly to him.

The DA had come through with a search warrant for Ross's cabin at the equestrian center. No gun was found, but syringes and pipes had littered the place like confetti; in the wastebaskets, the bathroom drawers, even spewed over the coffee table. The real clincher was the crude but workable meth lab in the cabin's kitchen.

Poor Lynn Traxler had stepped into her nephew's cabin like a woman stepping onto an alien landscape. On the kitchen's tile countertop were coffee filters stained scarlet from iodine and red phosphorous. Tablets of ephedrine were scattered next to bottles of battery acid, antifreeze, lye and Drano, a toxic mix that created the poor man's cocaine: methamphetamine.

The drug enforcement officials on the scene had told a pale Aunt Lynn that she could touch nothing because the hazardous materials team would have to be called in. The fire department had warned her to evacuate the horses until the place was cleaned up, because clandestine meth labs often caused explosions and fire. The tears that had ran down Aunt Lynn's face matched the glint coming off the rock "candy" shining in small glass vials stored on the top shelf of an otherwise empty food pantry. Lynn's husband, Jim, reacted by punching a hole in the cabin wall and he had to be subdued by officers.

Dash sat in the chair next to Ross. "Where were you on November twenty-eighth, Ross?"

"Uh, I worked, I believe." Ross scratched his arms.

Gabriel glared at him, shaking his head. "Try again. That was your day off."

"Did you leave your cabin at the equestrian center on the twenty-eighth?" Dash asked reassuringly.

Ross wiped the sweat off his upper lip with his hand. "What day was that?

"It was a Sunday."

"Sunday, Sunday..." Ross slapped his thigh. "I know! I was mostly with my pal, Jerry, go-carting."

"Can Jerry vouch for that?" Dash asked.

"I didn't do anything."

Nervous ticks, itchy arms, Gabriel observed. Drug enforcement officials called it tweaking. Ross was in bad need of a fix.

"Quite a setup you have at your place," Gabriel said.

Ross made no reply.

"Do you use all the product you cook or do you sell some on the side?"

"I want a lawyer!" Ross blurted. "Where's Aunt Lynn?"

Gabriel stuck his face close to Ross. "She's upset with you, Ross. She's wondering how her favorite nephew could manufacture drugs at the very place she hoped would rehabilitate him."

Ross glared back at Gabriel but said nothing.

"Tell us about Tara Samuels," Dash prompted Ross. "Is she nice to you?"

No reaction.

"You used to follow her around," Gabriel chimed in.

Silence.

Dash moved closer. "Did you follow her on November twenty-eighth? Out onto the trail?"

Ross sniffed, wiping his nose with his hand. "Uh, I—"

"Did you?" Gabriel pressed.

"Uh, fuck, I can't even remember what I did yesterday. No, I did not."

"Are you sure?" Dash asked.

"Uhhh..." Ross scratched his arms, wiped his face, and slapped his thigh.

"Did you follow Mrs. Samuels on that Sunday?" Gabriel asked.

"I was with Jerry."

"What's his phone number?" Dash readied a pen and paper.

"Fuck if I know it by heart. I don't."

"You lying little shit," Gabriel muttered, infuriated with the boy's melting skin, the rashes standing out on his arms, and his nervous twitching. "You left a calling card near a dead girl's body."

"The fuck I did!"

"You like working with baling wire, Ross?" Gabriel leaned close.

"I don't know what you're talking about, man."

"Let me clarify it for you then. I'm talking about working with wire, particularly around a young girl's throat."

Ross stared at him. "You're freaking out, dude. You're fucking nuts."

The anger struck, stark and quick. The thought of this wiry scumbag, too doped out to remember, attacking Tara, made Gabriel want to puke.

"I want a lawyer," Ross whined. "I didn't do anything! My Aunt Lynn won't take this shit. By the time she's through with you, you'll be holding a 'will work for food' sign near the freeway—"

Gabriel grabbed him by the neck, gripping him hard, and Dash immediately pushed himself between the two men. He pulled Gabriel off as Ross's thin T-shirt ripped and exposed more sores and needlepoints along a hairless chest. Gabriel shook Dash off and backed up to the door. Seizing the opportunity, Ross busied himself with scratching his sores.

"You're in for it now, dude," Ross yelled, spittle flying from his mouth. "Work for food! Work for food!"

Dash gestured angrily for Gabriel to leave.

Gabriel eased out of the room to find Ramirez watching through the one-way glass.

"Damn, you are like a *pinche* pit bull, McRay," Ramirez said, turning his short frame toward Gabriel. "What're you gonna do? Kill the kid?"

Gabriel reddened. "I'm sorry, sir. He's obviously lying."

Ramirez peered through the window once more, rubbing his chin. "I don't know. He looks pretty strung out to me. What's with you anyhow? Man, you go back and see Dr. B and maybe he can shrink your head again or something. It's always trouble with you, *cabron*, always trouble."

"I'm sorry, Lieutenant."

Ramirez nodded in agreement. "Yeah, you're sorry, all right." He gestured to Gabriel's bitten earlobe.

"Cut yourself shaving?" he asked, sarcastically.

"Yeah."

Ramirez gave him a long hard look. "You fucking frighten me, McRay. Get lost. I'll take it from here. Why don't you go charm those Tapia Park rangers? They're giving us a hard time."

"How so?"

"They don't like us nosing around their turf, I guess." Ramirez watched Gabriel as he collected his coat. "And get that loose screw in your head tightened!"

Gabriel had every intention of driving to Tapia Park, but instead he found himself driving back to Hidden Springs. He felt compelled to explain to Tara why she felt the need for a man to abuse her. He decided her behavior had to be some strange manifestation of her rape. Gabriel also decided that their affair must end. This relationship was not doing either of them any good. Tara would have to find a sense of security elsewhere.

An accident slowed traffic on the road. Drivers sat in their vehicles, jabbered on Bluetooth, and looked like schizophrenics talking to themselves. A silver Land Rover impatiently swerved past. Gabriel grimaced at the driver and felt a chill run through him. At the Land Rover's wheel sat Andrew Pierce.

A double take made Gabriel realize the driver was merely a scruffy looking teenager who resembled Andrew. Shaken, Gabriel reached for his cell phone and punched in a phone number. Before he realized whom he had called, a woman's voice answered.

"Hello?"

Gabriel opened his mouth but couldn't speak.

"Hello?" the woman repeated. An elderly crack cut through her voice, a sign of age Gabriel had never heard before.

"Ma, it's Gabriel."

"Hi, honey! Where are you? How are you? Want to talk to Dad?"

Getting off the phone already?

Gabriel frowned. His mother didn't want to deal with their issues any more than he did.

"Actually," Gabriel said, "I'm in the car right now and can't really talk. I just thought I'd say hello."

Her voice faltered. "Well, that's great, Gabe. Gosh... You sure you don't want to talk to Dad? He would be thrilled to hear from you. Wait, I'll get him—"

"No, it's okay."

"Pete!" Gabriel heard his mother call. "Gabe's on the phone!"

"I really can't talk."

"Oh, just one minute; he's coming."

Gabriel caught the eye of the driver in a Prius and, again, saw Andrew staring back at him. Shocked, Gabriel nearly slammed into the car ahead of him.

"Can't talk now, Ma. Tell Dad I called."

Gabriel flipped the phone shut. He took a shaky breath and wiped his sleeve against a band of perspiration that had broken out on his forehead. He should see Dr. B. But if he saw his therapist, he'd have to tell him about Tara.

Gabriel pulled into the Samuels' driveway.

A cold wind had kicked up as Gabriel parked and exited his car. He knocked lightly on the front door, waiting. He heard Rosa's Spanish from inside and carefully entered the house. Gabriel was about to announce his entry, when a male voice stopped him in his tracks. Rosa was just within view, standing under the archway to the kitchen.

"Come on, Rosa."

Marc Samuels was home. Gabriel swallowed. He had no idea Marc was back in town. Just this morning, he and Tara...

Suddenly, Gabriel felt exposed, standing uninvited in the entry. He backed up toward the front door.

"*¿Porqué no me paga?*" Rosa was asking Marc.

"*Pronto*," Marc answered, condescendingly. "*Dame tiempo*, Rosa. *La Señora* needs you."

Gabriel slipped outside and quietly closed the door. He counted to ten and then rang the bell. The chimes of Westminster rang gracefully from somewhere inside.

Rosa answered the door. Angry lines crossed her face but she made an effort to be cordial as she moved aside to allow Gabriel entry.

Marc Samuels joined them immediately. "How you doin', Detective?"

Marc shot out his hand and Gabriel took it, receiving a hard handshake. Marc's model good looks, all hustle and bustle, exuded an energy that had been absent moments before, when Gabriel had stood surreptitiously inside the house.

"I'm sorry to disturb you, Mr. Samuels. I thought I could ask Tara some more questions."

"Tara's not home. She's out shopping at the mall or something. Spending my money, that's all I know. But hey, gotta keep the little woman happy, right?"

Gabriel could only stare at him.

"So," Marc said, steering Gabriel into the den. "Tell me what's going on with the case."

"Well, we've—"

"You got someone nailed, right? Come on, you guys have been working on this long enough. You have to have someone in mind by now, don't you? I mean, what have you been doing all this time? Playing with your balls?"

Gabriel studied Marc's tan eyes and skin. "We're working hard to bring in a suspect. She's lucky, Mr. Samuels. The other victims weren't left alive. Did Tara—Mrs. Samuels, tell you anything more about the man who abducted her?"

Marc shook his head. "No, she hasn't talked about it. Honestly, we both kind of avoid the subject." He sighed dramatically and then stood up. "Well, keep me posted. I'll try to get more out of Tara. Deal?"

Gabriel rose from his seat, fixing Marc with a distasteful eye. "Please let Mrs. Samuels know I was here."

"Oh, sure, you got it," Marc replied, looking at his diamond Rolex, his mind obviously on the next order of business.

As Gabriel exited the front door, he saw Rosa hovering at the end of the long corridor, looking as if she had something to say.

Gabriel paused; giving her time, but the housekeeper dropped her eyes and walked out of view.

CHAPTER 12

The laboratory technicians cut Ross's donated dark hair strands into one-centimeter sections and then put the hairs in an enzyme solution. Ming watched their progress at the downtown police lab, always yearning to learn more about her trade.

The human head hair typically grows one centimeter every month. Hair analysis permits the forensic scientist to identify many substances that get into the hair bulb from the bloodstream. These substances then remain locked in the hair shaft as the hair grows. A strand taken from the scalp can be read like a timeline, providing valuable information on an individual's history of drug use. Ming wanted to prove that Ross had been taking methamphetamine at the time of Regina Faulkner's death. This, added to his fingerprints and his blood type, would be further proof that the syringe found at Wagon Wheel was his.

Ming watched the lab techs with their test tubes and droppers, but found it difficult to concentrate. She kept thinking about Gabriel dating someone else. Who was the mystery woman? Someone in the bureau? And how could Gabriel so easily throw his relationship with Ming away?

"Now we're going to place the hair in a mass spectrometer and vaporize it," one of the scientists said to Ming. "We'll soon see if there are trace amounts of methamphetamine in the section of hair pertaining to late November. That's what you want to know, right, Dr. Li?"

Ming looked at the scientist, but kept pondering the identity of Gabriel's new girlfriend.

"That's what I want to know," she echoed.

As Gabriel drove to Tapia Park, he wondered what Tara's housekeeper was hiding. He wondered what Marc and Rosa had been talking about. He also wondered if Rosa knew Gabriel had been in Tara's bed.

Tapia Park lay under a canopy of oaks. Mist lay calmly on branches made black by the rain. The few sycamores that dotted the campground were draped in autumn colors.

Gabriel found Dash near the ranger station, engaged in a heady conversation with a park ranger. A group of Sheriff's investigators stood idly by, watching the discourse. The park ranger was a thick man, who alternately smoothed his military crew cut and shaped his large handlebar mustache with a meaty hand.

"We're fully capable of dissecting this park and looking for any trouble, dead or alive," the ranger told Dash. "You guys wouldn't know where to look."

Poor Dash's Adam's apple was bobbing overtime. "Well, we appreciate any assistance, but this is really our job."

"Your jurisdiction ends the minute the parkland starts," the ranger argued. "You ever woke up a mountain lion before?"

"Excuse me," Gabriel said, jostling in beside his partner. "We're experienced in the parkland areas."

The handlebar eyed Gabriel as if he were shit on his shoe. "Day hiking doesn't cut it, Sergeant. We're going to have to contact Fish and Game if you guys mess with the creek. That's a protected watershed, you know."

"Okay," Gabriel said, annoyed and unable to control himself. "I know you love your job, but take your fucking soapbox and move aside because you are blocking my way."

Gabriel commanded the teams of detectives to search a two square mile area from the main road. He turned to the handlebar. "If you want to help, now's the time to do it. But if you disrupt my officers in any way from conducting their search..." Gabriel left off, arrested by the sight of a blond woman walking a dog. He was so reminded of Tara that he forgot what he was going to say.

"Just don't interfere," Gabriel finished, still eyeing the blonde. He finally turned to the ranger, but the man had already ducked out of sight. Sighing, Gabriel returned to the task at hand.

The officers searched the park as best they could, but the search ultimately proved fruitless. They stumbled upon the bones of a deer and the rotting carcass of a coyote, but no human remains were found.

At nightfall, Dash offered to buy Gabriel dinner. The two detectives went to a little sushi place in Malibu.

They took seats at the counter and nodded a hello to No, the sushi chef, who was reputed to be short-tempered.

"What's in your seaweed salad?" Dash asked No.

"Take it easy on him, Dash," Gabriel advised.

"Seaweed," No answered. "Very good for you."

"Yeah, well, we'll see about that," Dash answered, squinting and shaking his head at the hand-written menu.

Heading off a confrontation, Gabriel said quickly, "I'll have the spicy shrimp hand roll to start and an Asahi."

"Could I have a California roll with none of that crab crap in there?" Dash asked.

No slashed with his long knife. "How 'bout a Stupid Roll for you?"

Dash glared at him. "Excuse me?"

"A Stupid Roll. Lots of request for it."

Dash nodded, smirking. "Okay, I'll have it. See? I'm adventurous. Do you have bottled water?"

"Only tap." Slice went the knife.

"How can you not have bottled water?"

"It L.A. water. Very high standard." No dipped his hand in a steamer of rice and pulled out a sticky white plug.

Dash rolled his eyes. "I'll have decaf coffee." He nodded toward Gabriel. "So, what's going on with you? Everything okay?"

A beaded curtain parted and a kimono-clad young woman set down Gabriel's beer and the coffee for Dash.

"Are you sure it's decaf?" Dash asked the waitress. "Caffeine makes me edgy."

"And you make everyone else edgy," Gabriel scolded mildly.

Dash inspected the cup's rim for dirt and said to Gabriel, "I don't want to be nosy but, are you still bothered by, you know, that loss of memory?"

Gabriel sipped his beer and the cold liquid went down too fast. Thinking of those lost hours last summer, that panicky feeling at discovering a new set of clothes on his body, clothes he couldn't remember putting on, sent a chill through Gabriel that was colder than the beer. The memory lapses had been a terrible symptom of his post-traumatic stress disorder. Since his recollection of Andrew Pierce and the repeated molestations, however, the blackouts no longer plagued Gabriel. Still, Gabriel kept his fingers crossed on a continual basis, taking one sane day at a time.

"I'm fine, Dash. Really."

His partner nodded with a questioning look, obviously dissatisfied with Gabriel's answer.

"Go on and ask," Gabriel acquiesced. "I know you want to."

"Is it Ming?"

"It's not Ming."

Dash nodded knowingly. "I thought you were seeing someone new. I didn't know you and Ming had broken up. When do I get to meet her?"

Grateful that his friend did not further question the breakup, Gabriel took another swallow of beer and answered, "You won't be meeting her. She was... temporary."

Dash received a page and dialed a number on his cell phone. He listened to a message and then spoke to Gabriel. "They've found the father of Regina Jones in Morro Bay. I guess her real name is Regina Faulkner. One of us is going to have to go up north and talk to him."

Three young women dead, thought Gabriel, and the only witness is fragile, unbalanced Tara. *Not only did I sleep with her, I punched her in the face. At the very least, I'll lose my job.*

Gabriel took a deep swallow of the Asahi and volunteered to drive up north.

ॐ ॐ ॐ

A few miles away in a silent warehouse district located in Canoga Park, a couple exited a black Rolls Royce. The moon shed silvery light on the car and glinted off a bottle of Dom Pérignon the man held.

The couple approached one of the buildings. The lobby door was unlocked as they were told it would be, and the couple walked through a suite of offices that led to the warehouse. They giggled and wobbled on unsteady feet, swilling the expensive champagne straight from the bottle.

Malcolm Dobbs wore Versace pants and designer loafers. His bride of three months, wrapped in mink, wavered clumsily on her skyscraper heels. At the back of the warehouse they saw another door and knocked loudly.

The door opened and their host ushered them inside a large room. The first thing the couple saw was a wrought iron four-poster bed, which was anything but ordinary. A large mirror loomed above for the entertainment of the bed's occupants and a variety of thin chains and iron manacles hung, forming a canopy under the mirrored ceiling. Hanging from studs running along the walls were cat-o-nine tail whips, dog chains, horse reins, leather collars, masks, and various other restraints. On a shelf were poised a selection of sex enhancers. Still and video cameras were poised on tripods facing the bed.

The couple looked around in amazement.

"Wow," the woman said, "A pleasure dome."

"Quiet," Malcolm told her. "You'll speak when we tell you to."

The woman giggled and pushed her hand in front of her mouth.

"Ready for some fun?" their host asked as he opened another bottle of champagne that had been cooling in an ice bucket near a television set.

"Always." Sparse dark hair wrapped the sides of Malcolm's balding skull and a middle-aged paunch peeked over his belt.

"She ready?" the host asked, indicating the woman.

Malcolm turned to his mink clad companion. "Go ahead, Lena. Show him your pretty titties."

The woman let the mink fall luxuriously around her jacked up ankles. Except for black leather thong panties, she was naked underneath.

"Aren't they gorgeous?" she gushed, playing her fingers around her nipples. "I just got them." She giggled again and gave Dobbs a quick, grateful peck on the cheek.

Malcolm put an arm around her, grinning and then turned to the man. "We were sort of expecting something more." Malcolm's eyes surveyed the room curiously, like a little boy anticipating a fine present.

"Gotcha," their host said and went to a side door. "Is this what you were thinking of?"

With a grand sweep of his hand, the man opened the door to a mauve boudoir and bathroom. Like a fancy club, the pink marble counters were bedecked with gold baskets heaped with mouthwash, scented soaps, lotions, cigarettes, Cuban cigars, candy bars, aspirin packets, chewing gum, mints, joints, pipes, condoms, and various flavored lubricants.

Malcolm and Lena Dobbs peeked inside and saw something else reflected in an ornate gilt-framed mirror. A wide, boozy smile splayed over Malcolm's face.

"Now, that's what I like. Yeah, that's perfect."

⁂ ⁂ ⁂

In the morning, Gabriel was called into Ramirez's office and found a trim, thirty-something woman clad in Levi's and a worn leather blazer, sitting across from the lieutenant. Ramirez was hanging up the phone.

"Man, you don't quit, do you?" Ramirez pointed a finger at Gabriel. "I give you chance after chance and all you do is embarrass me. I got a call from the National Park Service wondering why we're abusing their rangers. Did you bitch-slap the guy or something?" Ramirez indicated for Gabriel to take a seat.

"No, sir, I did not," he answered warily as he sat down.

"Too bad." Ramirez smiled and leaned back. "You must be getting soft, McRay. A year ago, you would have decked him. Those *culos* better stay the hell out of our investigation." Ramirez nodded at the blazer-wearing woman. "This is Patty Brisbane. She works for a shelter in Hollywood." Ramirez handed Gabriel a business card.

"Children of the Night." Patty offered her hand, which Gabriel gently shook.

"Pleasure to meet you."

Ramirez took the card back from Gabriel. "Sergeant McRay is lead detective on the case, Ms. Brisbane."

Gabriel looked at the shelter volunteer questioningly, and she took her cue to begin.

"I'm the one who sent your partner that snapshot of Regina Jones—er Faulkner," Patty explained, nervously twisting a loose button on her jacket. "Children of the Night is a non-profit organization that works to save kids from the streets. You probably never saw Regina on a missing person's list because she's over eighteen and estranged from her father."

"What put her on the streets?" Gabriel asked.

"No work." Patty shrugged. "No money. She came to Los Angeles to pursue an acting career, but she couldn't get an agent and she refused to hold a day job. We picked her up one night while she walked Santa Monica Boulevard, right there with the other boys and girls."

"Was she turning tricks?" Ramirez asked.

Patty shook her head. "No, I don't think so. But she was close. She was desperate and prostitution is usually the next step. She was grateful for the shelter, though. Regina and I hit it off. She had confidence in herself, which is something you don't see often in the kids. At some point, she told me she had hooked up with some nice people who cared about her. Good role models." Patty shook her head at the loss.

"Then what happened to her, Ms. Brisbane?" Gabriel pressed.

Patty shrugged again. "I wish I knew. I still can't believe she's dead. The last time I talked to Regina she told me she had an in."

"What 'in'?"

"I don't know. I think maybe for her acting."

"Did Regina take drugs?" Gabriel asked. "Meth in particular?"

Patty shook her head. "Never. That's why I thought she would one day stand on her own two feet."

Ramirez reached for his Winstons. "Did she ever tell you who these people were that were nice to her?"

"No." Patty glanced at the "No Smoking" sign and then watched Ramirez light up.

After taking a contemplative drag on his cigarette, the lieutenant rose from his chair. Following his signal, Patty and Gabriel also stood.

"Thanks, Ms. Brisbane," Ramirez told her, and walked the shelter volunteer to the door.

"Well?" Gabriel asked Ramirez when she had gone.

"Well, nothing. We gotta talk to the father."

"I would think this Patty would know more about Regina than a father with whom she had no relationship." Gabriel spoke from the heart. His parents knew nothing about him.

"He may know something." Ramirez took another puff. "By the way, our friend Ross was definitely not at the go-cart place on November twenty-eighth. The go-cart people confirmed that. So his alibi is shit. We've got Ross with the syringe and his access to baling wire. But I want to know what ties him to the dead women."

"Me, too," Gabriel murmured. "It bothers me that no suspect prints were found at the crime scenes, except on that syringe."

Could Ross have killed two women and left no prints? A killer that left no prints was careful and Ross seemed sloppy. Still, like Ramirez said, the syringe at the Wagon Wheel Ranch nailed him.

"Lieutenant?" Gabriel began.

Ramirez nodded.

"What does 'may-pahga' mean?"

"*Me paga*," Ramirez said as he exhaled gray smoke. "Pay me. Why?"

Gabriel shook his head, watching the smoke undulate around them. "Nothing. Thanks. I'll call you as soon I wrap things up in Morro Bay."

When Gabriel returned to his apartment on Bay Street the sun was shining warmly and the bicyclists and joggers were hitting the wet pavement in abundance. Gabriel was making himself strong coffee for the ride north when heard the rumble of a truck's engine. He held a mug in his hand and watched through the window as a brown UPS truck parked next to a thick group of white oleander bushes. The driver got out and walked toward Gabriel's apartment. Gabriel met him at the front door. He wasn't used to getting packages.

After signing for the light rectangular box, Gabriel carried it into the kitchen. The package had been sent from Seattle, Washington. His parents had settled there years ago to be close to his sister Janet and her family. Janet had made numerous attempts to draw Gabriel back into the familial fold, but Gabriel always resisted.

He placed the package on the kitchen table and stared at it. Just seeing his parent's names on the return address label caused memories to rise to the surface of his mind, memories of Andrew.

Memories like the Melody Theater excursions where seven-year-old Gabriel had been treated to a Disney movie and a hand job. Memories of Gabriel's hand caught in Andrew's iron grip, tucked deep into Andrew's pants as the older boy whispered instructions while Gabriel tried to make sense of a sexual act he couldn't really comprehend. And memories of the pain—the pain that happened in the pastel-colored house with the rabbit-eared TV and Brady Bunch couch. Andrew's cajoling, "It's okay, my ma won't be home for another hour." Andrew's threats, "While you were sleeping, I implanted a bomb in your dick. One word to your parents and it blows off." Gabriel remembered one threat rather vividly: "If you tell our secret, Little Buddy, I'll drown your sister in my pool and everyone will hate you because you caused your little sister's death."

Andrew Pierce, the Skipper, barking orders. Gabriel, the First Mate, fearing for his life, but wanting to die.

Gabriel ran a pensive finger along the taped seam of the box. He rose, grabbed a steak knife, and cut the tape. He hesitated before opening the package, absently testing the knife blade against his palm.

How could his parents not have known?

At first, Gabriel recalled being terrified that any insurrection on his part would result in his sister's death. Eventually, he began to wonder why his family was not rescuing him. Why his mother left for work every morning leaving Gabriel vulnerable to the perverse advances of a teenage pedophile.

And then, when Andrew and his family moved away one wet spring morning, dismantling the small, sad Doughboy pool which had stood in their meager backyard, nothing was left as testimonial to the traumatic few months of Gabriel's seventh year. Life simply went back to normal. Gabriel continued to wait on the steep granite steps of his own doorstep after school, anticipating the sound of his mother's car returning home. They continued to have family dinners and celebrate holidays. Only, Gabriel continued to wet his bed. Eventually, that stopped too when his mind decided that Andrew had never happened.

Last summer, the Malibu Canyon Murder case had blown open the taped seal on his own memory box and what had come unwrapped in that package, besides the horrible remembrances, were the angry bones of betrayal. How could his parents not suspect that something bad was happening? How could his mother throw bloody underpants into the laundry and never ask a question? Or the time Gabriel poked himself with his math compass and bled all over his homework; his mother had asked why he did it and he had answered truthfully, "to drain out all the rotten stuff." That must have served as an adequate enough answer because she never questioned him further. Gabriel remembered his father knocking persistently on the bathroom door, demanding to have his turn, angry about Gabriel's continuous episodes behind the door.

Dad had worked in a downtown department store in the ladies shoe department and often worked double shifts. Mom was a teacher. Child psychology was in vogue back then. How could they not have known?

Gabriel was angry with Janet, too. He had suffered at Andrew's hands to protect her. Janet's boy must be around eight years old now. She had a daughter, around four. Gabriel saw the boy once. He had never met his niece.

The coffee was cold. Gabriel dipped his hands into the box and pulled out a large tissue-wrapped bundle. He gently removed the tissue to reveal his father's navy pea coat. Why did they send him an old coat?

Dad had been an officer stationed at the Presidio during the Vietnam War. It was a proud time in his life and he had loved the pea coat. Gabriel shook it out, expecting moths to fly from the dark blue folds, but none came. A card fluttered out with a tiny typed poem by William Wordsworth, "The World Is Too Much With Us."

"The world is too much with us, late and soon. Getting and spending we lay waste our powers..."

Mom, the teacher—always trying to broaden Gabriel's horizons. Well, there were some very good reasons why the world was too much with him. Some very cherry good reasons, Ma. Maybe if you hadn't been so busy all the time you would have...

Gabriel suddenly caught the clear scent of his father's after-shave, something he hadn't smelled for years. He lifted the coat to his face and took a deep breath. Suddenly, he was reminded of walks on Fisherman's Wharf and the duck ponds of Golden Gate Park. He could clearly recall a family trip up the Lost Coast to Mendocino. Janet and his mother had stayed behind to sip afternoon tea at one of those Victorian bed-and-breakfast places, while Gabriel and his father took a walk through town. Dad had worn the coat. He had placed his arm around Gabriel, hugged him close, and told him how good it was to hang out together, just the two of them. Gabriel had smelled his father's aftershave then. He would always associate that scent with the feel of his father's arm around his shoulders.

Gabriel studied the dark blue weave of the fabric and then caught sight of his wristwatch. Freeing himself from the grip of memories, he decided it was time to get on the road.

CHAPTER 13

Gray clouds rested over the eucalyptus and palm trees and the sunlight threw a gold cast over the freeway. The Pacific was as blue as Tara's eyes and seemed to hold as many secrets. As Gabriel approached Santa Barbara, he thought about Marc Samuels's conversation with Rosa. Gabriel knew '*porqué*' meant why. No meant no. Rosa was asking Marc why she wasn't getting paid. That caused Gabriel to chuckle. King Midas was having trouble paying his domestic help.

As he passed the University of Santa Barbara and Goleta, Gabriel's amusement at Marc's possible financial distress had dwindled and he became more curious as to why things didn't add up. Perhaps Marc was cheap with his employees, having less respect for people who "served" him and this was simply employer abuse. Perhaps Rosa and he were discussing a pay raise that Marc felt was premature. Then again, Marc Samuels was such a showoff; he could be running one step ahead of his creditors. Gabriel made a mental note to do a background check on Marc's business and financial history. It wouldn't do to ask

Tara, as Gabriel was certain that Marc Samuels was the type to keep the "little woman" blind to their predicament.

Gabriel pushed a random CD into his player to get his mind off Tara. The quirky music of Stéphane Grappelli and Django Reinhardt filled his car. Ming had introduced Gabriel to Grappelli's violin and The Quintet of the Hot Club of France.

If Ming were with him right now, Gabriel thought, this drive would be filled with her eclectic chatter. She would be rambling on about the forensic data that could be gleaned by the breeding cycle of flies and their tissue-eating maggots. Gabriel grinned. Ming enjoyed turning his stomach.

His grin slowly faded. Ming had always been his friend. They'd had their troubles, but at least their relationship had a solid footing. Gabriel's strange entanglement with Tara Samuels left him feeling derailed.

Perhaps Ming would help him sort out his thoughts. She was a straight shooter and he could always count on her sensible opinions. When he stopped in Buellton for an early dinner at Andersen's Pea Soup, Gabriel took out his phone and called her.

Ming was still at work, about to perform the autopsy on the latest victim, but she took Gabriel's call.

"What's up?" she asked, trying to keep her emotions out of it.

"Can you talk?"

Ming took a seat behind her desk. "Well, I'm about to examine Paula May."

"That's right. I'm sorry, I can't be there."

"I'm not surprised," Ming said.

"What do you mean?"

"That you're not attending the autopsy. You've been avoiding me like the plague ever since you started seeing someone else."

Gabriel was silent. Ming sensed his surprise. Did he honestly think she wouldn't figure out what he'd been "busy" with?

"She has nothing to do with me missing the autopsy," he said at last. "I'm on my way to interview a relative."

"Then why are you calling?"

"I wanted to talk with you, that's all."

Ming took up a pen and absently tapped it against the desk. "Where's your new girlfriend?"

"She's not my girlfriend. If anything, she's a person who confuses the hell out of me."

Ming rolled her eyes. "Uh-huh."

"You've always been good at seeing through bullshit," he continued. "I thought maybe I could talk to you about it."

Ming laid the pen down and pursed her lips together in anger. Gabriel wanted to talk to her about his problems with other women. What did he think she was—a doormat he could step on? How could he think of Ming as a mere friend after everything they had shared?

"Well, good thing you have a therapist," Ming commented callously. "You can discuss your confusion with him."

"Why do you have to be such a hard ass?" Gabriel asked her. "Why do you always have to act like you don't need anything or anybody?"

"I guess that's because you're needy enough for the both of us."

As soon as the words left her mouth, Ming closed her eyes and wished she could take them back. She had never truly considered Gabriel a needy man, no matter how troubled he'd been. She silently cursed her inability to control her mouth. All those focused years of study and hard work had left her badly lacking in social skills. She was about to apologize, when Gabriel spoke.

"Goodbye, Ming," he said. "I should have known this was a bad idea."

She heard the phone disconnect and he was gone. She'd had him, but now he was gone.

Why do you have to act like you don't need anything or anybody?

Ming put on her mask and entered the autopsy room. Forcing back the tears that threatened to blind her eyes, Ming made herself concentrate on the woman lying placidly on the steel examination table before her. The victim was Paula May, the girl found at the Hindu Temple.

The sight of this corpse was enough to make Ming forget her own problems. It took all of Ming's professional calm to deal with the manner in which Paula had been killed. She had been strangled with the baling wire, but not before the poor girl had been sodomized and one breast ripped repeatedly with what Ming could only surmise to be pliers. Tears and abrasions along the vagina indicated that she had been penetrated, but as with Regina, no semen was apparent.

Ming found several other wounds along the body corresponding to acid burns, although she had no clue yet as to what sort of acid was used. Ming studied the girl's hands and arms. Ligature marks appeared on both wrists and ankles. Straight cuts indicated manacles or handcuffs of some sort. Other than the mark of her binds, the dead girl's arms and hands were clear of trauma, which Ming found strange. The girl had no defensive wounds. Why didn't Paula fight her attacker before she was cuffed?

Ming heard the hydraulic hiss of the door opening and looked up to see Miguel Ramirez wearing scrubs and a mask. Ming immediately averted making eye contact.

"*Hola. ¡Qué tal!*" he called out to her merrily.

Ming shook her head in annoyance. Ramirez was aware that Ming downplayed her Mexican heritage and he loved to tease her about it.

"What do you want?" she asked curtly.

"I'm here for the autopsy. Filling in for McRay. The relatives want to know when we can release the body."

Ramirez made a cursory view of Paula May. *Dios mío,* he uttered to himself, thinking of his wife and his innocent daughter who had recently celebrated her quinceañera, her fifteen-year-old birthday. Look what a beast had done to someone's daughter... Ramirez definitely needed a cigarette.

"She was garroted with baling wire," Ming relayed to him. "Death came relatively quick. With garroting, the victim loses consciousness rapidly because the blood supply to the carotid arteries or jugular vein is cut off, unlike manual strangulation, which is death by asphyxia. The victim has time to struggle and panic. Of course, death would have come as a release from the other trauma she suffered..." Ming left off. She held a hand against her mask as if she had a headache.

"Want some fresh air?" Ramirez suggested, knowing he could use some. He was sure the dedicated medical examiner would say no, but to his surprise, she ripped off the mask and called for her deputy coroner to take over. With the mask off, Ramirez could clearly see Ming had been crying.

"Let's take a walk," he offered.

Outside, Ming plopped down on a grassy rise overlooking the skyline of downtown L.A. and the busy freeway. Soon, her shoulders began to quake. Ramirez watched her rifle through her purse. Finally, Ming found the object of her search, a tissue.

"I know you'll use this against me," she said as she blew her nose.

Ramirez cocked his head cheerfully as he sat down beside her. "Probably."

Ming opened her mouth to speak, but then swallowed her words and gazed sadly at the moving cars.

"What is it?" Ramirez asked.

"I'm not discussing it with you. I'd rather die."

"Smoking will kill you faster." Ramirez reached into his jacket and pulled out a pack of Winstons. He offered the pack to Ming, who simply shook her head. Ramirez lit up anyhow.

"Do you mind?" Ming asked testily.

"Not at all," Ramirez replied, and patiently waited for Ming's witty retort.

But none came. He took a deep drag and surveyed the running freeway. From the barrio nearby, sounds of Norteño music drifted toward them. A mural on a wall of a distant store depicted Jesus, his arms spread amid a riot of colored paint: Savior Nuestro.

"You know what they call two Mexicans playing basketball?" Ramirez asked.

Ming did not answer.

"A Juan on Juan," Ramirez said, nudging her. "Get it? A Juan on Juan."

Ming scowled and turned to face him. "Know why a man has a hole in his penis?"

Ramirez's smile faded under the glare of her ebony eyes.

"To get some air to his brain," Ming answered sourly and turned toward the freeway.

Ramirez took a thoughtful puff on his cigarette.

After a moment, he ventured a question. "Why is it you don't tell nobody that you're half Mexican? You ashamed or something?"

Ming appeared startled at the direct question and that pleased Ramirez since he enjoyed catching people off guard.

He'd done it to Gabriel McRay umpteen times and it amused him to no end.

"I'm not ashamed, even though I was taught to be."

"You could use it to your advantage, you know."

"Did you, Lieutenant?" Ming asked maliciously.

Ramirez stood up and unzipped his pants.

Ming surveyed him. "Are you trying to get me to laugh?"

Ramirez turned around and showed her a keloid scar on his lower back. "This is only one bullet hole. Nearly put me in a wheelchair for life. No, everyone thinks I got promoted for being Chicano, but I've got scars that say otherwise." Ramirez zipped up. "So, who taught you to be ashamed?"

Ming picked at the tissue in her hands and little white shreds fell onto her lap like snow. "My father. He's Chinese and always felt he was superior to my mother. She was the one who was Mexican. From Jalisco."

"Oh, yeah?"

"Only she wasn't allowed to speak Spanish in our home. She wasn't allowed to share anything of her heritage with me." Ming watched the freeway. "Sometimes I wonder why he married her. Just to treat her mean?" Suddenly, Ming began to cry again, and Ramirez ventured to put an arm around her. She immediately recoiled.

"Go away! Why do you of all people have to see me like this?"

"You got me wrong, homegirl. *No te preocupes.* I won't tell anybody you cry your eyes out over McRay."

Ming stopped, staring at him with red-rimmed eyes. "You are pond scum."

"I got you to stop crying, didn't I?"

Ming dug miserably into her purse again and pulled out another tissue. She blew her nose and dabbed at her eyes. "What about you, homeboy? For someone who is proud of his heritage, you sure do a lot to make a parody of it in front of people."

"No, I don't."

"You sure as hell do. You're a walking spoof of a Chicano. You don't even let us see your wife. Why is that, Miguel? Is it because she's a real basket-weaving tortilla-slappin' mamasita?"

Ramirez took an angry puff, but remained silent.

"I'll bet you know every great Mexican food joint around here. But you'd never let anyone know, would you?"

Ramirez looked genuinely miffed and Ming gave him a smug smile.

"Why are you upset with McRay?" Ramirez asked, deciding to thrust his own dagger.

"None of your business."

"Come on, Dr. Li. I know you've been *novios*. It's no biggie. I don't care. But I don't think you should go out with a lunatic. You're too smart for him."

"Please stop," Ming told him. "I don't want your opinion. And Gabriel is very intelligent." More tears welled and she sniffled. "He's seeing someone else, that's all. If I'm so smart, how come I didn't see that coming?" The tears streaked down her face. "He thinks of me as a friend. Only I don't want to be just his friend."

Ramirez put an arm over her shoulders, and this time she let it stay.

"Don't say anything to him, okay?" Ming pleaded.

"*Te lo prometo*."

⚛ ⚛ ⚛

Gabriel drove by stretches of cattle ranches and vineyards, and passed the signposts for Atascadero, the mental hospital for the criminally insane, which stood amid graceful slopes and eroded sandstone outcroppings. A large abandoned white house, a leftover from the 19th century, sat lonely on a hill. A land developer's name was printed on a sign at the hill's bottom. So much of California history had disappeared under the backhoes and bulldozers of builders, which is why Gabriel didn't mind working in the Santa Monica Mountains, the last bastion of preserved land amid sprawling Los Angeles County. Passing San Louis Obispo, he made the turnoff toward Morro Bay. Morro Rock, a huge stony mass, jutted from the ground up ahead.

Gabriel glanced at the passenger seat on top of which lay Regina Faulkner's case file. Dash had spoken with Regina's father by telephone and the man had told him Regina was a chronic runaway. She had called him from Los Angeles during the summer and that's the last her father ever heard from her.

Gabriel continued driving until he saw a tract of houses packed between the freeway and the beach. He exited and drove up a small cul-de-sac to a joyless one-story clapboard home.

Christmas lights adorning the other houses on the block bathed the misty street in a cheerful, multi-colored glow. Lights also hung from the Faulkner house, but they weren't on. Gabriel exited his car and, feeling the salt spray on his face, pulled on the blue pea coat. It fit well and the scent of his father's aftershave comforted Gabriel. He knocked at the front door.

A man with red cheeks and a slight widow's hump opened the door.

"Mr. Faulkner?" Gabriel asked, hugging the pea coat to his body.

"You the detective who called me?"

"That might have been my partner, Sergeant Starkweather. I'm Detective McRay."

The man squinted at his identification. "Yeah, he told me you'd be comin'."

He lightly shook Gabriel's hand and let Gabriel pass into a modest house that smelled of the beach and oatmeal. It wasn't a bad smell, homey, sort of, and made Gabriel wonder why Regina ran away.

"They tell me they found my daughter." The man's lips trembled but his eyes remained dry.

Gabriel nodded. Dash usually handled grieving relatives. Gabriel put tight reins on his many questions, allowing Regina's father ample time to absorb the tragedy.

"I didn't go see her myself. I had a friend do it. She was strangled, right?"

Gabriel nodded again.

"They said with some sort of wire."

"Yes, sir."

Mr. Faulkner seemed to age ten years in a span of ten seconds, and he asked, "Can I get you something to drink, Sergeant McRay? I have Coke or beer. Coffee? What can I offer you?"

"I'm fine, thank you. Is Mrs. Faulkner around?"

"Regina's mom died two years ago from cancer." The man went to the window. "I'm a bit older than my wife and always thought I'd go first. Kind of funny..." He pulled a handkerchief from his bagging trouser pocket and wiped his mouth, staring at the gray ocean beyond the street.

Gabriel absently fingered the blue fabric of the pea coat. His father, too, was a quite a few years older than his mother.

"Regina and her mom were very close," Mr. Faulkner said. "Maybe that's why Regina couldn't find it in herself to hang around much after her mother passed. Regina, she got bored; nothing much to see here except for tourists. I tried to get her to go on to Cal Poly over there in SLO but she wasn't in'nerested. She and I used to argue about it."

He continued to gaze out the window, tucking the hankie away and seeming to forget about Gabriel, who took the opportunity to survey the small house. Like the outside, the inside had a clean but neglected look. Missing the female touch, Gabriel supposed. Both the house and its occupants never stopped mourning.

"Did Regina ride horses, Mr. Faulkner?"

"Hmm?" the man said, turning from the windowpane. "Horses? No, she never went for that. She was into music and movies. Wanted to be a rock star. Then she wanted to be an actress. Had high ideas about herself."

Gabriel felt disappointed. Of course, it would have been too easy to unearth a clean connection to Ross. Gabriel asked Mr. Faulkner a few pointed questions relating to the equestrian center, but they went dead cold. He asked if Regina had any friends who fit the description of Ross, but the answer was negative.

"May I see her bedroom?"

Mr. Faulkner led Gabriel down a short hall with stained beige carpeting and ushered Gabriel into a room that produced an instant headache. Regina's room was painted completely in black and slathered in rock posters, postcards, bumper stickers, and various gothic memorabilia.

"Screams at you, doesn't it?" Regina's father stood at the doorway. "Told you she was into music."

Music and more, Gabriel thought as he entered cautiously and headed to the dresser. A sticker-covered jewelry box held all sorts of rings and earrings, silver trinkets, skulls and lightning bolts. He slid open a dresser drawer to find various bras and underwear; mostly lacey black thongs. Another drawer held hair paint and body glitter. He ran his hands along the inside of each drawer, hoping to find stray note papers, phone numbers, matchbooks, receipts, anything that could tell him a story. His search proved fruitless.

Sighing inwardly, Gabriel moved to the small closet. A few clothes hung on wire hangers; black leather, some vintage dresses, funky cheap platforms, and lace-up work boots.

Eager to quit Regina's room, he scanned one last time the riot of black bold swear words, heavy metal posters, and images of death and destruction, and his eye fell upon a single postcard glued among several on the wall nearest the dresser. Gabriel approached it, peering closer. On the glossy red background Gabriel saw a golden cross with a black snake draped across it.

"May I take this one?" he asked Mr. Faulkner.

"Why not? Ginny won't be missing it no more."

Gabriel's reaching fingers paused, feeling the tenderness in those last words, and then he carefully peeled the postcard from the wall. Turning the card over in his hands, he read in the upper left hand corner, "Greetings from the Cloister."

CHAPTER 14

A terrified Lena Dobbs looked up from her supine position on the bed. She couldn't scream for the gag in her mouth and she couldn't move for the manacles that clamped her wrists and her ankles. She lay spread-eagled and naked on a bed stained with her own juices and blood. Hanging dead on a hook against the wall was her husband. Malcolm had crapped his pants on his dying breath and the odor in the room was ripe. Lena could even smell her own fear. Also hanging on a hook was her shiny mink coat, looking out of place in this hellhole.

What day was it, she thought desperately? How many days had she been trapped here?

Terrified, she jerked her head toward a sound at the door and gave a little groan of despair when she saw the man enter with a navy ski mask over his face. His eyes were merry under the mask.

He hovered over her body momentarily then ripped off the mask, and said, "Oops! Now you've seen me."

The man grasped Lena's manacled arm, and his touch sent a volt of terror reverberating through her. "You can't please a man for nothing, you old bitch. And I don't think I want you anymore."

❦   ❦   ❦

Gabriel returned home after midnight, pulled his car into the carport, and collected his briefcase, gun pouch, and his father's coat. He walked to his front door, put the key into the lock, and instantly felt another presence.

A rain gutter ticked like a clock and low clouds ebbed and flowed about him. Bay Street was not what it used to be, and the Venice gangs didn't stick strictly to Venice. Gabriel gently unzipped the gun pouch and pulled out his service revolver.

He heard a barely discernible footstep behind him. God, he hated people sneaking up on him… He allowed his anger to consume his fear, and in one swift movement, Gabriel whirled himself and the gun around.

Tara grabbed him.

"Tara!" Gabriel instantly lifted the gun to the sky; worried his quaking heart might shake his trigger finger. "What are you doing? Why are you—?"

"Help me," she whispered frantically, clutching him. "I don't know what to do! Marc's back and he's being so mean. I had to get away!"

"Shhhh," Gabriel said, mindful of the neighbors. He took hold of her hands. "You're freezing. How long have you been waiting out here?"

Once inside, he poured them each a whiskey from the bottle Ming had given him. Gabriel stood before Tara as she sat on the couch. She quietly sipped her drink and stared into the amber depths.

"Did Marc hurt you?" Gabriel demanded.

"No." Tara kept her eyes on the floor. "He's just, he's been acting odd ever since... You know."

"Would you like me to drive you to a hotel?"

She looked up at him with her luminous blue eyes. "Can't I please stay here?"

Gabriel did not reply. He reached for his revolver to return it to its case.

"So what did Ross say?" Tara patted the space next to her, indicating that Gabriel should sit. "You never called me."

"He wasn't very forthcoming." Gabriel remained standing. The buttons on Tara's tight blouse strained against her cleavage.

"What did he say?" Tara pressed.

"He denies any involvement."

Tara appeared to absorb that for a moment. "And what do you think about that?"

He gave her a sardonic look. "Most suspects deny involvement."

An uncertain expression clouded her features and then Tara perked up and grinned. "Can I see that?"

At first, Gabriel didn't know what she was referring to, until he remembered the gun pouch in his hand. "This?"

"Yeah, the gun."

Gabriel made sure the safety was on and then leaned over the coffee table to give it to her. It was a Smith and Wesson Military and Police semi-automatic pistol.

Tara hefted the weapon in her fist. "I think a man with a gun is very sexy."

"I bet you like uniforms, too." Gabriel joked and then noticed a spot of red on Tara's neck. "You're bleeding."

Tara immediately placed her hand over the spot and rubbed it away. "It's nothing. Probably a spider bite I scratched too much.

"Are you sure that had nothing to do with Marc?"

Tara smiled and pointed the gun at Gabriel. "Bang."

"Answer me."

She fiddled with the safety lever. "How do you...?"

"Don't do that." Gabriel reached for the pistol, but Tara flicked the safety off and put the barrel of the gun against Gabriel's forehead. He froze.

"You're under arrest, Detective McRay." She took hold of his shirt and pulled him down to the couch.

"This isn't funny. Give me the gun, Tara."

She giggled and pressed the gunmetal against his flesh.

"Give me the fucking gun," Gabriel demanded tensely.

Tara's smile broadened and she shook her head. Gabriel's hand flew up and grabbed her wrist with a vice-like grip. He yanked her arm and the gun away.

"Oh, there he is!" Tara appraised his fist clamped tightly onto her wrist. "I knew the lion was hiding somewhere in the lamb."

Her semi-biblical inference made Gabriel pause, perplexed by her once again.

Tara's eyes went dreamy and she pushed her body against his. "Doesn't this make you hot?"

Gabriel swallowed. He could feel her heartbeat.

"Here," she whispered and let the gun dangle from her finger.

As Gabriel took the weapon from her, Tara immediately covered his hand with her own. She began to guide his hand, still gripping the revolver, down toward her crotch.

"Put it in," she urged softly.

"Okay, enough." Gabriel forced himself to pull away from her.

She regarded him with concern. "What are you doing?"

He stood up, returned the pistol to its pouch, and retrieved his car keys. "Get up. I'm checking you into a hotel."

"I don't understand," she said. "We're just having fun."

"Fun? Jesus, Tara. Haven't you been roughed up enough?"

"I'm not being roughed up."

"You were hurt with a gun, remember?"

"This is just a game." Tara rose from the couch and walked over to him. "Play with me."

"No."

"Why not?"

"Because…" Gabriel glanced toward the couch and his words halted in his throat.

Andrew Pierce was sitting there, casually nodding his approval.

"What is it?" Tara asked.

Gabriel stared frozen at the longhaired specter. Wearing ripped jeans and an auto-grease stained T-shirt, Andrew Pierce pulled off a plug of black licorice and chewed it slowly, his eyes drilling a hole through Gabriel.

Gabriel felt a spider crawl up his back and he jumped.

"What's wrong?" Tara asked, her blue eyes sailing in her face. Her hand remained crouched like a spider on Gabriel's shirt.

He closed his eyes and felt a small pulsing in his skull. He counted to five. When he opened his eyes again, the place where Andrew had sat was empty.

"Are you okay?" she asked him.

"The gun," Gabriel said in a shaky voice as he turned towards her. "You want me to repeat what happened to you with the gun. Somehow you want to relive your rape and make it acceptable in your mind. But it's not! It's not supposed to be acceptable." Gabriel glanced with haunted blue eyes toward the couch. "I know what you're going through and you can't handle this alone."

In his head, he heard Ming reminding him that he was not a therapist and shouldn't act like one. He shook his head to clear it of Ming.

"I know Jonelle Williams has spoken to you about a victim's advocate," Gabriel continued. "I think—"

"It was Ross."

Gabriel blanched. "What?"

"Ross… It was him. Even with the mask, I recognized his voice."

Gabriel stared at her. "Why didn't you say so before?"

"I couldn't be clear, but I remember it now." Tara returned to the couch and sat in the spot vacated by the ghost of Gabriel's molester. She began to rock back and forth. "I felt him shaking against me. He was thin and smelled like the stables. I know it was him."

Gabriel, emotionally raw, stared at her, knowing he needed to call Dash and Ramirez right away.

❧   ❧   ❧

The following morning, Thursday, Gabriel and Dash arrested Ross, charging him with Regina's murder and the sexual assault on Tara. Nothing tied him to Paula May, the young woman found near the Hindu temple, and efforts to press Ross to identify the recreated female head sitting on Gabriel's desk had been in vain.

That afternoon, the detectives went to the condo Paula May shared with two roommates to see if they could provide any link between Paula and Ross.

Paula's roommates, one who worked as a producer's secretary at Fox Studios and the other who sold insurance, were very cordial and understandably upset at the fate of their friend. They allowed the officers to search Paula's room and again, Gabriel found evidence of the party life.

"She enjoyed going to clubs," the studio secretary informed the detectives.

"Did she ever mention something called the Cloister?" Gabriel asked.

Both women shook their heads.

"What clubs did she frequent?" Dash asked.

"The Sunset Room, Club Naked, Garden of Eden, the Highland..." The insurance broker shrugged. "You name it, she was up for it."

"Was she up for kinky sex?" Gabriel asked.

The girls shared guarded looks. Dash rolled his eyes at Gabriel, but Gabriel stayed on track.

"Come on, ladies," he said, prompting them. "You lived with her. Isn't there something you could share with us? She's not going to care anymore, especially if it helps us nail her killer."

"She was a real freak, but you can't let anyone know," the insurance broker said tentatively. "People think she's a golden girl."

"We'll try our best to keep the media out of her bedroom."

The girls led Gabriel to a computer they shared in a small nook off the living room that had been converted into a tiny office.

The insurance broker shrugged apologetically. "My computer crashed and she let me use hers. I hit her personal bookmarks one day—by accident! And this website popped up."

Whether or not her story was true, Gabriel could immediately tell what hooked the roommate's interest. The website was for the Land of Dor.

Gabriel sat down at the small desk and read the history of the site, taking a crash course in Dorean philosophy. He learned that women were slaves and men were masters. Gabriel felt a chill ripple down his body as he read about punishment and love, pleasure and pain, all one and the same. Meant to be fun and games by most people's standards, Gabriel knew the chat rooms on these websites provided hiding places for real deviants.

"I want to subpoena a member list from the website," Gabriel told Dash as they exited the condo complex and walked to Dash's Cutlass parked on Wilshire Boulevard. "I want to know every name. Tenant can get it for us."

Ralph Tenant was a federal agent who had worked with the two detectives on the Malibu Canyon Murder case. Gabriel had already enlisted Tenant's help on a more private matter. He'd asked the Fed to gather some information about Marc's business affairs. Gabriel feared that Samuels would recklessly drag Tara into financial ruin.

Tara...

The Land of Dor reminded Gabriel of last night and how Tara was drawn to rough sex. He was sure she was erotizing her rape in order to find a way to cope with it mentally. But was there a chance that Tara actually enjoyed being abused? Could she possibly be tied to the victims in this way?

"What is it?" Dash said.

Gabriel eyed his partner, longing to tell Dash everything, knowing that he should.

"Nothing," Gabriel replied.

As soon as he and Dash parted ways, Gabriel drove to Tara's house. He wanted her to give him some background. Where did she learn to play these "games," as she called them? It also occurred to Gabriel that he'd never thought to ask Tara, his one and only witness, if she had ever heard of the Cloister.

When Gabriel pulled up the Samuels' driveway, Gabriel spied Marc cleaning his Mercedes.

What, manual labor? Gabriel thought derisively as he pulled on his pea coat against the cold.

He approached Marc Samuels, who immediately jumped out of the car, wiping his hands. Marc wasn't his usual ebullient self. He seemed more like Ross, sweating and nervous.

"Hello, Mr. Samuels," Gabriel said. "Is Mrs. Samuels home?"

"Nah," Marc said, shaking his head. "She's out riding. What do you need?"

"I need to talk to her." Gabriel studied Marc for a moment. "I have to ask her a question."

Marc licked his lips, shifted edgily, and said nothing.

"Maybe she's mentioned something to you about this." Gabriel pulled out the postcard depicting the snake and cross from Regina Faulkner's bedroom and handed it to Marc. "Some of the victims are tied by this symbol."

Greetings from the Cloister...

Gabriel and Dash had consulted everything from Google to the FBI. No one knew about the Cloister. The only lead Gabriel had was the fact the postcard had been glued next to a card depicting the Viper Room in Hollywood. If Regina had gotten the postcards around the same time, then Gabriel needed to check out the Hollywood club scene.

Although Ross was in custody, tied by a syringe and Tara's own words, Gabriel didn't like having any loose ends. The snake symbol had been found on one dead girl's body and in another dead girl's bedroom. He needed to tie Ross to the Cloister, whatever it was.

"Ring a bell for you?" he asked Marc.

Marc handed the postcard back to Gabriel. "Nope."

Marc looked once at his Mercedes and then back at Gabriel. "I heard you have the dude that did it in custody."

"We have a person of interest."

"Tara is sure it's Ross."

The sun, bright and blinding, winked at them from behind a cloud. Gabriel squinted at Marc. "You know Ross?"

Marc shook his head, crossed his arms, and fixed Gabriel with hard eyes. "I don't see much of Sergeant Williams these days. She's not working this case?"

"This case has gone beyond Sex Crimes, Mr. Samuels. Sergeant Williams doesn't handle homicides. I do."

"You have your man. Haven't you got enough clues? What more do you need from my wife?"

"I'd like to know if she knows about the Cloister."

"She doesn't."

"Thanks, but I'll ask her."

"You know, I've done some investigating of my own and I don't think I want you hanging around Tara anymore."

Gabriel was caught off guard. "Excuse me?"

"Oh, yeah." Marc nodded eagerly. "I've heard you shoot civilians and shit. I went on the web and found some interesting stuff about you. One Halloween, you shot a guy dressed up as a cop for waving a plastic gun in your face. Then you hit some old black woman. That lawsuit was all over the Internet. I also read how you had some sort of breakdown last summer and you're under a doctor's care. How do you still have a job?" He pointed a finger in Gabriel's face. "Stay away from my wife, understand?"

Marc turned away and threw his arms down as if he were shaking off Gabriel's scent. "We're done here. I'm busy and I don't need some psycho on my property."

The normal Gabriel wouldn't take that from anybody, but he was far from normal right now. He stood humiliated in the driveway as Marc drove the Mercedes into one of his four garages.

❧ ❧ ❧

Gabriel waited nervously in the psychiatrist's small lobby, his insides like jelly. He'd been putting off seeing Dr. B for weeks, but Marc's diatribe regarding Gabriel's checkered past had thrown him for a loop. Seeing Andrew Pierce sitting on his living room couch didn't help matters either.

Dr. Raymond Berkowitz was happy to squeeze Gabriel in between appointments. Why Gabriel had been avoiding therapy when he'd been progressing so nicely was a mystery to Dr. B, and he stood to greet his patient warmly when the detective walked into his office.

"I like your coat," Dr. B said. "I haven't seen a true navy pea coat in years."

"I know I look old fashioned."

"No, it makes a statement."

"An old-fashioned statement," Gabriel said, taking his seat. "But it keeps me warm."

"Where did you find it?"

Gabriel hesitated and then said, "My father sent it. It was his."

Dr. B raised an eyebrow as he lowered himself into his own armchair. "You're speaking with your folks then?"

"Not exactly."

"And when you called to thank them, what was the conversation like?"

"I never thanked them."

Dr. B nodded. Gabriel remained silent.

"What makes you want to wear the coat?" Dr. B asked quietly.

"I told you. It keeps me warm."

Dr. B waited for more commentary, but Gabriel was closemouthed.

"Is there another reason you like the coat?"

"It's just a damn coat, Raymond. Why are you reading the world into it?"

"That's my job."

Gabriel rolled his eyes, rose out of his seat, and poured himself a glass of water. "It reminds me of San Francisco," he admitted finally.

"How does it remind you of San Francisco?"

Gabriel focused on the rough fabric; the smell of his father's aftershave still stamped on it, or was that his imagination? "It reminds me..."

He remembered chasing his sister Janet through the short halls of their flat, wrestling her to the floor and laughing. His mother would ask if either of the two kids wanted to help with dinner, and Janet would retreat to her room to play while Gabriel traipsed happily into the kitchen. His mother would ruffle his dark hair, and say, "You're an angel and a good chef!"

"It reminds me of happy times," Gabriel whispered. He took a deep breath and then regarded Dr. B. "I got a break on the case I'm working on. We've got someone in custody who's been identified by the witness, the one who was sexually assaulted."

Dr. B waited.

"You know the witness I'm talking about?"

"Of course. Tara Samuels," the psychiatrist prompted.

"Her husband is a real piece of work." Gabriel gave a little laugh that had no mirth. "They have this incredible wealth. You should see their house. You should see the two of them together. He looks like an actor and she..."

Gabriel paused and slowly met Dr. B's eyes.

To Dr. B, they were the eyes of a drowning man.

The psychiatrist wasn't sure where Gabriel was going with this, but he considered the subject a lead that he, as a mind detective, should follow.

"I guess everything isn't truly great with them, is it now? They're both dealing with her rape."

Gabriel swallowed noticeably. "I don't know that they're dealing with it. She's badly affected."

"Are you identifying with her, Gabe?"

"How so?"

"Well, you're still dealing with your own rape issues."

Gabriel winced at Dr. B's words. "It's not the same thing."

"Whether it happens to a man or a woman, rape is rape."

Gabriel narrowed his eyes at Dr. B, annoyed by his questioning gaze. Marc's sneak attack was bothering Gabriel, too. The man was a true asshole. Just thinking about Marc got Gabriel angrier by the minute.

"You know," he told his psychiatrist. "Just once I'd like you to not treat this so casually."

"Why do you feel I'm treating it casually?"

Gabriel's demeanor darkened. "It's easy for you to toss off a 'rape is rape' and then go back to your secure little world where you can thank your lucky stars that you're not me. I'm trying my best to make a go of things, you know; and your indifferent attitude really pisses me off."

Dr. B pushed his glasses up the bridge of his nose and said calmly, "Who do you think, Gabe, is being indifferent about your trauma? Your mother? Your father? Why didn't you call them about the coat? You're not giving them the chance to say they didn't betray you, to explain."

"Fuck their explanations!" Gabriel yelled, standing up and upsetting the water. "They didn't see what was in front of their own eyes? My poor mother, always complaining; she left me alone every day to be mauled by that freak across the street! And my father? What a fucking pathetic wimp. He never would have had the guts to put a bullet into Andrew Pierce's brain."

Dr. B clasped his bony hands together and regarded Gabriel. "Is this the reason you became a cop?"

Gabriel's shoulders slumped and he sat back down. He pulled some tissues from a box on Dr. B's desk, and, in resignation, wiped up the spilled water.

"Shall we continue?" Dr. B asked as he got up to refill Gabriel's fallen glass.

❦ ❦ ❦

The Paramount Ranch off Kanan Road in the Santa Monica Mountains was used as a movie set for many years but now stood abandoned. The ranch was rented out on various occasions, and this season the city intended to put on a holiday festival there. An appointed group of local denizens were browsing around the property on this cold Saturday morning, looking for various locations in which to place the strolling Dickens carolers, the concession stands, game booths, and, of course, the giant Christmas tree.

And a *menorah* of all things, thought Mrs. Kinsinger, a venerable matron and one of those denizens. She wore a knitted sweater decorated with sparkly Santa's elves and a fat faux-pearl necklace over her ample bosom. She moved about the ranch with an air of purpose and self-importance.

Of course, Mrs. Kinsinger had no prejudices about people. But the next thing you know, they'll want her to put up some Kwanzaa thingie. How many ethnic groups was she supposed to please anyhow?

Mrs. Kinsinger walked toward a wooden stage, thinking this may be a perfect place for the bell choir, when she saw a lone woman wearing a mink coat leaning back in one of the plank seats facing the stage.

Mrs. Kinsinger knew that today Paramount Ranch belonged to her, and took it upon herself to oust the sloppy-looking intruder who obviously didn't belong to her volunteer group.

"Excuse me, Miss," she said officiously. "May I ask what you're doing there?"

Rude, the woman didn't even turn around to grace Mrs. Kinsinger with a reply. Mrs. Kinsinger's breasts bobbled under the elves as she strode imperiously toward the woman.

"Excuse me, but we're here to..." Mrs. Kinsinger came around to face the woman and her words escalated into a high-pitched scream, for the seated woman was naked and dead under the mink. Nudity would have been enough to rock Mrs. Kinsinger's world, but the swollen white flesh alone wasn't causing her screams. A damp breeze ruffled the lifeless woman's hair along a bruised and battered face marred by foraging insects. Through the open fur coat, Mrs. Kinsinger clearly saw rust-brown blood.

Mrs. Kinsinger screamed again and ran off, her pearls flying back behind her.

CHAPTER 15

Knowing the media would have a field day with this latest victim, Ramirez requested Ming to perform an immediate autopsy on the woman found at Paramount Ranch. He also scheduled the task force to meet on Sunday, the following day.

The crime scene investigators had supplied Ming with a preliminary report which she read as she stood over the body. The victim on her examination table had been identified as Lena Dobbs. Her expensive mink coat was being examined at the lab. She had been found with no other clothing. Unlike Paula May and the other women, Lena had not been strangled to death. The hole in her chest was indicative of a gunshot wound.

Assisted by Geoffrey, Ming went to work.

A mass of maggots nested in the wound site, already in the pupal stage. The pupae were rounded on both ends, which meant the adult fly had not yet emerged. The crime scene report included the temperatures of the insect mass, the soil, and weather data. The CSI techs had also supplied Ming with a "killing jar," a glass container filled with cotton balls soaked in fingernail polish remover. Flies, taken from around the body, now lay immobile on the cotton.

Forensic entomology, or the study of insects in legal investigations, was nearly an exact science. Bugs made excellent timetables.

Ming began the autopsy by extracting fifty pupae from the maggot mass in Lena's chest. She placed each of them in boiling water for thirty seconds. The forensic entomologist who would study the maggots told her that boiling them first resulted in good specimens. Ming collected more of the pupae and placed them in special containers for live shipment.

Today is Saturday, Ming thought. Assuming Lena's body had been dumped at night and because of the colder weather, Ming surmised the flies would have arrived six to ten hours after the dumping, in the warmth of morning. After another eight to fourteen hours, the eggs would hatch. Add another eight hours for the first instar, or life cycle, to complete its development. Second instar larvae would fatten for forty-eight to seventy-two hours before they were ready to develop into pupae. Ming estimated that Lena Dobbs had been killed sometime Wednesday.

When Ming was finished, the packages of insects went off to the entomologist for further examination, and Ming continued her work on Lena Dobbs.

The woman's body was marked with the killer's same signature of torture, including a circlet of nail holes. These wounds had recently bled. Ming shook her head at the damage done to the woman's body.

Ming was able to extract a few yellow blanket fibers that were common to the other victims from the nail holes. She also discovered a number of blue fibers between the toes of the victim's feet, one even caught on a polished toenail. She carefully packaged the fibers for transport to the evidence lab.

With the pupae removed, Ming could inspect the entry wound from the gunshot. She then turned the body over to examine the exit wound. Ming's finely arched eyebrows furrowed curiously. Something about the angle seemed unusual, not a point-blank shot to the chest, as she expected. Ballistics would know better how to handle her findings.

"Hi, Ming."

Ming looked up to see Gabriel McRay step inside the room, wearing gloves and a mouth covering.

"Hi. I didn't hear you come in." Ming couldn't help but gaze at him. She hoped she didn't look as relieved as she felt. She was so happy to see him.

Gabriel's blue eyes were bright with some unexpressed worry and Ming fought the urge to ask him what was on his mind. He'd made it clear that it wasn't her business anymore.

Suddenly, Ming wanted to talk to him about anything—the weather, his cooking; anything that would make him stay, but when she opened her mouth to speak, Ming told him only of her findings about the dead woman on the table.

"I found six fibers; the same yellow cotton blend. These fibers have been consistently found on the victims, but never where they were..."

"Dumped."

"Dumped, right." Ming held his gaze and then said, "Which means this must be an item belonging to the suspect."

"I would agree. Unfortunately, we've looked high and low for yellow cotton items and we haven't found anything near Ross. He didn't kill them in his cabin, that's for sure. It's a pigsty, but not a torture chamber."

"I also found some blue fibers on her feet." Ming indicated a small plastic bag on a table near Gabriel.

He nodded and picked up the bag, studying the small fibers. Gabriel then regarded Ming above his mask. "How are you feeling?"

"Great," she answered promptly, honored to have his attention and berating herself for it, knowing her self-esteem was in the toilet. She wasn't doing great, of course. She still had moments where she thought she couldn't breathe, and everything was made ten times worse, knowing the man she felt the safest with was seeing another woman.

"How about you?" she asked and then added awkwardly. "Still confused?"

"I'm fine."

But he wasn't, Ming could tell. He had a dark cloud hanging over him. Ming moved slowly to the instrument tray. Gabriel had a suspect in custody, which meant the case was progressing well, so that wasn't bothering him. Maybe, Ming surmised, he still had girlfriend problems.

"That's good," she said, more to herself, and held up a scalpel. "I'm going in now. Look closely and you'll see what she ate for her last supper."

"Thanks for the warning."

Ming could tell that Gabriel was smiling underneath his mask.

Taking up her scalpel again, Ming began a "Y" incision, slicing the body from shoulder to sternum and then down the middle.

She was conscious of Gabriel close by her side, watching and listening as she made verbal notes into the microphone pinned to her scrubs. Feeling his energy, standing elbow to elbow with him, made Ming want to meld against him and take shelter against his chest.

When the examination was concluded, Ming stepped back, removed her mask and trashed her gore-stained gloves. "The mechanism of death was a loss of blood and shock secondary to a traumatic hemorrhage of the lung. The manner of death was homicide."

Next to her, a small steel table ran red from the bloodied instruments. Other than the sound of the water draining from under the steel table, the autopsy room was quiet.

Ming went to the sink and began washing her hands. She didn't want Gabriel to leave. "Guess what?"

"What?" he answered, as he removed his mask.

"I cooked."

"You cooked?"

"I did. And I want you to try it."

"What did you make?"

"Spaghetti pie."

Gabriel glanced at the victim's stomach contents lying in a steel bowl. "Only you could bring up the subject of spaghetti pie during an autopsy."

"Is that bad?"

Gabriel gave her an amused grin. "It's what I've always liked about you."

"Will you try it?"

"Yeah, only not here."

"Well, of course not here." Ming swallowed. "I could bring it over, or you could come to my place; or we could picnic, you know, whatever."

"How about bringing it to my place? I bet your dishes are still in their original boxes."

"Ah, you know me well. Tonight, then?" Ming asked brightly.

"Yeah, tonight."

"Okay. I'll be there."

Gabriel nodded and headed toward the exit.

"Get ready to pig out!" she called after him. Ming watched the door close and then looked down disdainfully at the stained scrubs she wore.

Look how he always sees me, covered in gore.

Ming promised herself that tonight she would wear something Gabriel McRay wouldn't know too well; something that would keep his blue eyes focused only on her.

⚘ ⚘ ⚘

Later that evening, at the apartment on Bay Street, Gabriel opened a decent bottle of red wine and set it on the tiled counter to aerate. Through his window, he could see a spectacular sunset. Too bad it was cold outside. His excuse for a patio might have come in handy for al fresco dining.

Gabriel had made an arugula salad to go with Ming's Italian dish, but he didn't overdo it because he wanted Ming to have the limelight. And why was Dr. Li cooking? Ming hated to cook.

Whatever it tastes like, pretend you like it.

Gabriel chuckled to himself and set the table. He was glad they had made this date. He was determined to keep his problems off the dinner table and keep things light between them. As he was putting out a baguette of bread, he heard the knock on his door.

"Okay, I'm ready to pig out—"

Gabriel swung open the door and Tara Samuels fell into his arms.

"He told me what he said to you and I'm so sorry!" Tara threw her arms around Gabriel's neck.

"What?"

"Marc!" she said emphatically. "He told me how he insulted you and threw you off the case!"

"Wait a minute, Tara." Gabriel pulled her delicate arms from his shoulders. "Marc can't throw me off the case."

"Yes, he can. He said he was going to pull some strings and get you fired from the force!"

Big shot, Gabriel thought.

"Not likely."

"What a relief." Tara nestled against him, resting her head on his shoulder. "I was worried. I wouldn't want to cost you your job."

"My job is fine. Look, you've got to go now—"

"Marc can be so forceful when he's not getting his way. Thank goodness I have you!" Tara lifted her face to his and gave him an impassioned kiss.

As Gabriel pulled away from her grasp, he spotted Ming standing in the doorway, staring at them, and holding her foil-wrapped spaghetti pie. She wore a tight red sweater dress with a revealing décolletage that seemed as out of place on Ming as Tara being here tonight. Gabriel could only stare back, unable to speak.

Abruptly, Ming turned and stomped to her car. Tara threw her arms once more around Gabriel. She didn't notice Ming at all.

လွှ လွှ လွှ

Dr. B should have known the task force meeting was not going to go smoothly. The tension between Ming and Gabriel was palpable and Gabriel, who normally kept open channels of communication with Dr. B, refused to meet his eyes. Sitting between Gabriel and Ming was Dash. He must have felt the heat too, because his normally peachy complexion was splotched scarlet.

Ramirez read a newspaper with the latest victim splashed across the front page, and the way he was cursing in Spanish under his breath, no one had to guess that his superiors had already reamed him.

In the middle of the table, like a morbid centerpiece, perched Tapia Park Jane Doe's reconstructed head. Her glass eyes regarded the entire company and her clay lips fixed them with a Barbie doll smile.

Ramirez slammed the paper down and barked an order to a clerk to get some coffee. He turned to Gabriel with a scowl. "The D.A. wants more on Ross. You're the lead investigator on this case. What have you got? Somebody give me something!"

"Okay," Dash said quickly. "One of the victims, Paula May, liked to dabble in cyber slavedom on the Internet."

Ramirez roared for coffee again and said to Dash. "Cyber slavedom? What's that?"

Dash told them about the Land of Dor website and the role-playing of masters and slaves. He also informed the group that his research on the Dorean lifestyle was stilted due to the fact that members and chat room participants all used pseudonyms.

"What does that have to do with Ross? Ah, forget it. Just keep on that track." Ramirez then asked Ming to pass around the autopsy photos of Lena Dobbs, the woman found at Paramount Ranch.

"Lena Dobbs, our latest victim," Ramirez continued. "Late-thirties but looked much younger thanks to a Beverly Hills plastic surgeon. She was married to Malcolm Dobbs, an entertainment lawyer. Both she and her husband were known swingers. Answered kinky personal ads; loved to party."

"Did she ride horses?" Dash asked, making notes.

"Why don't you find that out, Señor Spiceless? They went out for some kicks one night, according to the maid, and never returned. The lawyer husband is still missing. And if you think tackling a couple is a new and interesting twist for this *pendejo,* then get this: the wife here was shot to death.

Ballistics was able to tell us the weapon used was a Smith and Wesson .357 Magnum revolver. No baling wire was found on or around the victim."

"Then how do we know it's the same killer?" asked Dr. B.

Ming answered him. "Yellow cotton blend fibers were found on Lena Dobbs's body, just like the other ones, and of course, the signature of torture is the same. The lab analyzed some blue fibers I found and informed me that they originated from a Dupont brand of automobile carpeting."

A shaky clerk came in balancing coffee cups.

"Automobile carpeting," Ramirez murmured. "Blue fibers, okay. So we know Lena Dobbs was transported to Paramount Ranch, but the evidence suggests she wasn't killed there. So, we've got a car with blue carpeting that transported the body."

"Excuse me," Ming said. "But would a dead woman's toes dig into a car's carpeting? I believe Lena was alive in the car when she was transported."

Dash shook his head. "How do you know? If she was alive in the car but dead at Paramount Ranch, then where was she killed?"

"Maybe she was shot in the car," Ming offered.

"Check out Ross's car and get me some fiber samples," Ramirez said.

"But we didn't find a gun at Ross's place," Dash said.

Gabriel flipped through the report. "Ross's uncle is a troubled veteran. Maybe he has guns and Ross borrowed one."

Ming rolled her eyes at Gabriel. "There's a troubled soldier in the picture? Why haven't we heard that before?"

Dr. B watched Gabriel cringe slightly at her tone.

"Stick to your job, Dr. Li," Ramirez warned. "McRay will stick to his."

"Fine." Ming trembled like a taut wire as she turned toward Ramirez. "No foreign bodily fluids were found on Lena Dobbs, even though there was evidence of sexual assault. Just like the others. Because the maggots found on her body were already in a pupal stage, I estimate she must have been killed Wednesday night."

"And we arrested Ross Thursday morning," Dash muttered. "Just too late."

Ming turned a kinder face to the thin detective. "Thank goodness he's out of business. I found that circlet of punctures, similar to the wounds on Regina Faulkner, only these marks were brand new."

Ming passed out more photos of both the victim's wounds for comparison. Lena Dobbs's punctures were vicious and fresh. Two sets of them adorned her right buttocks.

"May I see the photo of the Wagon Wheel victim?" Dr. B asked, and studied Regina Faulkner's wounds. "Piquerism," he murmured.

Everyone looked at him.

"Piquerism is the act of deriving sexual pleasure from puncturing or jabbing yourself with sharp objects," Dr. B explained. "Albert Fish, an infamous and perverted killer, used to flagellate himself with a nail-studded board. Perhaps Regina Faulkner participated in this sort of paraphilia willingly by—"

"Para what?" Ramirez asked.

Dr. B pushed his ever-slipping wire-rims up the bridge of his nose. "Paraphilia. This is the technical term for sexual deviation." He thoughtfully eyed Gabriel and Ming who seemed to be pressure-cooking. "It really means 'abnormal love.'"

Gabriel turned toward Dr. B. "Why would you suggest that the first victim, Regina Faulkner, willingly poked herself?"

"She wasn't the first victim," Ming stated testily and then indicated the disembodied head on the table. "Jane Doe here had been killed months before."

"I got that, Ming," Gabriel said.

"Well, don't confuse everyone," she countered.

"I think everyone knows what I meant."

Ramirez's head swiveled between the two of them. Dash, caught in the crossfire, slid low in his chair.

"When you're calling the second victim the first victim," Ming argued, "you're screwing with everyone's timeline."

Gabriel shook his head. "Everybody's stupid, huh?"

"Not everybody," Ming said and eyed him menacingly. "Just you."

Ramirez leaned toward them. "What's going on here?"

Gabriel looked away.

Ming answered tightly, "Nothing."

Unconvinced, Ramirez continued to stare the couple down until Dr. B cleared his throat.

"Going back to Gabriel's original question," the doctor said coolly. "The puncture wounds on Regina Faulkner are too old to have been caused by the suspect, so she must have participated in this activity on her own, at a prior time. Isn't that right, Ming?"

Ming nodded. "Regina's puncture wounds are old. However, they are in the same exact pattern as the wounds on the other victims."

"Then was Regina his prisoner for a long time?" Dash asked the group.

Gabriel rubbed his temples, suddenly worn out. Masters and slaves; pain for pleasure... Gabriel envisioned slugging Tara. He felt the grip of his fist entwined in her hair. He cleared his throat, unable to clear his head.

He recalled the hurt behind Ming's eyes as she watched Tara kiss him while the spaghetti pie congealed in her hands. A headache now pulsed at the top of his scalp. Gabriel closed his eyes, willing the pain away. When he opened them, he saw

Jane Doe's reconstructed head slowly revolve on the table until she faced Gabriel with her vacant stare and toothy smile. Her clay features began melting and blending into the countenance of Andrew Pierce. His doll's eye winked.

"Gabe?" Dr. B asked concerned.

"Earth to McRay!" Ramirez shouted.

Gabriel took a shaky breath and pulled his eyes away from Jane Doe's head, which he discovered wasn't facing him at all.

"Regina wasn't his prisoner," Gabriel said finally, forcing the words from his mouth. "She couldn't have been his prisoner; she spoke to a shelter worker over the summer."

"That's true," Ramirez agreed. "So, that means she knew the suspect."

Dash shook his head. "But Ross won't admit he knows Regina. He draws a blank whenever we show him her picture."

"What about Tara Samuels?" Ramirez asked Gabriel. "Is she giving you anything?"

A sharp slap was heard and they all turned toward Ming. She had slammed shut her briefcase.

Gabriel eyed Ming guardedly. "She claims her assailant is Ross."

Dr. B sensed some unspoken, secret knowledge pass between Gabriel and Ming.

"It says in your report she smelled him," Ming piped. "Don't tell me you're taking that to the D.A. I'd say she's not the most reliable witness."

"Give her a break," Gabriel responded in a low voice. "Mrs. Samuels has been through a horrible ordeal."

"Smells don't hold up in court, Gabriel. You should know that." Ming sneered at him. "Or perhaps you're still confused. Would you all excuse me?"

Ming scraped her chair away from the table and made for the exit.

Watching her abrupt departure, Ramirez called out after her, "Come back when you've pulled that giant bug out of your ass!"

Dr. B looked at Gabriel who was staring at the opposite wall with a flat expression.

CHAPTER 16

Ross was housed temporarily in a padded cell because the tremors of his forced withdrawal sent him careening around the room. He had vomited a number of times and an officer would hose down the floor at intervals, all detritus swirling into a drain near the room's center.

Gabriel entered carefully and saw Ross rocking back and forth on a cement bunk, scrunching a brown blanket as though he were kneading dough.

"You got anything new to tell us, Ross? About Paula May? Regina Faulkner? Lena Dobbs? How about the identity of the girl you dumped at Tapia Park?"

"Fuck you!" Ross screamed and a long moan escaped him. "I need some. I'll tell you all kinds of shit if you get me some crank."

Crank meaning meth, Gabriel knew. "No can do, partner. You're going to tell me everything I want to know anyhow. That hypodermic found at the Wagon Wheel Ranch has your prints all over it, your blood, and your drug of choice. To put it simply: you're fucked. So, talk to me, Ross." Gabriel took a seat next to him on the bunk. "Tell me about the Cloister."

"I'm not saying anything without my lawyer!" Ross's voice escalated. "Where's Aunt Lynn? Are you keeping her away from me?"

"You ever take her to the Cloister, Ross?"

"I don't know what you're talking about!"

"Let's get back to the girls then. Do girls get you mad sometimes, Ross? What do you do to girls that don't behave?"

Ross started shaking and his face twisted into a grimace. He gagged once and scratched his arms. "I don't hurt anybody." Tears ran down his face. "I never hurt no one." Then he turned on Gabriel, spittle flying from his mouth. "Get me some ice, fucker!"

Gabriel left the cell, shaking his head and looking at Dash who was waiting outside. "Your turn to play good cop. I need a shower. He's truly disgusting."

"Since when are you so paranoid? I thought phobias were my claim to fame."

"That's not it." Gabriel rubbed his eyes in frustration. "The killer leaves no sweat, no blood, no prints; he doesn't ejaculate on or around his victims. We don't have one scrap of DNA evidence in four rape cases."

"He's careful. We know that about him."

"Dash, if the suspect was really that poor sap in there, we'd have an avalanche of DNA."

"What are you saying, Gabe? We found a syringe at the crime scene with Ross all over it. Your witness has identified him. What more do you want?"

Gabriel walked absently down the hall, shaking his head. "I want the killer."

The heavy sky broke as Gabriel returned home late; the rain pattered manically on the roof. It had been an excruciatingly long week, and even though Gabriel had stopped at his gym to work out, he couldn't sweat out his frustration.

As a last effort to relax, he attempted to concoct a meal. He hoped his busy hands would free his mind. Gabriel decided on eggplant Parmesan and set all his ingredients on the counter. He washed the eggplant and began cutting it into neat, thin slices.

Ross seemed to be the perfect suspect. He was addicted to a drug known for causing violent and aggressive behavior. Tara had fingered Ross, but was she a reliable witness? Ming's concerns about Tara may have had their roots in jealousy, but they were valid concerns nonetheless. And Ross wasn't careful. That bothered Gabriel as well. He breaded the eggplant and turned the fire on under a large oiled skillet.

Ross seemed to know nothing about the Cloister. What was the Cloister anyhow?

And then there was Ming, catching him and Tara. Gabriel sighed as he placed the breaded eggplant into the skillet and watched the hot oil bubble. A witness could hug the detective working her case, couldn't she? Gabriel began shredding mozzarella cheese, knowing that Ming wasn't that stupid.

Across town, Ming sat in her spacious dining room, with its rich woods and soaring ceilings, and listened to the rain while she thought about Gabriel.

Maybe she was plagued by a biological clock. Maybe the need to create a nest with the male of her species was so primal an urge even Ming's practiced discipline couldn't control it.

Frustrated, she walked to her kitchen with its stone floor, Wolf range, and Sub-Zero refrigerator. Wouldn't Gabriel have a field day cooking in here? It was ironic that they always cooked in his tiny kitchenette.

Ming's space was filled with trophies of her success, overwhelmingly so. The testimony to her success was a cold, unwelcoming cavern.

No wonder he feels intimidated.

Gabriel had fallen for Tara Samuels. How could he have done such a thing? Didn't he know what he was risking? A knot of jealousy wound around Ming's stomach.

Okay, so she's beautiful. She's got enough of that vapid look about her to make a man feel superior.

Gabriel had defended Tara by saying she had been through a horrible ordeal. Well, what about Ming's horrible ordeal? How could he sympathize with a stranger over her?

I know I don't exactly play the damsel in distress, but...

Ming leaned against the kitchen counter and glanced at a framed photo of her father and mother. Even posed for a photo, her father did not smile. And her mother... Her mother simply looked defeated, beaten down by life and a lousy marriage.

The knot of jealousy faded and suddenly Ming felt like crying. She turned her parent's picture facedown and pushed a potted plant in front of it.

She refused to be beaten down. She refused to cry. She had cried enough. After all, Gabriel was the one who was blowing it.

He thinks he can fool everyone, but he's forgetting that I'm nobody's fool.

Ming's stomach growled, reminding her it was dinnertime. She picked up the phone, intending to order a pizza, but found herself dialing Lieutenant Miguel Ramirez's voicemail instead.

"Miguel," she began as she visualized Tara kissing Gabriel. "There's something I think you ought to know."

⚜ ⚜ ⚜

About midnight, Gabriel finished scrubbing the last dish and placed it in the dish drain. The rain had abated somewhat and through his kitchen window a bright moon peeked behind fast-moving dark clouds.

Taking the pea coat from the couch, Gabriel headed into his bedroom. He walked to the closet, opened it, and the hairs stood out on the back of his neck.

What? Gabriel asked himself silently and peered into the black depths of the closet. Jeepers Creepers, he thought and yawned. He hung up the coat, got undressed, brushed his teeth, and fell into bed, exhausted.

His eyes opened and found the bedside clock. The digital numbers read two ten. Gabriel sat up on his elbows, light-headed with sleep, and wondered what awoke him. The apartment was silent. No, Gabriel did hear something. Water running... He looked around, trying to determine the source of the water.

The shower. He quietly opened the nightstand drawer and took out his Redhawk. Holding the gun, Gabriel edged along the wall into the hallway. His heart did a backflip when he saw the bathroom door tightly closed with steam issuing from under the door.

Swallowing, Gabriel reached out his hand, turned the doorknob, and slowly pushed the door open.

Through the opaque glass shower doors, clouds of steam undulated like harem dancers. Gabriel raised the gun with one hand and reached for the shower door with the other.

It's Andrew again, Gabriel thought wildly. I'm sleeping and I'm having a nightmare. *I'll kill him this time. This time, I'll make a victim out of him.*

Gabriel threw back the shower door and saw a torrent of water hitting the empty shower stall. His hand clumsily fumbled with the knobs until only a series of staccato droplets hit the tiled shower floor.

Like Chinese water torture, Gabriel thought. Had he left the shower on? Did he take a shower? Was he blanking out again like he did last summer? What did Dr. B call those episodes of lost memory? Fugue states...

Frightened more by the possibility of his own wretched psychosis than by the thought of a midnight intruder, Gabriel took deep inhalations as the steam caressed him.

He listened intently for any sound, but could only hear the incessant tap-tap-tap of water. Reaching inside the shower, Gabriel twisted the knobs more forcefully until the dripping ceased. As he stepped back into the vapory silence, he felt his body come into contact with a solid form behind him.

Gabriel spun around to see Tara Samuels standing before him like a mist-clad phantom, naked and wet. The fingers of her right hand dripped in red and held a razorblade. She screamed in his face.

"Filthy! Filthy! Filthy!" she shrieked and her wet arm flung out and furiously slashed at Gabriel with the razorblade.

Keeping the gun raised, Gabriel willed himself to get over the shock. He felt his flesh rip and he tossed his gun into the sink, worried he'd shoot her. He quickly grabbed at Tara's flailing arms and then squeezed her wrist hard until she dropped the small blade.

Shaking her, Gabriel yelled, "Tara, calm down! It's me! It's Gabriel!"

She fell sobbing into his arms and he sat her down on the closed toilet seat. A number of cuts magically appeared up and down her legs and blood ran down her skin. Gabriel jerked a towel from the rack and dabbed wildly at the cuts; there seemed to be a hundred of them, all bleeding. Gabriel caught sight of his own startled blue eyes in the mirror as Tara sat weeping and he thought:

What the hell?

❀ ❀ ❀

Gabriel stood above Tara as she sat on his bed, wearing his robe and holding a glass of cognac.

"Have you been in my apartment this whole time?"

Tara's legs were dotted with Band-Aids. "I thought I'd come and say hi."

"Come and say hi...?" Gabriel's mouth hung open like a broken door. "You scared the hell out of me. What did you think you were doing with that razorblade?"

She reached out a finger and touched a cut on his chest. She stared at his blood on her finger.

"Tara, what is going on with you?"

She smiled dreamily, stood up and put her arms around him. She pressed her lips against his. Gabriel pushed her away and regarded her, noticing for the first time a purplish bruise around her left eye.

"Did Marc do that to you? Is that why you came here?"

"Marc's away on business." Her eyes were like roulette wheels, daring him to place a bet. "Please, don't be mad at me. I meant to call you, I did. I came in through the window because I felt so alone." She touched the bruise under her eye. "Do you know how it feels to be out of control?"

She laid her head against the cut on his chest and seemed to drift off.

Yes, I know that feeling well, Gabriel thought.

I'm feeling it right now.

With a sigh, Gabriel put Tara in his own bed where she immediately fell asleep. He spent the remainder of the night sitting on his living room couch. He kept a watchful eye on his closed bedroom door and listened for any unusual sounds. He'd had enough surprises for one night.

CHAPTER

The following morning, Gabriel drove Tara back home to Hidden Springs as she was without her car. Tara refused to give Gabriel any further explanation regarding her nocturnal visit. He watched Tara's lithe figure walk the brick steps and disappear behind the heavy front door. Through the dining room window, Rosa stood sentinel, watching him.

Gabriel drove the Ventura freeway east and exited at Coldwater. As he took the winding road into the city, he felt nauseated. Was it the road or the events of last night that sickened him? By the time Gabriel arrived at the Dobbs's house in Beverly Hills, he was pretty sure that it was Tara's weird behavior that soured his stomach. He'd made a bad mistake getting involved with this witness and now he didn't know how to get away from her.

Malcolm and Lena's housekeeper couldn't offer much to Gabriel. When asked if she knew anything about the Cloister, the Philippine woman shrugged her shoulders, saying the private lives of her employers were just that: private.

She allowed Gabriel to search the premises. The Dobbs house had once belonged to a forties starlet and had a pool out back that featured a tiled mermaid at the bottom.

Despite his best efforts, Gabriel's mind kept wandering back to Tara. What time had she snuck into his house? He had been home all evening. Had she escaped a beating from Marc? If so, why did she tell Gabriel that Marc was away on business? What did Tara mean when she called Gabriel filthy? Gabriel longed to discuss this with Dr. B.

Instead, he continued his inspection of the house. He did not find anything related to the equestrian center or to Ross. He entered the master bedroom and found nothing of interest, which sort of surprised him.

Lena had a huge walk-in closet filled with all the accoutrements of a trophy wife: furs, elegant evening gowns, designer clothes, and shoes, maybe a hundred of them. In built-in bureau drawers, Gabriel found sexy lingerie: red lace and black satin, a few sachets, thongs, and, not surprisingly, a vibrator.

Gabriel opened another drawer and saw a treasure trove of sparkling diamond jewelry. He stood in the middle of the closet, sensing the very personal effects of a person no longer here. The Dobbs couple might have been into unconventional activities, but their home could have easily appeared in *Good Housekeeping*.

Gabriel turned to leave when his eye fell on a fox fur coat. Remembering the only article of clothing Lena Dobbs had been found in—a fur coat, Gabriel walked over to the fur and began rifling through the pockets. He pulled out a crumpled cocktail napkin and unfolded it. Behind a lip print left by the dead woman's red lip color, the napkin bore the unmistakable insignia of a black snake coiled around a golden cross.

The Cloister again, Gabriel mused as he drove through the city. In many of the cases he had solved, Gabriel had learned the value of patience. A poem his mother had framed and hung in his teenage bedroom had made an impact on him, even though he had never told her so. The poem was by Longfellow and entitled, "A Psalm of Life." The line that most impressed Gabriel was, "Let us then be up and doing, with a heart for any fate; still achieving, still pursuing; learn to labor and to wait."

Gabriel was waiting. Soon the mysterious Cloister would reveal itself. In the meantime, he would continue his labors. Lena's Cloister napkin sat bagged in his briefcase. He drove the Celica under the twin gold dragon gates of Chinatown. Just short of the beige arches of Union Station, Gabriel parked the car and headed into an L.A. landmark restaurant, Philippe the Original. Finding the napkin must have cheered him, because his stomach pains had turned into growls of hunger.

Supposedly, in 1918, Philippe Mathieu was preparing a sandwich for a policeman and accidentally dropped the beef sandwich into a pot of hot gravy. The cop agreed to eat the sandwich anyhow and found it delicious. Thus, the French-dip sandwich was born at Philippe.

Ralph Tenant and Dash were waiting for Gabriel at the ordering counter. Gabriel ordered a lamb sandwich and practically salivated when they handed him the plate dripping with au jus sauce. Ralph Tenant, an FBI agent Gabriel had met on the Malibu Canyon Murder case, was a chunky, porcine man who wheezed like a bellows. Tenant had initially irritated Gabriel until they had seen past each other's crummier exteriors. Tenant ordered a standard beef dip with two pickled hard-boiled eggs, two bags of chips, and a wedge of cheesecake.

Dash was next and addressed the blue-haired lady behind the counter.

"What's in the beef sandwich?"

"Beef."

"I know—beef. I'm asking what's in the sauce; a lot of salt?"

While Dash wasted time at the counter, Gabriel and Ralph made tracks across the sawdust-covered floor and set down their trays at a long wooden table shared by other patrons. The table afforded them a view of the white pointed tower of City Hall.

"Your friend must be sweating bullets," Ralph said as he sat down, his bulk draping over the wooden stool.

"What friend?"

"The guy you had me look into, Marc Samuels."

Gabriel bit into his sandwich. Chewing, he said, "He's no friend of mine. His wife is a homicide witness."

"Too bad, because she's in for more tough times," Ralph said, biting off half an egg. With his other hand, he pushed a file folder across the table to Gabriel.

Gabriel tucked the folder away and glanced back at Dash, who was placating the angry, hungry people standing behind him as he continued to argue with the blue-haired employee.

"Why do you say that?" Gabriel asked, turning back to Ralph.

"Hedge, Inc., that's Marc Samuels's company, is in the business of selling promotional items. In the past, Hedge had some quality clients, mostly entertainment people. Production companies that buy gadgets from key chains to coffee mugs to plug their latest TV series or flick."

Gabriel nodded. He could just see Marc schmoozing the movie execs and loving every minute of the glamour.

"Problem is," Ralph wheezed, "The studios buy large but pay slow. Throughout the years Hedge kept outlaying money for products to supply the studio demand, but it wasn't getting steady revenue in return. Hedge's debt to the bank kept growing. Now, with this economic slowdown, promotional items are being cut as the corporations tighten their belts."

Gabriel wasn't a businessman and didn't pretend to be. "So, what does that mean?"

"Well, the production companies say, 'times are tough and we'll pay you within the next six months. By the way, that order we made last week, cancel it, 'cause we've got no budget for it.' That's what that means."

"Not good."

"Not good at all. Hedge is left with a huge receivable in one hand, a huge inventory from cancelled orders, and a waning income in the other. The result being that Hedge owes a debt of nine million dollars to its bank. A bank, my friend, which is becoming increasingly agitated with Hedge." Ralph slathered hot mustard on his sandwich and looked satisfied at his meal. "Still, I wondered how a company could incur so much debt, so I delved a bit further."

Dash was approaching, carrying his tray; as people griped at him and the blue-haired lady muttered swear words under her breath.

"What did you find?" Gabriel asked Ralph.

"That the CEO, Marc Samuels, has been taking large chunks of the pie for his personal use, a factor that the IRS is keenly interested in, interested to the point of an indictment. And all that ill-gotten cash appears to have been blown, because the bank is about to take everything they own."

Pleased with his rhyme, Tenant took a huge and happy bite of his sandwich.

Gabriel studied his own sandwich. The fact that Marc Samuels was draining his troubled company did not surprise him. The man was too obsessed with being a blowhard to think rationally. But Gabriel felt bad for Tara, who was already unstable. Marc would take her down with him.

Dash took a seat, some dry-looking turkey resting on his plate. He reached for the mustard. "What'd I miss?"

Late that afternoon, Gabriel sat in the armchair of Dr. B's office, his mind rolling over the predicament of Hedge Incorporated, Marc Samuels, and of course, Tara.

"Where are you?" Dr. B asked.

Gabriel shook himself out of his reverie. "Sorry."

"Any update on the pea coat?"

It took Gabriel some time to figure out that Dr. B was asking about his parents. "Ah, no. I haven't called them. I've been preoccupied."

"It's been a while since you got their present. Are you still punishing your parents?"

Gabriel checked his watch. He really had too much on his mind. "Are we back to that again?"

Dr. B nodded. "You need to give them the opportunity to reestablish their protection of you."

"What?"

"Let them in, Gabriel."

Gabriel sighed and rose from the armchair. "You know, I better leave. I've got too much on my plate to handle a session right now."

"Really? What else is on your plate?"

"I made a mistake. I shouldn't have come."

"Why not?"

Gabriel fixed Dr. B with a curious look. "Are you baiting me? Look, just leave me alone. Tell me about your life for once. What's it like in Safetyville?"

"Now you're not letting me in either."

"What do you care? I'm just a few dollars to you."

Dr. B knew that it was crucial to make Gabriel trust him. Gabriel had transferred the sense of betrayal and resentment he felt toward his parents to Dr. B. If Gabriel could accept that Dr. B truly cared about him, then Gabriel could more readily allow his parents back into his life. But how was he going to win Gabriel's confidence?

"My father always knew I wouldn't make much money," Dr. B said wryly, folding his hands together. "He laughed when I said I wanted to be a cop."

Gabriel hovered over the armchair. "You wanted to be a cop?"

Dr. B smiled, pausing for a moment. "I didn't have the balls. So I got degrees in medicine and psychiatry instead and now I have lots of capital letters following my name. Dad always judged me though—negatively. I think I got into psychiatry to figure out why he enjoyed belittling me. It took me some time, but now I know he was just a brat stuck in adolescence who had to be better than me. By putting me down, he affirmed his own capabilities. All those years, I thought he was critical of me because he desired to see me succeed in life. Now I know he was wrapped up in his own trip and I was simply an easy mark. It's a nice life in Safetyville. Thanks for asking."

Gabriel slowly returned to his seat. He gave his therapist an apologetic look.

"Last summer, you told me that someday I would be in a better place to help others, but first I ought to help myself. I'm sorry, Raymond. I guess I'm still not there."

"Do you trust me enough to tell me what else is on your plate?"

Gabriel searched for the words. "I—I'm realizing all that glitters isn't gold."

"A true enough statement, but sadly one that most people don't realize. Can I ask why it's on your mind?"

"Tara Samuels," Gabriel said frankly and eyed Dr. B.

The psychiatrist knew Gabriel was expecting some sort of reaction from him, so he kept a poker face. "The witness and rape victim. Also half of the couple that you considered quite blessed at our last session."

Gabriel guffawed. "I was wrong. I was envious of their life."

"It's easy to take someone at face value especially when that person is good at self-promotion."

Gabriel let his eyes drop to his lap. "I had an affair with Tara Samuels."

Dr. B went a shade paler and his hands busied themselves with the papers from Gabriel's open file.

"I'm not telling you because I think you're some priest and I want absolution," Gabriel said. "I'm telling you this because I thought you could enlighten me as to how to handle her." Gabriel knew he looked desperate; he couldn't help it. "She's acting bizarre."

Dr. B seemed to be struggling to find the appropriate answer. It was a long time coming. "In what way is she acting bizarre?"

Relieved that he hadn't been judged, Gabriel spoke eagerly. "She likes sneaking up on me. Just last night I woke up to the sound of my shower running. I go in the bathroom and she's hiding, holding a razor. She starts calling me 'filthy' and then attacks me. I almost shot her! I didn't know she was in my apartment! And she's been cutting herself. I can only guess she must have post-traumatic stress, like I did, right?"

Dr. B stared at Gabriel, trying to take it all in. "Well, her behavior is certainly unusual. Would you consider this liaison with Mrs. Samuels a healthy one?"

Gabriel shifted his gaze to the hands of the wooden desk clock. "Not exactly. Every time I get around her, I feel like I've boarded the wrong train."

"How so?"

"You take a seat. You get comfortable and then you realize you're heading in the wrong direction."

"Why the wrong direction?"

"She's a witness, first off. I guess that's the most obvious reason this is a train wreck. She's married. That reason speaks for itself. But she's so troubled, Raymond. She witnessed a murder and was raped by a frigging sadist. She can't even talk about it. I've told her to get help, but she changes the subject." Gabriel thought for a moment. "Just like Ming,"

He stood up and began pacing the room. "I know Tara knows more about this case than she's letting on. All the victims seem tied by this rough sex stuff—what did you call it? Abnormal love?"

"Paraphilia."

"I'll tell you, Tara has a liking for that kind of game playing. But I think it's a reaction to her rape." He halted and looked at Dr. B. "What do you think?"

Dr. B calmly regarded his patient. "Have you participated in the game playing, Gabe?"

"Of course not. Well, one time she asked me to hit her and I did, not purposely, but I did." Gabriel crossed his arms defensively. "At first, I thought hey, maybe this is good for me, you know, to be in control for a change, to not feel like a victim."

"Whoa," Dr. B said. "Back up. Hitting someone is not being in control. It's hurting someone. Look, Andrew made you feel like a victim. That's your reality. But dominating someone, acting like a perpetrator, is not going to make that reality any easier to live with."

"What are you talking about?"

"Let me explain. The School of Individual Psychology, which I follow, believes in something called fictionalism. You can set positive future goals for yourself by using fantasy as a tool."

The puzzled look remained on Gabriel's face.

Dr. B continued. "An example would be a person who is down on herself, thinks everyone is better than her. She fantasizes on a continual basis that she's royalty—a princess, and builds around it. Soon, her inner self begins radiating toward the outside. People look at her differently; maybe treat her with more respect. Do you see? Her fantasy has impacted her reality. In your case, it's all right to employ fantasy as a tool. Go ahead and imagine yourself empowered sexually, but don't put yourself in the real role of an aggressor."

"Believe me, I've learned I'm not comfortable in the role of a…" Gabriel paused as the realization of what he was about to say took root. "A rapist."

Dr. B waited, allowing his patient time to let it sink in.

Gabriel swallowed. "But I think Tara wants me to play that role. I think she's trying to work out her trauma through me. Does that make sense?"

Dr. B pushed his wire-rims up the bridge of his nose. "If you'll pardon my opinion, I think you are projecting your own issues onto Mrs. Samuels."

Gabriel blinked at him.

"Not only can you jeopardize your case by sleeping with a material witness, Gabe, but you can jeopardize your own personal recovery. You don't know what her issues are. The woman herself is unstable. Certainly her behavior suggests she's under extreme duress."

"Because of what she went through."

"You're assuming that. You don't know."

"What else could it be?" Gabriel asked. "Look, can you tell me how to handle her? I'm in a bad predicament. She's my key witness and now I've… I can't alienate her, Raymond. I need your advice."

"Here's my advice," Dr. B said, and his brown eyes locked on Gabriel. "Don't handle her at all. Leave Tara Samuels alone."

❦ ❦ ❦

Dr. B sat bleary-eyed at his desk, listening to the wooden clock chime a late hour. Gabriel had departed hours before, but Dr. B was still trying to sift through the fallout left from the bomb Gabriel had dropped. Suddenly, everything made sense now: the cancelled appointments, the newly untapped anger, and the guilty postures.

Dr. B felt a heady conflict of interest. After all, Tara Samuels was a witness in a case he was profiling. Yet he couldn't compromise his confidentiality with Gabriel, his patient.

Dr. B removed his glasses and rubbed his eyes. Laurel and Hardy couldn't have scripted the scenario better. "Well, it's another fine mess you've gotten me into..." he said aloud.

And what of Gabriel forging this unhealthy bond with Tara Samuels, a married woman and a victim herself? Cutting her flesh, screaming at Gabriel, attacking him. Dr. B retrieved his glasses and scanned Gabriel's case file. Instead of concentrating on Gabriel, he allowed his professional mind to drift toward Tara Samuels. Cheating on her husband, and yet worshipping him. All that glitters isn't gold... Self-mutilation...

Something nagged at Dr. B. He tried re-reading his handwritten notes but the words blurred before his tired eyes. As he closed the file, he wondered what it was about Tara Samuels's issues that had snared his attention.

CHAPTER 18

After his session with Dr. B, Gabriel returned to his desk in Commerce and opened his case file. It was late now and the building was nearly deserted, but Gabriel had no desire to return home. He was afraid that Tara might be waiting for him and he had no idea how to act around her. So, he studied the victims, what they did for a living, who their friends were, and the S&M tie. What linked them together? The newspapers were hounding the Traxlers for information on Ross. *Ross...*

The Tapia Park Jane Doe's reconstructed head sat on his desk. Under the clay was a real woman's skull. Who was she? Her glass eyes stared unblinkingly at Gabriel. Although the forensic anthropologist was a good artist, facial reconstructions were at best sketchy, mainly because the tissue thickness had to be guessed. A couple of decent facial reconstruction computer programs were available. Unlike the clay models, they produced less artificial-looking results. Then again, having a girl's actual head on your desk was a good impetus to hurry up and solve the case.

A message beeped on his phone and Gabriel checked the call log. His mother had phoned. Unable to deal with all the females that were pulling at him, at least for tonight, Gabriel snapped the file closed and shut down his laptop. He decided to take his troubles to Hollywood and ferret out the Cloister.

Gabriel exited the 101 Freeway at Hollywood Boulevard, and caught sight of the gray dome of the Griffith Park Observatory topping the distant hills. Hollywood's eclectic mix surrounded him. Homeless souls squatted in front of abandoned theaters. Exotic boutiques, tattoo parlors and head shops stood out in neon against fading Art Deco buildings from the thirties. Super-sized record stores and tourist traps like "Ripley's Believe It or Not" added just the right amount of tackiness. Gabriel drove past an impeccable Dolores Del Rio mural gracing the side of a building off of Hudson. Murals like these had become L.A.'s unique contribution to the art world: vibrant original pieces adorning freeways and boulevards, artwork often tagged with graffiti more colorful than the mural's original pigment. Gabriel turned north to Sunset Boulevard.

The bohemian turned trendy with cafés and corporate stores lining the streets. The lights twinkled around celebrity-rife Le Dome restaurant and intermingled with the marquees of rock clubs like the Whisky, the Rainbow, and the Roxy. Long lines of kids stood waiting in the still, cold air for bands Gabriel had never heard of. The buzz of their talk and laughter was a constant sound down the boulevard. Stretch limos and luxury cars cruised by, their passenger windows tantalizingly dark.

The Viper Room's black façade was an unobtrusive mole on the otherwise glowing skin of Sunset. One would walk right by it if he didn't know it existed. But Gabriel didn't walk by. He stood in line like anybody ordinary and got in. Maybe his pea coat was just raggedy enough to be considered chic and his black hair, needing a wash, curled around his face in a manner rebellious enough to be cool.

The bouncer, a bald-headed African-American man wearing a diamond-studded ear gauge and a jaded expression on his face, allowed Gabriel to enter what was essentially a small theater with standing room only. A four-piece band played hollowly while some people danced or watched with nodding heads and glazed eyes. Gabriel spoke with the manager and bartender. Neither claimed to know anything about the Cloister.

Gabriel wandered outside and stood in front of the club, hands in his pockets, and listened to the muffled bass chords issuing from within.

A sandy-haired young man with pockmarks and a round belly stood to Gabriel's right, holding a sign that read, "The Fires of Hell Burn All Sinners!"

Gabriel sighed and walked carefully by him.

"Repent!" the sandy-haired fellow yelled after him. "The Lord sees your evil ways!"

Gabriel returned home around eleven thirty at night.

The Lord sees your evil ways. So did Dr. B.

With the music of the club still echoing in his head, Gabriel scrolled through the contacts in his cell phone. He wanted to talk to someone... anyone. He paused at Ming's number and then passed it. He selected another phone number and called it.

He heard a ring three times and then a woman's sleepy voice answered.

"Hello?"

"Hi, Ma," Gabriel said.

"Gabriel?"

"I'm sorry to call so late."

"It's okay." Her voice began escalating, the pitch rising as the dreams of sleep drifted away and reality set in. "Did you get the coat?"

"Yes, I'm sorry I didn't let you know."

"I told Dad not to send it. I said, 'Pete, buy Gabe a new coat if you want him to have a coat,' but you know Dad… You want to talk to him? He's up."

"I guess we could talk first."

Pause. "Sure. How's work?"

Gabriel found it hard to elaborate on any one subject. He was beginning to wonder why he had made the phone call. He wanted to end it.

"Work is busy. I'm on a new case. How are things with you, Ma?"

"Oh, I'm busy as a bee. I work part time for the district up here and I make sure to volunteer every week in Liam's class."

"Janet's kid. She's got two now, right?"

"Amber is her girl. She's adorable, Gabe."

"How is Janet?"

"She's redecorating her house. Goodness, doesn't she send you pictures of the kids? I'll mail you some. We've got an adorable one from a portrait studio. They're such beautiful kids, but I guess every grandma says that. I baby-sit as often as Janet will have me!"

"That's nice you have time for them, Ma."

A pause. Gabriel could hear his mother catch her breath over the phone line. When she spoke her voice trembled. "Would you like to talk to Dad now?"

Gabriel hung up. He stared at his hand covering the telephone and knew he had stabbed her through the heart. He simply couldn't take the useless back-and-forth banter any longer. Gabriel hated when someone hung up on him, but his burgeoning anger made him afraid he would say something to his mother that he'd regret.

Gazing at the phone, Gabriel wondered if it would ring and he waited for the shrill sound to pierce his eardrums. Outside a whippoorwill called and still he sat. Canned laughter from a neighbor's television bubbled through the thin wall separating them, and a plane rumbled in the sky above.

Gabriel waited, hoping his mother would call back and berate him for hanging up on her. She would tell him they needed to talk. Tell him that perhaps she devoted herself to her grandkids to make up for the lost time that she didn't spend with him and Janet. Maybe she would ask Gabriel why he hated her. Maybe she would convince him to tell her the secret he'd kept for nearly thirty years.

Gabriel was still sitting by the phone as the sun rose the following morning.

❧ ❧ ❧

Dash stood alongside a prison guard, observing Lynn Traxler speaking quietly and earnestly through a glass partition to her nephew. Tears ran freely down her cheeks, but the woman was holding herself together. Dash admired that.

Ross didn't look so hot. He was recovered enough from his methamphetamine withdrawal to be housed in county lock-up, and while he wasn't shaking or picking imaginary bugs off his skin, the face under his dark hair was ashen and morose.

Dash checked his watch. Gabriel was supposed to meet him here so they could talk to Ross about the Cloister. Gabriel was late. Although Dash claimed to know Gabriel the best of anyone in the bureau, partnering with him was a bit like looking into the Magic 8 Ball. One never knew what would surface.

Lynn Traxler slowly rose. She hung up the phone she had used to communicate with Ross as if she were cutting an umbilical cord. Ross watched her cut their connection and his face turned another shade of gray. Finally, a guard led him away.

Dash heard footsteps approach from behind and he turned around. Gabriel looked weathered, wearing an old navy pea coat that might have come from a thrift store. He's not even in a suit and tie, thought Dash, and he sighed, knowing that some mental malaise was once again burdening his partner.

"Hey," he ventured warily to Gabriel. "Everything alright?"

"I haven't slept much lately. Sorry I'm late." Gabriel was now looking past Dash at Lynn Traxler, who was approaching the two detectives, her face set in anger and disappointment.

"I told him I've given all I can give," she confessed with finality, using a tissue to dab the water from her eyes. "He's wanted for murder. I simply can't help him anymore. Those chemicals to make his drugs... Do you know we had to shut down the stables? Men wearing space suits came to clean out his cabin. Equestrians are very particular regarding their show horses. This is killing our business. And my husband, well, Jim is just having a terrible time with this. It's breaking his heart and not helping his—well, I've told you he suffered a bit in the war."

"Of course," Dash offered sympathetically.

Lynn sniffed, and tucked the tissue away. "The phone calls from the news agencies don't stop. I keep thinking about those girls and what their families must be going through. I told Ross he's on his own now."

"I'm sorry, Mrs. Traxler," Gabriel said. "I know this has been difficult for you. I have to tell you, I'm not entirely convinced of your nephew's guilt."

Lynn jerked her eyes toward Gabriel, hopeful. To her credit, she waited for him to continue.

"Strong evidence against Ross was found at one crime scene. But there have been other crime scenes..."

"Yes?" Lynn asked, her bright green eyes assessing Gabriel carefully.

"I need to know what Ross knows about this place or thing called the Cloister. Has he ever mentioned it to you?"

Lynn looked at the floor and then shook her head tiredly. "No. But he never talked much to me about his private life. I guess that's obvious."

"But through all his foibles, Ross still has respect for you, doesn't he?"

"I suppose so. You should have seen his face just now when I told him I was through with him."

Gabriel studied Lynn. "Then I wonder if you would come with me and ask him about the Cloister? Maybe he would open up to you."

Lynn's searching eyes traveled between the two detectives. "I'll ask him."

The prison guard accompanied Dash, Lynn, and Gabriel down a hall where inmates sat sullenly on bunks or hung their arms out between the cell bars and made comments to those passing by. Gabriel hoped Ross would cave in more easily, knowing his aunt was seeing him behind bars.

"Ross," Lynn began loudly as they neared his cell, ignoring the crude words of the other inmates. "I'm here with Sergeant Mc—"

The words froze in her throat when the party assembled in front of Ross's cell. Lynn's nephew was neither reclining on his bunk nor stretching his arms through the bars. Ross was swaying back and forth, feet floating above the ground, having hung himself from the light fixture with his bed sheet.

Jonelle Williams tapped her gold tooth in satisfaction as she sat in Ramirez's office. Jonelle was campaigning hard for a transfer from Sex Crimes to Homicide and was a frequent visitor to Lieutenant Ramirez these days.

"As far as I'm concerned the streets are safer now that that dude has met his maker," she said, and tossed a newspaper recounting Ross's suicide across the desk to Ramirez.

The Chicano lieutenant eyed Gabriel, who stood stoically near the doorway. "Sergeant Williams has put her seal of approval on this one. As far as she's concerned, Ross saved the taxpayers money."

Gabriel caught an unknown fire lurking behind Ramirez's eyes, but he ignored the flames and said to Jonelle, "You're completely convinced?"

"The syringe, Gabriel," Jonelle spoke to him as if he were a child. "Didn't you hear the latest? The DNA report on that syringe found near Regina one hundred percent belongs to Ross. Aren't you satisfied?"

"Hell, if everyone else is, I guess I should be too, right?"

Jonelle guffawed. "Nice attitude."

"I don't like loose ends. What about the yellow blanket? What about the Cloister?"

"The Cloister is some private fixation you have, Gabriel," Jonelle said primly. "The yellow blanket could have been destroyed by Ross days ago, or buried in the hills. Mrs. Samuels identified her attacker. I'm satisfied." She rose to shake Ramirez's hand. "Good job, Miguel. You must be the pride of the barrio."

Gabriel watched Ramirez bristle noticeably. The most amazing thing about the melting pot that comprised Los Angeles was the way each ethnic group managed to spotlight each other's differences.

Jonelle innocently strutted her ample ass toward the door. Gabriel was sure she felt she'd given Ramirez a prize-winning compliment.

When the door closed, Ramirez took a deep breath. "Why did you jump on Sergeant Williams like that, McRay? You need a vacation again? Didn't you take one last summer?"

"I was busy getting stabbed by Victor Archwood, remember?"

"I pulled you out of the ocean, remember?" Ramirez sneered. "So *nasty* with our friends from across town... What's your problem today, McRay? Think like all the other WASPS that I stole a promotion out from under you?"

"What does that have to do with this case, sir?"

"I asked you a question."

Lots of talk surfaced throughout the force how minorities were pushed faster through the ranks. But just because Jonelle had wound him up, Ramirez didn't have to hassle Gabriel.

Ramirez pulled a cigarette out of his ever-ready pack. "I worked my ass off for this job, McRay. No one made it easy for me, I'll tell you that. You got a problem with Mexicans?"

"No," Gabriel replied and turned to leave. He'd had enough. "But I'd say you do."

Ramirez smiled maliciously. "Ah, that's real good. That's profound, McRay. Sit down. Go on, take a seat."

"What did I do now, Lieutenant?" He sat in the chair warmed by Jonelle.

"This Tara Samuels, are you still trying to get information from her?"

Gabriel's heart pounded. The thing with Ramirez was that he enjoyed throwing people off. Gabriel forced calm shoulders and a poker face and nodded affirmatively to Ramirez.

"What else are you getting from her?"

Gabriel felt his knees go weak. Ramirez was going to slam him with suspension at the very least.

"Ahh, I don't care who you fuck, McRay. You're just *loco* enough to bang a witness. Maybe she'll open her mouth as well as her legs and give you some insight about this Cloister you're so worried about. That's it, isn't it? You're not satisfied because..."

"Listen, Lieutenant—"

"Don't talk. I'll do the talking. You're lucky I trust your instincts, McRay, you silly fuck. I'm telling you once before this leaks out: you cut it off with that woman or you'll be cut from your job. Let's hope and pray this witness doesn't sue your ass in the meantime. As part of my team, you're my responsibility, and I'm not taking any shit for you!"

Gabriel sat motionless as Ramirez lit up and dragged deeply on the Winston.

"Can I give you some advice, McRay? I can't imagine anything more sickening than hooking up with a woman who handles dead people all day long, but Dr. Li, she's a quality woman." He exhaled and the smoke traveled up Gabriel's nose. "That's all. Get out and find the Cloister."

CHAPTER 19

Gabriel tread on Nicholas Cage and Jack Nicholson and other celebrity stars as he made his way toward the Mood Club along Hollywood Boulevard. He had visited three clubs already, asking patrons and club employees alike if they'd heard of the Cloister. The answer was always negative.

A light rain, barely a mist around the streetlights, damp-ened Gabriel's face. The Mood Club was of Balinese design and quite chic, part of the facelift Hollywood had undergone. In the darkened club, Gabriel questioned the young patrons. Nobody had ever heard of the Cloister and looked at the detective as if he had fallen from the moon.

Outside, Gabriel rocked on his aching feet and thought about his conversation with Ramirez. Dr. B wouldn't have dared discussed Gabriel's relationship with Tara, so that left only one person. Like the ultimate woman scorned, Ming had gone behind his back and told on Gabriel to his superior.

For all his bombast, Ramirez still had a leader's loyalty to his team. He was obviously going to let Gabriel slide, but only because he trusted Gabriel's hunches. To that end, Gabriel was grateful to his moody lieutenant.

At a sex shop across the street, a girl wearing a feathered boa over her skimpy T-shirt attempted to wave passersby inside. Gabriel watched her as she taunted a round young man who hovered near the entrance. He was the same sandy-haired fellow Gabriel had seen outside the Viper Room.

"God watches you, slut!" the kid warned the girl.

She shook her fanny in his face. "He made my ass cute, that's for sure!"

"Repent now or die with your sins!"

Gabriel caught the green light across the street.

"Hey," he called to the sandy-haired kid. "Can I ask you something?"

Gabriel broke out his department badge. The girl quickly retreated inside and the kid tucked his sign under his arm and began hobbling down the wet sidewalk, his legs splaying in funny angles. Gabriel wagered he suffered from some sort of spinal problem.

"I only want to ask you a question. You want to hold a sign, I don't care."

The kid kept shuffling and Gabriel kept right up with him. "I'm investigating a murder, and if you want to really send a sinner to hell, then help me do my job."

The boy stopped and looked at Gabriel with wild brown eyes, magnified by the thick lenses he wore. He was a painful reminder to Gabriel of Ross, young and shaking.

"Have you accepted Jesus into your heart?" the boy asked Gabriel accusingly.

Gabriel thought about it. "Why not?"

"What do you want?"

"The Cloister. Have you ever heard of it?"

"Sodom and Gomorrah," the kid said without hesitation. "A den of depravity."

Gabriel's heart skipped a beat. "You've really heard of it? You're not lying?'

"Liars are the minions of Satan."

"A den of depravity," Gabriel repeated. "Full of sinners?"

"All of them destined to burn."

"I can help shut them down," Gabriel said, knowing he was dealing with someone whose toolbox might be short one wrench.

The kid tossed back his unkempt hair passionately. "The Lord will see that their evil disintegrates. They will beg for mercy under the fires of His divine power!"

"What's your name?" Gabriel asked him.

"Why?"

"I'm not writing it down, okay? I just want to know what to call you."

"Danny. And that's all you're getting."

"Danny. Okay, take it easy, Danny. What's the Cloister?"

"A den of—"

"I know, a den of depravity. Is it a club? Like the one across the street?" Gabriel gestured toward the Mood Club.

"It is."

"*Good.* Where is it, Danny? Please, tell me."

Danny's eyes narrowed. "Why?"

"No one else will help me."

"It moves. Only sinners in the know attend."

"How do you know about it then?"

"I make it my business to save souls in peril." Danny turned and headed down the street with his stilted gait, slipping on the sidewalk cracks and holding his sign like a shield.

"Wait, come back!" Gabriel pursued him. "When and where will it be next?"

Danny stopped and gave Gabriel a look that hovered somewhere between haunted and crazy. The boy then turned his head toward the sex shop. The girl with the feathered boa had emerged and loitered out in the street once more.

"You can see her tits through that shirt," Danny muttered, staring at her.

Gabriel shrugged amusedly. "Well, it is cold outside..."

Danny turned back to survey Gabriel. After a moment, he spoke.

"Meet me at the corner of Hollywood and Orange tonight at twelve thirty. Bring no one else!"

Gabriel let the boy amble away, until Danny disappeared down a silent, darkened side street like a thief into the shadows.

Gabriel resisted the urge to follow him, trusting that the odd, crippled fellow would keep their rendezvous. He called Dash, informing him of this latest break and then looked at his watch. The hour was late, but Gabriel still had time before his meeting with Danny to take care of a little private matter of his own.

As was her habit, Ming worked into the evening hours, and penned her signature on the death certificate of a female gang member whom she had just examined. The girl had been shot three times in the abdomen. She had only been fourteen.

An air purifier hummed in the corner; other than that, her offices were quiet. Ming made a cursory review of the certificate, then placed it in her outbox. She gasped to see Gabriel McRay standing motionless in front of her.

"Why did you tell Ramirez about Tara and me?"

Ming's heart thudded mercilessly, a storm within her breast, but she managed to gracefully swing herself up from the chair and busy herself at the file cabinet.

"Because what you did was detrimental to the case," Ming replied without looking at him.

When she turned back around, Ming found herself pigeon-holed between the cabinet and Gabriel, who now stood right next to her.

"What else is it detrimental to, Ming?" Gabriel angrily cocked his ear toward her. "Come on. Say it. To us, maybe?"

"Back off." Ming bravely pushed past him. "You know you're acting stupid. I can't let you risk your job and everything that's meaningful in your life. I can't believe you, Gabriel. She's married; she's a witness! Besides, there's something very odd about her."

"It's called being traumatized, something I know you don't want to talk about."

"Don't start with me. I'm trying to help you."

"Did it ever occur to you that I can help myself?"

Ming pretended to organize the papers on her already neat desk. "Not when you act like an idiot. How did you think this would all come out? You think she would ever leave her rich husband for you?" The papers fell and as Ming bent to retrieve them, she saw Gabriel stiffen with anger at that last remark.

"This isn't about me or my job. You're jealous, Ming."

She snorted despite the truthful statement. "And your head is so far up your ass, you can only think with your cock."

"Watch your mouth," he growled.

"Fuck you! How's that for watching my mouth?"

Gabriel slammed his fist into the file cabinet and left a good-sized dent. He grabbed Ming's shoulders and steered her into the leather chair. She gaped at him in astonishment, but a sudden thrill rushed through her, starting at her hammering heart and ending in blossoming warmth between her legs. At that moment, Ming knew she would do anything for him, to feel his strong hands on her shoulders again, to capture the attention she craved from him.

He brought his face close to hers and the anger sharpened his features.

"You're not so tough, Dr. Li," he told her in a low, even voice. "Are you forgetting I held you when you were choking on sand and puking up saltwater? You begged me like a little girl not to leave you alone."

Ming saw the ocean in his eyes, remembered the salty air and the taste of brine. Suddenly, she felt as disjointed as a broken mannequin.

Gabriel brought his face even closer. "You clawed at my eyes, thinking I was him, didn't you? What's it feel like to be buried alive?"

"Don't," she whispered.

"Did you forget, Ming?" He shook her, branding her with his glare. "Did you forget the one moment we had where I was a hero instead of some unfortunate jerk, and you..." Gabriel searched her face. "You were a woman who needed me."

Silence fell as they regarded one another. He glanced at his hands, tightly gripping her shoulders, and guiltily released her.

"I'm sorry," he said quietly. "I didn't mean to make you cry."

"I'm not crying."

With a slight shake of his head, Gabriel gazed at Ming with something like pity; then he straightened up, stuffed his hands in the pocket of the pea coat, and walked to the door.

As Ming watched him leave, she realized that tears were streaming down her face.

CHAPTER 20

Gabriel glanced at his watch. It was already a quarter to one in the morning and an El Niño rain was pelting him. Black water overflowed the gutters and fanned across the sidewalk. He was tired of standing in his soaking shoes. Los Angelinos were never prepared for inclement weather, certainly not rain like this.

He saw Dash laughing at him from the warmth of an unmarked car, and Gabriel raised his middle finger, a gesture that caused Dash to bust up even more. Gabriel was in no mood for jokes. He felt badly that he had wounded Ming, but her stubborn resolve made it impossible for him to communicate with her.

Think of something else, Gabriel told himself as the rain crept wetly into the collar of his pea coat. *The Cloister, the cross and the snake. Ross swaying two feet above the earth in his cell. Aunt Lynn's face.* The poor woman had to bear up under a drug-addicted nephew and a husband. Gabriel considered Jim Traxler, the veteran with emotional instability. Jim had as much access to baling wire as Ross had.

At that moment, a green VW Bug with patchwork paint pulled up and Danny gestured for Gabriel to get inside. Feeling the revolver snug in his shoulder holster, Gabriel made a mental note of the license plate and then ducked into the passenger seat. The peeling black vinyl seats were piled with markers, poster boards, pamphlets, and crosses. A Madonna hung from the rear view mirror and a dog-eared bible lay on a cracked dashboard. The car smelled of sweat.

"How are you doing, Danny?"

Danny didn't answer. A crazed look hung in his brown eyes and his mouth was working, but making no sound.

Remembering that Danny was crippled, Gabriel asked, "Are you able to drive?"

Again, Danny grumbled silently. Gabriel regarded the kid for a minute then tossed a concerned glance to the passenger side mirror to make sure Dash was really following them.

They traveled across Los Angeles and ended up in the historic West Adam's District, a neighborhood of Victorian mansions dating back to the nineteenth century. In this gang-infested area close to USC, some houses were beautifully restored, while others sat sadly dilapidated.

Danny parked curbside of a decaying mansion with boarded up windows. The rain had abated and under the misty glow of the streetlamp, Gabriel made out quite a few cars parked out front. "This is it?"

Danny reached into the backseat, rifling through the debris.

"If this is a private club," Gabriel continued, "how do we get in?"

Danny pulled out a bundle and handed it to Gabriel. "Put this on."

Gabriel shook out the coarse brown fabric—a monk's cloak. He gave Danny a strange look.

"Put it on," Danny hissed and threw on his own cape, carefully lowering the hood over his face. "Follow me."

He stepped out of the car and Gabriel followed suit.

As Danny swayed and limped up to the house, Gabriel called after him. "Is this some sort of joke?"

The boy immediately swerved back and quickly hobbled up to Gabriel. "Don't talk from this point on, Mr. Policeman. This isn't a joke. I assure you that you won't find anything remotely funny in that house."

Gabriel could feel Danny's hot breath on his face.

"Take it easy, sport," Gabriel said, eyeing Danny's spittle-flecked mouth, the only thing he could make out under the monk's hood.

The crippled fellow turned and headed toward the house again. Gabriel followed, pulling on his cloak. He grimaced. The cloak was ripe with body odor.

Danny knocked on the door. A hooded figure opened the door and Gabriel caught a smile under the hood.

"If it isn't Danny Ray Hart!"

An unearthly growl seemed to escape Danny and he quickly whispered something about an interested party. The figure turned toward Gabriel, surveying him, although Gabriel was identically frocked. Finally, the two of them were allowed to pass.

The living room was painted black. Candles were lit along a portable black bar, illuminating bottles of liquor and various glasses. On the bar were cocktail napkins, similarly embossed like the one in Lena Dobbs's coat pocket. Gabriel eagerly tucked a few under his cape.

"Sacramental wine, gentlemen?" A male voice purred from under a cloak behind the bar. "Or is it ladies?"

Gabriel shook his head, following Danny's example. The monk-bartender chuckled softly and wiped a cloth across the ebony surface. Strange music drifted down from a decrepit wooden stairwell and waxed and waned against murmuring voices. Gabriel soon recognized the music: Gregorian chants.

The medieval church music was set against a pulsing bass and a backbeat, which made for a provocative mix. Gabriel wondered what lurked upstairs.

Danny was talking to himself, damning this and hell-firing that as he climbed cumbersomely up the stairs. Gabriel followed Danny, sidestepping two cloaked figures whispering on the steps. He wanted an opportunity to talk to Danny or anybody else about Ross. So far, Gabriel didn't see much of an opportunity for talking of any kind.

A series of closed doors ran along a corridor, which splintered off to the right and to the left. The faded wallpaper was peeling in places, exposing wooden two-by-fours underneath. Gabriel was reminded of a haunted mansion attraction and would not have been surprised to see a ghostly candelabra floating in the hallway. The music was louder here, but did not mask a squeal of ecstasy or an occasional drawn-out moan coming from behind closed doors.

"Open a door," Danny whispered. "Or they'll start getting suspicious."

Danny quickly loped down the hall and turned right, disappearing.

Gabriel warily opened a door and entered blackness. A claustrophobic sensation enveloped him; the air was thick with incense. As his eyes adjusted, Gabriel became aware of a censer swinging back and forth from the ceiling. On pillows laid out in front of him a man was having intercourse with a woman who had her mouth glued against the crotch of another man. Behind the music being pumped in was the sound of their quick gasps. The standing man getting the blowjob kept banging his head into the censer causing it to swing. He suddenly noticed Gabriel.

"Hey, there's always room for one more," he said in a rasping voice.

Gabriel shook his head, pulling the hood down lower, and stepped back toward the door.

"Watch it!"

He looked down to see a gorgeous naked woman, one hand at her groin, legs splayed. The other hand held a smoking pipe. The woman broke into a seductive grin. "I mean, watch it, if you like."

Gabriel stepped over her and into the hallway, closing the door behind him. He took a deep breath. He felt himself growing excited, that beautiful woman in there, but knew he had to keep his wits about him. No one on the force had ever mentioned something like this, and Gabriel wondered how the Cloister had managed to keep itself so secretive.

"Danny?" he called tentatively into the hallway. Candle sconces threw an eerie light, causing shadows to bob up and down. What a fire hazard, he thought. This place was like some strange dream.

"Here." The voice came from behind a closed door.

Gabriel walked over to it and put his hand on the knob. Another hand immediately crawled around the doorknob like a crab and long black nails dug into Gabriel's flesh. Before he could pull away, someone grabbed his hood and hauled him inside.

Immediately, Gabriel was thrown to the floor and felt a slap on his chest. If not for the cloak, Gabriel imagined he'd be in stinging pain. A flashlight beam was fixed on his face and he shielded his eyes from the glare.

"Don't speak, worm."

The flashlight did a 180 and landed on the face of a sharp-nosed woman, not unattractive, with full red lips, wearing a black leather corset and hip-high stiletto boots. In one hand she held the flashlight. In the other she held a cat-o-nine tailed whip.

"I've got everything prepared for my dearest doll-face." She smirked and sauntered over to the far wall, sweeping her beam over a spike-covered chair and two shackles hanging from the wall. "Or maybe you prefer this..." Like a game-show hostess proudly displaying the grand prize, the leather-clad dominatrix traipsed to a bondage bed.

Gabriel's eyes fanned over the fur-lined handcuffs and tie-up rings. A length of black rope was coiled on the bed like a snake.

"Now, don't cause a fuss, doll-face." The dominatrix pulled a collar-to-wrist restraint from a hook on the wall. "Or things may go worse for you."

Immediately, Gabriel stifled a laugh; the whole setup was so inane. But then a sense of revulsion began creeping into his gut. Behind his eyes, a familiar headache was beginning to bloom, the seeds of which were planted a long time ago when...

He was raped.

Don't think of that right now, Gabriel told himself. Think only of how pathetic these people are. Get something solid about this place; it's connected to a majority of the victims—then get out.

Do it in a hurry.

"I'll play," Gabriel said, standing up. "But first you need to answer a question."

The whip sizzled through the air and landed across Gabriel's cheek. Again, the hood provided a modicum of protection, but not much.

"Hey!" he yelled, feeling the anger strike.

"I give the orders, you little shit!" the woman shouted back. "I don't answer any questions! Now turn around before Mommy gets mad."

She tried to push Gabriel around, but he stood his ground and she cracked the whip over his head.

Gabriel fended off the blow with his arm. "Cut it out!"

"Turn around!" she screamed and whipped him again.

Gabriel backed up and tripped over something dark lying on the floor. When he fell on his rear, his hand felt the strap of a woman's purse.

"Okay, 'Mommy,'" Gabriel muttered, fighting hard to keep the sarcasm out of his voice. "Don't use the whip."

"You be a good boy and I won't have to. Now stand up. I don't want to hear one word from you."

Gabriel stood up. As he did, he tucked the purse under his cloak. While the flashlight beam stayed on the bed, presumably to light Gabriel's way, Gabriel sidled toward the door.

"I have lots of toys we're going to play with," the Dominatrix said. "But if you whine too much, I'll punish you. I'll have to—"

Gabriel quickly slid out the door and shut it, half-running down the hall. A fun house, Gabriel decided. For those into kinky sex, or was it called alternative lifestyles nowadays? Something about her use of the word "mommy" bothered him. He didn't like to think of a mother like that. No wonder religious fanatic Danny Ray was so repulsed by this place. But he must have come before, and often enough, because not only did the bouncer know Danny's full name, he let him bring a friend. What exactly did that mean?

Gabriel shoved himself into an alcove and quickly rifled through the purse, straining his eyes in the dim light. The murmuring Latin words echoed around him; the heady smell of incense and drugs made him dizzy. He finally pulled out a wallet and tossed the purse on the pitted wood floor. Let the dominatrix think a common thief had robbed her. He tucked the wallet into his own pants pocket and then made his way down another hallway.

Suddenly, a door flung open and Gabriel jumped to one side. A naked man ran out wearing a collar and a strap that encircled his erect penis. His hands were tied behind him and he laughed, "Kick me, you bitch! Kick me!"

Gabriel shook his head as he passed. A second cloaked figure soon followed, yelling in a high falsetto, "I'm coming. Oh, am I ever coming!" The hood fell back as the cloaked one pursued his quarry, revealing a dark colored ski mask. The masked fellow was swinging a paddle back and forth. Soon, he had disappeared around the corner.

Tara had mentioned a ski mask. Could the masked one be her assailant? Gabriel made a move to follow when a grunt of pain issued from the closed door next to him. This was followed by a long wail. Gabriel's head was thumping now. He didn't need his own madness to rear its ugly head, but the cop in him felt obligated to vet that painful cry. Gabriel took a steadying breath and turned the knob.

A single candle illuminated the room. A man was tied, bent over, to a swing-like apparatus, which swayed to and fro. He wore his cloak but his naked buttocks were exposed. In the background, a cloaked figure was flagellating the man's flesh with a nail-studded board. Droplets of blood dotted the floor around the candle. The two seemed oblivious to Gabriel.

Which one of these people was the suspect? All of them? He needed to get out and get his mind clear then return with some backup and—

Under the couch was a puke-colored rug and Gabriel could smell the black licorice near his face. Lie still, Little Buddy. My mother won't be home for another hour.

Gabriel backed up, exiting the room. He threw his hood back and wiped his forehead clean of perspiration. He'd had enough of the Cloister. His heart was racing. Another yowl of pain issued from the room he had just vacated.

Gabriel turned away only to come face-to-face with a cloaked figure standing inches from him. His heartbeat skipped and his first instinct was to free his revolver and start shooting anything that moved. Using all of his willpower, Gabriel slowly replaced his hood. The other figure grabbed his arm and Gabriel thought of his gun again.

"It's me, Dash."

Gabriel couldn't keep the relief out of his voice. "How did you get in?"

"Two guys walked out drunk as skunks and one of them dropped this outfit on the curb. I snuck past the bouncer who was too busy getting a blowjob to notice." Dash gestured around him. "Interesting place, huh?"

"Interesting isn't the word. Remember the victims with the nail holes? Well, go through door number two and you'll see it live in action."

"Thanks, I'll take your word for it. What are we supposed to do?"

"Talk outside." Gabriel nodded toward a shrouded figure standing motionless at the opposite end of the hallway. Whether the figure was a guard, a client, or a statue, Gabriel did not know, but it gave him the creeps to see someone standing so still and so silent, facing his way.

"I'll meet you out there in five," Gabriel told him. "I'm gonna look for the kid."

Gabriel walked past his partner. Down the hall, he passed by an open door and whispered, "Danny?"

Someone immediately grabbed him and threw him into a pitch-black room. Gabriel smelled expensive cologne and instantly felt hands roving over his body. He heard a woman's giggle. Gabriel shoved the fumbling hands away, conscious of the gun tucked into his shoulder holster.

"Hey, it's just fun," a man's voice cajoled.

A match was lit, quickly illuminating the face of a fat, middle-aged man. "Give him to me." His voice slithered like a snake.

"No, this one's for all of us."

A hand slid up Gabriel's cloak and he jumped away.

"Hey, no fair. You're wearing pants."

Two lighters were lit and displayed more faces. Gabriel counted three in all—two men, one woman. He turned toward the direction of the door, but he was confused in the darkness. He heard the unmistakable snap of handcuffs and quickly raised his arms, holding his hands high. If he couldn't see them, they couldn't see him. He didn't like this. He didn't like the dark and the hands.

Gabriel felt sweat running down his back. He inched forward and bumped into someone. He heard a match strike and saw the lowered hood of a grinning figure. The figure slowly lifted his face and panic swept through Gabriel as he beheld the visage of Andrew Pierce.

"Stay away from me," Gabriel told him.

The features molded into that of one of the two men.

"Oh, come on," the man replied. "Play with us."

I have to get out of here, Gabriel thought, feeling the headache thunder forth. He winced under the pain and, pushing the man aside, Gabriel scrambled out of the room. He rammed into another cloaked figure that landed against the wall as he scurried down the hall. Gabriel skidded to a halt as he passed a skinny figure with a prominent Adam's apple under his hood— Dash. He was standing motionless and staring intently into the darkened doorway of another room. Gabriel pulled at his arm.

"Has it been five minutes already?" Dash asked, entranced and still gazing over the threshold.

"Come on!" Gabriel steered his partner downstairs and out the front door.

❦ ❦ ❦

CHAPTER 21

"Looks a little less ominous in the light of day," Gabriel said, reassuring himself.

He and Dash sat in an unmarked car down the street from the boarded-up house. The morning light glistened off the rotting timbers, the bottles, and the broken glass that littered the overgrown lawn.

"You had to pull me away."

Gabriel smiled and shook his head. "Enjoyed yourself, did you?"

"Ah, forget it," Dash muttered. "Who owns this dump anyhow?"

Gabriel popped the top off a soda. Breakfast. He offered it to Dash. "Wells Fargo Bank."

"A foreclosure," Dash said as he took the can. "I'm assuming the bank has no clue the place is being used as Club Kinky."

"Of course not." Gabriel took a swig from his own soda. "Ramirez wants to know why we didn't bust it last night."

Dash shook his head, surveying the house. "Did you tell him they'd scatter like cockroaches at the first flashing light?"

"I did. 'We need to infiltrate the place,' I said, 'not raid it.' I told him we're not going to get much information from a couple of empty vodka glasses and leather whips."

"Ball stretchers, body harnesses, gladiator cuffs…"

Gabriel gave his partner a sideways smirk. "You an expert on this, Dash?"

"I go on the Internet from time to time."

"What would Eve say?" Gabriel clucked.

"She goes on with me."

"See? You never know about some people." Grinning, Gabriel pulled a driver's license from his back pocket. He displayed the picture of a good-looking brunette to Dash. "Take her for instance. Looks like the girl next door, huh? You wouldn't know she parades around in a leather teddy and a whip, would you? Her name is Jill Bennet and she works a day job as, believe it or not, a Beverly Hills masseuse. Someone should pay her a visit today. Course, one of us has to stay here and watch the house."

Dash narrowed his eyes at his partner. "I suppose that someone is me. You know I'll be bored."

Gabriel reached into the backseat and pulled out his laptop. Handing it to Dash, he said, "Surf the net, dude."

As Gabriel drove toward the Beverly Hills day spa that employed Jill Bennet, he called in for his messages. His voicemail held two calls, one from Ming and the other from Mrs. McRay, Gabriel's mother.

He waited a moment and then reluctantly dialed Ming's number.

She took the call on the second ring. Gabriel heard an uncomfortable tremor in her voice but somehow, that made him feel more at ease.

"I owe you an apology," Ming told him. "I'm not sorry for telling Ramirez about you and Mrs. Samuels. That was completely unprofessional of you, Gabriel. I'm apologizing for being jealous. I got all female on you."

"Isn't that what you are?" Gabriel asked.

He sensed her silent, internal struggle over the phone.

"It's embarrassing how I act around you!" she blurted. "I don't like feeling this way, feeling out of control."

"I know you don't."

Ming was quiet again. Gabriel patiently waited, moving through the traffic along Wilshire Boulevard.

"Are you in love with her, Gabriel?"

Tara.

"Ming…"

"Please answer me. I'm standing here with two examinations on my table this afternoon and a hospital administration meeting tonight." He heard her sniff and then, "Do you? Love her?"

"No. I blew it, okay? I admit it. But that night you came over, we weren't—"

"People meet each other through unlikely circumstances. I need to know how much she means to you."

Gabriel crossed Canon and pulled into a public parking structure. The cellular reception crackled. "Ming, I'm losing you."

"Do you know how hard—me to say—things to you?" she asked.

He drove deeper into the structure. "Yes, I do. To be honest, I like seeing you a little unsteady on your feet."

"What? I ca—hear you."

Then the call was lost.

Serenity Spa was in a small cottage type building that once was a fancy restaurant. New Age music wafted and a heater blew drafts across lit candles and rustled the leaves of fake ivy covering the walls. A receptionist with clipped brown hair, hip clothes, and exceedingly long French-tipped nails stood behind a counter chock full of lotions, bath salts, creams, and other sundries. Gabriel scanned the prices for the services. *Out of his league.*

"Is Jill Bennet working today?"

"She's giving a massage right now. Do you have an appointment?"

"No." Gabriel walked right past her and opened the door. The receptionist protested, but Gabriel ignored her.

He was about to open the first door he saw, when a voice from down the hall said, "I'm just going to get your oil, doll-face."

Mommy, Gabriel thought with a grin and walked in the direction of the voice. Ignoring a sign that read: Quiet Please, Gabriel threw open the door. The client was face down on the massage table with a sheet draped over her back.

"Excuse me!" Jill exclaimed indignantly.

Jill Bennet wore little makeup in the light of day, and looked altogether wholesome, very unlike her dominatrix persona.

"Excuse me," Gabriel echoed. "We need to talk."

"What are you doing in here? Marguerite!"

Marguerite, the long-nailed receptionist, ran up to the door. "I tried—"

"Get out or I'll call the cops!" Jill yelled to Gabriel.

He promptly stuck his ID in her face and then turned to the receptionist. "You're dismissed, Marguerite."

Marguerite gaped at Gabriel, gaped at Jill, and then slowly retreated to the front desk again.

"You'll need to wait, Sergeant—" Jill read his identification. "McRay. I'm with a client."

"We talk now or I tell your high-priced clientele how you moonlight as Sally the Sadist."

Jill looked at him in shock and then her eyes slid warily toward her client, still face down. Gabriel regarded the client as well. He could see those back muscles tensing.

In a controlled voice, Jill said, "I'll be just a moment, Mrs. Bradshaw."

Jill stepped out into the hall with Gabriel, angrily wiping the oil off her hands with a towel. "What's this about?"

"Have you ever heard of Paula May or Lena and Malcolm Dobbs? How about a Regina Faulkner?"

Jill licked her lips nervously and then shook her head. Gabriel wasn't convinced.

"Where do you store your leather outfit, Mommy?"

Jill gasped. "You can't do this to me. I—I just do that for extra money."

"I don't give a rat's ass how you make ends meet. I'll ask you one more time, and then I advertise all over Beverly Hills how proficient you are with a whip."

"You stole my wallet, didn't you?"

"Here's your wallet." Gabriel fished it from his pocket and handed it to her. "I only want information. Do you read the papers? Do you know the people I mentioned were murdered?"

Jill went a shade whiter but her expression did not change. She was used to acting tough. "I've heard of them. I mean, they came by the club once in a while, but I didn't know them personally. They never, well, they didn't seek my services."

"Whose services did they seek?"

Jill hesitated then looked squarely at Gabriel. "If you think Beverly Hills is the only place you can find high-priced clientele, then you are one naive cop. Those people you mentioned could pay big bucks to party."

"Paula May paid big money? How? Regina Faulkner was a runaway, a Hollywood street teen."

Jill glanced down the hall and lowered her voice. "Paula May was a wannabe, a secretary or something. A nobody on the fringe, but she was a cute little twat and willing. So was Regina Faulkner. Both of them were connected. The Dobbs— they could afford bigger action."

"Have you seen Malcolm Dobbs recently?"

Jill shook her head, so Gabriel asked, "What's meant by bigger action?"

With great effort, Jill said, "There's this guy who comes in off and on. Paula and Regina—they were his friends, okay? He brought them in. Anyhow, this guy could hook people into serious kicks. At least he said he could."

As if the Cloister wasn't serious enough.

"What is his name?" Gabriel asked, thinking of Ross. "Can you describe him?"

Jill sighed, shaking her head. "I don't know his name. We don't use names. And he never took off his hood. Obviously he didn't want to be seen." Jill paused worriedly. "Did you already shut down the Cloister?"

"Not yet. Would I be able to lock into this guy tonight?"

"Maybe. He doesn't come in all the time, but he always seems to find us. We're like a private club. We never stay in one place long. Just wherever someone finds us a viable location."

"This man, is he a member of your club?"

"I guess so. I never speak to him. I don't make personal friends there. For me, it's just business."

"Who pays you?"

"We take our money from the kitty at the end of the night."

"I got in free."

"Lucky you." Jill frowned at him and then walked back into her room.

�֍ ✖ ✖

Gabriel gave Dash the update via cell phone. Dash then informed him that Ramirez was insisting on raiding the Cloister tonight whether Gabriel wanted to or not. He wanted to sweep the place and pull everyone in for questioning.

Ramirez always wanted to go right for the jugular. These people, Gabriel guessed, would simply clam up under pressure. They most likely led ordinary lives outside the Cloister and would not want those lives intruded upon. And if a couple of them were rich enough or important enough to pay "big bucks to party," then even Ramirez might not be able to get at them. A better move would be to infiltrate the club. Gabriel sighed in frustration, but let it go. Right now he needed to talk with Tara.

Play with us...

Hadn't Tara used those words?

It's just fun...

Gabriel was sure she knew something about the Cloister. She could very well provide the link between all the victims. Besides that, he wanted to check up on her. Although Tara denied it, Gabriel had a feeling Marc beat her. Strangely enough, Tara's phone calls and midnight visits had suddenly stopped. Gabriel hadn't heard from her and he was concerned.

The sun was beginning to set, tinting the sky pink and turning the clouds purple. Soon the revelry of the Cloister would begin—and end when the place was raided tonight. Gabriel drove the corral-fenced streets and turned up the winding drive of Tara's home.

Whispers of winter hung on the breeze, rippling across the koi pond and causing the tree branches to rustle against the eaves of the house. The home had a hollow aura about it, or maybe Gabriel felt differently because he knew foreclosure was imminent. Gabriel rang the bell, which played "We Three Kings."

Rosa answered. "*¿Sí?*"

"Is Mrs. Samuels home?"

"No, nobody here."

The woman's eyes seemed to plead with Gabriel. He took the bait.

"Rosa, is there something you want to tell me? Where is Mrs. Samuels? Is Mrs. Samuels alright?"

Rosa pursed her lips together and whispered, "*Ella necesita ayuda, su marido la golpea.*"

Gabriel shook his head, not understanding. Rosa searched his face and then in a louder voice, she exclaimed, "Nobody home."

Gabriel held up a finger indicating that Rosa should wait, and he moved away from the front door. He punched a few numbers into his cell phone and reached Ramirez.

"I need your help," he told his lieutenant. "I've got an opportunity right now to interview Tara's housekeeper who has something to say, only I don't understand her. I'm going to put her on now."

Gabriel handed the phone to Rosa.

"*¿Bueno?*" she asked timidly and listened for a moment. Rosa then spoke in hushed and hurried Spanish. She quickly handed the phone back to Gabriel and promptly shut the door in his face.

"What did she say?" Gabriel asked as he faced the closed front door.

"She wants to quit," Ramirez told him. "But she's afraid Samuels is going to call the INS on her. She's illegal. She wants to know if we can help her."

"Is that what goal-payah means? Because she told me, *la golpea.*"

Ramirez was quiet for a moment and then said reflectively, "He hits her."

I knew it, thought Gabriel. "Did she say where Mrs. Samuels is?"

"No," answered Ramirez. "What does it matter?"

"I believe Tara knows something about the Cloister."

"We'll get everything we need about that place tonight," Ramirez assured him.

He told Gabriel the raid tonight would be coordinated with the LAPD, the Bureau of Alcohol and Firearms, and the DEA. Ramirez also mentioned that he ran Danny Ray Hart's license plate through the DMV. He gave Gabriel the address.

"Thanks," Gabriel said, jotting it in his notepad. Danny could be instrumental in identifying the "friend" of the murdered women that Jill had described. Surely, Danny must know things if he could walk into the Cloister without paying admission. And besides that, Gabriel wanted to warn the kid. He didn't want the crippled boy to be around when the fireworks went off tonight at the Cloister.

By the time Gabriel parked in front of Danny's apartment off La Brea Avenue in the Miracle Mile district, the moon was a yellow balloon in the sky. He rang the bell three times and then gave up contacting Danny the conventional way. Gabriel loped around the side of the Craftsman style building and spied an open window. A warped, torn screen hung halfway out.

"Danny?" Gabriel called softly. "It's Sergeant McRay."

Silence. A pigeon cooed from its niche in a nearby wall, and Gabriel peered through the dirty screen. He saw a bed so spare it would make an army cot look luxurious, and scattered along the floor were wires, fuses, and dynamite.

Gabriel stepped away, blinking, wondering if his eyes were deceiving him in the dim light. He jogged back to his car, grabbed a flashlight, and then returned to the window. He reached up and carefully removed the screen. Shining his light inside, Gabriel could now see everything clearly: all the makings of a bomb, including some bolts, nails, and scrap iron to serve as shrapnel. Some of the dynamite sticks were sweating nitroglycerin.

"Oh, shit." Gabriel hopped off the window ledge. Suddenly, he remembered Danny's raging promises about sinners disintegrating and fires burning. "Oh, Danny, no…"

Gabriel raced to his car.

Dash sat in his unmarked car in front of the Cloister. From behind the boarded up windows came the lulling, but barely discernible sounds of Gregorian chants. Dash smirked, reflecting back on what he'd seen go on in those rooms.

"Get ready for one hell of a wake-up call, jackholes," he said to no one.

A group of gang members loitered noisily down the street. The young men were oblivious to the growing number of unmarked cars and agency vans now parking along the side streets.

"Children behave," Dash said, watching them. His cell phone rang. He peered at the display and flipped the phone open. "Hey, partner."

"Get everyone outta there!" Gabriel yelled as he tore up Western Avenue. "Clear it now! The kid's gonna blow the—" The call suddenly dropped. Cursing, Gabriel tossed the phone and stepped on the pedal.

He honked at cars, passing them wildly, and then slammed on his brakes as he came upon traffic backing up from an accident. He fumbled for his light beacon, slapped it on the roof of his car, and then rode half on the sidewalk, half on the street, until he cleared the traffic. He raced toward the West Adams district, burned rubber around the street corner, and breathed a sigh of relief to see the decrepit mansion still standing.

His car screeched to a halt and Gabriel tumbled out of his car. He yelled for everyone to get back. The gang members, thinking Gabriel a deranged soul ambled toward him, yelling obscenities. The officers in the unmarked cars could only trade incredulous looks, perplexed as to why their compatriot would blow their cover.

Dash exited his car and shrugged at Gabriel. "What are you doing?"

Gabriel's words were lost amid the threats of the gang members, who now surrounded him.

"Get everyone out of here! We've got—" The edge of Gabriel's vision caught a hooded figure running from the site with a stilted gait. "Danny!"

The hobbling figure whipped back his hood and yelled in a thunderous voice, "May God have mercy upon their—"

With a blinding explosion, the mansion blew apart. Glass and splintered wood shot out and rained down in a hailstorm. Cars were blown to their sides, the Celica's tires popped and the unmarked car's windows blew out, firing glass at the officers trapped inside. The roaring blast threw Gabriel backwards into two gangbangers, who collapsed to the ground. Gabriel shielded his eyes from a searing heat and bullets of wood.

When he finally opened his eyes, he lay at the edge of a disaster area blanketed by debris. What was left of the Cloister was a burning bier. He thought he heard people yelling, but his ears were plugged, so he couldn't be sure. An intense heat surrounded his face and he stood up. As he wobbled on shaky legs, Gabriel lowered his watering eyes to the ground. At his feet lay a fleece-lined handcuff with a bleeding hand still attached at the manacled wrist.

CHAPTER 22

Gabriel sat in the homicide bureau gazing pensively at the front page of the Los Angeles Times, which read in bold lettering: "Ravers Die in Abandoned Mansion."

The article suggested the "freak accident" was caused by a gas leak, but an investigation was pending. Someone had done one heck of a cover up job. Names of the "ravers" were withheld.

The snapshots of Regina Faulkner, Paula May, and the Dobbs couple faced Gabriel. Jane Doe's clay head regarded him merrily from her spot upon his desk.

His notes were scattered in front of his computer. Ever since his lead of the Cloister literally blew up in his face, Gabriel felt as deflated as his car's tires. He absently rubbed at the scabs on his face, party favors from the explosion. He blamed himself, and not knowing what else to do, he left a message for Dr. B.

The psychiatrist called him back within minutes.

"It's not your fault," Dr. B told him over the phone.

Gabriel gazed at Jane Doe's head. "I should have seen it coming. I wondered why Danny was getting in for free. I thought he was some type of religious policeman or something, infiltrating the place like me. I thought that was kinda funny. But then I had this notion that Danny Ray Hart might actually be a customer. He knew everyone there. Now all his connections have died with him."

"That must have been such a paradox for him," said Dr. B. "Here is this fanatically religious fellow most likely carrying deep issues from his upbringing and yet…"

Gabriel finished for him. "And yet he can't help but indulge his nastier habits."

"Who would suspect he'd bomb the place?"

"You know as well as I, Danny fit the profile of a human time bomb."

"Can't you cut yourself some slack?"

Gabriel thought of Ming. Somewhere in the notepaper piles was a message from his mother. "No. I think I'm a real dick sometimes."

"Well, welcome to the human race, Gabe. We all do a good job being our own worst critics. The challenge is to find a way to feel good about yourself, truly good."

Gabriel looked up to see Ramirez smoking a Winston.

"I gotta go," Gabriel told Dr. B and hung up the phone. He met his lieutenant's eyes and waited.

"Case is closed, McRay. You found the Cloister. It led nowhere."

"Ross didn't do it."

Ramirez regarded Jane Doe's head then nodded at Gabriel's notes. "What's in there that convinces you that the suspect is still at large?"

"A guy that knew Paula May and Regina Faulkner. Possibly the Dobbs as well. A guy that may or may not have been Ross. And by the way, I can't locate Tara or Marc Samuels."

Ramirez rolled his eyes. "What are you trying to find them for? We already have Mrs. Samuels's statement that Ross was her attacker. Marc Samuels can't tell us nothing. He was at home with the housekeeper the day of his wife's abduction."

"You know Rosa is terrified of Marc Samuels. She'd do or say anything he wanted."

"Who cares, McRay? A syringe with Ross's prints, blood, and DNA was found directly beside the Faulkner girl. Why can't you leave the Samuels couple alone?"

Gabriel looked away.

Ramirez took a puff and exhaled too quickly. "Christmas is coming. I thought we'd have a little party here. Any comments?"

Gabriel shook his head.

"Great. You bring sodas the twenty-third."

Sensing discomfort radiating from Ramirez, Gabriel looked back at him curiously, but the short dark man had already walked away, leaving a trail of cigarette smoke behind him.

The syringe, the baling wire, and Tara's witness testimony tied Ross to the crimes. Gabriel turned toward the reconstructed head of Jane Doe, still unidentified under her fake hair and glass eyes, not pictured in Missing Persons. Who was she? What story would she have told?

Gabriel gazed at the mess on his desk and saw the Cloister postcard depicting the snake coiled on a cross. *Kinky fun. Serious kicks.*

Something was missing. Gabriel felt like he was on the wrong track. What had he missed?

Cloaks and disguises. Ski masks and rough sex. Gabriel quickly leafed through his notepad and read, "Conversation with Ralph Tenant about Hedge, Inc. Foreclosure imminent."

Gabriel reached for Ralph Tenant's file and looked up the bank that was foreclosing on Tara's home. Wells Fargo Bank. That was the bank that was foreclosing on the Cloister as well.

Gabriel quickly collected the notes, checked his gun, and left word for Dash that he was heading to one of L.A.'s more upscale suburbs, Encino.

As he walked out the door of the bureau, he was surprised to see Ming loitering out front.

"Hey," Gabriel called to her.

"I heard about what happened," she said. "Are you okay?"

"I'm okay."

Ming hugged herself self-consciously, as if she were cold.

"So," she began, keeping her eyes on the ground. "I've still got these test results pending at ballistics on Lena Dobbs and I'm waiting on an entomologist's report."

"Why bother?" Gabriel asked dryly. "Ramirez says the case is closed and we're having a Christmas party." He glanced at his watch, eager to get over to Encino.

"I have some questions about Lena Dobbs."

That got his attention. "Anything you'd like to share?"

"Not until I get my answers."

Gabriel surveyed the parking lot, wondering why Ming had not come inside to talk. The answer soon became apparent when Ming's lower lip began trembling and she started to cry.

"Ming," he began and moved close to her.

"I hate this," she said, between her tears. "I hate missing you. Am I such a bitch that you had to go to her?"

Tell her, Gabriel thought. Now's the time to open up like Dr. B wanted you to. Tell her it's not her. Tell Ming it's you. Tell her you can't stand to look weak in her eyes.

But he said nothing.

Her voice hitched as she spoke. "I came over to tell you I'm sorry. I don't know what else to do."

A couple of officers strolled out of the building and Ming quickly turned away. The officers nodded at the couple and then moved off to their cars.

"Do you want to take a ride?" Gabriel asked her tentatively. "I need to check something out."

Ming nodded and wiped her eyes.

They drove together in silence. Ming was no longer crying, but she was staring silently out the passenger window.

Gabriel felt like a complete jerk. He had turned a beautiful, confident lady into an emotional mess, just to appease his impaired ego. He had resented her self-assurance, so he successfully destroyed it. As if it was Ming's job in life to make him feel important. If that wasn't weakness, Gabriel didn't know what was.

He didn't know what to say, so he reached across the seat and took Ming's hand. She didn't resist, but kept her eyes pinned on the outside scenery.

He held her hand in silence, until they pulled up to an office building on Ventura Boulevard. The sun was masked by black clouds, which rolled past the building's mirrored exterior. The moving clouds reminded Gabriel of Tara and how she said she didn't like the winter.

"What are we looking for?" Ming finally broke the silence. Working together was like a salve on their wounds.

"Like you, I have some questions that need answers."

"Where are we?"

"Marc Samuels's office."

Ming raised her eyebrows at him, but made no comment.

They took the elevator up to the highest floor and walked into the lobby of Hedge Promotional, Inc. A large circular oak receptionist's desk was unoccupied. No lights lit the phone. Gabriel and Ming stood idly by for a moment in the empty room.

They heard a female voice echoing down the hall, talking about a tea called "Smooth Move" that aided constipation. Figuring the receptionist was otherwise occupied, Gabriel motioned to Ming to follow him through a set of rich oak double doors, which opened into a hallway.

"What are you doing?" Ming whispered to him.

"I need to find out something."

"Do you have a search warrant?"

"I'm not searching. I'm visiting. If I see Marc, I'll ask him my questions."

Ming took a hold of Gabriel's sleeve as they treaded quietly down the carpeted hall.

Gabriel poked his head into each office. Many desks were cleared. The ones that looked occupied were messy, as if the occupant had left in a hurry. One computer monitor showed beach scenes and sunsets—a screensaver. Gabriel heard mechanized fast-talking and moved to another office, only to see a portable radio sitting on a credenza, the channel tuned to a news station.

It's like a nuclear bomb went off, he thought, and felt locks of his hair lift as the building's central heating came on. They continued moving down the hallway toward another set of double doors. Gabriel opened them carefully and stepped into a large suite.

Modern leather chairs presided over Persian carpets. Slashes of red paint intersected at black angles on a huge painting that dominated the room. The overall design seemed off-kilter, as if these expensive items were thrown together for show. Through tinted windows, the dark clouds rolled.

Ming tugged at Gabriel's sleeve and when he looked at her, she pointed at something across the room.

Behind the expansive wooden desk, framed photos of Marc the Model adorned the wall from floor to ceiling. Marc posing at the beach, Marc shaking hands with the mayor. The blond bride Tara, linking arms with Marc, who wore a dashing tuxedo. An entire wall transformed into a veritable shrine to Marc Samuels.

"What a narcissistic pig," Gabriel stated as his eyes scanned the wall in disbelief.

He moved to the giant desk. No desk calendar. No notes. Gabriel warily glanced at the door and then began opening each drawer of the desk.

"You're searching," Ming warned.

Gabriel didn't reply. Most of the drawers were empty. He saw an autographed baseball and a Waterford crystal paperweight engraved with the name "Tara."

Ming hovered near Marc's Wall of Fame, and her nervous eyes roamed the many photos as she waited for Gabriel to finish up.

Gabriel went through another drawer and saw a file of invoices stamped in red: Past Due. Flipping through them, Gabriel saw that most were from mortgage companies and referenced various warehouses throughout the Los Angeles area.

No other invoices were found. Why did Marc keep these warehouse bills in his own private drawer? Gabriel surveyed the desk, fighting the urge to access Marc's computer. Ming was right. He'd be done for without a warrant.

A female laugh issued from down the hall and a light blinked on Marc's phone.

"Gabriel." Ming shuffled anxiously on her feet.

The receptionist must have returned. Gabriel knew they should leave before she found them snooping.

He chewed his lower lip, ran his eyes along the desk, and stopped when his gaze fell on a Rolodex. Gabriel quickly went through the cards, some of the names and numbers were typed, and others were scrawled in what could only be Marc's erratic handwriting.

Suddenly, a name flipped past Gabriel's eye and his heart jumped. He quickly backtracked to it. May, Paula.

Gabriel stared at the handwriting. Next to her name was "Venus Productions." Gabriel's throat felt dry as he looked under "D" and found Dobbs, Malcolm, Esquire. His fingers flew through the "f" but no Faulkner was listed. It didn't matter.

Gabriel had been following the wrong lead. He'd been lured by the hook of the Cloister and the S&M games and didn't see what was right in front of him all along. Jill the Dominatrix had mentioned Regina and Paula as being connected. Gabriel had assumed she meant into serious kicks. He had been wrong. They were connected to the movie and music industries. Dobbs was an entertainment lawyer. Paula May, a production secretary. All the victims were tied to the entertainment industry... and so was Marc Samuels. Regina Faulkner had wanted to become an actress. She would have glommed onto that group.

Marc Samuels.

Gabriel stood motionless under the weight of what he had just discovered. Marc Samuels was tied to all the victims, but what about Ross? If Ross wasn't guilty, what did he kill himself for? What about Tara?

"Gabriel," Ming repeated.

That Marc had a secret life didn't surprise Gabriel, he'd had plenty of experience with criminals leading double lives, but would Marc have abducted his own wife?

Serious kicks.

"Gabriel!" Ming whispered more forcefully and he turned around. "Look." She pointed to one of the photographs.

Gabriel moved over to it.

The photo displayed Marc with some buddies in a Las Vegas casino. Marc stood at a craps table holding out a huge stack of chips. He boasted a dark tan and white teeth. His buddies were caught in mid-cheer, one of them slapping Marc's back. And just behind grinning Marc, standing too close to be a stranger, was a cocktail waitress holding a tray of drinks... Jane Doe of the reconstructed head fame.

❧ ❧ ❧

A couple of days later, Dash and Gabriel waited outside one of Marc's foreclosed warehouses in Canoga Park, not a far drive from Encino. A deputy was coming to unlock the chain on the front door. The rain had taken a reprieve and the sun was bright and blinding, beaming off of every dewdrop and mirroring the wet pavement. Still, the air was chilly, like an eastern fall day, and Gabriel buttoned his pea coat, his dark hair reflecting the sun.

Marc was not at his house and repeated calls to Tara's cell phone proved fruitless. Gabriel had real fear for Tara's safety and Ramirez had granted him carte blanche for the rest of the investigation. Gabriel demanded every warehouse in Marc's name be searched immediately and this time he was prepared with a warrant.

This particular warehouse had the aura of Marc's corporate headquarters: vacant and dead. The detectives felt like they were raiding a tomb. Two squad cars had accompanied them as backup and waited patiently for marching orders.

Gabriel stood at the open trunk of his Celica, getting out his Mag-Lite and pulling a photograph from his evidence kit. Las Vegas Metropolitan PD had researched the photo of Marc and the cocktail waitress. After identifying the casino as the Venetian, they had an easy time tracking down Jane Doe. Once identifying her, LVMPD e-mailed Gabriel the woman's high school graduation picture, which he now held in his hand.

"It's definitely her," Dash commented, looking over Gabriel's shoulder at the picture.

"The name is Delia Marks. Las Vegas PD claims she was never listed as a missing person because the few friends and relations she had, and supposedly you could count them on one hand, knew she had left Vegas with a rich boyfriend to start a new life. No one really expected to hear from her again."

Dash gazed at the picture. "We'll still need to talk to her people, no matter how few they are. I'm sure they've got a story to tell about this rich boyfriend."

"No doubt," Gabriel said, gazing at the color photo.

The doll's head on his desk depicted a scary, waxy Delia Marks. Her senior picture radiated youthful innocence and beauty. Delia hadn't started a new life, had she? Instead, she had been brutally murdered, and no one familiar with her was even aware that she was dead.

To Gabriel, that factor was pathetically sad because he was reminded of his own family relationships. He could disappear and really, who would know? His own parents wouldn't know if he were dead or alive. His nephew and niece wouldn't know their uncle if they passed him on the street. Gabriel felt a strange, empty hole in his gut.

Like Delia, he could count those he was close to on one hand: Dash, Dr. B, maybe Ramirez and Ming. Yes, Ming would move heaven and earth to find Gabriel if he were to go missing.

Gabriel sighed. He and Ming had gotten so caught up in the case after their foray into Marc's office; they hadn't had the chance to address any of their personal issues.

We never get a chance. We never get a break.

"Here's the deputy now. 'Bout time," Dash said, pulling Gabriel from his thoughts.

The deputy strode up to them, boasting a muscular upper body over wiry thin legs that reminded Gabriel of wrestler action figures. Deputy Tom Lewitt made a show of carefully examining the warrant and then breaking the lock, not wanting to undermine his importance in the venture.

The two detectives walked into the dark warehouse, now bank-owned, and asked for the lights to be turned on.

"Sorry," Lewitt said. "Electric's been turned off. If I'd had more advanced warning the bank could have arranged something with the DWP, but you guys were in such a hurry..."

Gabriel rolled his eyes. The deputy's need to feel important was grating on his nerves. Everyone had to be a VIP. Look where that attitude of self-importance had gotten Marc Samuels.

Gabriel and Dash walked inside the dark warehouse, training their flashlights here and there, rolling the beams over pallets of boxes that resembled hulking animals asleep in the dark.

Gabriel switched open his pocketknife and cut into a box. He pulled out a ceramic coffee mug adorned with the logo of a major television network and a sitcom that had been cancelled weeks ago.

"I want every box opened," he told the backup uniforms. "Let's get another team down here to help."

"I'll call Ramirez," Dash offered and reached for his radio.

"Uh…" Deputy Lewitt stepped forward. "This is bank owned property. I don't—"

"And you." Gabriel motioned to Lewitt who backed up, crossing his burly arms defensively. "You get these lights turned on."

Gabriel continued his trek deeper into the warehouse where the sunlight from the open doors could not reach. Some of the aisles were empty of product and in others, one or two sleeping monsters rested. Gabriel heard a scratching noise down one dark aisle and followed the sound. His light passed over a shrink-wrapped stack of boxes stamped with a shipping label dated four months ago. Everything was dusty and dated, as if time had stood still. Gabriel was reminded of ghost towns and graveyards.

Rssssss! The scratching noise came from a box near the top of a pallet farther down the aisle. Gabriel approached it and then jerked left in response to another rustling sound. He pulled out his Redhawk .44, a pistol chosen with care to stop Marc Samuels in his tracks.

"Marc?"

No response. Gabriel approached the boxes to his left. *Rssssss!* His hearing became keener as his vision waned in the stretching darkness.

His sense of smell was becoming sharper as well, because now he was aware of a sickly sweet odor permeating the aisle.

Rsssss!

With shaky fingers, Gabriel reached up and pulled at one carton. With a ripping sound, the cardboard gave way and the box immediately tumbled onto Gabriel, showering him with its contents of popcorn padding and rotted candy.

A squeaking hit his ears as two rats pounced on him, their claws digging in his cheek as they raced down his body and scampered off into the black recesses of the aisle.

Gabriel yelled in disgust and in a minute he heard rapid footsteps heading his way.

"Gabe?" Dash called, staying low as he quickly approached, his own .38 Special drawn and ready. "What is it?"

"Rats," Gabriel said grimacing and pushed a half-gnawed chocolate bar off his coat.

"It stinks back here," Dash observed.

Gabriel opened his mouth to complain about the candy but then sniffed the air. The candy wasn't causing the smell. The hairs saluted on Gabriel's neck and he eyed the lone stack of boxes piled at the end of the aisle. The two detectives exchanged glances and then quietly walked toward the stack. The scratching sounds began in earnest again.

Gabriel halted in front of the cartons. A rat ran across his shoe and disappeared behind the stack. He looked at his partner and shrugged.

Wedging himself against the wall, Gabriel trained his light on the space behind the boxes and saw a large trunk. Silver duct tape wound around the trunk in a tight seal. The stench was strong here.

"What do you see?" Dash asked him.

"Trouble," Gabriel answered. "Help me move these boxes."

When the two detectives had unblocked the aisle, Gabriel put on his latex gloves and broke out his pocketknife. He carefully sliced the duct tape and grimaced from the noxious vapor that oozed out of the trunk. Gabriel opened the lid and Dash gagged. Gabriel's flashlight fanned over a wallet, shreds of pinstriped fabric, and pair of shiny men's shoes all neatly sitting on top of a badly decomposing corpse. Giving his Mag-Lite to Dash, Gabriel reached in and shook open the wallet.

"It's Malcolm Dobbs."

The time the entertainment lawyer had spent in the airless and musty trunk had reduced him to offal, a veritable stew of bones and gore.

"What's HAZMAT doing here?" Gabriel asked Ramirez as they watched the Hazardous Materials squad arrive and park amid the coroner's van, the Crime Scene Unit vans, the fire trucks, and the many police cruisers.

"Just a precaution." Ramirez shook a Winston from his pack. "Who the hell knows what other kinds of garbage, besides lawyers, Samuels had boxed up in there?"

Ramirez lit up and gave Gabriel an apologetic nod. "You were right to follow your gut. We've got a warrant to search the Hidden Springs house and we've already impounded all the vehicles, although the leasing companies are fighting us. Samuels defaulted on all his leases. I hear the bank has already begun eviction proceedings."

Poor Tara, Gabriel thought.

"Any word from Mrs. Samuels?" Ramirez asked, seeming to read Gabriel's mind.

"Not one," Gabriel answered, and knew his face betrayed his worry.

⚜ ⚜ ⚜

CHAPTER

23

Gabriel joined the search through the Hidden Springs house in hopes of finding some clue as to where Tara and Marc had disappeared.

The detectives crawled over the place like ants on a picnic, but unlike the warehouse, the mansion held no dark secrets. Just more pictures of Marc adorning the walls. A whole row of professional black and white shots hung on a guest room wall across from the bed. Any unsuspecting guest would be forced to stare at Serious Marc, Playful Marc, and Sexy Marc with his bicep at center stage. A bronze bust of Samuels was spotlighted in the master bedroom. Gabriel could only shake his head at the unabashed narcissism. And yet, he'd bought Marc's brand of self-promotion lock, stock, and barrel. He'd bought it big-time.

Rosa was nowhere to be found. God only knew what happened to her when the house of cards crashed down.

Samuels was capable of brutalizing his wife, of that Gabriel was sure, but would he go so far as to actually stage a rape and allow his wife to witness a murder? Usually these men hid their sleazy secret lives from their spouses, but Marc was into sex games, wasn't he? Perhaps his sick fantasies included kidnapping his own wife in disguise and raping her. But now the game playing had reached its end. The house was empty of its occupants. Food rotted in the refrigerator, dust was settling on the Navajo print couches, and the Evening Primrose plants were wilting in their pots.

Frustrated, he called Ming at work.

"Do you have anything?" Gabriel spoke desperately into his cell phone. "Anything at all I could use?"

"The yellow blanket. And those blue automobile carpet fibers."

"What questions did you have about Lena Dobbs?"

"It's about her being shot in the car. The bullet trajectory doesn't quite make sense. Ballistics needs a suspect vehicle."

Gabriel recalled seeing Marc cleaning his own car, nervous and agitated.

"I've got a suspect vehicle for you."

Gabriel jogged to the driveway, bypassed Dash, and opened the backseat doors of Marc's Mercedes Benz. He took out his blade and cut a wide swath across the expensive leather seats.

"What are you doing?" Dash called, walking over to Gabriel. "The lenders are collecting these vehicles tomorrow afternoon."

"Not this one," Gabriel answered.

Leather repels a lot of liquid, he thought, but it isn't waterproof. Gabriel ripped back the leather. On the padding beneath, two ugly brown blotches stood out under the fading sun.

❧ ❧ ❧

Forensics calls it projectile trajectory testing. In plain English, Gabriel knew it to be tracking a bullet's path from the point of impact back to the point of origin. To understand better the details of Lena Dobbs' last moments, officers reconstructed the crime.

At the impound yard the following day, technicians took a mannequin and carefully marked the positions of Lena's entrance and exit wounds. Next they positioned the mannequin against the bloodstains that had saturated the padding of Marc's Mercedes. Although it was too early to get results from a DNA mapping, blood analysis had already been done. The blood type on the padding matched Lena's.

Judging from the points of impact and the blood spatter, the ballistic experts determined the killing shots had been fired from Lena's right. The shooter had sat in the passenger seat.

Ming and Gabriel sat at the counter of a burger stand near the impound yard, digesting both the trajectory results and chiliburgers.

"Why would Marc be sitting in the passenger seat of his own car?" Gabriel asked Ming.

Ming shrugged and wiped chili from her chin. "Maybe he had to move over to get a better shot at Lena."

Gabriel shook his head. "Not likely. Bucket seats make it hard to move over."

"Maybe he first sat in the passenger side and shot her, then went around to the driver's side to take her to the dump site…"

Gabriel was shaking his head.

Ming took a sudden intake of breath and leaned towards Gabriel. "Then you know what this means, right? Everything falls into place now."

Gabriel regarded her dark, intelligent eyes, the way the wheels turned in her mind. Ming tossed her dark hair over her shoulders, and it fell in a cascade down her back as she presented her hypothesis.

"Marc had a partner. You always wondered how one suspect could handle both Tara and Regina."

"Tara said Regina was already subdued when she got to the Wagon Wheel Ranch," Gabriel reminded her.

"You sure Tara didn't mention another man?"

"Never."

Ming bit her hamburger and chewed thoughtfully. "What about subduing Lena and Malcolm? How can one guy handle that?"

"One guy and a gun can handle that."

"Gabriel! What about Ross? There's your Ross connection. I'm sure there were three people in the Mercedes the night Lena was shot; one driving, one in the passenger seat with the gun, and Lena in the back—" Ming abruptly left off.

"What?" Gabriel urged, reading a lost expression on her face.

Ming swallowed and set down her burger. "I was just thinking of Lena in the backseat, digging her toenails into that blue carpeting and being terrified." Ming paused and then looked miserably at Gabriel. "It reminds me of—of when the water began filling around the pipe. I tried to get my hands free but no matter how hard I tried, I couldn't do it. I couldn't do it, Gabriel. I knew I was going to die!"

He watched her shudder and then ventured an arm around her. He wondered if she would pull away. She didn't.

"I don't know which was worse for me. Realizing I was going to drown or realizing I had lost control of the situation." Ming gave him a sad, incredulous smile. "I am a terrible control freak, aren't I?" Then the phony smile faded and tears filled her eyes. "It's funny how we manifest the thing we fear the most."

Gabriel nodded, agreeing.

"I did it," she told him. "I made an appointment with Raymond. Just to talk."

"I'm glad," he said gently and was about to release her, when Ming spoke again.

"Please do not let go of me."

Gabriel pulled her close and held her until she stopped trembling.

Later, he drove along the winding roads of the Santa Monica Mountains. The winter was playing tricks again; the mischievous sun had come out and the temperature rose and warmed the basin. Bicyclists and hikers braved the mud and rode the hills. Behind Gabriel, the beach was mist-free and shining like a star.

The equestrians were back at Blue Sage Stables. Apparently, the reputation of the center was still sterling and the negative history had been swept under the rug. Gabriel saw the Saddlebreds, the English, and the Western riders all paying tribute to a beautiful day.

Gabriel's thoughts, however, were not on the blue skies. If three people had sat in the car the night Lena Dobbs was killed, then that would explain Ross's involvement in the murders. Ross had left drugs at the crime scene. Ross had access to baling wire. Marc and Ross made a good team because Marc could always hang the crimes on his drug-addicted partner.

Marc looked me in the face, that bastard, and asked if we had enough clues.

Gabriel's cheeks reddened with humiliation and he felt his anger stirring. He wanted nothing more than to have a private sit-down with Marc Samuels.

He was admitted into Lynn's plush office with its Laura Ashley prints, rich green leather, and darkly polished wood. Jim Traxler and Felipe sat on one of the couches. Traxler appeared worn and deflated and Gabriel wondered how he could have suspected the war veteran.

"I'm worried Mrs. Samuels is in danger. Has she contacted you?"

The Traxlers shook their heads.

"Please be honest with me. I know she might have come here. She loved her horses."

Lynn shook her head. "We haven't seen or heard from her. What a terrible time this has been, hasn't it? All this with Ross and now Tara is missing."

Traxler cleared his throat and when he spoke his voice was surprisingly deep and dangerous. "If we'd never taken in that no-good drug fiend—"

Lynn put a hand on her husband's arm. "Please, Jim. He's gone."

Traxler looked down at his lap and said nothing more.

Gabriel readied his notepad and asked, "How often did Marc Samuels hang out here with Ross?"

"Mr. Samuels?" Lynn traded disbelieving glances with Felipe. "Why, never."

Gabriel looked curiously at Felipe, who nodded, agreeing with Lynn.

"Only the missus," Felipe offered. "She come here caring for her horses, jus' like always. But Mr. Samuels, he never come here. I never seen him here."

"Did Ross ever mention him?"

Lynn shrugged. "No. Why would he? They didn't know each other."

Gabriel thoughtfully tapped his pen against his notepad. That wasn't the answer he had been expecting.

Walking back to his Celica, Gabriel squinted under the bright sun, bothered by the brief interview. Ross must have met Marc at some point, but obviously Ross and Marc rendezvoused elsewhere. And that brought something else to Gabriel's mind. None of the victims had been killed where they were dumped. So where would two murderers meet to carry out their deeds?

Gabriel's cell phone rang as soon as he cleared the mountains. He maneuvered through the cars on Pacific Coast Highway and flipped open his cell phone.

"Hello?"

"Gabriel?"

He fumbled with the phone. *Tara!*

"Tara, where are you?"

"Oh God, Gabriel, I'm sorry. Marc's been insisting on living in hotels for the last week. He said the house is being painted and he didn't—"

"What hotel? Where?"

"What's the matter?"

"Where is Marc now?"

"Well, that's just it. He left me at the Bel Air hotel for the last two days and I haven't heard from him. They're bothering me about the bill and—"

"Stay there! I'm coming."

"Can you pay the bill?"

Gabriel was flustered. "Tara, stay put. I'm coming to get you."

"I'm not at the hotel! I—Marc called and told me to wait at a restaurant for him."

"Which restaurant?"

"Why? What's wrong?"

"It's Marc, Tara. I don't know how to tell you this, but you've got to stay away from him. He's in big trouble and he might act very desperate."

"What are you talking about?"

Gabriel paused. "Your husband knew the victims, Tara."

"He couldn't have."

"He's involved. You have to stay away from him."

She was silent and Gabriel heard static. "Hello? Tara? Are you there?"

"I'm here," she said weakly. "Are you saying Marc murdered those girls?" She was silent a moment and then screamed, "That's a lie!"

"I don't know the extent of his involvement, but a body was found in his warehouse. And right now, the police are crawling over everything he owns. Tell me where you are and I'll come get you."

"No!" she blurted hysterically. "This is impossible! Marc didn't do it! You're lying!"

"Tara, calm down."

"Are you going to arrest him? What are you going to do?"

"Tara."

"I've got to go now," she said in small, tremulous voice. "I've got to go."

The phone went dead. Gabriel quickly redialed her cell phone, but got her voicemail. Gabriel slammed the phone against his dashboard in frustration.

Tara was unstable from the get-go. He should have never dropped that bomb on her. Worse, Gabriel had his chance to arrest Marc, and now Tara might warn her husband, thinking him innocent. Cursing as he drove, Gabriel stepped on the pedal, wondering what he should do and berating himself for what he had already done.

CHAPTER 24

The Bel Air hotel confirmed that Marc and Tara had checked in with a cash payment for the first night. Marc's promise of a credit card for subsequent nights never materialized, and the couple had been asked to leave.

Detectives in San Diego, where Marc's family lived, had interviewed relatives who claimed to have no knowledge of his whereabouts. The San Diego Police Department did what they could and then sent their files over to the L.A. County Sheriff's office.

"Wanna hear some background on Marc Samuels?" Dash asked Gabriel as they sat at their desks in Commerce.

Distinctly absent from Gabriel's desk was Delia Marks' clay visage, now tucked away in an evidence carton. Gabriel had been in a funk since he had spoken to Tara. He'd mismanaged the whole conversation with her. Now she was out there, probably still with Marc. On Gabriel's conscience was the possibility that Marc might kill Tara if she began to question him.

Dash was talking. "Supposedly he was a happy kid, a perfect child. Polite, well-mannered in school. Very cute. He also had a good head for figures."

"What?" Gabriel looked curiously at Dash.

"Marc Samuels," Dash answered emphatically. "Have you been listening?" With a sigh, Dash continued. "When Marc Samuels was eleven years old, he found out he was illegitimate. Relations between him and his mother went sour. The news must have affected him really badly because he grew up to be one helluva jerk. Our friends in San Diego tell me that Marc's old college girlfriends claim he was into forceful anal sex and enjoyed humiliating them publicly."

Gabriel shook his head. Was Tara still alive?

"Supposedly Marc has always had a voracious appetite for sex, fancy toys, clothes, and money," Dash said, finishing.

"Did friends or family mention Tara at all?"

Dash scanned the notes and shook his head.

Gabriel rubbed his temples, frustrated. On the phone, Tara said she had to go. Perhaps she had fled to her family in Nevada. They were the Nevada Bannings, after all, and would have the resources to protect their daughter.

Gabriel left Dash and walked into Ramirez's office.

"I need to go to Las Vegas," he announced.

To Gabriel's surprise, Ramirez gave the trip his blessing, saying they were obligated to give closure to Delia Marks' relatives anyhow. In private, Dash agreed to handle the Marks interview in order to free Gabriel so that he could search for Tara. If he found Tara, he could probably locate Marc. And nothing would please Gabriel more than arresting that bastard.

Gabriel kept trying her cell phone. He contacted her service provider and researched all incoming and outgoing calls. There weren't many. Mostly to her own home phone number, presumably to remotely retrieve messages from her home answering machine. The home phone bill had been paid and was currently tapped by the FBI.

Tara had also called Marc's cell phone. On a whim, Gabriel tried Marc's cell phone, too. It rang until his voicemail came on. Once again, Gabriel heard the confident swagger in Marc's voice: Mr. Important. Gabriel made sure Marc and Tara's cell phone bill was paid up, determined to keep the account alive, hoping for more activity.

The following morning, early, Gabriel stood in his bedroom, packing a duffel bag. He and Dash were booked on an eleven a.m. flight to Las Vegas out of LAX. Between traffic and the tightened security at the airport, Gabriel knew he needed to hustle.

He was throwing the bag over his shoulder when he heard a timid knock at his door.

He ignored it. He wasn't expecting anybody and didn't have the time for Girl Scout cookies or whatever anyone else was selling. Nine twenty on his wristwatch. Again somebody knocked and Gabriel froze in mid-stride. Tara...?

He loped to the door in seconds flat and tore it open. He expected to see a blond waif-like woman, but instead beheld an elderly woman with medium-length black hair run through with gray. Tears stood in blue eyes that matched Gabriel's.

"Hello, son."

Gabriel beheld his mother, so in shock he couldn't invite her in. She held the handle of a rolling suitcase and mustered a sad smile.

"Ma... What are you doing here?"

"May I come in?"

"Sure, sure." Gabriel stepped aside and stared at her as if she were an alien that had just landed. Mrs. McRay was stooped a little in the shoulders and her arms seemed much frailer than Gabriel remembered. He took the suitcase from her.

"This is a surprise," he said quietly.

"Please don't kick me out."

His mouth fell open. "I wouldn't kick you out. Jesus, Ma... Sit down. Can I get you something?"

"You weren't answering my phone calls." She took a deep breath and sat lightly on his couch. "I wanted to see you."

Gabriel took a seat next to her, unable to stop staring. She looked older, but her nose was still pert and, under dark lashes, her beautiful Irish blues still twinkled.

"Where's Dad?" Gabriel asked, eyeing the door.

She paused and then said, "He couldn't come, Gabe."

Gabriel was about to ask why not, but his mother took one of his hands. "Maybe I should have written you a note, but I wasn't sure if you'd read the mail." She gazed at his hand. "Do you know how long it's been since I held your hand?"

Gabriel felt a pit yawn in his stomach and he fought the urge to pull away. He couldn't help shaking his head. "This is very unexpected."

"I've been in therapy, Gabriel. My psychologist has been urging me to talk with you."

Now Gabriel did retract his hand and said sharply, "So, you're here on the advice of a therapist?"

"I've wanted to see you for years. My therapist gave me the strength to do it. That's all."

"And what did you need strength for, Ma?"

"To break down the wall you've built against me and your father." She regarded him with a slight resentment that mirrored his own. "I knew that if I told you I was coming, you'd get conveniently out of town."

Out of town... Gabriel checked his watch. Nine forty-five. He looked desperately at his mother and gathered the strength to say words that did not come naturally to him.

"I want you to stay. I have to go, but I'll be back tonight."

"You have to go?"

"I've got this case—"

"No, you don't." She looked away.

"I swear I do. Look," Gabriel displayed the duffel bag. He took out his airline ticket and held it under her eyes with shaking hands. "My flight is in an hour. I've got to meet Dash, my partner, at the airport."

Mrs. McRay blinked tiredly at him, and a rush of emotion ran through Gabriel. He had expected anger, but instead, felt the need to draw her fragile shoulders close to him. She looked so vulnerable, not at all like the mother he remembered— strong, smart, and independent. The career woman. Just like Ming.

"I know you want me to leave you alone," Mrs. McRay said. "But I need—we need to talk, son."

Gabriel took her hands in his own, giving her a steady gaze. "I promise I'll be back tonight. I want you to stay here and wait for me. Will you do that?"

She nodded and a tear rolled down her cheek. Gabriel smoothed her hair. "Why are you crying?"

She shook her head and said, "I'll be here."

Gabriel stood, backed toward the door, talking quickly. "I'm glad you came. I'm going to call a friend and she'll come over to keep you company." He smiled nervously at his mother. "Stay here, okay?"

His mother looked pleased when she saw Gabriel pull on the pea coat. He kissed her quickly on the cheek, an action that caused both of them surprise, and then Gabriel departed in a whirlwind. He couldn't believe that his mother was sitting in his apartment.

Driving toward the airport, a million thoughts drummed against his brain, each vying to get his attention. Would his mother rifle through his things, trying to learn more about her estranged son? Would she call a taxi and leave, promising herself she'd never speak to her outrageous offspring again?

Would she cook herself dinner? Did he have enough food in his pantry? Oh, why did he leave like that?

A headache was sprouting, feeling like the bad old days. Gabriel reached for some aspirin and realized he didn't carry aspirin bottles with him anymore.

He pulled onto Century Boulevard and joined the line of cars nearing the airport terminals. He dialed Ming at the coroner's office and a morgue assistant offered to find her when Gabriel said it was an emergency.

Ming came on the line breathless. "You found Tara?"

"No. But I have a real emergency and, Ming, you've gotta help me."

"Oh God, what's wrong?"

"My mother's in town!"

The United Airlines plane winged its way into Nevada and landed at McCarran Airport. From the air, the passengers were treated to the sight of the pyramid-shaped Luxor Hotel, the medieval castle of Excalibur, and the Eiffel Tower of Paris. Las Vegas, the ultimate adult sandbox, pulled out all the stops to separate a fool from his money.

Gabriel and Dash were given a Ford Taurus, courtesy of Las Vegas PD. They were also given the address of Delia's old roommate. Delia had been closer to the roommate than to her few relatives. Unfortunately for Gabriel, Las Vegas PD could offer no leads on Tara's family, the Bannings.

After dropping Dash off to speak with Delia's roommate, Gabriel went online to find the Banning's phone number and address. He found a couple of Bannings listed but none he called had ever heard of Tara.

He then went to the Hall of Records and tried to look up the "Nevada Bannings." The person in charge of records, a young man with premature balding offered to help Gabriel.

"I can't find anything," the young man said, his glasses glowing from the light off his computer monitor.

"Are you sure? They were a wealthy, influential family. I believe they owned a ranch, lots of land right outside Las Vegas, maybe in the late seventies, early eighties?"

The young man shrugged. Gabriel's cell phone rang and he answered it.

Dash relayed to Gabriel his conversation with Delia's roommate, who was a showgirl at the Rio. Delia allegedly loved to party and was quite smitten by a high roller she had met at the Venetian Hotel and Casino. The roommate described him as tall, movie star handsome, and free with his money.

"Sounds like our man, doesn't it?" Gabriel asked. He felt a tug and turned to see the young bespectacled record-keeper smiling at him. "Uh, Dash, I gotta go. Think you can catch a cab to the airport and I'll meet you there?"

Gabriel hung up.

"What did you find?" he asked the young man.

"I researched the county parcel maps from the late seventies and found a track of land out near Red Rock Canyon that was once owned by a Banning family."

He gave Gabriel the address.

"Does it say anything more about them?"

"Let me access more about these particular Bannings..." The boy's fingers tapped rapidly on the keys. "I have a record of a Scarlett Banning filing for divorce in 1986. Looks like she later remarried a Peter Shechter. Their last known address was in Henderson, Nevada, not far from—"

"Thanks, I got it," Gabriel said.

Scarlett? The irony wasn't lost on Gabriel, who was familiar enough with *Gone with the Wind*. Tara had been the name of the plantation beloved by the heroine, Scarlett O'Hara. Gabriel quickly checked the yellow pages once again and jotted down the address of S & P Shechter. They were still residents of Henderson.

He drove the Taurus out of Las Vegas and headed toward Henderson, a growing suburb of Las Vegas.

He found the Shechter condominium and parked in the red, as all the guest spots were taken. The condo complex was ordinary, tidy and well kept. Nobody was at home, however, and Gabriel paced around, feeling helpless. He looked up at the darkened windows with the hope that Tara's face would appear.

Finally, he got back in the Taurus. Even though the ranch was no longer Banning property, Gabriel was curious enough about Tara to check it out. He had to burn time anyhow before he tried the condo Shechters again.

As he drove toward Red Rock Canyon, Gabriel called his mother. She assured him she wasn't going anywhere. She was being babysat by an intense Asian woman who asked a lot of questions and fed her take-out food. Gabriel smiled. Ming had come through.

Gabriel called Tara's cell phone once more and got her voicemail. No surprise. He called Marc's cell phone for the hell of it, and this time Gabriel left a message.

"If you hear this, Marc, you'd better give yourself up. We know you're involved and things will go easier for you if you come forward." Gabriel left his cell number urging Marc to set up a meeting.

As twilight descended, a cold desert wind kicked up, buffeting the car as it moved along a narrow two-lane highway. Finally, Gabriel pulled up alongside a dusty dirt road bordered by a rusting chain-link fence. A dented mailbox stood lonely at the side of the road, and painted on it was the name "Martinez."

Gabriel glanced once more at the address; sure he had taken a wrong turn somewhere. This, however, was the right address.

He exited the car and looked around, perplexed. Gabriel walked down a long dirt road while the wind blew dust flurries around him. The place looked thirsty, no greenery, no trees. Someone had dumped drywall on the road; the broken pieces lay in a smashed and abandoned pile. Gabriel soon made out a small tract house in the flying dust. As he approached, he could see that the house was in disrepair, slipping off the foundation from what appeared to be old earthquake damage.

What a lifeless dump, thought Gabriel. He could see nothing grand about the house, even when he tried to envision it as brand new.

Nothing was here, just a vista of desert backed by the red mountains. An old truck rusted near a pile of broken metal parts covered by a tarp that flapped in the wind. A barn stood a distance away with half of its roof caved in. Tumbleweeds bounced merrily by. Gabriel shook his head in disbelief. This was the utopia Tara had described?

He headed back toward the car, hair full of dust, and drove back to Henderson. During the ride, Gabriel stared at the road ahead, disturbed by his findings about Tara's "rambling" ranch. The only thing rambling there were the tumbleweeds.

When Gabriel arrived at the condo, he was able to park in a vacant guest spot. He walked up a narrow path to the front door and knocked loudly.

An overweight short woman with no front teeth opened the door.

She looked him up and down and said curtly, "Yes?"

Gabriel showed her his ID, and immediately she barked behind her, "Pete! It's for you."

Gabriel eyed her curiously and waited.

A long stick of a man, sporting a tan, rough-hewn face and a scraggly gray-brown beard, came to the door. Faded tattoos graced sinewy forearms. When he spoke, rubbing his chin in reflection, Gabriel saw the fellow was also shy a few teeth.

"I already told the other cop I had nothing to do with that stolen car."

Gabriel gazed at him. "I'm not here about a car."

The man took his hand from his chin and smiled genially. "Oh. Well then, how can I help you, Officer?"

"Sergeant McRay," Gabriel said, extending his hand. The skinny man shook it heartily and invited Gabriel in. Gabriel viewed a decent space filled with flea-market furniture. HUD housing, Gabriel surmised. Government assisted.

"I'm looking for a woman named Tara Samuels."

"Scarlett, you'd better get in here."

The short, fat woman reentered the room. "Tara? What about her?"

Gabriel could see that the front of the woman's floral-print housedress was covered in cat hair. "Do you know her?"

"She's my daughter."

"You're Tara's mother?"

"How's she doin? She ain't in any trouble, is she?"

Gabriel looked around. "Is Tara here?"

"Hell, no." The woman grunted and smiled snidely. "We don't talk. She up and married some rich fellow years ago and that's the last we all heard of lil Tara. You think she'd ever share the wealth? Not that one. You know between Pete and me we got fourteen kids? That's right, Sergeant. Fourteen. Pete's got five of his own from previous marriages, and I had Drew and Jonah from my first marriage. Then I had Ashley, Rhett, and Tara, from my second. I just had to do something with *Gone with the Wind.* My mama was a big fan and named me Scarlett after you-know-who. And Pete and I have three more together—June, Jordan, and Julia. Julia is my baby. She's sixteen and already wants to marry. Pete here tried to talk her out of it, but it did no damn good."

"I did try," Pete said, holding up a finger at Gabriel. "But I got married young m'self at seventeen to my first wife. So how can I tell Julia not to do it? But I'm making her promise, *promise* to use birth control until she's at least eighteen." Pete shook his head.

Gabriel eyed them both. "What do you do for a living, sir? May I ask?"

"I got nothin' to hide." He exchanged sly glances with his wife. "I'm a forklift driver. Do most of my work with the union when the trade shows come through Vegas. Good pay." He winked at Gabriel. "We used to live in trash, I tell ya, but look what Scarlett and me saved up and did. We got us this condo. And I plan to put a spa out back just as soon as I can afford it. 'Nother couple o' months or so."

"And you, ma'am?"

"I worked as a telemarketer for a few years. Mostly I been busy with babies."

"I imagine." Gabriel paused to let his eyes scan the room once more. "And Tara hasn't contacted you?"

"Nope. As I said, her and me don't talk. It ain't her fault. I was a young mother. I'm much better with mine and Pete's kids. But that girl is no saint neither."

"How so?"

"Fucking tramp, mind my language. I couldn't keep that girl's pants up faster'n she could take 'em down. An' Tara was thick as a brick too. Just plain stupid. I can't tell you how many problems I had with that girl. When she left I said, 'God bless me, I'm free.' No lie. I said that." The woman spoke fast and spittle escaped from the space where her teeth had been. "Now her daddy was a real mean son of a bitch, never did an honest day's work in his life, and left me to raise the kids, so's I don't blame her none for wanting to cut out. But Pete here knows how to build confidence. Don't you, Pete?"

"I do try."

"He does try. June and Jordan finished high school with good grades. I mean it! Now if we can just get Julia to finish before she marries that oaf, Frank, we'll be a pair of proud parents. You understand where I'm comin' from, Sergeant?"

Gabriel nodded, gazing at the two of them. He gingerly wiped her spittle off his pants with his sleeve. "Here's my card. If Tara does contact you, please let me know right away."

"Why? Is somethin' wrong, Sergeant?" Pete asked. He walked Gabriel to the door with his hand on his back, as if they were old friends.

"Yeah. Something's wrong. Something's not right at all."

CHAPTER 25

The following afternoon Gabriel sat in the armchair opposite Dr. B. Thoughts of Tara, her mother, Marc, and Gabriel's own mother whirled in his mind and he had trouble focusing on any one thing in particular. For all Gabriel knew, Tara was dead.

Gabriel had left his mother to walk the Venice boardwalk by herself, but he reminded her that this wasn't Seattle. She was not to talk to any person eating fire or selling voodoo dolls. His mother was entranced by the locals and shooed Gabriel off, eager to start her new adventure.

So far they hadn't talked much. Not about the serious stuff that had driven her down to California in the first place. Ming hung around a lot, injecting her quirky humor into the conversations and for that, Gabriel was grateful. But tonight he planned to cook one of his gourmet feasts so he and his mother could talk alone, which is why he booked an emergency session with Dr. B.

"So, your mother is in therapy too," Dr. B stated, clasping his bony hands together. "She's been here how long?"

"Two days."

"And how has it been?"

"Good. I've told her about the cases I've worked on. We've gone to Chinatown, Thai Town, Little Tokyo, and Olvera Street. You name the part of the world, we've been there."

Dr. B nodded, studying him.

Gabriel shifted uncomfortably. "I plan on confronting her tonight. Not confronting, but..." He sighed. "Opening the door."

"I know you have a lot of anxiety about this. But this is a necessary step in your adjustment phase—to iron out the family relationship that was spoiled by Andrew Pierce. On the outside, Gabriel, you're a grown man with a career and a life. You've made important progress regarding your feelings about sex, about managing your anger, and addressing the source of the post-traumatic stress disorder that has plagued you. But on the inside, there is still a little boy who feels betrayed by his parents. Yes, you open the door. Would you rather do it in a controlled environment like this? I'm happy to be of service."

Gabriel shook his head and cast a sideways smile toward Dr. B. "I'll cook. I'm fine when my hands are busy."

"Try not to attack."

"I know. I keep reminding myself of that. I'll be very controlled."

"This is big." Dr. B thought a moment. "And I've heard the news about Marc and Tara Samuels. They've both disappeared, correct?"

"She's in danger," Gabriel said plainly. "Her husband is our main suspect and he's still out there somewhere, hiding with her. I knew there was something rotten about that guy the minute I laid eyes on him. I should have followed my instinct more thoroughly."

"Wait a minute. Are you saying he staged the rape of his own wife?"

"Why the hell not? The Cloister, remember? This guy had a real sense of humor when it came to sex. Now, with the walls closing in... God knows what he's doing this time to Tara. I tried to track her down in Las Vegas. I even spoke to her mother. No luck. She's gone."

"And what did Tara's mother have to say? You told me her parents were wealthy socialites."

Gabriel guffawed. "Hardly. Seems like everything Tara told me about her parents was a lie. The father she supposedly adored was a scumbag who abandoned the family. And the mansion they supposedly lived in wouldn't house your dog. Her mother... her mother could make a dentist's career."

"Why do you think Mrs. Samuels would lie to you about her background?"

"I don't know," Gabriel answered. "I only know she's in trouble now."

Dr. B scribbled something into his notebook and then reflected on it.

"What?" Gabriel asked the psychiatrist, concerned.

"Well, from casual observation, I think Tara's psychological issues range beyond her rape. Obviously, she was a troubled person before this trauma occurred."

"So?"

Dr. B shrugged innocently. "Nothing. But my experience with pathological liars makes me wonder if Tara isn't delusional, creating and believing her own take on a less-than-perfect past."

Anger flooded Gabriel. "And what do you think I did? I did the exact same thing as her. I blocked out a bad part of my past and told myself it didn't happen. Am I a pathological liar?"

"I think you know that answer. You two have different issues, Gabe. Please don't let your empathy for another

273

victim get in the way of seeing the facts as they really are. I'm going to ask this again. Do you think it's possible that you have been projecting your own trauma and symptoms onto Mrs. Samuels?"

Gabriel stared at his therapist but did not reply.

Dr. B clasped his hands in front of him and said gently, "I think you better look at that possibility very seriously."

When Gabriel left, the anger shadowed him like a stalker, but as he drove the freeway home, he wondered if Dr. B was right.

There's something very odd about her. Ming's words bounced around in Gabriel's skull.

Please don't let your empathy for another victim get in the way of seeing the facts as they really are.

Gabriel had convinced himself that Tara was working out her problems through him. Maybe all along, he'd been working out his problems through her. Gabriel took a deep breath and worried over that prospect. He didn't want to think about all the mistakes he might have made. Besides, tonight he had bigger worries. Tonight he was going to have a showdown with his mother.

❦ ❦ ❦

Gabriel had chosen salmon en papillote, or salmon baked in paper, for tonight's dish, and his mother helped him unpack the grocery bags.

"This all looks so interesting," Mrs. McRay said. "I remember you enjoyed cooking as a boy."

"It's like meditation. Helps me relax." He laid out his ingredients and then turned to his mother, braving himself for the inevitable. "Why did you need strength to come see me?"

She seemed taken by surprise. Holding up a salmon filet, his mother asked, "How should I season this?"

Gabriel always thought that when he finally spoke with his mother, his rage would surge up and grab him by the neck, shaking him until he lashed out at her. He always thought he would confront her with blame blazing in his eyes.

But he remained perfectly calm. "I asked you a question."

Mrs. McRay set the salmon down on the counter and stared at the white tiles. "Someone needs to scrub the grout. Boraxo does a good job."

Gabriel ground his teeth, eyeing his mother thoughtfully. Perhaps he should have taken Dr. B up on his offer to mediate.

Finally, Mrs. McRay pulled up a kitchen chair and sat down like a wilted flower. She met his eyes with her cobalt blues. "I don't know what we did, your father and I. I've been fully armed for a war, but I don't know why I'm fighting."

Gabriel leaned against the counter, gazing at her. He didn't respond.

Mrs. McRay stared at a point on the kitchen linoleum. "I'm proud of you, you know. Even though friends called me and told me about your troubles, what the local papers printed about you, I knew in my heart you did well."

Gabriel shifted and crossed his arms, but his face remained impassive.

She paused, struggling for the right words. "Even when you changed from a sweet sociable boy into a—a withdrawn, solitary child, I just thought it was your development." She shrugged, smiling apologetically, but the tears were brimming now, ready for escape. "I worked, and your dad worked, and everything was normal." She shook her head, looking far away into her memory. "I knew something was up with you, but I guess I didn't want to pay it much attention. You never talked about it to us."

"That's because Andrew told me—"

"And then you wanted out of our lives." His mother looked at him quizzically. "Andrew? Who's Andrew?"

Gabriel steeled himself. "Andrew Pierce. Across the street from the house on Irving."

Her brows furrowed and she shook her head until the memory dawned on her. "The Pierces. Oh, but they moved out of the neighborhood many years ago."

Gabriel swallowed, taking in her puzzled expression, and recited his words as if they were well-practiced. Were they?

"Andrew was their son. You used to call him a dropout. Tinkered a bit with his car?"

"I think I remember him."

"Try. He played a very pivotal role in my childhood." Sarcasm darkened his tone. Gabriel couldn't help it. Could his mother truly have had no clue?

"What role?"

Gabriel knelt down in front of her, trying to read her, looking for signs that she knew what had happened to him. "He molested me, Ma, starting when I was seven."

Her eyes widened. "What are you talking about? The Pierce boy...? I—" She shook her head, not willing to comprehend.

"Yes. While you were at work. For months. Right up until the time they moved away."

"Oh my God..." She pursed her lips, searching his face. "You wouldn't be making this up, would you?"

Gabriel felt a cold anger flare in his heart, but he suppressed it, keeping his composure. "It's the truth."

"Gabriel, why didn't you say something? Why didn't you tell us?"

"Because he threatened to kill Janet if I did. He said he'd drown her in their pool." Gabriel stood up and took a deep breath. "Kind of a joke, looking back on it. They had this broken down Doughboy that would crowd a hamster..."

Mrs. McRay began to cry. Gabriel watched her suffering, unable to comfort his mother. He himself felt numb.

"I can't believe it," she said through her hands. "But it makes sense now, doesn't it? Oh my God... Why didn't you tell us, Gabriel? Why didn't you say anything—anything at all?"

Gabriel pulled a paper towel from the rack and handed it to her.

"Ask your psychologist, Ma," he said quietly. "I can't go through this again."

"That's why you withdrew." She suddenly looked up at him over the paper towel. "You blamed us."

"That came later." Gabriel went to the window and watched the ocean mist roll up the street, feeling it dampen his soul. "My life had changed forever, and yours, Dad's, and Janet's continued like normal. It wasn't fair. No one said anything. Nobody noticed or asked questions." He turned back to his mother. "How could you not ask questions? All I saw of you was that you were on your way to work or on the phone or busy with this or that, and forever complaining of how much you had to do."

Mrs. McRay shook her head; her tear-stained face implored her son. "That's not fair, Gabriel. You don't go around thinking your child is being hurt in his own house!"

"In Andrew's house or sometimes in the movie theater."

"What?" she blurted.

"That's what I could never figure out. The signs were all there, Ma. You just never made time to look."

She stared at him, as fat tears rolled down her cheeks. "I never would have let anyone hurt you!" She turned her eyes toward the linoleum. "No wonder you hate us."

"I don't hate you." Gabriel walked over and slumped into a chair next to hers. "I'm just tired and I don't want to talk about this anymore."

Mrs. McRay sniffed and said, "I was busy. I was young when I had you kids and maybe I felt a little robbed. I was still young enough to have a lot of dreams. I tried to be a good mother. I never, ever would have stood by while my child was being hurt. You have to believe that, Gabe. You have to. All this time your dad and I never knew what we'd done to make you hate us so much. You never called, and when we called you, you were so tight on the phone—so angry or worse, you were indifferent, as if you didn't care if we lived or died." She wiped her tears. "Can we press charges?"

"He's dead."

She looked at him, wanting more information. Gabriel complied.

"I believe it was cancer."

His mother digested that. "Is this the reason you picked a profession in which you can protect people?"

Gabriel said nothing, but inside, he was surprised at the question. It was the second time someone had asked him why he became a cop. He watched his mother twist and fold the damp paper towel over and over. Outside, the rain began to fall. He reached out and took her hand.

"What made you come down here, Ma?"

Mrs. McRay studied their held hands. Gabriel was convinced she wasn't going to reply when she spoke.

"Once I had a little boy whom I loved very much. One year, he drifted away from me." She looked gently at Gabriel with wet eyes. "I've come to get him back."

�֍ ✖ ✖

The rain gutters ticked like clocks as Gabriel sat at his desk in Commerce. His mother's face still etched in his mind. The rain had arrived again and with it a fresh batch of memories.

First Andrew had told Gabriel that his family would die if Gabriel ever said anything, but then he drilled it into Gabriel's head that his parents did know after all, and that they approved of Gabriel's repayment of Andrew's "friendship."

So much was twisted and unresolved, but the conversation with his mother had lifted one veil from his eyes. Gabriel realized now how hard it had been for his parents. He had always viewed his actions as natural, considering what had happened to him. He had ignored his parents for reasons so deeply buried; Gabriel forgot why he ignored them.

Dr. B said it was important that his parents create a way to "protect" their son again, thereby allowing Gabriel to trust them. How that would happen, Gabriel didn't know. All he knew was that having empathy for them "losing a son" felt better than the endless blame he carried around.

On his desk lay a blueprint of the warehouse in which they had found Malcolm Dobbs. Notes containing names and phone numbers of all the area hotels lay scattered over the blueprint. Copies of Marc and Tara's credit card bills were stacked nearby. Everything had been double-checked but no leads had surfaced. Officers staked out Marc's home, his office, and his warehouse. Friends in Marc's photos had been questioned. No one had heard from the "big guy."

Gabriel dialed Tara's cell phone again. When he heard her voicemail, he left a single sentence message, "Talk to me."

He dialed Marc's cell. No answer. Had they left the country? Could two people vanish into thin air? Gabriel leaned back in his chair and closed his eyes.

"Looks bigger on paper, doesn't it?"

Dash stood before him, holding a to-go bag from Michael's, a meat and potatoes eatery in Commerce.

"Whatcha got in the bag?" Gabriel asked him.

"Two tuna sandwiches. Light mayo."

"No steak?"

"I did your heart a favor." Dash set a food carton down before his partner.

Gabriel flipped open the lid. "Not even potato salad."

"That's gratitude for you." Dash snorted and opened his own carton.

"What looks bigger?"

"The warehouse." Dash laughed. "You should have seen your face after the rats fell on you."

"Ha ha. If it had happened to you, you would have dove into the nearest acid bath."

Gabriel took a bite of his sandwich and gazed at the blueprint. He realized Dash was correct.

"It is bigger on paper. We walked every square inch of this place, didn't we?" He pointed his sandwich at the blueprint.

"Yeah, so?" Dash murmured as he chewed.

"Look at this." Gabriel set down his food and wiped his hands. "Do you remember this area here?"

He took a pencil and circled a fairly large area that jutted from the rest of the rectangular building.

Dash shook his head.

"Me neither. I don't remember making any turns. And look, here's obviously a bathroom. You remember seeing a bathroom on the north side of the warehouse?"

"I can't remember."

"Well, I do, and there was no bathroom."

"The area must have been blocked off," Dash said. "I wonder why."

Gabriel picked up the plans and folded them under his arm. "Let's find out."

∿ ∿ ∿

CHAPTER 26

The two detectives arrived in Canoga Park as the muted sun was setting. Traffic had been miserable with a multitude of accidents glutting the freeways. They ducked under the crime scene tape surrounding the warehouse and began walking its perimeter. When they reached the back, they noticed the square addition abutting an empty field.

Gabriel and Dash then returned to the front and entered the building, flipping on the lights. Much of the warehouse had been emptied by evidence collectors and then by the creditors who had made claims on the merchandise. Only a few lone stacks of boxes remained between the tall racks.

Gabriel unrolled the blueprints on the smooth, cold floor and then stood above them, studying the building. He nodded toward the north side of the structure.

"There should be a whole other area to the back left. The plans show the location as a separate suite of offices."

They walked north, their shoes making noises on the cement floor. Their trek was halted by what appeared to be the exterior wall.

"Should we call in a demo service?" Dash asked.

"No," Gabriel told him as he walked along the wall, running his hand along the plaster. He stopped at a pile of wooden pallets blocking his path. Upon closer inspection, Gabriel noticed that the pallets were neatly nailed together. Gabriel pushed his foot against the bottom pallet and found that it was on wheels.

"Give me a hand."

They pushed the stack of pallets, which rolled easily to one side, to reveal an ornately carved wooden door.

"Holy secret passage, Batman." Dash whistled and pulled out his .38.

Gabriel followed suit and pulled the Redhawk from its holster. The two detectives stood on either side of the door.

Dash whispered, "Samuels couldn't be in there. We've been crawling all over this building for days."

"Samuels!" Gabriel yelled anyhow. "Come out of there."

Gabriel regarded his partner and the two of them waited. No noise issued from behind the door. Gabriel tried the knob, but it was locked tight. He motioned to Dash who took a ready stance and aimed his firearm at the door. With his lips set in a determined line, Gabriel hauled out and kicked in the door. It flew open with a splintering sound.

Both detectives pitched to the side, guns focused, but were met only with darkness. With Dash covering him, Gabriel reached in his hand, searching for a light switch. He found one and flicked it on, jumping to the side again like a jackrabbit.

Nothing happened. Gabriel and Dash peeked inside.

A large room was bathed in soft light. A black bookshelf lined with sleeveless videotapes was mounted above a large color television upon which sat an old model VCR. The entertainment center faced a king-sized bed covered in crumpled, taupe silk sheets. Four fluffy down pillows in matching silk cases were plumped up against a carved headboard. Next to the bed, a small refrigerator hummed and a counter with a sink and two-burner stove stood next to that. A microwave sat on top with what appeared to be a half-cooked bag of popcorn still inside.

Gabriel's eyes panned across the room. The other side was decidedly less homey. Staring at it in mute fascination, Gabriel was reminded of a scene from a medieval depiction of hell. Manacles and chains hung from the walls near a four-poster double bed with cuffs at all four posts. A steel grid was positioned above the bed with various chains and ropes hanging down. The mattress was bare but marked with numerous brown stains. The wall behind the bed was blood-spattered. An arc of dried arterial splatter crisscrossed the ceiling.

A whoosh of air drifted past the detectives and they both ducked instinctively. A heater had come on and the cords hanging from the steel grid began swaying gently. Again, Gabriel was reminded of the Cloister and the swaying censer, the flapping robes.

Serious kicks. Real action.

Gabriel began moving through the room, gun drawn. The place had a strange toxic smell of burnt popcorn and a mix of something animal and chemical. A couple of video cameras were primed and ready, aimed at the soiled bondage bed. A solitary fly buzzed around a crumpled yellow blanket covered in hardened brown stains that lay on the floor next to the bed.

"Radio Ramirez," Gabriel told Dash quietly as he spied another closed door. As he moved toward it, his eyes were drawn to the numerous perversions in the room. Screwdrivers, drills, pliers and other tools were scattered on a carpet mottled with stains. A table held battery acid, hydrochloric acid, Drano, and syringes, reminding Gabriel of Ross's methamphetamine lab. Rubber tubing and various canisters held strange liquids and the bad odor was more palpable here. Hanging from one wall, was a paddle with a familiar circlet of nails on one end. The nails looked dark—used. Someone had been doing terrible, secretive things in here. A monster's private lair, thought Gabriel.

They'd found the killing room.

Despite the warehouse chill, perspiration beaded on Gabriel's forehead and his head felt dizzy from the smell. As Gabriel approached the pattern of dried blood on the wall, the droplets began to move and metamorphosed into a face—a rust red depiction of Andrew Pierce. Gabriel jerked his eyes away and looked back toward the closed door.

He heard Dash talking fast to Ramirez, who was responding by promising backup.

A droplet of sweat coursed down Gabriel's face, and he brushed it away. He stood to one side of the closed door and said, "Marc, you've got nowhere to run. Come out."

He waited. No answer, no noise. Gabriel looked back at Dash who nodded. Gabriel reached for the doorknob and this one turned in his grip. He pushed the door wide open, ready for anything, but nothing happened. Gabriel turned on the light and saw a bathroom decorated like a whore's boudoir. He saw his nervous reflection in a large gilded mirror hanging over a divan. The walls were covered in a brushed silk, padded fabric. The stark contrast between the rose-colored bathroom and the chamber of horrors struck Gabriel as freakish.

Dash crept up behind him. Ahead were a toilet, a bidet, and a large tub with a closed shower curtain. The two detectives exchanged knowing glances and Gabriel immediately swept back the shower curtain.

Their eyes were met only by a row of ladies underpants and thongs hanging on a line. Gabriel knelt down and checked the bottom of the bathtub for blood evidence. He saw a few strands of brown hair caught in the drain. The crime scene unit would perform a more diligent check.

"You gotta look at this," Dash said from behind.

Gabriel stood up and joined Dash at the marble countertop. Baskets were arranged one after the other, most of whose contents had been plundered. Still the detectives could see candy wrappers and gum, mints, mouthwash, toothpaste, brushes, condoms, sex aids, lotions and oils, and then an assortment of pills, bags of marijuana, rolling papers, and brown medicine vials half-filled with crystals and powder. Gabriel used a tissue to open one and inspected the contents.

"Meth," he murmured to Dash.

Get me some ice!

Hadn't that been Ross?

"This place is too much," Dash said. "A frigging pervert's paradise." He opened a cabinet under the sink and found a stack of clean yellow blankets. "Hey, check this out."

Lying atop the blankets was a wooden dowel. Remnants of baling wire were wound around both ends.

"For the garroting," Dash murmured.

"Let's grab our kits," Gabriel told him, meaning the evidence collection bags they carried in the car. He needed to get some air. "That's our smoking gun, right there."

"One of many." Dash picked up a vial of powder. "This should convince you that Ross was part of this after all."

Gabriel looked longingly at the exit. "Marc must have supplied Ross with drugs and, in exchange, Ross partnered with Marc."

I never hurt no one!

"This is ugly shit, you know what I mean?" Dash muttered, shaking his head. "I mean really twisted."

"I wonder where Tara is." Gabriel didn't even try to estrange himself from her, and Dash eyeballed him but said nothing. In the distance, they heard the howling of sirens. "Let's move."

The two detectives headed out of the bathroom when a firecracker pop split their ears, and instantaneously Dash was on the ground, writhing next to Gabriel and cursing in pain. Stunned, Gabriel looked up but saw nothing.

"My leg!" Dash yelled.

Willing himself to defrost, Gabriel pushed his partner into the cover of the bathroom. Dash's blood left a swath across the floor. Gabriel's eyes jerked around the room as he fumbled for his gun, his ears piqued for any sound.

"Marc?" he yelled and then dared to glance behind him at his partner. Dash was groaning holding a leg that was leaking red all over the bathroom floor. "Hang in there, Dash."

Holding the gun in one hand, Gabriel reached for his radio. "Officer down, Code Three" he said, and absently rambled off the location as his eyes riveted around the room. The dispatch officer crackled a response that help was already arriving. Gabriel barely understood; his senses were keen on finding where the shot had come from.

"Marc!" he yelled again into the large room. His eyes swiveled to the bookcase and then to a closed wardrobe. He began to make his way there when another shot rang out, and Gabriel heard a plunking sound as the plaster behind him was nailed with a bullet.

It's low, he thought frantically, and his eyes dropped in surprise to the silk-sheeted bed. A waft of gun smoke escaped from under the taupe skirting.

Jesus Christ he's been in here the whole time under the frigging bed!

Another shot rang out, and Gabriel jumped on the filthy bondage bed, knowing he was playing hell with evidence, but he couldn't risk getting shot in the ankles and going down. "Get your ass out of there, Samuels! Get it out now or so help me I'll shoot that bed into Swiss cheese. Toss your weapon out before you move!"

Silence. Only slight squeaks and gasps issued from Dash in the bathroom.

Gabriel licked his lips nervously and then stepped forward on the bed, which creaked dramatically. At once, a volley of shots rang out from under the other bed, ricocheting off the walls, chinking and overturning the tray of tools.

Gabriel didn't hesitate and emptied the chamber of his Redhawk into the silk-sheeted bed. His .44's plunged into the pillowcases, hurling white feathers toward the heavens. Finally, the smoke cleared and an unearthly silence fell like a pall. Goose down moved ethereally through the air.

"Gabe?" Dash called in agitation from the bathroom. "Answer me!"

"It's okay," Gabriel replied, not taking his eyes off the bed as he rapidly reloaded the cylinder. He carefully stepped down and walked gingerly toward the mauled, silky bed. Dropping down on all fours, Gabriel reached for the bed skirts, knowing any minute he might receive a bullet between the eyes.

Gabriel took hold of the fabric and realized blood was dripping from his shoulder. He felt no pain. The wonders of an adrenaline punch, he thought, and lifted the skirt. He saw a shock of brown curling hair and a limp arm. Gabriel positioned the gun against the head.

"You're finished, Marc. Crawl out of there, you piece of shit."

Marc didn't move. Gabriel grabbed his arm and pulled. Marc Samuels appeared halfway out from under the bed with blood pooling on his back. Gabriel stared at him for a moment and then heard Dash groan again. The sirens were loud now.

"They're comin' now, Dash. Hang on."

Gabriel pulled Marc out all the way and nudged him with the gun. "Marc, where's Tara? Where's your wife?" Gabriel pushed feathers from his face in frustration. "Damn it."

He walked over to the bathroom and caught sight of his bleeding shoulder in the gilded mirror. He set his gun down and hoisted Dash up to a sitting position. Gabriel fashioned a tourniquet from one of the yellow towels. "Like the fucking O.K. Corral, huh?"

Dash managed a weak smile, and Gabriel watched it transform into a mask of astonishment as he stared past Gabriel. "Look out!"

Gabriel turned around to see bloodied Marc smiling wickedly and leveling a gun at Gabriel's face.

"Fuck you," Marc said and pulled the trigger. The gun clicked—empty.

Gabriel lunged at Marc and pushed him out of the bathroom, but the other man held on like a half-dead heavyweight boxer clutching his opponent. Dash grappled with his gun, dragged his body to the open doorway, and took aim at Marc. He fired off a shot and Marc jerked, but held tight to Gabriel.

"Where's Tara?" Gabriel pressed.

Marc smiled through bloodied teeth. "I put her where you'll never find her."

The two men fell against the table holding various chemicals and Marc grabbed a small brown bottle. He tried pouring the contents on Gabriel, but Gabriel swatted the vial, and battery acid flew upwards. Marc screamed and went down on his knees, clutching his face. In one movement, he collapsed forward... dead.

Rapid footsteps sounded and two uniformed officers sprang into the room shouting warnings. Their words were lost on Gabriel. He was too busy watching the acid eat away Marc's good looks.

CHAPTER 27

Ming stood at the doorway of Gabriel's apartment, toting a bag of deli takeout and a prescription of antibiotics.

Mrs. McRay answered the door and smiled. "We've been expecting you. Come on in."

Ming entered Gabriel's apartment and was amused to see the feminine touch already permeating the bachelor pad. Fragrant flowers were arranged prettily in a vase on the coffee table and a tasteful cloth covered the small kitchen table. Gabriel ordinarily kept his kitchen clean enough, but today the counter and sink fairly sparkled.

"I see things are going nicely here."

"He's being taken care of," Mrs. McRay answered, taking the deli food into the kitchen.

"Of that I'm sure. Where is the Sun King?"

"Watching TV in bed."

"Didn't he give you the bedroom?"

"He tried, but I find the couch much more to my liking."

"That's a good lie."

"It has a comfortable mattress, really. I made us all lentil soup. Gabriel used to love it as a child..." Her voice trailed off.

Ming walked over and planted a kiss on her cheek. "It's good you are here for him, Mrs. McRay."

Gabriel's mother nodded. "Such a horrible thing to have happened, so frightening! What a dangerous profession he's in. His partner, thank goodness, is recuperating, from what I understand."

"Yeah," Ming grinned. "Dash is driving the hospital staff crazy. They'll need to be hospitalized themselves by the end of the week.

"At least he's with people. I can't imagine Gabriel being by himself. I know he was stabbed last summer and he recovered alone."

Ming felt her good mood slipping away. "He wasn't alone."

Mrs. McRay eyed her but didn't press the subject. "I'll be leaving soon—as soon as Gabriel's better. Janet, Gabriel's sister, is helping me out up north, but I've got to get back to my husband."

"Why doesn't Mr. McRay join you down here?"

The other woman paused, her back toward Ming. "Gabriel's father isn't well, Ming."

"May I ask what's wrong?"

Mrs. McRay faced her, holding soup bowls. "He's in the early stages of Alzheimer's. Janet and I both felt that he might not be able to be much support to Gabriel right now. And I came down here expressly for my son." She busied herself with setting the table.

Ming watched her, realizing where Gabriel got his strength. "Does Gabriel know?"

"No, no..." Mrs. McRay moved past Ming to the stove, stirring the soup. "He's got a lot on his plate right now. I'll tell him in time. Please don't mention it before I do."

"Of course not. I'm so sorry. They're making some positive headway with Alzheimer's medication. Please let me know if I can be of help."

Mrs. McRay turned toward Ming and gazed at her. "Thank you. Thank you for being here for my boy."

Ming nodded and shook the pill container. "I'm going to worship the Sun King for a while."

She wandered down the hallway, making tracks along the newly vacuumed runners. She knocked at Gabriel's door and went inside.

He lay on the bed. Under his shirt, a bandage was visible, taped to his muscular chest. His blue eyes had a glazed zombie look as they watched the television. Ming thought about Gabriel's father and wondered how Gabriel would react to the news.

Bolstering up her confidence, she announced, "Wake up, Oh Majestic One. I bring drugs."

Gabriel was galvanized then; he fumbled for the remote and immediately turned off a VCR player. Ming raised her eyebrows.

"Did I interrupt?"

Gabriel looked ashamed for a moment and then gestured toward a stack of videotapes neatly stacked in a cardboard box near the TV. "Not for civilized eyes."

Ming shook her head at him. "You never quit, do you?" She sat on the bed. "You need rest, Gabriel."

He noticed the prescription bottle. "Painkillers?"

"I'm not that generous. I refilled your antibiotic prescription. Lucky for you the bullet passed right through. We're entering it into evidence in case you want to know. I think I'll wear it as a lucky charm."

"You're weird," he said, taking the prescription from her.

Ming's eyes traveled warily to the box of videos, a hellish Pandora's box. "Speaking of weird. What's in there?"

Gabriel returned his gaze to the now black television screen. "So far I've only seen Lena Dobbs. Hers was the most recent video."

Ming looked ominously toward the TV as if it were a venomous snake about to strike. "You're not going to watch them all, are you?"

"Someone has to."

"But it's over," Ming told him squarely and then her shoulders slumped in defeat. "I guess you think you can find something in there that will tell you where she is, huh?"

Gabriel didn't answer. He tossed the remote onto his nightstand. "You're staying for dinner, right?"

The only thing worse than breaking up, thought Ming, was playing pretend at a relationship that was already over.

"I don't think so," Ming told him.

He looked patently disappointed. She was disappointed too. It was cold outside, and Ming could think of nothing better she'd like to do than to eat Mom's soup and snuggle for hours under Gabriel's good arm.

"I don't want to be just your friend," she said.

Ming stood up and Gabriel took hold of her wrist. "What makes you think I'd only want to be friends with you?"

"The way you could toss us aside and go for her."

Gabriel reflected on that, but said nothing. Still, he wouldn't let go of Ming's wrist.

Ming held her ground. "Do you still have feelings for her?"

"No, not like you think. She was just so... frail, Ming. She was looking for protection. Now she could be in a trunk somewhere like Malcolm Dobbs."

Ming nodded. "I know. And I know you'll use every effort to find her."

"She thought she would be safe with me..." Gabriel let his voice trail off.

"I'm sure she did." Ming gazed at him wistfully. "I know I do."

Gabriel met her eyes.

Ming gently pulled her wrist from his grasp. "The thing is, I don't like the shape of my romantic relationship to be in a triangle. I prefer a one on one." She grinned. "A Juan on Juan."

"What?" Gabriel asked.

"Nothing." Ming kissed the top of his head and then moved to the door. "Your mother is trying hard to do right by you. It's obvious to me she loves you very much. You're a lucky man, Gabriel." She gave him a sad smile and slipped out of the room.

🎄 🎄 🎄

Festive decorations didn't mesh well with the pictures of victims and crime scenes hanging on the walls of the homicide bureau, so the Christmas party was held at headquarters in Monterey Park.

Usually, Gabriel volunteered to work around Christmas and be the one left in Commerce to answer the phones. This time, however, everyone knew his mother was in town, (knowledge Gabriel was sure that Ming had spread), and his coworkers urged him to bring Mom to the party.

It would be the first Christmas Gabriel had spent with any member of his family in over fifteen years. A large tree festooned the small lobby and tables were laid with a variety of food, drink, and decorations. Someone had put on a generic Christmas CD, and "Holly Jolly Christmas" played. Detectives from the contract cities of the Sheriff's Department, such as the Malibu substation, joined the party to celebrate the closing of the Samuels case.

For Gabriel, their presence was a constant reminder that one part of the case remained open. They had not found Tara, and Gabriel burned with many unanswered questions. Why did she lie to him? Why fantasize about her past? Was she alive? If he'd used Tara to work out his own problems, was he now responsible for her predicament?

When the other officers shook his hand and made jokes about Marc the Model being reduced to Marc the Mush, Gabriel averted his eyes and frowned.

Watching the grisly video of Lena hadn't helped his holiday spirit either. Marc had been rather careful to keep himself out of the spotlight. He obviously preferred to see his victims surprised, scared, or begging for their lives on camera. The next tape he'd watched seemed almost innocuous by comparison. Marc had taken a video of Malcolm cuffing Lena to the bondage bed, which had a clean yellow blanket tucked over the telltale stained mattress beneath. She had been giggling, obviously drunk. Malcolm had been like a child with a new toy. Neither of them had had any idea what was in store for them.

Gabriel, having the unenviable privilege of sharing in Marc's dark entertainment, witnessed the game plan unfold. Playful nips and tickles had turned sadistic, although Lena didn't appear to mind. Then the sound of gunfire rang out with a close-up of Lena's tormented face as she watched her husband die off camera. Her shrieking and then her petrified silence as her husband's killer walked toward her and said, "Now that he's out of the way, we can have us some real fun."

Gabriel took a deep breath and leaned against a fake holly garland someone had taped to the wall. His eyes scanned the room and finally came to rest upon Ming.

She had pulled her long hair up into a French twist and wore a red velvet dress that hugged her curves and lit up her café-au-lait skin. She was animated tonight, talking easily with everyone, so opposite of somber Gabriel. If he allowed himself, Gabriel knew he could get caught up in Ming's joviality and by doing so, his spirits would lift. He did manage to return a smile as she waved to him. She had his mother by the hand and was introducing her to the group.

"How's your wound?" Dr. B appeared at Gabriel's side, holding a glass cup of pink punch with something frothy floating in it.

"Healing. How is Isaac? Is he home for the holidays?"

"You must be feeling better. You always ask about my son when—"

"When I can give my own head problems a rest. I'm a selfish bastard, I know."

"Selfish people wouldn't even bother to ask. Isaac is fine. I have to control myself from overwhelming him with things to do together and places to go."

"Home is a place to chill out, Raymond. Keep that in mind."

"I've missed him." Dr. B sipped his drink and then looking past Gabriel, said, "Well, what do you know?"

Gabriel turned to see Ramirez enter in a cheap but pressed suit, and at his heels was a small, dark-haired woman. Behind them walked two teenagers, a boy and girl, carrying in large trays of steaming tamales.

Ramirez motioned to the kids to put the trays on a table. He caught sight of Dr. B and Gabriel, and guided his family over to the two men.

"McRay, Doc..." the lieutenant nodded brusquely.

Gabriel could sense a disjointed nervousness about his superior, and that gave him a small sense of satisfaction.

"This is my wife, Pilar."

The woman didn't offer a handshake, but she nodded agreeably, smiling. She was attractive, and Gabriel could tell Ramirez was proud of her in a secretive sort of way.

"She made these tamales. It's a holiday tradition in Mexico."

"I can't wait to try them," Gabriel said. He could not remember a time when the lieutenant referred so openly to his heritage. Gabriel wondered what made Ramirez decide to unlock the door of his private life.

"Yeah, it took her all night to prepare these for you bozos."

"No..." Mrs. Ramirez shook her head shyly. "Not all night." She smiled again and positioned her son and daughter in front of her. "This is my daughter, Jessica, and my son, Francisco. You can call him Paco."

"Pleased to meet you, Paco." Gabriel shook the boy's hand. Dr. B repeated the gesture. The two men nodded a greeting to Jessica.

"Paco here is going to be a real doctor when he grows up," Ramirez told them and then eyed Dr. B. "One that heals real wounds."

Dr. B grimaced at Ramirez, who smiled mischievously and continued. "These two are gonna support their old man, right?" Ramirez clapped their shoulders and then turned to another officer. "Hey, *vato*, have a tamale." He then directed his children's gazes back toward Gabriel. "Watch out for this one. What he has might be contagious."

Gabriel rolled his eyes. Dr. B shook his head.

Ramirez leaned close to Gabriel and whispered, "Listen, stay away from tall buildings. You know what they say about depressed people during the holidays." He lifted his finger into the sky and then plunged it downward with a whistle.

"Thanks for the advice," Gabriel said, and Ramirez, satisfied, blustered off, his family in tow.

"He's in fine form tonight," Dr. B said. "He must be feeling especially insecure."

"It's a vitamin to him." Gabriel watched Ramirez harangue another colleague.

Dr. B nodded. "Miguel will never suffer a heart attack. He'll just give them to everyone else. Speaking of heart attacks, I think I'm going to chug more of this liquid ice cream."

Dr. B headed for the punch bowl while Gabriel walked over to his mother and Ming, who chatted with Rick Frasier, a boyish blond detective whose preppie attire never ceased to irritate the rest of the crew.

As Mrs. McRay talked with Rick, Ming pulled Gabriel aside. "Are you still watching those tapes?"

"I've managed to get through one and a half. Hard to stomach, I'll tell you."

"You have another notch on your stick, Gabriel. You brought Marc Samuels down."

Gabriel leveled his gaze at her. "Spend Christmas with us, Ming."

Ming shook her head again, but Gabriel could see in her eyes that she wanted to. Let her be, he told himself. Let her go.

Gabriel glanced up to see Ramirez approaching his mother. "Uh, oh. I'd better intervene." He looked back at Ming. "You look beautiful."

She nodded sadly and watched him go.

His mother wanted to return home by the New Year. Now that Gabriel's arm was sufficiently healed and they were on good speaking terms, Mrs. McRay felt it was time to get home. The day after a quiet Christmas, she set her clothes out on the coffee table and packed her one suitcase.

"You can come up anytime," she told her son. "To see Janet and her family, you know."

Gabriel sat next to a small tree that his mother had adorned with twinkling lights. Blue, red, and green colors shone in an alternating pattern against the black of Gabriel's hair. "I guess

I could take a few days off and do that. Why didn't Dad come down?"

Mrs. McRay lowered her eyes. "I guess this is as good a time as any to tell you. Dad's ill, Gabe. He's got Alzheimer's."

Gabriel was felled, unable to speak. He watched his mother pack, again struck by her strength.

"How long?" Gabriel finally asked.

"We noticed his symptoms getting worse this last year." She stopped packing. "I have a confession to make. I wanted to try to work things out with you so that you could have a meaningful dialogue with your father while he..." She sighed. "While he still could."

Gabriel shook his head in disbelief.

"He's well taken care of, Gabriel."

"You're not going to handle this all by yourself, are you?"

"We're fine. I only want you to be able to talk to him, that's all."

His mother so reminded him of Ming, endeavoring always to be strong.

Gabriel sat on the couch with his head in his hands. So much time had gone by. So much time had been wasted, and now he would be robbed of his father. Now he knew why his mother had sent him the navy coat. His father! What a terrible fate to endure. Gabriel had heard stories of untold frustration and anger bent against family members, frustration from forgetting. And with the loss of memories came the inevitable loss of self. Gabriel was reminded of Lynn Traxler and how she had asked him if he had ever lost someone to drugs. What about to disease?

I don't have a lot of time.

Gabriel rose from the couch and walked over to his mother. "Ma, how much is Janet able to help you?"

"Oh, lots. She's got the kids, of course, but..."

"And she works, too, right?"

"No, she volunteers—"

"Janet needs to spend time with her own kids."

Mrs. McRay turned around and faced her son. "What are you getting at, Gabe?"

"I can talk more about it when I visit you."

She smiled widely. "You're coming? Dad will like that."

He drew his arms around his mother. "I'm here now, okay?"

She hugged him tightly and a strange sort of contentment washed over Gabriel; a contentment borne out of being needed.

CHAPTER 28

It was late when Gabriel returned from the airport. The apartment still glistened from his mother's presence but felt empty. The colored lights on the tree did their holiday best to cheer him, but Gabriel felt a pang of sadness and realized he missed her. Soon, a new year would begin and he had to be sure to keep his resolutions. Gabriel was going to pay more attention to his family. His father needed him.

Gabriel grabbed a soda from the refrigerator and noticed many neat foil-wrapped bundles of food. For once, Gabriel had let someone else do the cooking, and his mother had made her old standbys.

He wandered down the hall, passed the bathroom, and then steadfastly backtracked and inspected the shower. He entered his bedroom and opened the closet door. No monsters under the bed. No blond wraith-like women either.

A chair thudded from the upstairs apartment and the sound of laughter drifted down. The neighbors were in the holiday party spirit. Gabriel was comforted by the sounds of people surrounding him. He turned around and his sense of comfort faded. Across the bedroom floor stood the box of videos, waiting for him.

Gabriel pulled a video from the middle of the stack and pushed it into the VCR. He sat on the edge of his bed, holding the remote, and pressed 'play.'

Ming returned home to her Los Feliz house, tired. Catastrophes didn't take off for holidays and Ming had spent the entire day working at the hospital. Only one person would have kept her from her job, but he had spent the holiday alone with his mother.

Ming craved a little R&R and when the phone rang, she was annoyed to hear Ron Goldring, the entomologist, on the phone.

"You weren't at your office," Ron scolded.

"I just left. I don't live there, you know."

Ron Goldring was a dedicated scientist like herself. He wasn't bad looking either, for an overweight forty-something divorcee.

"Want to go to a New Year's Eve party with me in Holmby Hills? Big bash at a doctor's place." He croaked a nervous laugh. "You gotta see this house, Ming. It's huge. I hear he's going to have buckets of Veuve Clicquot and lobsters, all you can eat. Want to come?"

None of that impressed Ming, but she weighed her options. Talks with Ron were not a waste of time. He liked bugs and Ming needed to broaden her entomology horizons.

"No thanks," she said, finally.

"Really?" Ron sounded disappointed and then he said in a voice tinged with vengeance, "So, how did you feel when you saw you were off your mark?"

Ming was too worn out to play touché with Ron Goldring. "What are you talking about?"

"That's really why I called. I sent you the Lena Dobbs report by e-mail and snail mail. Obviously, you didn't get either."

"What do you mean I was off my mark?"

Ron seemed to relent a little. "Ah, I'm just giving you a hard time. Rejection, you know. My bruised ego."

Ming was not amused. "How was I off my mark?"

"No biggie, Dr. Li. You were off by twenty-four hours, that's all. Blame it on Sarcophaga Haemorrhoidalis."

Ming sighed, waiting.

"The red-tailed flesh fly. See Ming, you estimated the instars, quite accurately I might add, of the common blowfly. But the blowfly isn't what we're dealing with."

Ming dragged a chair toward her and sat down. "Explain."

"No offense, Ming, but the sample of adult flies you sent looked different from the common blowfly. Our red-tailed flesh fly friends have an abdomen ending in an obvious red speck. You missed that."

"I must have had something on my mind that day." Ming mentally kicked herself for not being more observant. But hadn't that been her pattern of late? She knew darn well what had occupied her thoughts each and every minute of the day for weeks: Gabriel McRay.

"No problem," Ron said genially. "That's what I'm here for. Uh, you sure you don't want to come to that party?"

"I'm sure."

"Oh. Anyhow, the female flesh fly appears on early and advanced stages of decomposition and skips the egg life cycle completely. In other words, the female deposits larva, which go directly into the pupal stage. That's why you were off by twenty-four hours. You counted in the egg stage and the subsequent development time."

Ming listened to Ron Goldring's words, trying to do the math in her head without her notes. She thanked Ron, told him to have a good time on New Year's Eve, and hung up. She stared at the phone as the news sunk in. After a moment, she quickly dialed Gabriel's number.

Paula May was chained to the bondage bed, naked. The games had gone beyond fun at the time Marc started taping, and the girl was looking haggard and ill-used. A pulsing rap song played, but Gabriel plainly heard Paula, as she looked at something off-camera.

"It's not funny anymore, Marc! You're hurting me."

Gabriel steeled himself for the inevitable torture. He could make out murmuring voices behind the music. Curious, Gabriel tried to see beyond the frame of the camera. In the few videos he had watched, he had never seen a glimpse of Ross.

I never hurt no one.

Again Gabriel's ears caught wisps of conversation off-camera. With a patient, pounding heart, he turned the volume up and waited.

A nude Marc Samuels stepped into the picture. Gabriel couldn't help but notice his toned physique. Marc aimed his penis at Paula and said, "You dirty little slut. You'll look better with my piss on your face."

A truly miserable look washed over Paula's features as she pleaded, "No, Marc, come on. Oh, yuck!"

Gabriel realized his fingernails were digging into his palms and stopped clenching his fist.

Filthy, filthy, filthy!

Gabriel heard the phone ring and answered it.

"Hello?"

"It's me," Ming told him. "What day was Ross arrested?"

"Why?"

On the video Paula was suffering abject humiliation.

"It's important."

Gabriel closed his eyes, trying to remember. "Thursday. We arrested him on a Thursday morning."

Ming didn't speak.

"Why?" Gabriel repeated.

"Lena Dobbs. I thought she'd been killed and dumped at the Paramount Ranch on Wednesday, but I was wrong."

Gabriel opened his eyes and saw Marc slap Paula across the face. He was barking orders to her, unintelligible to Gabriel while he was on the phone.

"I-I don't understand, Ming."

"Lena was killed late Thursday and Ross was already in custody."

"So? Marc disposed of her alone."

"If Lena was killed in the car before she was dumped, Marc wouldn't have been alone. Three people in the Mercedes, remember?"

Gabriel silently turned toward the video where Paula was looking at something off-camera again, fear growing in her eyes.

"If Ross wasn't in the car," Ming said, "then who was?"

Gabriel's eyes, glued to the television, widened as another person walked into view.

"That's right," he heard Marc say gleefully. "Get dirty, you bitches."

Tara Samuels, wearing only pink lace panties, sat lovingly next to a soiled Paula and kissed her mouth.

"My God," Gabriel whispered.

❧ ❧ ❧

Tara Samuel's status went from a missing person to fugitive on the run, and Tara had been afforded a lot of time to run.

Gabriel's mind was reeling as he sat in Ramirez's office. Next to him sat Dr. B.

"What about Ross?" Ramirez asked Gabriel, staring at his pack of cigarettes. "What about the baling wire and the syringe found at Wagon Wheel?"

"She supplied the baling wire," Gabriel told him and felt his stomach turn at each word. "She planted the syringe. The Traxlers told me they never saw Marc Samuels at the stables, but Tara was there—plenty; and Ross was interested in her."

Ramirez finally reached into his pack and pulled out a Winston. "Sorry, McRay. I can only imagine what you're going through."

Gabriel didn't reply. In his mind's eye, he replayed another tape he had watched. This one had featured Regina Faulkner with a gag between her teeth and her arms shackled. Tara had been an enthusiastic lesbian lover.

"She came over one time with blood on her neck," Gabriel admitted stonily. "She told me it was a scratch. Now I would lay bets it wasn't even her blood." He looked at Dr. B. "What did she want from me?"

Dr. B shrugged. "Maybe it was a mix of things, Gabe. Could be she wanted protection from Marc. You did say she had a black eye."

"Yeah, the maid said Samuels hit his wife." Ramirez kept his eyes on his unlit cigarette.

"Could be a subconscious part of her wanted out and she saw you as an escape route," Dr. B continued. "Or maybe she used you to keep tabs on the investigation."

Gabriel tried to ignore the fact he might have been used. He focused on the scenario of Marc being abusive instead. "Why not just leave him? Or make an anonymous call to the police?"

Gabriel knew he sounded naive, but he couldn't help it. He had been so blind. He had been so used.

Dr. B looked sympathetically at Gabriel. "From what you've told me of Tara's background, it sounds as if she had low self-esteem and lived in a fantasy world, and she slept with a lot of men because she craved their affections." Dr. B paused, thinking. "Take a strong personality like Marc Samuels: good-looking, ambitious; he offers Tara what she doesn't have: riches and security. She's thrilled to have the attention of such a man. She'll do anything to keep him. Meanwhile, Marc Samuels is narcissistic, a very important characteristic here. If you mix narcissism with the need to control and be the center of attention, and add to that high intelligence plus violent sexual sadism, you get a very dangerous brew."

"We know about Samuels," Ramirez said. "Who we don't know is his wife."

Dr. B raised a warning finger. "Knowing Marc Samuels is the key to knowing his wife. Men like Marc start out pretending to be normal, but slowly they bring their wives into their perverse sexual lifestyles. At first Tara probably felt that Marc's dark side was very exciting."

Gabriel looked away. In his mind, he saw her hypnotic eyes. *We can play a game.*

Dr. B's audible sigh broke the stillness. "I should have questioned Tara's possible involvement once we suspected Marc. A man with Marc's traits wouldn't keep his secrets to himself for very long. He would need a lackey to support his grandiose self-perception."

"If anyone should have been clued into Tara Samuels, it was me," Gabriel admitted. "Only I could never read her. I guess I didn't want to." He glanced at Ramirez, sure his superior would take the opportunity to berate him, but Ramirez said nothing.

"Sex is an easy place to stay damaged," Dr. B said, almost to himself. "Our bodies are turned on while our minds our turned off."

Both Ramirez and Gabriel gave him a surprised look.

"In abusive situations," Dr. B continued thoughtfully. "The men make all the decisions and isolate their wives or girlfriends. Did Tara have any friends?"

"Not that I know of," Gabriel answered, still wondering if Dr. B's previous statement about sex had been about Tara or about him.

"Marc needed to be the sole person in her life. He becomes the center of her universe and she eventually finds herself doing things she never dreamed of doing before. Marc probably convinced Tara that in order to keep him, she would have to procure 'slaves' whenever he got bored or distracted, slaves like Paula May and Regina Faulkner."

Ramirez nodded at Gabriel. "Yeah, don't you remember that shelter volunteer saying that Regina had a role model, a friend that influenced her? Could it have been Mrs. Samuels?"

"Quite possibly," Dr. B replied for Gabriel.

Unbelievable, Gabriel thought. How could he have not seen her double life?

Because you thought she was a victim and you mistakenly identified with her.

But it was more than that. The need to dominate, wanting to be Tara's protector... Gabriel had subconsciously been doing all he could to be anybody but Andrew's victim.

"You'd have to think like Tara thinks," Dr. B said. "Inside Tara knows what she's doing is wrong, but Marc, who Tara worships, says it's okay. Tara has shown she's got a penchant for putting on rose-colored glasses. Look what she told you about the 'mansion' she lived in, the high-society family she sprung from. I'm sure she rectified the killings in her mind." Dr. B's wire rims slipped and he pushed the glasses back into place. "Now I think I know why Lena was shot and not garroted like the other women."

"Why?" Ramirez asked, fingering the unlit cigarette.

"Because Marc and Tara took a big chance on the Dobbs. This was a successful, wealthy couple, not the usual young wannabe. Since the pattern was skewed, Marc decided to dispose of them differently. You see, strangulation is a very personal way to kill. Malcolm and Lena were both shot to death, much more impersonal. That tells me the killer couple might have been subconsciously intimidated by the Dobbs."

"The killer couple?" Gabriel hung his head.

Ramirez finally lit up and then shook the match out. "McRay, let someone else track down Mrs. Samuels."

"No way."

"You sure you're up for this? I mean, she kind of played you for a *payaso*."

"A what?"

"A chump, McRay." Ramirez dragged deeply on the Winston.

CHAPTER 29

Gabriel wandered Abbot Kinney in the rain. A few cars rumbled over the wet, dark asphalt of the street. As he walked the row of cafés and specialty shops, Gabriel went over every word he could remember exchanging with Tara.

I feel safe with you...

Did she? Or did she simply want to glean information from the lead investigator on the case?

She played you for a chump, McRay.

And he'd acted like a chump. Had Marc put her up to it? The more Gabriel thought about it, the more convinced he was that Marc had pulled the strings. Still, Tara might have been reaching out to Gabriel from the crevice of her dark existence. If so, would she have left him a clue?

Gabriel paused near a bar; wondering if a drink might help sort his thoughts. His cell phone rang. It was Ming.

"I wanted to see how you are."

"I'm in Venice."

"I didn't say 'where' you are, Detective."

"Oh. Where are you?"

He heard Ming sigh. "Obviously not on your planet."

Gabriel shook his head. "I'm sorry."

"What are you doing in Venice?"

"Walking around. I can't seem to stay in one place. I keep trying to make sense of that fact that... Ming, I'm so sorry."

She was quiet for a moment and then said, "Hey, you acted the way any guy would. She was beautiful."

Ming waited for his response, but Gabriel made no reply.

"I'm sorry I didn't catch the fly discrepancy," Ming said tersely. "It was my job to tell you that Ross couldn't have part-nered with Marc the night Lena was killed. I've been kicking myself all—"

"For God's sake, how can you work with me?"

Dark clouds rolled above Gabriel's head and he looked up into their rapidly moving depths.

I hate the winter.

"I like working with you," Ming said softly.

"Ming," Gabriel said suddenly. "Have you ever heard of movie called '10?'"

"What?"

A passing car sprayed oily water near Gabriel, but he didn't care. "I think it's set in Mexico."

❧   ❧   ❧

Ming stood in Gabriel's bedroom and watched as he packed his duffel bag.

"You're crazy. She could be anywhere! Why do you have to go to the ends of the earth?"

"I know where she is."

"She's a manipulative killer." Ming was at his heels as he moved around the room. "And she knows how to manipulate you. Let someone else go. If you think you've got a lead, then let Ramirez follow it."

"I've got to do it."

"Now I know," Ming said sullenly.

"You know what?"

"How women become idiots for the men in their lives. Look at her, look what she became. Look at me. I can't stand this anymore. Why do I have to love you?"

Gabriel regarded Ming. She had never told him she loved him. He walked toward her, but she retreated from him.

"I wanted to celebrate the New Year together," Ming said, wringing her hands. "Make a new start of things."

"We will. New Year's Eve, we'll start over."

"How? You're going to another country."

Ming backed against the wall, looking as vulnerable as a wounded fawn. Gabriel went over to her. He put both hands on the wall, trapping her between his arms.

Looking her in the eye, he asked, "Does one night mean that much to you?"

"It means that much to me."

He nodded. "Then I won't be late."

Gabriel backed away, took up his duffel bag, and walked out the door.

The plane to Mexico appeared to be second-hand and the cabin smelled of stale food with a slight hint of insecticide. The turbulence over Baja California caused the plane to shake, rattle, and roll. Yet despite the dingy outward appearance, the stewards were well dressed and courteous.

And all that glitters isn't gold, thought Gabriel.

The plane made an easy landing on a single airstrip bordered by the Pacific Ocean on one side and a mango plantation on the other. The heat blasted Gabriel as he exited the plane, eighty degrees with eighty percent humidity. The sweat began percolating on his forehead and under his arms as he stood outside in a single line awaiting the immigration desk. Mosquitoes battled around him as Gabriel flagged down a cab and headed for the beach resort of Las Hadas.

Gabriel had picked Las Hadas, despite its expense, because the resort had been featured in the Dudley Moore movie, "10." If Tara didn't like winter, this was the place to be. The ocean breeze sent the mosquitoes adrift, and from Gabriel's room he could see the warm ocean and a marina filled with yachts.

After changing into shorts and a T-shirt, Gabriel wandered into the large lobby. Twin statues of fairies, *las hadas*, kept watch over a sign that advertised a gala New Year's Eve bash. Gabriel wondered if, indeed, he would be able to apprehend Tara and still make it back to meet Ming's deadline. It was silly for Ming to impose such a thing on him, but Gabriel understood her reasoning. She was testing his love for her. This time, he could not fail her.

Gabriel approached the hotel manager and showed him Tara's picture, but neither the manager nor the concierge recognized the pretty *"rubia,"* or blonde.

Unfazed, Gabriel walked outside to the pool, past the sunbathers with their dark tans, bikinis, and gold watches. He gratefully downed a Margarita and a free shot of Patron tequila (for being a gringo cop), but both the bartender and the guy manning the towel booth had never seen Tara.

Gabriel walked down to the marina, peering onto the luxury crafts, thinking he might spot her resting onboard. He saw a couple of pretty women, but neither were Tara.

That night, Gabriel found himself walking the main street of Manzanillo, the city nearest the resort. A musical group played on a bandstand surrounded by dancing young couples. The sound of laughter and whistles filled the starry evening.

The smell of barbeque drifted toward him, and Gabriel's stomach rumbled in response. He'd been warned by Ramirez to put a lot of lime on the food as a natural disinfectant and to eat "where there were lots of people and the chef was cooking up a storm."

Gabriel followed his nose to a crowded taco stand called Tacos Ramon. He ordered tacos *al pastor* and two bottles of beer. He sat down at a wobbling metal table and watched the happy folks revel in the street. After finishing his meal, Gabriel pulled out his cell phone and made a call to Seattle. After greeting his mother, he asked to speak with his father.

Gabriel gazed at the empty beer bottles and crumbled the tortilla crumbs before him. He heard the phone being passed around and then a man's throat cleared.

"Hallo?"

"Hey, Dad. It's Gabriel."

"Well!" He heard his father happily tell his mother that it was Gabriel on the line. "Gabriel, how are you? You still with the police force?"

"Still with the police force." Gabriel bit his lower lip. "How are you?"

"Oh, you know, I'm hanging on like always. Gosh, it's great to hear from you. How the heck are you?"

"Good. I'm actually calling you from Mexico."

"Mexico! How do you like that?" Gabriel heard his father tell his mother that Gabriel was in Mexico. "Watch out for those pretty senoritas, son. Whew! I was in Mexico in '68 with a bunch of friends and whew, I tell you it was some time…"

"I'd like to hear about it," Gabriel said, squishing the tortilla bits with his thumb.

"Let me tell you, it was some time. Well, it's really nice to hear your voice. So, are you still with the police force?"

Gabriel swallowed a lump forming in his throat. "Yeah."

"Well, that's just fine, just fine. When are we going to see you?"

"When I'm finished here, I'm going to visit you and Ma. Would you like that?"

"Would I like that? Of course, I would!"

When Gabriel hung up a few moments later, he paid his bill and walked down to the beach. Shedding his sandals, he waded into the dark water. He stood there and let the surf caress his legs as he thought about the lost years.

Close to midnight, Gabriel drifted into a nightclub and watched the couples dance from a safe position at the bar. He ordered a Don Julio and silently toasted Ming.

Had he truly broken her strong spirit? He hadn't even told her that he loved her back. He wouldn't even give her that much strength to go on. His father, Ming... How much did he extract from those closest to him? Too much, thought Gabriel.

A balding little man wearing a dapper suit took a place at the bar next to Gabriel.

"Lots of hotties here tonight, huh, my friend?" His accent was more Persian than Mexican.

Gabriel nodded genially.

"Hey, what's up with you?" the man nudged Gabriel. "How come you don't have a woman with you? Me? I got three hotties here tonight." The little man nodded to the barkeep. "One *vino tinto*, one champagne, and one vodka with soda." He smiled at Gabriel. "I can barely keep up with all my women."

"Don Juan," Gabriel murmured behind the loud music.

"Excuse me? My English is no good."

Gabriel shook his head and watched the bartender fill the man's drinks. An idea struck him and he said to the little man, "You know a lot of women around here?"

"My name is Emil and a lot of women know me!"

Gabriel dug in his pocket for Tara's photo. "Emil, you ever see this woman?"

Emil's thick eyebrows rose approvingly. "She's some beauty. You know I saw a hottie like that in Barra de Navidad."

"You sure?"

"How could I miss her? Every man in the street nearly fell over when she walked by."

The following afternoon, Gabriel sat under the *palapa* of a beach café called Panchos. His bare feet rested in the sand that made up the giant coastal bank of Barra de Navidad, so named by the Spanish explorer whose ship nearly capsized on the sandbar one long ago Christmas day.

On the rough wood table before Gabriel sat a plate of spicy shrimp, *coctel de pulpo*, or octopus salad, and a basket of tortillas. Beyond the sand, the warm Pacific beckoned lazily.

Despite the paradise surrounding him, Gabriel felt frustrated and guilty. Tara could be anywhere in the world. Barra was a small village, a couple of quiet streets really. Gabriel had haunted the beach all day long, showing Tara's picture to tourists and to the vendors that walked the hot sand and hawked bead necklaces and hammocks.

Nobody recognized Tara. No one admitted knowing her. Gabriel was a cop with a badge, after all, and most cops in Mexico were looked upon with fear and distrust. Gabriel might also be an abusive American husband tracking down an estranged wife. People kept quiet. If they only knew the truth, thought Gabriel.

Tonight was New Year's Eve. Gabriel had booked a late plane flight back to Los Angeles, but dreaded leaving without some sort of closure. He hated loose ends.

After viewing a dramatically red sunset, Gabriel walked through the sleepy village one more time. He wandered down a dusty residential street and tried to convince himself that Tara had disappeared for good. He needed to get on that plane and let someone else handle the fugitive.

Gabriel paused near an abandoned construction site, some investor's half-done dream of a condominium complex, now left to rot away. All that remained were stubby gray concrete slabs, one on top of the other, with rusting rebar sticking out everywhere.

A new SUV swerved onto the dirt road, kicking up dust. The driver talked animatedly on his cell phone. The tires skidded suddenly and the SUV went into a shallow ditch.

"Nice going." Gabriel shook his head in amusement at the driver who hopped out to survey the damage and, unbelievingly, didn't end his phone call.

Gabriel's eyes dropped to the cell phone clasped to his shorts. Slowly, he released it and dialed Tara's number. To his surprise, it rang. Gabriel hung up and on the edge of the disconnection; he could swear he heard a separate ringing. Gabriel redialed and this time held his own phone away from him. Again, the echo of another phone rang nearby. He followed the sound and ended up standing outside the wrought-iron gate of a small bungalow that fronted the beach. Gabriel ended his call, and the ringing from inside the house ceased.

His heart pounded. He heard a woman's familiar voice talking in Spanish, and Gabriel ducked behind a large palm tree. Rosa, holding a canvas bag of groceries, approached with another Hispanic woman.

Rosa entered the house and said "adios" to her companion, who bypassed Gabriel without a glance.

Gabriel waited until the street was empty, weighing his options. Technically, Tara was a fugitive and Gabriel was out of his jurisdiction. He should alert the Manzanillo police.

Tenant and the FBI needed to be notified to begin extradition proceedings. He knew he should call Ramirez immediately.

Instead, Gabriel snuck into the house.

It was very simple and small. Maybe two bedrooms, Gabriel thought as he crossed the white marble floor. He saw Rosa busying herself in the kitchen and he darted across the entry hall to a sliding glass door. Outside, a small patio faced the ocean. In the dusk, the sand looked like blue-patterned glass and the water, not yet moonlit, undulated softly, secretively, unwilling to provide Gabriel with any clues. An evening breeze played with his dark hair. Gabriel quietly reentered the house and peered into the kitchen. The groceries lay half-bagged on the counter. Rosa was nowhere in sight.

Gabriel turned around and saw the housekeeper standing a few feet away. She held a butcher knife. Gabriel's hand automatically went for his holster, but froze when he remembered he was armed with only shorts and a T-shirt.

"What are you going to do, Rosa?" he asked calmly.

Her mouth was set in a tight line, but her eyes were wide and frightened. She raised the knife, and it trembled in the air.

Suddenly, Gabriel smelled lavender. A cool hand crept serpent-like around his neck from behind and caressed him. He jumped forward, practically into Rosa's blade. He turned to see Tara Samuels smiling opposite him, wearing a black bikini. Gabriel was sandwiched between the two women: one a petrified housekeeper, and the other, a tranquil-scented killer. He waited for one of them to make a move.

Tara took the knife from Rosa and then looked at Gabriel. Clouds seemed to float across the sky blue of her eyes. She wore that trippy, dazed look that frightened Gabriel more than the knife in her hand.

"You should leave, Rosa," Tara said as she kept her eyes pinned on Gabriel.

Without another word, Rosa fled through the front door.

Tara put one arm around Gabriel's waist. Her other hand ran the knife up and down his torso. "You found me. I'm glad."

"I've come to take you home." Gabriel shifted his eyes downward, watching the knife skate along his shirt.

"I can't imagine what you think of me, running out on you like that."

Gabriel slowly moved his hand toward the blade. "Why don't you give me this and we'll talk about it?"

A seductive smile crept over her face. Instantly, Tara Samuels did an about-face and walked rapidly away from Gabriel. Stunned, he strode after her.

"Tara!"

She turned right and ducked into a room. Gabriel quickly moved to the doorway and saw her lie across a king-sized bed. She stretched out, her legs gliding along the bed linens, her stomach taut and tanned. Gabriel was reminded of how her soft skin felt against his own.

"Come over here." She patted the bed with the knife. From outside, the ocean spoke, the waves broke hypnotically.

Gabriel gave her a stony look. Tara seemed like a distant dream to him now. A cave he had tried to hide in as she pulled and jerked at the threads of his psyche. The train had wrecked. Gabriel was not about to count himself among the casualties.

"Get dressed, Tara."

"It's my fault," she said, pressing the knifepoint here and there along the bed. "I freaked out when Marc put the wire on Regina. She was like a little sister to me. I liked her. I asked Marc if we could keep her. He said no."

"Get dressed," Gabriel repeated.

"I didn't know what to tell them at the hospital," she continued. "Everyone was so nice to me. I thought for sure Marc was going to hurt me for running away. But he didn't. He understood I was scared. He was so smart about it, so calm. It became fun to him after a while."

"Fun," Gabriel muttered. "He had fun murdering innocent girls."

"Innocent?" Tara made a face and waggled the knife in front of her face. "Delia liked being choked with a scarf during sex. She said it turned her on. I didn't like Delia, but Marc did—a lot. I wanted her to go away. I was glad when she did."

Gabriel shook his head, marveling at how blind he had been.

"One day," she said conspiratorially, "Marc told me to get some wire. I didn't know why. Instead of a scarf, Marc put the wire on Delia's neck. She fought him, but you know how strong Marc is." The knife made imaginary circles on the bed. "She stuck out her tongue like a dog. She looked ugly."

"And where did Ross figure into all this?" he asked her. "Was he with you and Marc when Regina was killed?"

"Ross? He thought I was Mother Theresa. No, Marc had to cover for us because I ended up in the hospital. He went and grabbed something of Ross's to plant in the house. The equestrian center was nearby, and Marc is a very fast thinker." The blade in Tara's hand froze. "Marc is dead, isn't he?"

Gabriel nodded. Tara seemed to waver then and an unsure expression clouded her features.

"Give me the knife." Gabriel walked to the edge of the bed. Tara slid it across the sheets to him, and he promptly grabbed it. "Now, get dressed."

Tara nodded like a little girl and removed her bikini top. Gabriel instantly looked away from her bare breasts. He cleared his throat and moved toward the door.

"Two minutes," he told her, and closed the door to wait in the hall.

Gabriel silently congratulated himself as he placed the knife on a nearby table. He'd found her.

"Time to go, Tara."

He entered the room and saw instantly that Tara was gone. A lace curtain waved in the breeze from an open window.

Cursing his stupidity, Gabriel ran through the house and burst out the front door. He looked around wildly, trying to make out any movement in the darkening street. The palm fronds in the trees swished above him. A coconut hit the ground near the stranded SUV. He heard gravel crunching, and Gabriel glimpsed a blonde head moving through the construction site across the street. He watched unbelievingly as Tara climbed between the floors.

"Tara!" he called to her, but she kept climbing upwards. Gabriel immediately took off after her.

The entire front of the condominium building was open toward the ocean, awaiting oversized windows and balconies that would never arrive. In its abandoned state, the building resembled a dangerous dollhouse. Rugged cement stairs connected the first and second floors. Gabriel easily climbed those, stepping over cement chunks and fecal matter left behind by animals. To get to the third floor, Gabriel had to ascend a rickety wooden ladder.

"Tara!" he called out. He listened for sounds, but could only hear the breaking waves and the palms, agitated by the evening breeze. "It's no use to run!"

He walked carefully into the dark depths of the third floor condo unit, inching away from the moonlight. "Tara?"

Iron rebar poked out from the floors and the walls. Vines and weeds grew in sporadic clumps as Mother Nature reclaimed her property. Gabriel paused and listened. Something fluttered close to his scalp and he ducked. A bat flew erratically past him.

Gabriel returned to the front room where the ocean splayed out before him. Tara Samuels stood at the edge of a balcony, silhouetted by a round bone-white moon.

"Tara, come away from there." Reaching out his hand, Gabriel carefully approached her.

"I'm afraid."

"I know. Take my hand and we'll talk it over."

She took his hand, but pulled him close to her body and the ledge. "Will you help me?"

He nodded. She embraced him tightly and then suddenly pushed Gabriel as hard as she could. He teetered on the ledge—his arms flailing, as the waves cracked loudly against the shoreline. Gabriel reached out and grabbed Tara to keep from falling. Her bare feet skidded forward in protest. Lit by moonlight, her face was demonically beautiful. Tara gritted her teeth and violently shoved Gabriel again, only he had already regained his balance. He answered Tara's push by throwing her backwards.

She thudded against the rough gray wall opposite him and hung there for a moment. Gabriel stood immobile, breathing hard. Tara smiled and he braced himself, but she made no move.

Gabriel slowly approached her. Her eyes followed him until he halted in front of her.

He put his hands on her petite shoulders. "Let's go, Tara."

Gabriel attempted to steer her toward the exit, only she wouldn't budge. She was stuck to the wall.

"Tara?"

Gabriel looked on in astonishment as her eyes glazed over in front of him. The next moment she was like Delia Marks's reconstructed head—smiling and frozen.

His breath caught in his throat as he gripped her hard and pulled. She came away from the wall, and went limp in his hands.

Gabriel laid her down, turned her over, and was shocked to see two deep burrows in Tara's back. As he watched, they pooled with blood that bubbled with air. He jerked his eyes to the wall where two sharp and bloodied prongs of iron rebar poked outwards, beckoning to the ocean, and eerily reminding him of the twisted baling wire around the necks of Marc's victims.

A long death rattle issued from Tara's lips as Gabriel knelt beside her. He smelled the scent of coppery blood and over that, the unmistakable fragrance of lavender.

CHAPTER 30

The jet winged its way through slate-colored clouds and the pilot announced their final descent into the Los Angeles International Airport.

Gabriel looked out the oval window, feeling as dark as the clouds outside. Then like magic, the sky opened and the patina of lights, that infinite spread of urban Los Angeles, suddenly appeared, and Gabriel felt a familiar homecoming pang.

The roar of the engines and the squealing of the tires drowned his thoughts as the plane set down on the runway. He moved robotically through immigration and exited the airport. Wearily, Gabriel carried his duffel to the Celica.

Once inside the car, he looked at his watch. It was past one in the morning. He sighed.

Gabriel pulled onto Lincoln Boulevard and headed home. He would not ask Ming to forgive him for being late. He would no longer demand that she weaken herself to make him feel stronger. Still, there was something he needed to tell her.

At a red light, he pulled to the curb and punched Ming's number into his cell phone. He got her voicemail and left a message.

"I'm back," he announced. "Too late, I guess. Tara is dead, Ming. I had to stay and make arrangements. What else could I do?" Gabriel paused and said words that felt foreign to him.

"I've been thinking about what you said about feeling safe. I think we do that for each other. The world is kind of a scary place and maybe that's why the two of us connected. We make each other feel safe." He paused again. "I know I've disappointed you again. We really do manifest the things we fear the most. Wouldn't it be nice if you and I could get a break?"

Gabriel ended the call and tossed the phone onto the passenger seat.

When he arrived at his building, he pulled into his parking space and killed the engine. He grabbed his duffel bag and headed to the front door. A party was going on in a neighboring apartment. Gabriel heard the sounds of noisemakers and music. Suddenly, the music was turned down and voices began a countdown in unison.

"Ten!" they yelled.

Gabriel looked at his wristwatch. It was almost two o'clock in the morning.

"Nine!"

Then he remembered. He was still on Mexico time, two hours ahead.

"Eight!"

He'd made it back on time.

"Seven!"

As he slid the key into the lock, he had the feeling he wasn't alone. His heart began to pound.

"Six!"

He opened the door, and a footstep crunched the asphalt behind him.

Here we go again.

"Five!"

Gabriel turned around, fully expecting a phantom Tara to capture him in the cage of her slender arms.

"Four!"

A figure did stand in the darkness.

"Three!"

Ming stepped into the light, her hair hanging loose and thick. Her eyes were wet, but her expression was happy.

"Two!"

She held her cell phone in one hand and a bottle of cold champagne in the other.

From next door, the neighbors cried boisterously, "Happy New Year!"

Gabriel smiled and held the door open for her.

Victor Archwood is back in the next book in the series
and he is bent on exacting an elaborately designed
revenge on Detective Gabriel McRay.

Please turn the page for an exciting preview of
THE MASK OF MIDNIGHT

Coming in 2014

Gabriel met Ming at the bottom of Archwood's long driveway. She was wearing a Venetian style Mardi Gras mask replete with long feathers and sequins. He was wearing the clown suit that had been provided for him. The mask he wore was of a killer clown, sharp teeth, wicked smile -- but it was a clown all the same.

"Seriously?" Ming asked him when he approached her.

"Archwood handpicked it for me, I'm sure."

Gabriel held Ming's hand as they walked up the driveway. Slowly, a modern one-story house came into view.

"Good gracious," Ming said. "Where'd he get the money for this?"

Gabriel swallowed. He could barely afford his fixer-upper and Victor Archwood had built an architecturally stunning home. Rows of glass windows shined behind rich wood trim and elegant stonework. Looking around, Gabriel could already make out an incredible city view and they were only halfway up the drive.

"Didn't you know," he replied, staring contemptuously at the house. "Archwood is the shit nowadays. On everyone's A-list." He turned to his girlfriend. "Makes you sick, doesn't it?"

Ming squeezed his hand. "Come on. Let's see what he's hiding."

There were two bouncers standing guard at a solid steel front door, which was open. Gabriel queued up behind a row of people waiting to be admitted. As he neared the entrance, he craned to see inside the house. The stacked stonework reached beyond the exterior walls and wound itself into the interior, smartly bringing the outside in. Issuing from inside the house was the loud thump of bass and techno music. The place was overrun with people.

"Name?" a burly Polynesian man who was built like a sumo wrestler asked.

"Gabriel McRay." He brought Ming forward. "And guest."

Ming was reluctant to go inside and Gabriel pressed on the small of her back as the bouncer nodded and let them pass.

The couple stood awkwardly in the midst of what apparently was a rollicking party. The music thumped against their ears, competing for dominance over the sound of happy voices and clinking glasses.

A row of glass doors, now wide open, lined the walls across from them and beckoned the visitor to walk across a nicely appointed living room. Beyond the doors lay a sleek lighted pool and a spectacular view of Los Angeles. The city lights spread out below them like a blanket of sparkling gems. Near the pool, a bartender manned a well stocked bar, handing out drinks to those waiting in line.

Gabriel looked around, amazed. Didn't they know who was buying their booze? Didn't they care?

All the guests were masked. Many of the women wore elegant Venetian masks similar to Ming's. Still others had chosen costumes of the standard Halloween variety, frightening or grotesque. One guest was dressed like the Phantom of the Opera. Another wore the Scream mask with his mouth open in a frozen howl.

A woman rushed by them, calling to someone named Jim. She was dressed as a belly dancer and her diaphanous face veil trailed behind her. A man wearing a ragged beanie stared meanly at the newcomers from across the room. His face was replete with fake cuts bound by primitive black "stitches" that twisted his features. Although the man thought he was freakishly cool, his fake wounds reminded Gabriel of the autopsy images of Archwood's victims. Stab wounds had marred their bodies as well; only their wounds had been tragically real.

Ming shivered against Gabriel.

"Are you cold?" he asked her.

"Nervous."

He put his arm around her.

"Where do you think he is?" Ming asked.

"Hard to tell," Gabriel answered, still observing the man with the stitched wounds.

"Canapé?"

Gabriel and Ming turned to see a waiter wearing a tux under the Jigsaw mask from the movie "Saw." His pasty white face, red glowing eyes, and protruding red-spiraled cheeks made him a monstrously intimidating kitchen staffer.

"No, thanks," Gabriel answered flatly and watched the waiter move off.

He and Ming made their way through the living room, feeling out of place and vulnerable as two mice in a snake pit.

They peeked into an empty study. Here too, a row of glass doors lined one wall, which led to the backyard. The rest of the room was covered in panels of padded wine-colored leatherette. A large, single painting hung opposite Archwood's expansive desk. It was of a fey, big-eyed child with blood spilling from her eyes. The painting was eerily beautiful and looked expensive.

Ming couldn't tear her gaze from it, so Gabriel gently pulled at her sleeve. "Come on."

They returned to the living room and stood in the thick of the revelers. People sloshed drinks on them and the bass of the music mimicked their own rabid heartbeats.

Gabriel observed a group of people catering to a tall, black-shrouded figure whose back was to them. Gabriel nudged Ming and nodded toward the figure. At that moment, the dark one turned, and Gabriel saw Death.

The man inside the Grim Reaper costume apparently noticed Gabriel at the same time, and confidently strode over. Ming gasped and Gabriel took her hand. Archwood wore a hood over a grinning skull mask. In his hands he held a plastic scythe.

"I should have known," Gabriel told him when he joined the couple. "Death Incarnate."

"I'm Poe's Masque of the Red Death," Archwood said from behind the skeletal grin.

Gabriel remembered the story from his college English. "About the plague, right? That fits you, Vic."

Archwood chuckled. "I won't say anything about the clown costume. Welcome to my home, Sergeant McRay." He held out his black-gloved hand to Ming, "A pleasure, Dr. Li."

Unwilling to shake hands with the man who had tried to murder her, Ming took a subconscious step closer to Gabriel.

Archwood let his hand drop. "Would you two like a drink?"

Gabriel glanced at Ming who was frozen, the eyes behind her mask riveted on Archwood's grinning skull.

"No, thanks," Gabriel answered for her.

A sexy Cat Woman came up then and entwined her arm through Archwood's.

"You remember Andrea, don't you?"

"Shhh! You weren't supposed to tell!" she said as snuggled close to him.

"Sorry, Dre."

The Cat Woman nodded to Gabriel. "Hello, Detective McRay."

"Miss Leighton."

Andrea the Cat curiously cocked her whiskered mask toward Ming.

"Nice to meet you," Ming said mechanically and without introducing herself.

"Well," the Grim Reaper said, "Look at the four of us. We should go out sometime."

Gabriel suddenly felt claustrophobic. Was it due to the hot latex mask he wore or Archwood's suggestion of a double date? Ming must have felt it, too.

"Excuse me, I need to use the bathroom," she said, and instantly surveyed her surroundings.

Andrea took the cue and pointed left. "That way. First door down the hall."

Ming looked anxiously back at Gabriel. "How will I find you?"

He scanned the crowd with disdain. "I guess I'm the only clown around here. You'll find me."

Archwood snickered at that, but stopped when Gabriel swiveled his sharp-toothed clown face toward him.

Ming meandered off, looking furtively here and there, spooked at any little thing. Observing her, Gabriel regretted he had let her come. He knew he should take her home.

Archwood unraveled Andrea's arm from his. "Dre, go check on the food and make sure they've started serving the lamb."

"Okay." Andrea gave her hyper little wave to Gabriel. "Nice seeing you again, Detective McRay."

Archwood's death mask watched her bounce off and then it focused back on Gabriel. Behind the mask, Gabriel sensed Archwood bristling with energy, as though he could barely contain his excitement. And yet, the younger man was attempting to act very casual.

"Would you like a tour?" Archwood asked him.

"Sure," Gabriel said.

As they began walking, Gabriel reached under his clown vest and settled a waiting hand on the Redhawk. He quietly unlatched the safety -- just in case.

"Here's a room that would interest you," Archwood stated as they reached a closed door. He swung the door wide to reveal a large master bedroom with a king size bed, a grand fireplace, and more astounding views. Archwood paused at the threshold, holding the door open in invitation.

Discomfited, Gabriel continued his trek down the hallway, feeling exposed, as perforated as Swiss cheese, even behind his disguise. He heard rustling and in an instant, Archwood was by his side again.

"Pull something," Gabriel told the Grim Reaper. "Give me any reason; because you don't know how badly I want to take you down."

"Oh, I get that, Sergeant. But if I pull something on you..." Archwood wheeled in front of Gabriel and halted him in his tracks. "You'll never see me coming."

The younger man then turned and walked ahead. "So give the gun a rest, okay?"

Out in the crowded living room, Ming wandered around uneasily, searching for Gabriel. A man, wearing a mask that displayed only the bloodied upper half of a mouth, tipsily approached Ming.

"Hey, babe, can I get you a drink?" he slurred.

The forensic pathologist in Ming stared gravely at his mask, noting that a person who had truly lost half his face would have already expired from exsanguinations.

Ming shook her head, still studying the man's mask; and the jawless, would-be admirer moved off to greener pastures.

Gabriel stood and watched Archwood's flowing black robes disappear around a corner. What an arrogant bastard. Ramirez was right. Gabriel needed to avoid having anything to do with Victor Archwood. Being around the killer was toxic, and Gabriel would only poison himself by being near the other man.

He turned and headed back toward the main hall. Dr. B was right. By focusing solely on Archwood, Gabriel had not dealt with his anger toward Dash. He'd had enough therapy to know that ignoring his issues would not make them go away. Gabriel needed to get Ming, get out of here, and get on with his life.

He entered the thick of the party, fed up with the brazen masks and the thumping music. The partiers disgusted him. Archwood was a serial killer and these people were drinking his liquor and eating his food. They might as well have dressed like dogs, or pigs, or worms.

Gabriel searched the room and spied a woman with long dark hair and a feathered mask. He weaved his way through the partiers until he reached her.

"Let's go," he announced.

The lady turned to face him. She wasn't Ming. Gabriel mumbled an apology.

He began to circuit the crowded room, turning one Venetian mask around after the other, only none of the masked ladies were Ming. He thought he heard her call his name and he moved in the direction of the kitchen.

"Coming through!" a waiter dressed as Winnie the Pooh cried as he exited the kitchen, carrying a tray loaded with food.

Gabriel stepped back to let the waiter pass, and then swore he heard his name again.

"Ming?" he called toward a darkened hallway beyond the kitchen.

Gabriel entered a luxuriously long butler's pantry where glass-covered cabinets held china plates and twinkling crystal. At the end of the pantry was a closed door.

He walked over and opened the door. Gabriel felt for a light switch and flipped it on to reveal a large laundry room. It was empty, save for a lone Mardi Gras mask lying on the silent washing machine. Curious, Gabriel picked up the mask, which sparkled in his hands. It didn't belong to Ming.

Suddenly, he felt himself grabbed from behind and felt a sting in his bicep. Gabriel's arms immediately went up, clutching the person behind him.

"I said you wouldn't see me coming," Archwood whispered and retracted the hypodermic he'd plunged into Gabriel's arm.

Did you like this book?
Tell Laurie by visiting her website at
http://www.lauriestevensbooks.com

Read sample chapters
Find out when she's in your town

She wants to hear from you!

Connect with Laurie on Facebook at Laurie Stevens, author
Follow her on Twitter @lauriestevens1

ABOUT THE AUTHOR

Laurie Stevens is a novelist, screenwriter, and playwright. Her articles and short fiction have appeared in numerous publications. Her debut novel *The Dark Before Dawn*, is the first in a psychological suspense series. The novel earned the Kirkus Star and was named to Kirkus Review's "Best of 2011/Indie". Laurie lives in the hills near Los Angeles. To learn more about the author, visit her website at http://www.lauriestevensbooks.com.

CPSIA information can be obtained
at www.ICGtesting.com
Printed in the USA
FSOW02n1131140515
7159FS